New

Waite's eyes mov[...] her lips. As if drawn by some mysterious magnetic force, he lowered his face to hers.

Overwhelmed by sensations she had never experienced or even imagined, Mariah shut her eyes and let it happen. Just before his mouth touched her own, Mariah could have sworn the earth trembled once again.

Breath mingling, flesh against flesh, he kissed her thoroughly. If Mariah had thought she'd been kissed before, she'd been sadly mistaken. His hands were on her back, but it was as if he were touching her everywhere. One by one, and then all at once, pulses began hammering in her body.

Oh. Oh, my—!

"Sorry," Waite whispered hoarsely. "I never meant to—that is, I only came to see if you were—"

"I am," she assured him, disengaging herself from his arms. "Safe, that is. And thank you for offering to comfort me." She felt a slight urge to laugh. This was *comfort*? If what he'd offered was comfort, then heaven help her if she ever got any more comfortable. . . .

SEASPELL

by

Bronwyn Williams

A TOPAZ BOOK

TOPAZ
Published by the Penguin Group
Penguin Books USA Inc., 375 Hudson Street,
New York, New York 10014, U.S.A.
Penguin Books Ltd, 27 Wrights Lane,
London W8 5TZ, England
Penguin Books Australia Ltd, Ringwood,
Victoria, Australia
Penguin Books Canada Ltd, 10 Alcorn Avenue,
Toronto, Ontario, Canada M4V 3B2
Penguin Books (N.Z.) Ltd, 182–190 Wairau Road,
Auckland 10, New Zealand

Penguin Books Ltd, Registered Offices:
Harmondsworth, Middlesex, England

First published by Topaz, an imprint of Dutton Signet,
a division of Penguin Books USA Inc.

First Printing, August, 1997
10 9 8 7 6 5 4 3 2

 REGISTERED TRADEMARK—MARCA REGISTRADA

Printed in Canada

This book is dedicated
to the memory of all the keepers
of the Cape Hatteras Lighthouse,
their assistants, and the families
of those men who still
live on the Banks.

Authors' Note

In writing this story we've taken certain liberties. Near the turn of the century there was a one-room schoolhouse in Buxton Village where grades one through eight were taught. Before that, classes were taught in a private home. We not only supplied an earlier school but a teacherage as well.

Chapter One

Buxton, North Carolina

The wind was out of the northeast, bringing relief from days of stifling heat, but it was still hot. Storm-breeding weather. Waite stood on the dock and stared out across the ruffled waters of the Pamlico Sound. The mailboat had just swung into the channel and lowered her mains'le. He ignored the fidgety little man beside him. Newbolt had been a thorn in his hide for more years than he cared to recall.

"I'm counting on you to see to things, Mc-Kenna, same as usual," the magistrate said.

"Already done it. Roof's sound. Storm shutters battened back. No more mice than usual. Don't know what else you expect me to do."

"Just see to her comfort, answer her questions—you know how it is with off-islanders. Least little thing upsets them."

Waite turned slowly and pinned the local magistrate with a hard look. "*Her?* You went and hired on another female? Hellfire, Newbolt, I told you after the last one ran off that no city woman was ever going to last a full term. That little fool never quit whining from the day she set foot off the boat until the day she left again. If it wasn't the mice, it was the ticks. If it wasn't the ticks, it was the deerflies. I warn you, this one won't stick, either, and then we'll be without for another term. We've missed out on the whole blasted summer! Now the boys'll be stuck in a classroom when they should be out fishing."

Waite McKenna was a big man. He stood a full head higher than the magistrate. He was also a plainspoken man who had grown up without the gentling influence of a woman, his mother having run off when he was five, leaving behind a bewildered boy and an embittered husband to make out the best they could.

As it happened, they had made out quite well. At the age of sixteen, Waite had been introduced to the pleasures of sex by Miss Constance Devereaux, a visiting lady several years his senior. He'd been an enthusiastic student, and before the summer was over, Miss Devereaux had found herself with child. Waite had done the honorable thing. He had married her. For the next seven months, his bride had alternately cursed and complained. She had eventually died giving birth to their son, Nicholas.

Waite had reached the logical conclusion early in life that women in general were weak, city women the worst of all. Both his wife and his mother had been city women. Neither of them had had an ounce of sticking power.

"I did not specify gender when I advertised for a teacher, McKenna. It might not have occurred to you, but not every schoolteacher in the world is eager to move all the way out here to the Cape."

Maxwell Newbolt himself hadn't come willingly. A zealous young missionary fresh from the seminary, he'd been on his way to his first mission in Brazil when his ship had gone down just inside Diamond Shoals. He'd come ashore with two broken legs, clinging to a chunk of deck cargo. By the time he'd recovered his health, he'd been convinced that God had deposited him on the sandy spur of land that jutted out some thirty-five miles off the mainland for one purpose alone: to bring salvation, not to mention civilization, to what he considered to be a lot of heathen islanders.

And while he still enjoyed being a big frog in a tiny dab of a pond, much of his religious fervor had faded in the ensuing twenty-three years. He had married the fisherman's daughter who had nursed him back to health and proceeded to get himself five sons and a daughter with her before the poor woman gave up the ghost and went to her heavenly reward. Grateful to be relieved of duty, some folks said. Newbolt was not a wildly popular man. He was tolerated because his children were native-born Bankers, and because the people here were inclined to live and let live. An indifferent preacher, he lacked the patience to teach, but as magistrate he took it upon himself to secure teachers for the village school.

"We have a contract, McKenna," The older man reminded Waite.

"Contract, my ass. You asked me to keep an eye on your teachers, not change their damned napkins and wipe their snotty noses."

"It's a pity your mother didn't linger long enough to teach you some manners. Then again, I can understand her . . ."

Evidently, something in the lighthouse keeper's eyes made the older man rethink his statement. He cleared his throat. "Yes, well. From our correspondence, Miss Deekins seems a sensible sort. I believe you'll find her competent to change her own—that is to say, I don't expect you'll actually have to—"

Maxwell's plump cheeks reddened as he attempted to extract himself without further damage to his dignity.

"I give her three weeks," Waite said flatly.

"Her contract calls for eight months."

"You're real big on contracts, aren't you, Newbolt?"

"I am a magistrate, after all," the other man said pompously.

The man was nothing more than a jumped-up preacher, but Waite saw no future in badgering him further. In a war of words, Newbolt was bound to win. Waite was more a man of action, and action was what was called for in this case.

On first setting out from Elizabeth City after the train ride from Murfreesboro, Mariah had reasoned to herself that there was nothing at all to be frightened of. The mailboat was obviously solid. It had been plying these waters for goodness knows how many years. The mate and the captain appeared to be competent, and although the accommodations were rather spartan, she could certainly put up with a few hours of discomfort for the sake of a fresh start and an exciting new career.

True, she was terrified of water. Had been ever since, at the age of six, she had tripped over a cypress knee and gone headfirst into the Meherrin

River, dragged down by layers of heavy winter clothing.

It was that same river, ironically, that had claimed the lives of her parents only six months ago. Mariah was still trying to come to terms with her loss. After the first few unbearable weeks, she had numbly begun to piece together remnants of her life, and then, a few months later, all she'd been able to salvage from the ruins had come tumbling down all over again.

Desolate at having to leave behind her home, her friends—everything—she had failed to notice exactly when the mailboat had left the protected waters of the Pasquotank River for the more exposed waters of the Albemarle Sound until it was too late. Long before they reached the wild waters of the vast Pamlico Sound, she discovered that life had a few more rude surprises in store.

God bless the poor mate. He'd seen his duty and done it. Provided a pail, emptied it as often as necessary, and prevented his passenger from hurling herself over the rail.

Mal de mer. In French it sounded rather exotic. Even romantic, as if one were pining for a lover who'd gone to sea. Instead, it had turned out to be the most miserable, hopeless, helpless condition known to humankind.

Now they were nearing the landing. Mariah did the best she could with her hair, tucking it under her bonnet. But like everything else about her, her dark red, stick-straight hair was sadly bedraggled. Despite the towel wet with seawater the mate had provided, and the dipperful of drinking water he had brought her once he was certain she could keep it down, she felt stale and sour and woefully inadequate. Which was unfortunate, considering all the burned bridges she'd left behind.

The wharf was crowded with people. Children darted in and out among gingham skirts and denim-clad limbs. Most of them, she suspected, she would come to know quite well over the next few months.

Her stomach rumbled uneasily as she patted her bonnet and secured her umbrella under her arm. Thankfully, she was out of blacks, but she'd be wearing gray and lavender half-mourning for another six months.

Possibly for the rest of her life. Schoolteachers were expected to dress sedately. It was even more important for a woman in her circumstances.

Not that the good people of Buxton who had hired her even knew of her circumstances. With any luck, they never would.

Her stomach rumbled again as she did her best to repair the ravages of a nightmare journey before she stepped out to confront her future. Maxwell had promised to meet her. She looked forward with mixed emotions to meeting the man with whom she had corresponded over these past dismal few weeks. His letters had been the one bright point of her existence. He had described the local flora and fauna, some of which was familiar, most of which sounded quite exotic. He'd told her about the new teacherage that had been built on a piece of land near the lighthouse, which also sounded rather exotic. The lighthouse, not the teacherage.

She pictured him as tall, for no good reason except that as long as she was going to daydream, she might as well do a decent job of it. He would be dark, of course. She was partial to dark hair on a man. Dark brown hair, well groomed, but not heavy with hair oil. And nice brown eyes and long-fingered hands. A scholar's hands. His letters had sounded scholarly. She'd taken comfort in knowing there would be at least one kindred spirit among her new acquaintances. She only hoped he understood that she wasn't at her best after two days of traveling.

With the first touch of excitement she'd felt in many a day, Mariah stood on tiptoe and gazed out over the milling crowd, searching for a glimpse of a handsome, scholarly gentleman with dark brown hair.

Of course, his hair could be any color at all. All she had to go on was her feminine intuition, which was not always reliable. Which had lately proved sadly *un*reliable. She was still searching the crowd when something large and dark landed on the deck directly in front of her. She stepped back, tripped on a coil of rope, and nearly dropped her umbrella.

"Merciful heavens, do watch where you're going, sir!"

Dressed all in black, the man towered over her, his massive booted feet nudging the toes of her two-tone gray hightops. She gasped, inhaling the scent of wool, lye soap, and . . . lamp oil?

"I'll make you an offer, madam. I'll pay your passage if you'll turn around and go back to wherever you came from without setting foot off the boat. Do we have a deal?"

"I beg your pardon?"

With patience that obviously didn't come easily, the giant repeated his offer. He had a brogue that,

while not unpleasant, made him seem all the more
alien. "Oi said if you're willing to leave roight
now, Oi'll settle with the cap'n for your passage."

Mariah tilted her head back to take stock of the
creature who had dared accost her right in front
of the whole town. Windblown and unsteady on
her feet, she glared up at a face that was striking
for its raw strength alone. Weathered skin the
color of seasoned oak stretched taut over high,
sharply carved cheekbones, in contrast to sun-
bleached hair that was thick and a bit too long.
Crow's-feet fanned out at the corners of a pair of
dark brown eyes set in a sweep of black lashes.

"Well? Did you hear me? Do we have a deal?"

Maxwell, for heaven's sake, come rescue me!

"Certainly I heard you. You're practically shouting in my ear." In contrast to his roar, Mariah
deliberately moderated her own voice.

"Oi'm waiting for your answer."

"If you think I'm about to sail back across that
wretched sound, you, sir, are very much mistaken." His mouth didn't fit the rest of him. It was
wide and generously curved. A fluke, she told
herself. The man was obviously a barbarian.
"However, I do thank you for your generous
offer." She seldom stooped to using sarcasm, but
doubted if he'd even recognize it as such.

He smiled. She was not at all reassured. "You'll
never make it. D'you like mice?"

Mice? Clear gray eyes widening, Mariah said,
"I—I hope I'm able to tolerate all God's creatures." *Some more than others,* she didn't bother
to add.

"What about storms?"

"Storms never bother me in the least." Except

for the thunder and lightning. That, too, went unsaid.

"Then you'll not moind the critters that come into your house to escape the hoigh toides? They don't mean you harm, only you want to be careful not to back 'em into a—"

"Ah, there you are, my dear! Have you had a nice journey out? I must say, the passage is a great deal more pleasant this time of year than in the dead of winter. All that splashing and tossing about—one inevitably gets wet."

Mariah stared at the plump, fussy little man in the outdated clothes. "I beg your . . ." she began, when he took her hand in his and patted it. "I'm Maxwell Newbold, Esquire." She thought she heard the large barbarian snort, but then, Mr. Newbolt was speaking again. "And you, of course, are Miss Mariah Deekins."

This was her Maxwell? Her tall, handsome, courtly correspondent?

On the verge of correcting his error, she remembered the name she had used so impulsively on her application. Mercy, she'd better get used to it. It was the only name she was legally entitled to. "How do you do, Mr. Newbolt. I feel I should know you from your lovely letters." His letters had been addressed to Mariah Deekins, too. They'd been delivered with no problem, because of course by then everyone had known of her situation.

The yellow-haired, black-clad giant hovered over them like a bird of prey, blocking her access to the gangplank, which was no more than a narrow board tossed across to the wharf.

Mariah sent him a look that should have reminded him of his manners, but didn't. "If you don't mind," she said pointedly.

Maxwell Newbolt was bustling around, checking the tags on her baggage. "Step aside, McKenna, and while you're at it, would you mind transporting Miss Deekins's trunk to the teacherage? I'll see to the smaller things."

"Aren't you going to introduce me?" Planting himself between Mariah and the magistrate, the ruffian favored them with a truly wicked grin.

"Miss Deekins, this is McKenna. Lighthouse Service."

Mariah had thought a moment earlier that a grin couldn't be any more wicked. She'd been mistaken. The man leaned closer, so close she could see shards of gold splintering the dark depths of his eyes.

"That's *Lighthouse* Service, Miss Deekins. Not *schoolteacher* service. You'll not last out the week," he said, and spoken softly, his brogue sounded even more threatening. "It takes a certain kind of woman to stick, madam, and you're not that kind. Last teacher we had, she was big as a boar hog and mean as a weasel. She lasted nearly three weeks. One before only lasted two."

"Mercy, then you really do need a teacher, don't you? What a pity there were none to be found when you were young."

The flush on the keeper's weathered face was slow in rising, but the hard glint in his eyes never changed. Mariah deliberately stepped around him and hurried down the rickety gangplank, scrambling off onto the wharf with more haste than grace.

What on earth had she done to make the man

so furious? Surely word of her disgrace hadn't
followed her all the way out here. She wasn't accustomed to dealing with anger. False pity, yes.
Avid curiosity and outright rudeness, too, unfortunately, but not anger.

Yet, strangely enough, she discovered that of
them all, she much preferred honest anger, even
if she didn't understand the reason for it.

The small, plump man in the fusty-looking suit
was busy loading her smaller bags onto a cart.
Not a carriage. Not even a decent gig, but a
wooden cart of the type farmers used to bring
produce into town.

So this was Maxwell Newbolt. So much for her
womanly intuition, she thought wryly. Scholarly
and kind, he might be. Handsome, he was not.
However, if a monkey had leaped upon her shoulder and offered to lead her to a place where she
could lie down and close her eyes without fear of
rolling onto the floor, she would have gone with
him willingly.

Waite stood on the weathered landing and
stared after the pair disappearing down the narrow sandy trail. All around him people were beginning to follow the sack of mail to the new post
office. He loaded the freight he'd ordered onto the
cart and reluctantly hoisted the new teacher's
trunk onboard as well.

Another woman. Damn. Frail, prissy, she was
just like all the others. Wouldn't last the week.

This one was no beauty, either, for all she carried herself like she was wearing a bleeding crown
instead of that ugly hat. He wasn't partial to red
hair. Hers was the color of Honduras mahogany.

Still, he had to admit her eyes were uncommonly fine. Big, clear, and steady, they were the color of rainwater. The color of fog rising off the sea. He'd never seen eyes that color before, nor dark red hair so glossy it splintered the light.

Newbolt hadn't missed much, either. The lecherous old fool had practically peeled her right down to her underpinnings without even laying a hand on her. Waite figured Newbolt was still hoping to catch some poor woman off guard so he could talk her into taking on that brood of his. Why else would he keep on ordering female teachers out from the mainland when not a one of them was up to the job?

Because women teachers were always single. They also had to be pretty damn desperate to come to a place like this.

But desperate or not, they'd have to be weak in the head to take on the Newbolt litter. The three eldest were old enough to marry and have families of their own. Lazy as sin, but they'd come by it honestly. Maxwell had never been known to turn a hand to any task he could get another man to do for him. He could have hauled the teacher's trunk as well as Waite could, but then he might be expected to off-load it.

Like as not, Waite thought with a wintry gleam of amusement, he'd be toting the same trunk back down to the landing before the week was out. That was one task he was looking forward to because he'd flat out had his fill of frightened females coming after him day and night to fix this, do that, hold their hand every time the wind blew.

This time, he wasn't going to put up with it. He had a job to do, and it didn't include playing nursemaid to any damn schoolteacher.

* * *

The lighthouse towered over everything in the village. If Mariah had had the energy to be impressed, that might have done it, but by the time they had driven through what seemed miles of sandy track, past dense, brooding forest with only a few small, unpainted houses huddled in clusters here and there, she lacked the energy to do more than utter an occasional murmur to her escort's running commentary.

"Now, here we have the new post office."

It didn't look all that new to Mariah, but she supposed all things were relative.

"Called Buxton now instead of the Cape. Government's started giving the villages proper names instead of all the heathen names folks here on the Banks used to call themselves. Some of them weren't even pronounceable."

The Cape seemed perfectly pronounceable to Mariah, but she didn't feel like arguing the point. "Mmmm."

"Freshwater ponds over yonder. Boggy. Full of big bass, but they're not worth catching. Taste muddy."

"Mmmm."

They were almost upon the lighthouse by then. Mariah held her bonnet on with one hand and tipped her head back to stare. With its black and white spiral stripes, it loomed over the whole island, rising high above the woods and the small cluster of buildings near its base.

"Principal keeper's quarters." Maxwell Newbolt pointed to one of the two houses. "Assistant keepers live in the double house."

Mariah's tired gaze ranged over the patchwork

of houses, outbuildings, and neat picket fences. It was a small community in and of itself. Another time she might appreciate it, but not now. Now all she wanted was a bed that wasn't pitching and rolling.

"And here we have our brand-new teacherage," her self-appointed guide said proudly.

She twisted her head around and stared, dismayed at the sight of a tiny box on short stilts. Her mother's potting shed had been larger, not to mention more attractive.

"Built summer before last, hardly even been broken in."

"Mmm." She tried to sound appreciative, she truly did, but at this point it was all she could do to sit upright on the hard plank bench. A cow, a pig, two chickens, and a few shaggy ponies followed the slow progress of the wagon across the sparsely grassed grounds, as if hoping for a handout.

"Shouldn't they be fenced in?"

"They're fenced out. Gardens over there." Newbolt nodded to the neatly picketed rectangles beside the two houses.

Her stomach growled again, and she pinned on a smile that took every last shred of energy she possessed. "Yes, well . . . it's all lovely, but I'd best start unpacking and getting settled."

"I believe you'll find everything you need." The magistrate climbed down and came around to assist her. Then, with a grand flourish he opened the door. "You just let me know what else you require in the way of furnishings, my dear, and I'll see that it's provided."

The air inside was hot and stuffy. The room

smelled unpleasantly of mouse droppings and fresh paint. Maxwell bustled inside and began opening windows while Mariah stared in dismay at the tiny room that someone had tried to improve by painting the walls a painfully bright shade of blue.

"Had it all done up fresh as soon as we knew you were coming. Now, this is our kitchen." He pointed proudly to a minuscule cabinet, a small freshly varnished table, a galvanized sink with a pitcher pump attached, and a small, rust-coated range. "Bedroom's right this way—some of the ladies donated bedding." He made as if to lead her through the door, but Mariah dug in her heels.

"Thank you kindly, Mr. Newbolt. You've been most helpful."

"Call me Maxwell, my dear. If you'll recall, we've already progressed to first names in our correspondence. I must admit, I've come to think of you as Mariah. Lovely name, Mariah. I've always set great stock in a person's name. Give a child a proud name, I always say, and he'll live up to it. A man can't go wrong—"

A man most certainly could, Mariah thought. And this one had. The very last thing she wanted to do was discuss the matter of names. What she wanted was to be left alone to get her bearings in a place that was totally unlike anything she could possibly have visualized before setting out from Murfreesboro.

"Mr. Newbolt—Maxwell—there's nothing I want more than to sit quietly for the next few hours and enjoy being back on solid ground. I'm sure we have a lot to talk about, but could it possibly wait until tomorrow?"

As she was practically herding him toward the front door, there was no way he could mistake the message. *Get out of my house, Mr. Newbolt! Get out before I cry or throw up or do something else wildly unbecoming!*

He left, still talking. "Out back you'll find the necessary . . ."

The necessary? Good heavens, was she not to have even a decent bath?

". . . and a shed for your cart."

"My cart?"

"The pounding will take place in a few days, as soon as you're settled in. I'll come around after you've had time to rest from your journey and show you about the village. Such as it is," he added. "I'm sure you're used to something far more civilized, but then, those of us who've had the advantage of being born on the continent must share our blessings with these poor unfortunate folks."

On the continent? Did the man have no conception of geography? He had said more or less the same thing in his letters, but somehow it hadn't sounded quite so pompous written in a flowing copperplate with all the flourishes. "I'm sure you're right," she said, closing the door practically in his face.

She was sure of no such thing. All she was sure of at the moment was that if she didn't get something to eat soon she would faint, and she'd never fainted in her life. If the man had truly wanted to welcome her, he could at least have offered to feed her.

Chapter Two

Mariah sat in one of the room's two chairs and stared at the bright blue walls until her stomach threatened to rebel. Then she sighed and closed her eyes. *Merciful saints alive, what have I done?*

She was still sitting there, gripping the rocker's hard arms, both feet planted firmly on the bare floor, when someone pounded on the door. Her eyes flew open. Her arms flew out for balance. Startled, she yelped, "What? Who is it?"

"Do you want this thing or don't you?"

"Oh, for heaven's sake," she grumbled, hurrying to the door. It was the giant. The savage. The yellow-haired, brown-eyed barbarian. He was balancing her trunk on one massive shoulder, a fist lifted as if to pound on her door again. "Well, why didn't you say so?" she demanded.

Both his dark bushy eyebrows shot upward, and it occurred to Mariah that at one time, before his disposition curdled, he must have been a handsome devil. "Where do you want it?" He turned sideways to get through the door, and she backed up several steps and then gestured toward the bedroom.

He dropped the trunk on the bed. It was either that or set it down on the dresser, which didn't look up to bearing the weight of even the mismatched bowl and pitcher. There was hardly enough space on the floor.

"I suppose I can store it in the shed out back after I unpack," she said, half to herself.

"I wouldn't be too hasty. Like as not, you'll just have to pack it again in a few days."

Already busy with the straps, Mariah glanced over her shoulder. "Why on earth would I do that?"

Instead of answering, the man reached under the edge of the dresser with the toe of his boot and raked out a mousetrap, complete with victim. Her stomach gave a lurch, but she forced herself to ignore it. If he thought a little thing like a dead mouse was going to chase her away now, he was sadly mistaken. She might be no match for the man physically, but in determination—not to mention desperation—she was more than a match for any man, even one who, for some reason, seemed bent on scaring her off.

"Would you mind throwing him out the door? In this heat, he'll go ripe in no time at all."

To her surprise, she detected what almost appeared to be a gleam of appreciation in his eyes. He was at the door in three strides and returned a moment later with the trap reset.

"It isn't baited," she pointed out.

"Where's your cheese?"

"So far as I know, there's nothing at all to eat in the house. I don't suppose you know of a public dining room within walking distance?"

The look he gave her spoke volumes, none of it particularly flattering. "Maggie Stone takes in boarders. She might feed you if you were to ask her, but you'll have to hurry. Maggie sits down to eat at four-thirty sharp, and devil take the hindmost. It's gone past four already."

If she'd had the energy, she would have wept.

No, she wouldn't. She might have swatted that smug look off his face, but she was done with weeping. "I don't suppose there's a market within walking distance, either, then."

"A store? There's Cyrus's place. He'll have soda crackers, cheese, tinned food, salt meat—whatever you need. Just follow the road to the turnoff and take a left. You can't miss it."

Waite noticed a glittery look in her eyes and just the suspicion of a wobble to her chin. He waited for her to buckle, guilt nudging him in the backside like a cold-nosed hound dog.

"Well," she said. Just that. No more.

Against every grain of common sense he possessed, and that was considerable, Waite felt himself weakening. The woman couldn't help being female. That was pure luck of the draw. She couldn't help being city-bred, no more than she could help being skinny as a fence post, pale as a bedsheet, with hair the color of iron rust.

Reluctantly, he said, "You don't have to walk. There's a cart out back set aside for the use of whoever's staying here. The roan mare's yours, the rest belong to the lighthouse."

He waited for her to demand that he drive her. Instead, she swayed on her feet, closed her eyes, and reached out for something to hang on to. There were dark shadows around her eyes. He frowned. "Maybe you'd better sit down until you get your land legs under you. Takes longer for

some than others, after being on the water all
day."

He took her arm to steer her over to the chair
and was shocked at the sparsity of flesh covering
her frail bones. If she lasted out the week, he'd be
surprised. "Now, don't take me wrong, because
I'm not planning on making a habit of it, but if
you're not up to doing for yourself after jour-
neying all day—"

"Two days."

"—I reckon I could bring you over a plate of
supper."

Waite could tell by the way she hesitated that
she didn't want to take him up on it. Either she
was downright stupid or she had more pride than
was good for her. Unless he missed his guess,
she'd emptied out her belly more than once on
the way across the sound.

Newbolt should have seen to laying in supplies
before he brought her here. When it came to telling other folks what to do and how to do it, the
man was first off the starting line, but when it
came down to the actual doing, he wasn't even in
the running. If it weren't for that poor daughter
of his, him and his whole tribe would have
starved long ago.

Waite left her in the rocking chair that was just
about the only decent piece of furniture in the
parlor end of the room, promising to return directly with her evening meal. If Sarvice had baked
a fish, they'd fare well enough. Fish-cooking was
the one thing his first assistant was real good at
besides writing love notes and launching them
overboard in a bottle.

As it turned out, Sarvice A. Jones, whose turn

it was to cook, had set out a meal of white beans and cornbread. As usual, the beans were hard from being salted too soon—boiled bullets, Nick called them—and the bread was dry. At least it would fill her up, Waite thought an hour later when he walked across the barren stretch of sand between his house and the new teacherage with a bowl and a chunk of bread.

Not for the first time, he thought it was a damned fool place to build the teacher's residence, with the schoolhouse all the way over in the village. Land had been donated for the school, but nobody seemed eager to donate another plot for a teacherage. Some thought it was on account of Maggie Stone wanting the business, but none said it outright.

The magistrate had settled matters by taking over a scrap of land just outside the lighthouse property that was too swampy to be of much use for anything else. Folks squabbled over who owned it and how much, if anything, it was worth, but the fuss never amounted to anything. One thing the entire village agreed on was the importance of having a school and a teacher.

After allowing herself the luxury of a brief doze in the rocking chair, Mariah had forced herself to unpack her trunk, knowing that until she did, she'd have no place to sleep but the floor. And while she was tired enough to sleep around the clock on the naked pine boards, she didn't relish being run over by an army of mice.

Finding another burst of energy, she shoved the trunk, after unpacking her summer things, into the front room up against the window and arranged a few personal items on top: her favorite Wedgwood vase, which clashed horribly with the walls; the framed miniatures of her parents; and her journal.

Idly, she reached for the book. It fell open in her hands to the place where she'd described an excursion to Virginia Beach with her three best friends the year she had graduated from college. The trip had been one of several gifts from her parents, who hadn't wanted her to go to college in the first place, but indulged her whim because they'd loved her.

Dear Lord, it hurt to think about them. Her friends had rallied around her as soon as news of the double drowning got out. Mariah had been utterly stricken. Locked up inside herself, she had tried to deny first the loss, then the pain, and then the grief. Her three best friends had moved in and stayed with her through the funeral. They had stood by her during the endless weeks of trying to untangle her father's estate.

But once the lawyers discovered the root of the problem and the shocking news spread through town, they had begun to avoid her, using mumbled excuses a blind man could have seen through. Almost overnight, sympathy was replaced by embarrassment.

Mariah had felt like announcing to the whole town that she was still the same person she had always been, only she wasn't. Not really. And besides, she'd had too much pride to let them see how their desertion hurt.

Now, leafing through her journal, she bit her lips and choked back a sob of bitter laughter. Oh, heavens, had she really written all this drivel about Henry Lee, with his big blue eyes and his even bigger ambitions?

Henry Lee Ball had been her first and only beau. Unlike her friend Carrie, Mariah had never been a beauty. Nor was she witty, like Ada. Nor even half so well-to-do as Lottie, whose father owned the millworks and half of Hertford County besides.

But Henry Lee had chosen her, rusty hair, freckles, plain gray eyes, and all. He'd given her her first kiss. He'd escorted her to her first dance, and then dozens more kisses and dances. When he'd been promoted to head teller at her father's bank, he had celebrated by bringing her father a box of cigars, her mother a box of candy, and Mariah herself a tiny gold locket and a dozen roses.

Oh, what glorious plans they'd made that night.

And oh, what a glorious fool she'd been. The roses had wilted, the locket had turned green within weeks, but by that time she had already recorded every look, every sigh, every touch, and every false word of flattery that had ever tripped off his tongue.

As for his kisses, they'd been nice enough, but of course, she'd had nothing to compare them with. Nor was she ever likely to in the future, unless she decided to become a fallen woman.

She was still trying to convince herself she hadn't made a mistake—not that she'd had much choice—when her dinner arrived. Without asking, Mr. McKenna placed a thick white bowl and a slab of cornbread wrapped in a napkin on the kitchen table. Mariah wondered whether to offer to pay him or merely to thank him.

"If you want molasses for your bread, I'll fetch you the jug," he offered.

"Thank you, but that won't be necessary."

Without a word, Waite nodded and let himself out. He had left his own supper untouched. Nick hadn't come in yet. He'd been out late last night, as well. Waite knew better than most that a boy's natural urges could sometimes outstrip his common sense once he reached a certain age. Oh, yes, he knew all about that, all right.

They were going to have to settle a few things about that boy's summer schedule. A lighthouse keeper's life revolved around a daily routine. With lives and property depending on him, he couldn't slack off to chase down a wild, hell-raising boy, even when the boy was his own son. The trouble was, one of the two assistants he was allotted had gone down with a septic foot and decided not to return. His replacement was slow in coming. Service was a good man, for all he was inland-born. He'd been due to rotate to his next post, but he'd put in for an extension. The two men could easily do the work of three, but Waite alone bore the burden of responsibility.

And now he had another teacher to see to. Crumbling his cornbread in a bowl, he poured buttermilk over it and commenced to eat, wondering what she thought about her first meal on the island. If such plain fare was good enough for the head keeper, he thought grimly, it was good enough for the schoolteacher. After polishing off his supper, he washed his few dishes, dried them, and put them away, thinking as he hung the dish towel out on the back porch to dry that the days were growing noticeably shorter. Sarvice had already lit the tower lantern.

If Waite had a least favorite month, it would be August. For no real reason he could pin down, except that it was the end of summer, the peak of the storm season, and hot as hell.

Feeling unusually restless, he settled to his nightly task of logging the day's events. Diligently, he opened the ledger to the proper page and wrote, "August 3, 1886: Wind SW, light. Seven schooners laying offshore this morning. Five still there. No mail. New teacher . . ."

Here he paused to stare out the window toward the teacherage. There was no sign of light. He wondered if she even knew how to trim a wick, fill a tank, polish a chimney, and light a lamp. Probably used to having servants do those things for her.

Waite could still remember his wife complaining about having to wash her own dishes and mop her own floor. He had found a woman from the village to come out and clean once a week, and another one to do the laundry, but still his wife complained. The mosquitoes raised welts on her skin. The constant sound of the surf got on her nerves. The feel of sand underfoot, the smell of oil when he refilled the tanks, the weight of her own belly, where Nick was growing—she'd hated it all.

But mostly she'd hated Waite for getting her in the fix she was in. He'd refrained from reminding her that she'd played a small part in the matter herself. She'd been the one to seduce him, not the other way around. But Waite had never been a vindictive man. Hard, some said. That he'd never denied. Life either hardened a man or it defeated him, and Waite wasn't of a mind to give in or give up.

Dipping his pen in the ink jar, he wrote, "New teacher arrived. Same as all the rest. I give her a week. Nick rode up Kinnakeet way. Fishing he says. Courting, I reckon. signed, Waitefield B. McKenna, Principal Keeper, Cape Hatteras Light."

The next morning, Mariah was up early, having slept far more soundly than she'd expected. The bed was narrow, the mattress hard, the bedding that had been provided damp, although not actually wet. She was used to humidity, but out here on the Banks it was thick enough to drown in.

She rinsed out her personal things in a basin and then wondered if there was a line to peg them to. Her supper dishes were still in the sink. She had eaten as much as she could of the perfectly dreadful meal her neighbor had brought over, and scraped the rest outside rather than leave it for the mice.

She wished now she'd saved a bite of cornbread for breakfast. The first item on her list of things to do after hanging out her clothes was to locate the store that sold food. And then, heaven help her, she was going to have to learn how to cook before she starved. Poor Bathsheba, their old cook, who'd been part of the family for as long as Mariah could remember, had given her up for hopeless years ago.

It was thinking about the wonderful feasts Bathsheba used to prepare back in Murfreesboro that had first given her the idea of turning her home into a boarding establishment. She'd had some

idea at the time that between letting rooms and
teaching school, they would be able to manage
just fine.

But that was before the last few remaining
bricks in the safe, secure wall that had surrounded
her all her life had come tumbling down around
her. Before she, along with everyone else, had
learned that president of the bank and upstanding
citizen George Sawyer had never bothered to
marry Miss Lydia Deckins. Throughout all the
years they had lived together as man and wife—
as a family with their daughter—George's real
wife had been tucked away in a mental institution
in Massachusetts.

Even now Mariah had trouble realizing that not
only was she illegitimate, but her father's legal
wife had an older brother who would inherit, as
his sister's guardian, all George Sawyer's property, which included the house and all invest-
ments.

As an illegitimate daughter, she'd been gently
informed, Mariah had no standing whatsoever before the law. Nor in the community.

Briefly she had toyed with the vain hope that
the news of her mother's disgrace and her own
illegitimacy could be kept secret. That the real
Mrs. Sawyer's brother would forget all about his
unexpected inheritance, or else be so wealthy that
a three-story house in a small southern town, with
five dormers, a dozen stained-glass window pan-
els, and the loveliest millwork in all Murfreesboro
wouldn't be worth his bother.

She might as well have wished for the moon.
The news had raced through town like wildfire.
That was when Henry Lee had cried off. Not in

so many words—he'd simply stopped coming around. That was when her three best friends had suddenly grown terribly busy. When her parents' friends had stopped recognizing her, and merchants she'd known all her life had begun to frown at her when she'd sallied forth with her market basket.

A few days later the chairman of the local school board had notified her by letter that the committee no longer felt it would be in the best interests of the community for her to teach in the local school.

Mariah, stiff as a poker in her mourning black, had marched right into his office and demanded an audience. It had not been her proudest moment. Nor, she told herself, had it been his.

"For the sake of my past friendship with your father," he'd finally allowed, "I may be able to assist you in securing a teaching position in another area. Your credentials are impeccable, my dear, as is your personal character, I'm sure." She'd nearly strangled him at that point. "As for the other rather . . . um, unfortunate situation, I see no point in bringing it up. There are still a few places in our lovely state that are so isolated they have trouble securing teachers. The pay, of course, won't be generous, but then, I don't suppose you'll require much."

That very day, Mariah, using her mother's maiden name in an impulsive burst of indignation, had written to one Maxwell Newbolt, magistrate, at a place called Buxton.

And that, she mused tiredly, had been the start of it all.

Waving away a mosquito, she paced the area

between bedroom, living room, and kitchen, a matter of a dozen steps, at most. What she'd tried to think of as her Grand New Adventure was turning out to be rather less grand than she'd anticipated.

Surely things would look more cheerful tomorrow. They could hardly look *less* cheerful. Mr. Newbolt—she had already ceased thinking of him as Maxwell—had mentioned a pounding. Ministers and their wives were given poundings whenever they moved to a new charge. Mariah and her mother had always done their share, usually contributing a basket of eggs, a side of bacon, and one of Bathsheba's lovely Lady Baltimore cakes. Although, strictly speaking, one was supposed to bring a pound of this and a pound of that.

Evidently here on the Cape, teachers also rated a pounding. She would like to believe she'd be given a pound of fried chicken, a pound of roast pork, a pound of candied sweet potatoes, and a pound of butterbeans, all hot and swimming in butter.

But it would probably be the usual staples. For which she'd be grateful, even if she didn't know quite what to do with them. She would simply learn, that was all. If one balked at the first hurdle, one would never complete the course.

Eager to explore her new world, she dressed quickly and stepped outside. The house had only one door, so she squished her way through the dry sand around to the back. It seemed she lived on the very edge of a marsh. She could only hope it wasn't prone to flooding.

The cart alongside the shed wasn't pretty, but

at least it looked sturdy. The seat and sides had been given a fresh coat of paint, the same unfortunate shade that had been used inside the house. Remembering the neat little gig she had driven back home, and her mare, Merrily, she sighed and then took herself to task.

The past was gone. Sooner or later she would learn to forget. And while she was at it, she would learn to drive a wooden-wheeled cart through sandy ruts. And learn to cook, because it was either that or starve, and she'd never fancied herself a martyr.

There were several horses grazing on the skimpy grass, none of them particularly attractive. According to Mr. McKenna, the roan mare was for her use. She whistled, an accomplishment that had amused her father and horrified her mother, not that she was very good at it. According to Henry Lee, her pucker was all wrong.

Not a one of the horses looked up.

"Well, how am I supposed to call you when I don't even know your name?" Elmo had always seen to that sort of thing back home. Not that she couldn't have done it herself, but it was important for Elmo, who was old and slow as molasses, to feel needed.

She brought out her clothes and pegged them to the line and whistled again, with the same results. Lacking so much as a lump of sugar to attract the little roan, she would simply have to postpone her visit to the store. Meanwhile, there was another challenge still to be faced. The ocean.

While she hadn't actually seen it yet, she'd certainly heard it. That soft, swishy sound that she'd thought at first was the wind whispering through the pine trees, only there was no wind.

It was an old fear, the water. Living here, it was one she would simply have to confront and defeat. Fear, at least, didn't show. She didn't have to be ashamed of her weakness.

Several minutes later, after trudging through the deep, soft sand, she stared out across an endless, bottomless sea and wondered why on earth she hadn't applied for a position in the mountains. Better yet, in the middle of the nearest desert.

High above, at the tower rail, Waite shifted his attention from the ships passing offshore to gaze down at the new teacher. The little fool didn't even have sense enough to wear a bonnet. Didn't she realize how hot that sun was? With her pale skin, she'd be burned to a crisp in no time at all.

The wind had picked up enough to blow her gown against her body. It was a hot wind, out of the southeast. Hot and wet and good for touching off tempers. Which meant she probably wouldn't appreciate being warned against going out in the sun bareheaded, but he felt obliged to warn her anyway.

One hand sliding along the cool iron rail, he descended the 268 steps in less time than it took him to compose his speech, half hoping she'd be gone by the time he got outside.

She was still there, arms crossed over her chest, staring out at the water. He came up behind her, his footsteps silent in the powdery sand. When she turned her head slightly, it gave him a clear view of her profile. She wasn't pretty, not in the usual way. At least, not the kind of prettiness a man noticed right off. But there was a certain strength in the delicate set of her features that surprised him. Her neck was no bigger around than his forearm. The long glossy hair that blew across her face was almost the color of burgundy wine.

She was sweating.

But then, ladies didn't sweat, they glowed. His wife had told him that.

All right, so she was glowing. There were patches of glow in the small of her back, at the neck of her gown, and under her arms. "Ma'am, you ought not to be out here in the heat of the day without a bonnet."

She let out a yelp, making him feel guilty for startling her. But then, she'd have been just as startled if he'd spoken to warn her of his presence. There were times when a man just couldn't win, no matter which road he took.

Mariah recovered her composure quickly. Compared to something as vast as the Atlantic Ocean, the keeper didn't seem quite so terrifying this morning. She was even getting accustomed to his accent so that she hardly even noticed it. "Good morning, Mr. McKenna."

"Your nose is red."

"I beg your—"

"Yeah, I know—you beg my pardon, but ma'am, your nose is still red. Five more minutes and it'll be blistered. Next time, wear a bonnet."

Mariah told herself he wasn't being deliberately offensive, he was only trying to be kind. "Thank you, I will. I hadn't intended to be out this long. I merely stepped outside to see my cart and hang out my wash, and then I thought I'd better get

acquainted with the horse I'm to use. I'd been
hearing the roar of the ocean, so I came to
explore."

"You call this a roar? It's hardly even a whisper.
Madam, you'll know when she roars, all right.
She'll come right up and knock on your front
door."

"If you're deliberately trying to frighten me, Mr.
McKenna, you'll find that I do not discourage
easily."

His expression could only be called skeptical.
For several minutes, they stood side by side, a few
feet apart, studiously ignoring one another.

At least the keeper was ignoring her. He himself
was not so easy to ignore. She'd thought the last
of the pirates that had once haunted the area had
been hanged some half a century ago, but with
his shaggy, sun-bleached hair, his angular, sun-
bronzed face, and his forbidding expression, this
man might easily be a throwback to an earlier era.

Despite the oppressive heat, she shivered.

"I don't mean to be discouraging, but did Newbolt tell you why he can't keep a teacher here?"

"I didn't ask." Perhaps she should have. It simply hadn't occurred to her.

"They come down here expecting everything
the same as what they're used to. Looking for indoor plumbing and bottled milk. For paved streets
and fancy stores where they can buy fancy geegaws. They don't know how to dress sensible nor
eat sensible, and they don't—"

"By 'eat sensible,' you're referring to a diet of
undercooked beans and overcooked cornbread, I
presume."

He had the grace to look embarrassed. If she

hadn't been so miserable, what with the heat and
the lack of a decent meal in recent days, Mariah
would never have said it, but she was running
dangerously low on good manners. "Mr. Mc-
Kenna, I assure you, I'm here to stay, no matter
how much you might wish otherwise. I have all
the fancy geegaws I could possibly need. I don't
care for milk, bottled or otherwise. As for indoor
plumbing, I'm sure I'll adjust. In other words, sir,
you may do your best to drive me away, but
you'll not succeed, that I promise you."

And so the battle lines were drawn. Waite convinced himself it was for her own good that he
discouraged her from staying on. She would never
survive a winter on the island. Summers were bad
enough, with the air so hot and damp that half
the time a body needed gills to breathe. And then
there were the snakes, the mosquitoes, the ticks
and biting flies.

Winters were even more discouraging. While
there was seldom much snow or ice, the damp,
wind-driven cold cut right through to the bone.
The wind alone, even without a storm, could drive
the sound tide up the creeks and over the land so
fast a body could be trapped inside for days unless he wanted to wade. The island women waited
it out, doing whatever women did at such times.
His wife had complained. His mother had run off.

It was the isolation city women hated most, that
much he did know. The thought of being stuck
out in the middle of the ocean like a bit of flotsam,
subjected to constant howling winds and tides
that washed clean across the island . . .

He glanced over toward the teacherage, wondering how she would like being trapped inside for days on end, alone.

Not that she'd be here long enough to find out.

A handful of flimsy garments pinned crookedly to the wash line flapped disconsolately in the light breeze. Waite grinned. Mariah followed his gaze and blushed. And then, her back stiff as a flagstaff, she turned and trudged off, her narrow two-toned shoes sinking deeply with every step.

What she needed was some wide, flat-soled boots. Fancy high heels were no good for sand walking. His wife had worn shoes like that. "City women," he muttered, turning back toward the lighthouse. Halfway there, he glanced back to see if she'd managed to avoid the worst patch of sandspurs.

She hadn't. He should've thought to warn her about those, too. Looking about as substantial in her thin gray gown as a wisp of fog, she plowed right through the things. Too late to warn her now. Her skirttails would already be full of spurs. And her stockings. And however many petticoats she had on. More than one, he figured, from the way she was . . . glowing.

Determination was a wonderful thing. Mariah managed to lure her horse, hitch up her cart, and find her way unaided to Mr. Cyrus's store. But determined or not, she discovered that her cooking skills had not magically improved overnight, even though she'd spent hours poring over Bathsheba's handwritten recipes.

What on earth was butter the size of a walnut? An English walnut or a black walnut? Hulled or unhulled?

And a spoonful of cornmeal. What size spoon? A teaspoon? A soup spoon? A cooking spoon?

Three glugs of buttermilk? And what, pray tell, was a dollop?

She stocked up on soda crackers, shriveled apples, and strong cheese, which she shared with her mice. Actually, the tinned soup was quite acceptable, if one overlooked the scorched taste. She still hadn't quite mastered the stove.

She was losing pounds she could ill afford to lose. At this rate, she wouldn't have the strength to drive herself to school, much less conduct classes. Her gowns were hanging from her frame, and she lacked even the basic sewing skills to take them in. Back in Murfreesboro, dressmakers did that sort of thing. Just as cooks did the cooking, washerwomen did the wash, and housekeepers did the housekeeping. It was simply the way things were, she'd been told when she'd wanted to try her hand at everything, way back when she was hardly old enough to see the top of a kitchen table.

Her mare was called Conk. Mr. McKenna's assistant, who looked after all the animals, had said so. The mare was named not after the mollusk, but because you occasionally had to conk her on the head to make her settle down. She found that out soon enough, as well. In fact, after being on the island less than three days, Mariah had learned any number of useful things.

On the day of the pounding, she awoke with a headache. Wiping her temples with lavender water didn't help at all, nor did lying in bed in the stifling heat with a damp cloth over her eyes.

Knowing that within a few hours half the village would be showing up on her doorstep, ostensibly to bring offerings of food, but actually to look over the new schoolmarm, she got up, dressed in her coolest gown, a lavender lawn with loose-fitting sleeves, and selected her widest brimmed hat, a Milano straw with gray ribbons she could tie under her chin, for her morning walk to the shore. Fresh air and exercise might not help her headache, but it couldn't hurt. At least it would take her mind off her discomfort.

Mr. McKenna had been right about her nose. Not only had it reddened, it had peeled, and now it resembled a new potato. There was a fresh scattering of freckles across her cheeks and forehead, and even a few on her throat.

Not that she had ever been overly vain, but the effects of six months of mourning, followed by one shock right after another, and now all this relentless sunshine, were taking their toll on whatever negligible claim to beauty she possessed.

On her very first morning in residence, Mariah had resolved to face the ocean at least once a day on the theory that a fear unconfronted would remain unconquered. Standing well back from the reach of the waves, she assured herself she was perfectly safe. After the first few times, she even discovered a certain pleasure in watching the gulls swoop and dive, watching the children splashing about in the shallows, and a few of the older, bolder ones swimming out past the breakers.

They all swam like fish. They came roaring ashore on the backs of huge waves, washing right up onto the sandy beach, laughing and calling back and forth. Mariah promised herself that next summer—or perhaps the summer after that—she would take off her shoes and wade right out into the water with them. She simply would not permit fear to rule her life.

"You're wearing a bonnet. That's smart."

The voice came right out of the blue. She slapped a hand over her heart. "I do wish you would think to announce your presence!"

"I just did."

"Yes, well . . . you were right about the sun." She touched her peeling nose.

"It's not all that bad." He leaned forward and peered at her nose, and Mariah found her own gaze snared by those rich brown eyes of his, shot through with golden sparkles. She was coming to suspect that there was more to the man than a sharp tongue and a quick temper. Her gaze strayed to his mouth and then darted away again.

Stepping back, Waite cleared his throat. "I brought your mail." He handed her a heavy cream envelope addressed in a familiar hand. Mariah took it, glanced at it, and he stood there, almost as if he were waiting for her to open it and read it to him.

She knew what it was, of course. She'd been half expecting it. The real surprise was that it no longer even mattered to her that the man she'd once expected to marry was marrying her ex-best friend.

She never even noticed that the announcement was addressed to Miss Mariah Deekins Sawyer. Nor did she notice the puzzled look the lighthouse keeper gave her.

Chapter Three

The moment she got inside, Mariah tossed the envelope aside, unopened. She knew what it would say without reading it, and really, that part of her life was over. The best part was that she felt no great urge to swear or weep or throw something. By all rights she should be feeling a modicum of righteous indignation, yet all she could manage was a twinge of mild annoyance. Carrie could have him, and welcome. The world Mariah had left behind—a world of friends and family, of giggles and whispered confidences, stolen kisses and longing looks—now seemed so dim it was as if it had all happened to someone else.

As, in a sense, it had.

Quickly, she removed her hat and brushed her hair, arranging it in what she considered a teacherly style. Not that it would stay. Heavy and slick, there hadn't been a hairpin made that would hold it for very long. By the time the first of the pounders arrived, the headache she had walked to the beach to escape had completely gone, and she felt a surge of anticipation, not untouched by shyness.

Rhoda Quigley was a widow. "You'll have my three," she announced after setting two jars of fig preserves and a peck of meal on the table. "Mar-

shall, he's ten, Annie, she's nine, and Baby Jo-
cephus, he'll be seven come November. They'll
not give you any trouble, else you come to me
and I'll set 'em straight."

Mariah didn't believe in tale-bearing. While
she'd had no actual teaching experience, she was
convinced, however naively, that good intentions
would produce good results.

The widow Quigley examined everything in the
small room, which took less than a minute. "Last
teacher we had didn't last no time. Come late last
March, gone before the dust settled. Yonder comes
Malthea. Don't let her get off on that orange tree
of hers, or she'll talk your ear off. Thinks she's the
only woman ever sprouted a seed."

Malthea—Miz Malthea, as everyone called
her—came and stayed nearly an hour without
once mentioning her orange tree. She brought a
slab of salt-cured side meat and her husband
brought in a crock of salt mullet, after which he
blushed and backed out, hat in hand. Mariah
smiled and thanked them both, and then turned
to greet the next caller.

The women were friendly, if rather reserved.
From youngest to eldest, they bore themselves
with a quiet dignity that Mariah could only ad-
mire. She was treated with respect for her position, but it occurred to her that she would have
to earn their respect as a person. Somewhat to her
surprise, she found that she badly wanted that
approval.

By the time her last caller left, she was limp
with both fatigue and relief, but on the whole reassured that she had done the right thing by coming out here.

Her small cottage was crammed to the brim with comestibles, most of which were in their basic form, the most basic of all being the coop of chickens out back—two pullets, one rooster, and a layer, along with a sack of cracked corn to feed them.

Mercy, if she had to cope with much more island generosity, she didn't know where she would put it. She was still pondering that problem when Waite McKenna rapped on the frame of her open door and stepped inside.

"Newbolt's on the way. Got some papers he wants to go over with you." Coatless, he had obviously been working outside. Several buttons on his white shirt were open to reveal a sweat-damp throat. His sleeves were rolled up over dark, muscular forearms that glistened as if his skin had been oiled.

Mariah told herself that the reason she was having trouble catching her breath was that he had startled her, but the truth was, the entire room suddenly seemed to throb with his vitality. He was . . .

The phrase that came to mind was excessively masculine.

"Pounding go all right?"

"It was lovely. You could've come; I'm sure you'd have been welcome."

Waite tried to ignore the subtle scent that always seemed to surround her. Today the flowery odor was mingled with corned mullet, smoked bacon, and fresh-baked bread. He made a sound deep in his throat. "Pounding's more a woman's thing," he opined.

Not that he would have come in any case. He'd

never been one for socializing. Now, with only
two men to do the work of three, he scarcely had
time to eat, much less say grace. Aside from the
most important duty of all, that of keeping the
lantern burning, there was the bookkeeping and
maintenance, the oil to be toted up to the tanks
every day, wicks constantly in need of trimming,
and glass that salted up outside, sooted up inside,
and sometimes had to be polished twice a day.
Not to mention the heavy weights that turned the
clockwork gears that rotated the lens, which had
to be cranked all the way up to the top each
morning.

He looked at her and then looked away, uncomfortable with the images that peppered his mind
before he could shut them out. There was something about the woman that just plain drew a
man's eyes. All that gleaming hair. Those clear
gray eyes set in beds of black lashes. Not to mention her pink nose . . . thinking he could wrap
both hands around her waist and touch fingers
and thumbs, fore and aft . . . he wondered if she'd
been married, or if she was widowed, or if she'd
just forgotten her own name. Something was out
of kilter, but he wasn't about to question her. The
less he knew about the woman, the better he'd
sleep at night.

Shifting his attention to the assortment of
crocks, sacks, and baskets that cluttered her small
living quarters, he said, "They grubbed you up
right smart, I see."

Mariah took a moment to translate and then
acknowledged that everyone had indeed been
generous. "Although I'm not sure where I'll find

room to store everything. Some things can go in the shed, I suppose."

"Raccoons."

"Oh."

Outside the door, a horse whickered. Having livestock wandering at will took a bit of getting used to. Not only did she have to watch out for sandspurs and prickly pear cactus, she had to watch out for . . .

Well. She would simply have to watch her step, that was all.

Waite reached out and tilted the lid on a stoneware crock. "Mullet. Better drain 'em off and salt 'em down regular, else they'll not be fit to eat."

"The ladies explained all that. They were very helpful."

"Likely trying to bribe you to stick out the season. Last one didn't stay long enough to dust off the blackboard. One of the older boys set off a stink bomb under her chair." Waite didn't know why he was bothering to warn her. The sooner Newbolt gave up and sent for a male teacher who was both big enough and tough enough to handle those young hellions—his own included—the sooner he and his crew could go back to minding their own business.

"I was warned that the greatest pranksters are a pair named Dorien and Nick. Mrs. Quigley said I should start the day by whipping them good for all the devilment they'd be up to by dinnertime."

Out back, a hen cackled. A chorus of frogs in the nearby ponds called for rain. In the presence of the prim, delicate woman, Waite felt like a clumsy giant. Nevertheless, there was a quiet note of authority in the soft island brogue when he said, "High spirits never hurt a boy, Miss Deekins. You stick to book-teaching and leave any whippings to me."

"Nick is your son, isn't he?"

Mariah knew he was. By now she felt as if she knew all there was to know about every family in the village. She had been told that Waite McKenna had no use for women and that he had raised his son with a similar disregard. And that Maxwell Newbolt had six children, named in alphabetical order, and that the eldest three were handsome but trifling, the youngest pair had unspecified problems, and the one named Dorien was wild as a buck.

She knew that Cora Clark didn't care for Rhoda Quigley and vice versa, and that the woman who grew the biggest collards also bought paregoric by the pint. She still wasn't certain if there was supposed to be a connection between the two things.

"Leave Nick to me," Waite said quietly. "If you need a hand stowing your supplies, I'll send Sarvice over directly he gets done toting oil."

What was there about the man that never failed to put her on the defensive? Other than the fact that he openly expected her to fail, of course. "That won't be necessary. I'm sure I can manage."

Of course she could manage. All she had to do was find hammer and nails and build herself a raccoon-safe storage room in the shed behind her cottage. It was obvious that the teacherage had been designed and built by a single man, because other than the one small wall cabinet, there wasn't a closet or a shelf to be found, much less a pantry.

"Take my advice, get those chickens up off the

ground before dark. Even if a raccoon don't figure out how to open the coop, a rat snake'll likely get 'em. Be surprised at what one of those big ones can swallow."

Mariah caught a spark of sheer devilment in his eyes and knew he was trying again to frighten her away. Before she could tell him that snakes didn't bother her at all, Maxwell Newbolt arrived. He called through the door, "Good afternoon, and just how did the festivities go today, Mariah? Did you get everything you need?" Without waiting to be invited, he let himself in, as if he had every right.

And then he saw Waite and frowned. Waite frowned right back. "Don't let me keep you, Mc-Kenna. Mariah and I have business to discuss."

Waite looked for a moment as if he meant to stay, but then, without another word, he left. Feeling oddly deflated, Mariah watched through the window as he strode across to the principal keeper's house. Even from the back, he looked angry. But then, he almost always looked angry.

"Ruffian," Maxwell Newbolt muttered, recalling her to her manners. Removing a basket of sweet potatoes from the rocker, she invited him to be seated and sank gratefully onto the other seat in the room, a spoke-backed chair painted blue to match the walls.

"I was hoping to meet your children today," she said. Several of the women had been accompanied by young children, who had stared solemnly at the woman who would soon be drilling them in reading, writing, and arithmetic.

"Evie had wash to do. Franklin, my youngest, helps out."

"You have six children, I believe?"

Maxwell shifted position and crossed his left leg over his right. "Older boys rode down to Hatteras to deliver some papers for me. You'll soon come to understand, my dear, how much these people depend on me. My time is never my own." He sighed and set the rocker in motion, his face a study in martyred patience. "However, you'll be meeting my little family tonight. I came partly to deliver an invitation to supper."

Mariah glanced at the array of foodstuffs covering every available surface, including the floor. "Supper? That sounds delightful." Any meal she didn't have to prepare herself sounded delightful.

"Fine, fine. I'll expect you at five, then. First road to the left past the post office. It's the yellow house with the birdhouses. Only painted house on the road."

"I'm looking forward to it." She made note of the fact that unlike back in Murfreesboro, a dinner invitation from a gentleman did not necessarily include his escort. "You said you came partly to deliver an invitation? Was there something else?"

He rose and took a turn around the cluttered room, hands clasped behind him. Mariah pushed back the irreverent thought that he resembled nothing so much as a banty rooster.

One with exceedingly plump drumsticks.

Why on earth would any man with a grain of common sense wear a high-collared shirt, a tie, a vest, and a coat on the hottest day of summer? An open-throated shirt with the cuffs turned back would be far more comfortable.

And why on earth would she even be thinking about such things?

Maxwell cleared his throat. "There seems to be

a slight discrepancy in the records your college
sent. They just arrived on the mailboat. The school
office has been closed for the summer, which is a
deuced inconvenience, if you'll forgive my plain
speaking. Thing is, the records they sent are for a
Miss Mariah Sawyer. As was the letter that arrived
this morning."

It took a moment to register. When it did, Mariah took a deep breath and closed her eyes. Oh,
for heaven's sake, what had she been thinking of?

"Mariah? My dear, are you feeling faint?" Maxwell Newbolt whipped out a handkerchief that
reeked of stale cologne and flapped it in front of
her face.

"No, I—that is, I'm quite all right."

"Then there's been some mistake? Well, of
course there has. The idiots obviously sent me the
wrong records."

"No, they're the right records. I was known as
Mariah Sawyer when I attended college."

"I see," he said thoughtfully, when it was obvious that he didn't see at all. But before Mariah
could think of a delicate way to explain her situation, the magistrate did it for her, his damp face
red with compassion. "Oh, my dear girl, how very
tragic! You never mentioned your widowhood,
but I should have guessed. My only excuse is that
you look so lovely in lavender, it never occurred
to me that it was half-mourning."

Good Lord, what do I do now?

"You never actually mentioned your marital
status in your gracious letters, so naturally I as-
sumed—I mean, teachers are usually . . . But I
must tell you how I looked forward to each and
every one. Of your letters, I mean. Still, though

I've never claimed to be a wise man, my dear, I must admit, I sensed right off that there was something . . . an echo of tragedy in your lovely words, that spoke directly to my own heart." His voice dropped half an octave. "For I, too, have known great sadness."

Slightly dazed, Mariah thought, *Mercy! the man talks precisely the way he writes.* All those flowery words and phrases she had considered so courtly and romantic on paper sounded downright silly when spoken.

He rose and came to stand before her. Thinking he was about to kneel, she feared for the seams in his trousers. "I do believe," he said earnestly, "that it was your letters that made me select you from among all the many other applicants."

Well, what else would it have been? she wondered.

"It was as if I sensed somehow that you, a young widow, were reaching out to a kindred spirit."

He took her hand between his sweaty palms, and Mariah, too embarrassed to protest, repressed a shudder of distaste. His hands were warm, damp, and soft, his manner entirely too encroaching.

"There, now, we'll not mention it again, my dear. I can see you're still not over losing your helpmeet, but the Lord works in mysterious ways. Yes, indeed, He does. I believe He must have sent you to us for a purpose."

He wagged a finger before her face, and Mariah struggled to keep her eyes from crossing. A few minutes later she saw him to the door, wishing rather desperately there were some way she could

get out of the dinner engagement without jeopard-
izing her position.

On the other hand, a meal was a meal, and until
she mastered both cookstove and cookbook, she
couldn't afford to turn down any offer.

At half past four, feeling more than ever like an
imposter, Mariah buttoned up her gray twill with
the black military braid trim. It was too heavy for
the season, but entirely suitable for a young
widow. Heavens, how could she possibly have
made such a muddle of things? Through no fault
of her own, she had lived a lie all her life, but this
time, she had no one to blame but herself.

Were American schoolteachers in demand in
China? Or perhaps in Constantinople?

Against all reason, she knew that what she
dreaded most of all was not losing her job, but
hearing Waite McKenna say, "I told you so." Drat
his superior, mocking face. He was just waiting
for her to fail!

With a sigh of resignation, she turned her back
on all the sacks, crocks, and baskets yet to be put
away—or perhaps not—and pulled the door
closed behind her to keep out stray wildlife.
Sooner or later, the truth would catch up to her.
Truth always did, as she had learned to her sor-
row. But until then, she refused to run away. She
was weary of running.

When she went to harness up the mare, Sarvice
Jones was setting her chicken coop up off the
ground onto a makeshift platform. "I made a wire
latch for the door to keep the coons out, Miss Deekins. Them rascals'll get into things you'd ha'
swore was locked up tight. First chance I get, I'll

build you a bigger place, all wired in with a nest box and everything.''

She thanked him profusely, and he blushed. He was really a very nice young man. Painfully shy, but then, there were far worse sins than shyness. Arrogance, for instance.

After only two wrong turns, she located the Newbolt home. Unlike most of the other houses, which blended modestly with the wooded surroundings, the Newbolt house stood forth proudly. The yard was primped to a fare-thee-well, with shell-lined flower beds, half a dozen fancy birdhouses, a boardwalk path edged with upturned bottles, and every tree in sight whitewashed halfway up the trunk. She counted seven lightning rods on the roof and two on the washhouse out back.

Mercy! No tree would dare drop a leaf on this lawn!

The inside was every bit as meticulously kept as the outside. Maxwell met her at the door and ushered her into a room that struck her as utterly inhospitable. Varnish gleamed everywhere. Starched antimacassars perched stiffly on a plush upholstered sofa. A pair of straight-backed chairs stood at attention against the far wall, and two matched vases, both empty, a clock, and three china plates were arranged with mathematical precision on the mantel under a framed diploma from a small northern seminary.

''Evie'll be along with refreshments. Won't you take a seat?''

To tell the truth, she was afraid to, for fear of disturbing something. Her own home had been far more handsomely furnished, but there were

always newspapers that were never refolded quite
properly, occasionally a scattering of ashes from
her father's cigar, a book turned down, or her
mother's embroidery left spilling across a chair. In
summer, there were vases of fresh flowers on
every available surface, and as often as not a few
fallen petals beneath them.

Here not a single thing was out of place, not so
much as a speck of dust. She sat gingerly, feet
together on the red Turkey carpet. Maxwell
pinched the creases in his trousers and took his
place on the sofa. He smiled at her. Nervously,
she smiled back. Panic stuck like a dry biscuit in
her throat, and she wondered what would happen
if she were to blurt out the truth.

*As it happens, sir, I'm not a widow. Indeed, I've
never been married. Unfortunately, neither were my
parents. However, breeding notwithstanding, I mastered mental philosophy and moral science, physics and
botany, English literature and critical readings, zool-
ogy, geology, and physiology. In other words, sir, I am
a thoroughly qualified teacher.*

Would he be impressed?

Probably not.

"I take it you're settling in?" Maxwell inquired,
and she nodded.

"Everyone's been most helpful."

"I'll apologize for anything McKenna might
have said to upset you. The man's barely civil.
Comes of living out there all alone, I expect. Then,
too, there was his wife, poor woman. Not to mention his mother."

What about his wife? What about his mother?
And he was hardly alone, she thought, with Sarvice Jones and the other keeper, who, according

to Mr. Jones, happened not to be in residence at the moment. But before she could comment, a small girl with wild, carroty hair limped into the room carrying a tray that looked far too heavy for her skinny little arms to support.

"My goodness," Mariah cried, leaping up instinctively to grab it before it crashed.

The child flushed so that her myriad freckles looked pale green. Maxwell glared at her. "You should've made two trips instead of trying to bring everything in at once," he snapped.

"Yes, Papa," the child whispered. Mariah could have swatted the man. She looked around for someplace to set the tray, which was every bit as heavy as it looked, and Maxwell belatedly came to her assistance, clearing a place on a highly polished table.

Why couldn't he have done the same for his daughter? She didn't think much of a man whose manners were reserved only for strangers.

This child's problem was obvious as soon as she scurried from the room. In a dress that was both too short and faded almost colorless, covered by an apron big enough to wrap around her twice, the awkward twist of her left foot was painfully visible.

"Oh, dear, the poor child," she murmured. "Can nothing be done?"

Just as if she hadn't spoken, Maxwell clapped his hands. "Franklin, come in and pay your respects to Mrs. Deekins," he commanded, and a small boy wearing clothes that were both too old for his age and too large for his size peeped into the room, ducked his head, and mumbled something under his breath.

"My youngest son, Franklin. Franklin's somewhat slow, isn't that right, boy? But we have high
hopes you'll be able to bring him around, my
dear." His fatuous smile sparked a slow-burning
fuse inside Mariah that continued to smolder as,
over the next few hours, she met and dined with
the various members of the Newbolt brood.

Able was the eldest. She set his age at close to
her own. Tall, blond, and startlingly handsome,
he exuded the kind of easy charm that probably
made him a favorite with the girls. After the first
few minutes, Mariah didn't find him particularly
charming. He sauntered into the dining room after
everyone else was seated, sprawled in a chair with
neither apology nor explanation, treated her to a
slow, appreciative appraisal that stopped just
short of being fresh, and then proceeded to entertain them all with a tale about a dog that was
terrorizing an elderly widow.

Mariah didn't find the story amusing. Nor did
young Evie, who was in and out, fetching and
carrying for her father and brothers. Mariah offered once to help her bring in the platters, but
the poor child looked so stricken she quickly
subsided.

The second son was Baxter. He was almost as
tall, almost as blond, almost as handsome as Able,
but he was quieter. Mariah suspected that of the
two, he was the more intelligent.

And then there were the next two, Caleb and
Dorien. Caleb, whose age she put at about eigh-
teen, was every bit as attractive as his older brothers, but in a different way. With dark, wildly
curling hair and laughing blue eyes, he was, as
his father informed her, a caution, a rare caution.

Dorien, the jokester, lived up to his reputation. "Miz Deekins, have you ever noticed when a V-shaped flock of geese fly over, that one leg of the V is always longer than the other?"

Mariah truly hadn't, but said she had.

"You know why that is?" the irrepressible boy asked, and she shook her head, amused, but suspecting he'd be a handful to manage.

" 'Cause it's got more geese in it."

Able groaned. Baxter shook his head. Caleb said, "Shootfire, I told you that joke last week, now you go and tell it like you was the one that thought it up."

"You didn't think it up, either," put in one of the other boys. "I heard it down at the landing way back last spring."

Franklin piped up, "Papa, may I be excused? I hafta use the—"

"When everyone is finished with supper, boy."

"But Papa . . ."

Mariah wanted to say, *For heaven's sake, let the child go!* For someone who had never had the least experience with children, she was discovering that she had rather strong feelings.

"Evie, bring me some more biscuits!" Able called over his shoulder.

Evie brought in more biscuits, but she never joined them at the table. Not until midway through the meal did it occur to Mariah that with a guest present, there was no room for another chair. She felt dreadful. Felt like seeking out Evie and apologizing, at the very least. She wanted to believe there was a kindhearted cook out in the kitchen who was stuffing the poor child with chicken and greens and pudding.

"Evie, bring in the coffee!" called out one of the brothers.

The child hurried in with a heavy coffeepot, looking hot and harried and scared to death she might spill a drop.

"Go get the blackberry wine," Maxwell ordered.

"Yeah, and while you're at it, bring me some more of that pudding."

"Me, too, and I want some molasses on mine."

"Papa, *please*? I've got to go real bad." Poor little Franklin.

Mariah was beginning to believe the meal would never end when someone knocked on the front door. Maxwell called for his daughter to answer it, and Mariah barely managed to bite back the remark that rose to her lips. Listening to the uneven tread as the child hurried in from the summer kitchen, past the dining room, and all the way to the front door, she thought that she was going to do something for that child, one way or another, before she left the island.

There was a general scraping of chairs, then Maxwell, followed by the rest of the Newbolts, escorted Mariah out into the hall.

Waite McKenna stood just inside the door. In his dark lighthouse keeper's uniform, he was a formidable sight. He nodded to the little girl half hidden behind the door, removed his hat, and said solemnly, "Evening, Miss Evie." With a frightened look, the child scurried back to the kitchen. Waite turned toward Maxwell. "Newbolt, there's been some trouble down on Dark Ridge Road. Man got hurt real bad. Some question of how it happened."

"In case you haven't noticed, McKenna, I happen to have a guest," Maxwell said stiffly. And then, to the four stalwart sons flanking him, "Well? What are you waiting for? You boys ride on over and see what's going on." He turned to Mariah and took her hand in his own. "You see? It's just as I told you, my dear. A magistrate's time is never his own."

Mariah translated his words to mean *See how important I am?* and then felt ashamed of her own small-mindedness.

Able edged his father aside, took Mariah's hand, bowed low over it, and came up with a wicked twinkle in his eyes. "It's been a genu-wine pure pleasure, ma'am," he drawled.

Lordy, he must be a handful, she thought, unable to hold back an answering smile.

The two oldest boys left. The youngest dashed down the hall, and a moment later Mariah heard a door slam. "Poor little tadpole," said Caleb. "I reckon he peed his pants again."

Ignoring him, Maxwell said, "Was that all, Mc-Kenna? As you can see, the matter is being dealt with."

"If you call sending a couple of boys off down the ridge dealing, then I reckon it is. You're the magistrate." Waite towered over all the Newbolt men. He didn't need to raise his voice to command authority, nor did he.

"Drat it, McKenna, this can wait until morning! I'm not a physician. If the man's hurt, go tell Miss Agnes. She'll know what to do."

Waite continued to regard him silently. Caleb and Dorien looked at one another and shrugged. Then Dorien said, "I reckon maybe you'd better ride on down, Papa. I'll go with you in case you need a hand."

Maxwell, clearly furious, snapped that it wouldn't be necessary. "You boys see Miz Deekins home for me. A man can't even spend a quiet evening in his own home without—"

"I'll see Miz Deekins home," Waite said quietly.

Mariah could feel the atmosphere tighten around her. She felt the same way just before an electrical storm. "Miz Deekins can see herself home," she snapped, acutely aware of the metamorphosis of her title. She had intended to tell poor Evie how much she enjoyed her meal, but that could wait. The child would be one of her students. Thank heavens the older Newbolts would not.

Chapter Four

It was not quite dark, even though it seemed as if they had lingered at the table forever. Mariah did her best to ignore the man riding silently behind the cart as she followed the barely visible ruts out to the main road, but he was hard to ignore.

Instead, she thought about Evie. Was the child frightened, or simply shy? Or perhaps she was embarrassed by her affliction. One would think the only daughter in a family of sons would receive special treatment, even without her disability; but then, she herself had been an only child. She had no idea how larger families functioned. She did know, however, that she would never have treated a servant in her own home the way Evie was treated. The truth was, she'd been shamelessly indulged, even to the point of being allowed to attend the local college. None of her friends had attended. Her mother had said college was a waste of time for a girl.

Her father had said, "Oh, Lydia, let the girl give it a try if she wants to."

Her father had been like that. If she'd wanted to try harness racing, he'd have said, "Give it a go, honey!"

In the fast-fading light, Mariah savored the spicy fragrance of sun-warmed cedars, resinous pines, and wild grapes as her mind filtered through the impressions of the last few hours. The little mare twitched her ears, swished her tail, and plodded along the winding road, and Mariah made a diligent effort to focus her mind on the Newbolt ménage and not on the man riding silently behind her on his big, rangy gelding. Waite McKenna was not her escort. They simply happened to be going in the same direction.

"*Mrs.* Deekins?"

"What?"

"I thought teachers were supposed to be single."

Mariah detested lies, she really, truly did, yet somehow she'd managed to get herself trapped in a web of the nasty things. "Widows sometimes teach," she said, which was true enough.

"I reckon," Waite replied. To her relief, he seemed disinclined to prolong the conversation.

There was barely enough light filtering through the trees to make out the pale, sandy trail. Fortunately, the mare seemed to know her way home. Except for a deafening chorus of frogs and insects, and the constant murmur of the nearby surf, all was quiet. Almost too quiet. As if something were waiting to happen.

And then, somewhere in the edge of the woods, a chuck-will's-widow set up her monotonous threnody, and Mariah wondered with a desolate sort of amusement, *Whose-widow-am-I, whose-widow-am-I?*

Whose widow would she ever be? Although she tried not to dwell on it, the knowledge that she would never be free to marry and bear children saddened her almost as much as the loss of her family, her friends, and her home. Far more than the loss of her ex-fiancé.

When she had first learned the truth, she'd blamed her parents for living a lie and bringing a child, all unsuspecting, into that lie. Yet over time, her bitterness had faded, along with the first devastating sense of loss. Whatever had happened in the lives of Lydia Deekins and George Sawyer all those years ago was their story, not hers. She tried not to dwell on it.

From close behind her a horse whickered. Waite's gelding. Ugly creature, she mused. Unlike its rider. Should she make an effort to converse with him for the sake of politeness? Not that she thought for one moment he'd appreciate the gesture. If he had anything to say to her, she decided, he could say it, and she would respond. Evidently he didn't, so they continued to plod along in silence.

Back home in Murfreesboro, she thought nostalgically, the evening would be well under way by now, with gigs and carriages rattling past on their way to various entertainments. People taking the evening air on their verandas would call back and forth to one another. Dogs would bark, and the sound of Miss Penelope's piano and the choir practicing for Sunday service would carry clearly on the still summer air through the open church windows.

Here on this narrow strip of barrier island, the only sounds were of frogs, cicadas, and the occasional night bird. Except for the intermittent gleam of the lighthouse, there weren't even any comforting lights.

And then, suddenly, a jagged bolt of lightning streaked across the sky, followed almost immediately by a bone-rattling blast of thunder. The mare snorted and reared, causing the cart to lurch out of its sandy ruts. After one startled yelp, Mariah reacted instinctively. A few calming words, a firm hand on the reins, and the little mare settled down again, although getting the cart back in the proper ruts took slightly more effort.

Waite rode up beside her. "Move over. I'll drive," he said with what she considered unnecessary condescension.

"You'll do no such thing." Her heart was still throbbing like a kettledrum, but in the face of his attitude, anger quickly replaced fear. "It was hardly my fault the poor thing bolted. What sensitive creature wouldn't?"

Waite made a rude noise. "Sensitive, my—"

"I defy you to handle her any better than I did."

"Defy away. Leastwise I'm not afraid of a little lightning."

"Nor am I!"

She heard his snort of disbelief and couldn't much blame him. As it happened, she was terrified of lightning. Or, more specifically, of the thunder that accompanied it. Had been ever since she'd accidentally trapped herself in the attic as a child during a terrible thunder squall. She'd been playing dress-up because it was too rainy to go outside. At the first clap of thunder, she had crawled into a trunk, closed the lid, and been unable to lift it open again.

She hadn't been found until late that night, after half the town had spent hours searching the countryside.

All right, so after all these years, some things still made her somewhat uneasy. She was not afraid of mice. Didn't like them, but didn't fear them. That went for snakes and spiders, too. It was only loud thunder and large bodies of water that bothered her, but she'd be blessed if she would admit any fear, justified or not, to a man who was just waiting to pounce at the first sign of weakness.

Thunder continued to growl all around them like a slow-moving freight train. Lightning stabbed the horizon. Twice more the mare shied, and once would have bolted if Mariah hadn't kept a steadying hand on the reins.

"Shhh, Merrily, there's a good girl," she murmured.

"Her name is Conk."

"Her new name is Merrily. Conk is a ridiculous name for a horse. No wonder the poor beast balked."

A cannon blast sounded behind them as lightning struck a nearby tree. Mariah, her eyes wide and glassy, felt perspiration break out beneath her layers of clothing. It occurred to her that Maxwell might have had a very good reason for all those lightning rods on his roof. Everything, including the weather, seemed so much more immediate out here on this exposed strip of island.

"Dry shift," Waite said laconically.

"I beg your pardon?" At the rate she was perspiring, her shift was probably as damp as her palms by now.

"Wind's fixing to shift to the northeast. I doubt we'll have more'n a few sprinkles of rain."

"Oh." For a moment she thought he'd been re-marking on the state of her underwear.

Brilliant, Mariah! Your courage is almost as impressive as your intellect.

"Might want to throw a tarp over your chickens, just in case I'm wrong."

"You? Wrong? Heaven forfend," she said with a show of bravado. She thought she heard him chuckle. To tell the truth, she'd had so much to think about, she'd forgotten all about the poor creatures. "But thank you, I will."

"If you'd like a hand . . ."

Mariah had heard enough by now, both from the villagers and from Waite himself, to know how deeply he resented having to do anything for whoever happened to be installed in the teacher-age, simply because he was the nearest neighbor. "I'm perfectly capable of looking after my own chickens." They had reached the place where the path left the village and turned toward the light-house. "But again, I thank you," she added graciously.

"Might want to hang a weight on the corners, just to be sure your tarp doesn't blow off."

Her tarp. She knew what a tarpaulin was . . . vaguely. She was fairly sure she didn't have one, much less any notion of how to hang weights on the corners, but she would manage. She would manage just fine. She hadn't come this far to be frightened off by a bit of wind, some noise, and a few chickens.

Waite plodded silently along beside her until they reached the lighthouse clearing. Then, with-out a word, he turned toward his own house. Ma-riah stared after him for several moments, feeling vaguely disappointed. With an impatient snort, she drove around behind her cottage, jumped down, and began unhitching the cart. How many times had old Elmo been waiting to put away her mare and gig? How many times had she taken such services for granted?

She wished now she had expressed her appreciation more often.

Another bolt of lightning split the sky out over the ocean, causing the mare to shy and kick up her heels. Mariah murmured soothingly as she eased off the bridle. "Hush, now, darling, it'll be over before you know it. It's only a dry shift."

Which didn't make the lightning any less dangerous, nor the thunder any less deafening.

She was wondering whether or not she should lead the little mare under the shed, rub her down, and give her a handful of feed when Conk, newly rechristened Merrily, took matters out of her hands by wheeling around and galloping off toward a nearby cedar grove, where the ponies gathered during the heat of the day.

What a wild, strange place, she mused, not for the first time.

The low murmur of the chickens reminded her of what else she had to do. Hurrying around the cottage, head down against the wind and the constant flicker of lightning, she slammed up against something large, dark, and warm. Two hard hands bit into her shoulders, and she tipped back her head and stared up at the shadowy figure looming over her.

"Well, for heaven's sake, are you trying to scare me to death?"

"I thought you might need a hand."

Waite had thought she might need more than a hand. He'd been half expecting her to give up ever since she'd left Newbolt's place, what with the storm and that big cottonmouth that had been stretched across the road warming its belly. "Thought you might still be nervous about that snake."

"The snake?" Her voice was a breathless whisper.

"Cottonmouth. On the road. No cause to worry, though. They're not really aggressive except in mating season." She stepped away from his hands and he let her go, his palms missing the warmth of her skin under a thin covering of sleeve.

"I'm beginning to see why none of the other teachers stayed very long. You deliberately frightened them away, didn't you?"

Waite dutifully examined the accusation and accepted his rightful portion of guilt. "If I did, madam, I did it for a good reason. We need a teacher, all right, but we need a man for the job, not a timid female who's scared of her own shadow."

"For your information, I am not afraid of my shadow. Nor am I afraid of snakes."

Ignoring her remark, he proceeded on course. "My boy's starting to run wild for want of teaching."

"Then teach him. You're his father. You're supposed to teach by example."

"Dammit—begging your pardon, madam—I teach my boy what a father's supposed to teach, but there's some things he needs schooling to learn."

"Exactly!" She was good and riled now. Waite

was a little surprised to find that a woman who looked so frail could scratch up so much grit. "Which is precisely the reason I'm here," she said. In the distant flicker of lightning, he could see her hands on her hips. A wisp of breeze swirled her skirts about her limbs, and he did his best to ignore his body's instinctive response.

"What we don't need," he said evenly, "is another namby-pamby who'll throw up her soft little hands and hightail it back home at the first setback."

"So you make sure to supply a few setbacks."

"If you want to put it that way. No point in letting a woman think life here on the Banks is easy. It's not. Never was. Never will be."

"Well, thank you very much for your offer, Mr. McKenna, but—"

"My offer?" What he'd issued was a warning, not an offer.

"—but I'm perfectly capable of looking after my own chickens."

Mariah couldn't see his face clearly, but in the constant flicker of lightning out over the ocean she could see the breadth of his shoulders, the determination of his stance. A woman would have to be up to her neck in quicksand to ask a favor of a man who was just waiting for her to beg so he could turn away and gloat.

Arms crossed over her breasts, she bade him a stiff good night. Without a single word, he turned and stalked off. She sighed, wondering why every single thing the man did—or didn't do—should affect her so powerfully. He didn't want her here. He made no bones about that. She wasn't entirely sure what his reasons were, but he seemed to think, without even giving her a chance to prove otherwise, that she wasn't up to the job. He had judged her before she'd ever set foot off the mailboat. Judged her and found her wanting.

"Well, I've been judged before and found wanting," she said softly. "You're not the first and probably won't be the last."

Nevertheless, she was a little dismayed to realize that no matter how unreasonable—even if she might wish it otherwise—Waite McKenna's opinion mattered to her.

That night she opened her journal. For a long time she simply held it on her lap and thought about other times, other places. And then she uncapped her fountain pen and began to write.

Across the way, Waite watched through the window as the storm passed overhead and blew harmlessly out to sea with no more than a peppering of raindrops. As usual, his forecast had been right on target. He almost wished it hadn't. Almost wished they would have a real heller of a storm that lasted all night. Maybe then the stubborn woman would admit defeat and leave. The more he saw of her, the more urgently he wanted her to go.

Although a few of the reasons why didn't bear close examination.

The sun hadn't even lifted from the sea the next morning when Waite set out on his first rounds, after noting the weather and water conditions in his log. While Sarvice toted oil to the top of the lighthouse, Waite inspected houses, outbuildings, livestock, and gardens. Just last week Solon Benette's old boar hog had wandered out of the woods and broken a section of garden fence, allowing the deer to browse on the collard patch.

Come winter, Waite told himself, he'd have his share of smoked bacon and collard-fed venison. A man had to adapt if he wanted to survive.

The fence was intact, the grounds and outbuildings in good order, all livestock accounted for. Strictly speaking, the teacherage was not his responsibility, for it was not a part of the lighthouse grounds. But Waite had the disadvantage of being a conscience-driven man. He'd been asked to keep an eye on the house and its inhabitant, and he'd agreed to do it. What was right and what was regulation weren't always one and the same.

Besides, his own son had been partly responsible for driving off the last few teachers.

So he walked around the two-room cottage just to make sure it was all secure, which was how he came to see the yellow waterproof duster with the fancy braid trimming spread over the chicken coop. Little Miss Independent had set a chamber pot on top, tied a hand mirror to one sleeve and a ladle to the other, and then tied off the coattail with a pink ribbon, looping the standing end around the post.

He didn't know whether to laugh or swear.

He was unfastening the rigmarole when she came racing around the corner in her nightgown, her hair flopping down her back in a half-unraveled braid.

Rooted to the spot, he stared at the slender form silhouetted against the rising sun.

"Oh, for heaven's sake!" she cried. Wheeling around, she made a dash for the front door.

"I'm sorry, ma'am," he called after her.

He was sorry, all right. Sorry he'd already wasted so much time thinking about her. Sorry that, after catching her in that flimsy night shift, with her hair tumbling loose around her shoulders, he was probably going to waste a lot more.

Sorry she kept on reminding him that he still had a man's need of a woman, despite all his self-imposed rules and regulations. It had nothing to do with the woman herself. Being a widow, she probably had needs of her own. But because Nick was beginning to feel his oats and Waite had had to lecture him a time or two about keeping his britches buttoned up until he was old enough to know what he was doing, Waite hadn't felt right about visiting the woman who, for a fair and reasonable price, accommodated men in his situation.

Mariah, her fingers trembling, twisted the last tiny button through its loop, swearing under her breath at the man, the buttons, and those blasted chickens. She'd been afraid they might suffocate once the sun came up, it was that hot. And as it wasn't raining, and as she'd thought it was too early for anyone else to be up and about, she'd hurried out to uncover them before they succumbed to the heat.

She might have known her nosy neighbor would be snooping around, hoping to catch her in an indiscretion. What on earth did the man have against her? For all he knew—for all she knew herself—she could be the world's greatest teacher. Surely she deserved a chance to prove herself.

She dressed carefully for her first official duty as a teacher. Maxwell had promised to call for her this morning to drive her to the schoolhouse. She had lain awake most of the night, waiting at first for the storm to come back, wondering why the lighthouse keeper was so certain she would fail. Wondering why, no matter what she set out to think about, her mind always swerved right back to the same old topic. Waite McKenna.

To keep herself from thinking about him now, she reread the last entry in her journal.

"Tonight I met the remaining Newbolts. I believe the daughter, who can't be more than ten, actually cooked our entire meal by herself, which makes me feel even more inept. Something is wrong with her foot. Don't yet feel free to ask, but think I must soon, and not only out of curiosity. She's an appealing child. Hair needs attention, clothes truly dreadful. Why? Boys all dressed quite well, if not in latest fashion. Youngest stutters, has problems with bladder. I can't like Maxwell's attitude toward his youngest two, and don't really care for the eldest boy's attitude toward me. Too fresh by far, but an appealing scamp, for all that. So many questions arise."

Closing the leatherbound journal, she sighed. Not for the first time she wished she had spent more times with her friends' younger siblings. All she knew about children was that she had once been one. Ever since she'd made up her mind to become a teacher she had thought in terms of classrooms filled with adoring little darlings in ruffled pinafores and knee pants.

Obviously there was more to it than that. There would be Dorien Newbolt, for instance. And Nick McKenna. She wasn't sure about Caleb—she rather thought he was past school age. But then,

one would have thought Nick and Dorien were,
too.

As for the other two Newbolts, she might have
to deal with them on an altogether different basis.
The way they had looked at her she'd felt rather
like a bobtailed filly being shown off to a prospec-
tive buyer. She'd half expected Maxwell to repri-
mand them, but as the evening wore on she'd
come to realize that Maxwell saw only what he
chose to see. And what he chose to see was that
he had sired several big, handsome sons and one
useful daughter.

Funny, the way a person could form an opinion
from a few letters and have it turn out all wrong.
Courtly manners were all very well, as was lovely
penmanship and a poetic turn of phrase. But she
was beginning to suspect the man was nothing at
all like his letters. What man with a grain of sensitivity would call his son slow-witted in the child's
own hearing? And he treated his daughter as if
she were a hired servant. Or worse.

By the time the magistrate arrived, Mariah was
almost dreading the outing. So many questions
burgeoned in her mind, she didn't know where
to start.

Maxwell was at his best acting in his official
capacity as magistrate, which, as nearly as Mariah
could determine, included acting as mayor, police-
man, lawyer, school superintendent, and general
busybody.

"Up until a few years ago, classes were held in
a private home, but that was never a very satisfac-
tory arrangement," he informed her on the ride
through the village.

Mariah murmured something appropriate and

then asked, "How many children will I have to teach?"

"No more than a dozen or so, from first grade to eleventh."

"Mercy," she said, having no idea whether that was considered a lot or a little. Back when she'd been a child, only two or three grades were taught in a single classroom. This promised to be a challenge, to say the very least.

The schoolhouse was so new it still smelled more of raw lumber than of chalk and children. It consisted of one room, with three rows of high-low benches and a brand-new cast-iron stove in the middle of the space, with a section of stovepipe running up through the roof. There was a table and chair at the front of the room, which she presumed was for the use of the teacher. A large chalkboard and three plank bookshelves had been attached to one wall.

Maxwell proudly pointed out the new wood-stove, the tall windows, and the brand-new double privy set out behind the schoolhouse, one side for boys, one for girls, each with its own partitioned entrance.

Mariah thought about the fire hazards of the flimsy stovepipe. She thought about the drafts that would rattle the window and blow through the cracks between the floorboards. Her father had installed a new hot-air furnace and a lovely bathroom with all the modern conveniences years ago. Their tightly fitted windows had kept out all but the fiercest drafts.

But if this was what she had to work with, then work with it she would. They could all wrap up against the cold, and after all, in a place where orange trees grew and bore fruit, how cold could it get?

She took home with her a copy of each of the books that were to be used, none of them familiar, all dog-eared, each bearing several names. Some were adorned with hearts and initials, and several contained lists of wildfowl shot, including the dates and the number of each type.

What on earth was a coot?

There was a crude drawing on one flyleaf that she rather thought might be sexual in nature, but she couldn't be sure, thanks partly to the artist's lack of ability, partly to her own lack of knowledge.

Maxwell didn't offer to carry them out to the cart for her. She told herself, hiding her amusement, that a magistrate must always consider his dignity. Nevertheless, when he handed her up into the cart as if she were a fragile porcelain figurine, she had to admit he had lovely manners when he remembered to use them. She only wished he would use them with his two youngest children.

"When am I expected to take up my duties?" she asked on the way back to the teacherage. She'd hoped he might invite her to another meal. So far, her cooking skills had not noticibly improved, but she was working on it.

"The exact date hasn't been set yet. However, considering the proximity of the storm season, I believe we'd best not waste any more time. We always miss a few days on account of the tides."

The tides. Mariah stared down at the dog-eared copy of *Child Life, A Second Reader*, and tried not to envision water sweeping over the island, covering trees and entire houses. For the first time, it seemed that living right next to a lighthouse might have its advantages. If worse came to worse, she could climb the thing.

The opening day of school was set for the following Monday. Maxwell said he would post notices at the church, the post office, and down at the landing. Mariah made the most of the intervening days by unpacking the boxes that had come in on the latest mailboat, which only added to the clutter in the tiny cottage.

Her mother's china. Where on earth could she put it? She had yet to find room to put away all the staples she had acquired at her pounding.

And . . . oh, mercy, the portraits. She'd been of two minds about leaving them behind. They were so much a part of the house, and the house no longer belonged to her. In the end, she had left it up to Mr. Muncie, her father's lawyer, who'd offered to pack and ship whatever remained after he determined the proper ownership.

By the time the last streak of light faded from the sky, she was no closer to finding places for everything than she had been when she'd started unpacking. Mostly she just moved things from place to place, unable to decide whether she should set out her china—if she could find a place to set it out—and whether to leave her winter things packed away, and what to do with all her own books. The portraits were propped against the front wall, covering the entire space between door and window.

She might have known her nearest neighbor would choose the worst possible time to call. He caught her stalking from crate to box, a stack of embroidered pillow slips in one hand, a Jane Austen novel in the other, her hair sliding from its once neat arrangement, her clothes looking like something from the charity barrel.

"Oh, for heaven's sake, must you always catch me by surprise?"

"From now on," Waite McKenna said with that tantalizing hint of amusement in his dark eyes, "I'll whistle when I head out across the clearing."

"No, no, come in. I'm sorry—I don't mean to be snappish, but there's just so much to put away and not enough putting places."

He looked over the clutter of half-unpacked crates, opened boxes, and stacks of linens, dishes, and books. He studied the portraits in their ornate gold-leaf frames. And then he turned to the woman, his gaze assessing, giving away nothing of his thoughts. "I came to tell you we'll soon have another woman on the place. New assistant keeper's due in next week. Married man. No children. Thought you might want to know, in case you're still here when they move in."

It was the last straw in a day that had been filled with last straws. Mariah planted a pair of grimy hands on her dusty hips. "This will come as a great disappointment to you, I know, Mr. McKenna, but I'm here to stay. Come high water or whatever, I'm not leaving this house or this island, so you might as well stop trying to provoke me into giving up. Do we understand one another?"

"Yes, ma'am, I'd say we understand one another right well. Not that it's any of my business, but what are you planning on doing to earn your keep when school lets out for the year?"

"Lets out?" Her immediate goal was to get through the winter. To get through the next day, in fact. Beyond that, she hadn't a glimmer. "You're right, sir. It's none of your business."

"Maggie Stone might could use a hand in her kitchen, depending on how many boarders she has. Not too many folks come down here, even in the summertime, but there's always a few. Drummers, government folks, wreck commissioners and the like, mostly."

"I'm a schoolteacher, not a cook."

"As long as you can hold on to enough students to pay the school fees, you're a schoolteacher. I reckon what you do the rest of the year to earn room and board is up to you. I just thought if you're fixing to stay around, you might want to put in an early word with Maggie. She might offer you room and board in exchange for a hand in the kitchen or out in the laundry. Always a passel of washing to do in a boardinghouse."

Mariah regarded the man who had resented her before he'd ever laid eyes on her. She could feel the tip of her nose beginning to turn red, the way it always did just before the tears came.

This time, she refused to cry. She was flat out—as old Elmo would say—of tears.

Chapter Five

Mariah thought about what Waite had said. She was sorely tempted to tell the man she would hibernate. Like those smelly old black bears that had occasionally wandered into town from the swamp down near the Meherrin River. For someone who had graduated at the head of her class, she was incredibly ignorant. Here she'd been drifting along as if nothing at all in her life had changed. This time a year ago she would have spent her summer vacation visiting back and forth with Carrie, Ada, and Lottie. They might even have gone on another excursion to Virginia Beach.

Now, everything had changed. She had no home, no family, no friends—not even Henry Lee, who'd been on the verge of declaring himself when the news had leaked out about her illegitimacy.

So he had waited until she'd left town and declared himself to her best friend instead. And now here she was, living in a two-room cottage on the edge of a swamp full of noisy frogs and who knew what all, in a community full of strangers who were just waiting to see if she would swim or sink.

"Well?" Arms crossed over his truly impressive chest, Waite McKenna silently dared her to come up with an intelligent response. "I asked what you're planning on doing when you're done teaching. That's if you're still here."

"Do you know, I never even thought about where teachers went during their vacation." It was a mark of her distraction that she spoke without thinking. The truth was, she hadn't given a single thought to anything beyond securing herself a position before she ran clean out of money.

He shifted a stack of books and lit another lamp. She'd lit only the one because it was stifling inside the small cluttered rooms, and a lamp only added more heat. For a moment, as he leaned over to adjust the wick, yellow light illuminated his harsh features, reminding Mariah again of the pirates she had read about in a book on early colonial history.

"I reckon I could ask around for you. Someone's bound to need a hand with something."

Don't be so fanciful, he's only an ordinary man, she told herself. Although the word *ordinary* didn't quite describe him. "Thank you, but I'm sure that won't be necessary. I'm very good with figures, and my penmanship is excellent. I'd thought of offering my services to Mr. Cyrus." *My, what an accomplished liar you're becoming.* She'd thought of no such thing, of course.

"Cyrus has two sons and three daughters. If he needs any help in the store, he'll fetch it from the house."

She was determined not to look as defeated as she felt. The school year had yet to begin, and here she was worrying about next summer. "Yes, well . . . thank you for your concern, but I'm sure I'll find something when the time comes."

"If you're still here."

Waite regarded her steadily from under his dark, winged brows. She put him in mind of a deer scenting a hunter. Eyes wide, neck stretched to its limit. If her ears had been a bit bigger he was pretty sure they'd be twitching.

"I'll be here, Mr. McKenna," she said with a quiet composure that stirred his reluctant admiration. She might look as if she were no more substantial than one of those pink flowers that bloomed along the edge of the marsh, but he had a feeling she was more like a sandspur. Get too close and she'd reach out, grab hold, and hang on till hell froze over.

He left her standing in the middle of her sitting room, surrounded by the jumble of half-unpacked crates. Along with those two portraits that looked like the king and queen of high society.

An orderly man himself, Waite disliked clutter—although, to be fair, there really wasn't enough room in her quarters to swing a bobtailed cat, much less tuck everything away. He might send Sarvice over to hang her pictures on the wall and build her a . . .

Then again, he might not.

All the same, he was tempted to go back and tell her that, as nobody else would be using the teacherage once the school year was done, she might as well stay put. Halfway across the grounds he slowed his steps, but then he thought better of it. If he relented now, first thing he knew he'd find himself offering to store her gear for her. Next, he'd be offering to bring over her meals if she didn't feel like cooking. No telling what favors she'd be wheedling out of him before she was done. Women were like that. Always demanding special treatment. Whining, complaining . . .

Not that she had actually whined or complained, he admitted reluctantly. Hadn't even asked him for any favors, come to that. But she was building up to it. He could feel it in his bones, the same way he could feel a change in the weather before it ever happened. She was just biding her time, waiting to soften him up before she cut loose with a stack of demands.

He let himself into the dark, empty house, crossed to his desk, and lit the lamp. With a grim smile, he wondered what she would say if he were to tell her that, far from softening him up, she was having just the opposite effect.

It made him mad as the devil, too, because he was old enough to know better. Couldn't, in fact, recall the last time he'd been so stirred up by a woman's looks or the way she smelled. She didn't even have big bosoms. He liked big bosoms on a woman. Hers weren't much bigger than a pair of bay scallops.

Tossing his hat at the antlers on the wall, Waite slid his logbook across the table, unscrewed his ink jar, and commenced to write. He dated the entry, then noted the time of the sunrise and sunset. And then he wrote, "New assistant due in tomorrow, name of Claude Eustace Hardraker. Married."

God help the poor sod. Waite stared out the window, noted when the lamp in the front room across the way went out and the one in the bedroom was lit.

And then waited for that to go out. For a little while longer he allowed his mind to range freely, and then he reined it in. Dipping his pen in the ink bottle, he wrote diligently for the next few minutes, and when he was done, he read it over.

Sarvice aired out the other side this morning, ready for the new people. Two of Rollerson's boys got lost in Jenette's Sedge. Nearly set the woods on fire, but with the wind dead calm, it was put out before it spread. Treated cow for hoof-rot this morning. Believe it comes of standing in the water when the flies are bad. Glass falling. Smoke hanging low. By my reckoning it'll storm before morning.

Signed, Waitefield A. McKenna
Principal Keeper, Cape Hatteras Light.

He deliberately refrained from mentioning the new teacher. Mrs. Deekins. Mariah Deekins Sawyer. Mrs. Sawyer? He didn't have it straight yet, wasn't sure he even wanted to.

All the same, he found himself wondering, not for the first time, what kind of man her husband had been.

It was just after ten in the morning when Mariah met Evie Newbolt in front of Mr. Cyrus's store. The child was straining to lift a basket of potatoes. Jumping down from the cart, Mariah hurried over to her side. "Where's your cart? For heaven's sake, this is far too heavy."

The child blushed and then blanched. Pale as a bedsheet, with all that fiery red hair standing out around her face, she looked a sight. "My dear,

I'm Mariah Deekins, the new schoolteacher. Surely you remember—I had supper at your house just the other night?"

"Yes, ma'am, I remember, but I've got to go now. Papa don't like me to dawdle."

"I can't imagine why Mr. Cyrus didn't carry this out to your cart for you." The basket wasn't quite as large as a washbasket, but it was far too heavy for a child to lift onto the back of a wagon. "I'm sure Mr. Cyrus could load it for you, or perhaps one of your brothers could come for it?"

"It's not all that heavy. I can tote it home."

"To your cart, you mean." The store must have been all of a mile from Maxwell's house.

"Papa has to have potatoes with his stewed mullet, and I forgot to get 'em yesterday when I come for the side meat."

"That's all very well, my dear, but I'm sure your father wouldn't want you to strain your back."

She was sure of no such thing. The more she came to know about the magistrate, the more she found to dislike. There was no other wagon in sight, yet she found it hard to believe the child intended to walk all the way home carrying a heavy basket. Or that her family would allow it. She said as much.

"Baxter gave me a ride as far as the store, but then he went on down to the landing." The child was beginning to look agitated. "Please, ma'am, Papa gets real upset if dinner's late, and if I don't get my stew on the stove, it'll not be done in time."

"Then I'll drive you and your potatoes home."

"Oh, but—"

"Shhh. It's the very least I can do. Do you know,

I'm quite sure that if you hadn't fed me the other evening, I'd have starved by now? I've been trying my best to translate our old cook's recipe book, but between her handwriting and all those unfamiliar terms, I've ruined more dishes than you can imagine."

She swung the market basket up onto the back of her cart, climbed onto the bench seat, and held out a hand to Evie. "Come along, then. I'm trying to learn my way around the village, and I haven't explored the road between the store and your house. You'll have to direct me."

Evie clambered up beside her, and Mariah set out to put the child at ease. It wasn't easy. She chattered on about her miserable attempts at cooking, and when that brought no more than a few sympathetic murmurs, she switched to animals. All children liked animals, didn't they?

"My little mare was named Conk, but I call her Merrily after the horse I had back in Murfreesboro. I've always loved horses. They say my grandmother loved horseracing so much she once dressed as a boy and joined in a steeplechase. She won it, too. D'you like horses, Evie?"

"Yes'm. Take the next turnoff."

Mariah waited a few moments and tried again. "I always wanted a housecat, but cats made my father sneeze. Do you have any dogs or cats?"

"No, ma'am. Once I caught a baby rabbit. Her mama had got killed by a dog. I kept her in the henhouse until she grew up and I played with her every time I went out to collect the eggs or feed up, but then Baxter found her and skinned her out and I had to cook her for him. Baxter's real partial to fried rabbit."

Mariah thought that was the saddest, wickedest thing she had ever heard, but didn't say so. Instead, she snapped the reins over Merrily's shaggy croup and changed the subject. "Shall I tell you a secret? This is my very first teaching assignment, and I'm so afraid I won't know how to start out properly. Tell me how you like the different classes arranged. Front row, middle row, and back row? Or left side, middle, and right side?"

"I'm not sure how it is now," the child said diffidently, "but back when I went to school, the bigger boys sat in the last row, younger ones in the middle, and all the girls in front. When Miss Brown was here, she tried to separate us into classes, but after she left, everybody went back to sitting wherever they wanted to."

Neatly guiding the little mare along the narrow, pine-straw-covered road, Mariah glanced at the child huddled beside her. Evie was twisting her fingers. Head bent, her bony little neck looked incredibly vulnerable rising out of the frayed collar of that wretched dress.

What was she so frightened of? Why wasn't she dressed as befitted the daughter of the local magistrate? None of the boys wore faded and patched shirts. Their boots were shined to a fare-thee-well. Every one of them, except for poor little Franklin, strutted and crowed as if they owned the world and all its treasures.

Mariah ached to reach out to tug the child closer, to nestle that wild mop of hair against her bosom and promise whatever it took to make her smile—to erase the guarded look from her eyes. No child should look so forlorn on such a lovely morning.

And truly, it was a lovely morning. There was a golden haze over the sun. A light breeze whispered through the trees. Near the edge of a stand of cattails, a flock of tiny yellow birds fluttered and chattered, and butterflies drifted past like small windblown flowers.

"Evie, do you mind if I ask your age?"

"No, ma'am."

Mariah waited. "Then how old are you, my dear?"

"I'm twelve and a half years old."

Mariah covered her surprise. She'd thought perhaps ten. Although she acted older. Perhaps her infirmity . . . She wanted to ask about that, too, but didn't quite dare.

"How old are you, Miz Deekins?"

"How old am I? I'm twenty-two. An enormous age, I suppose," she said teasingly.

Solemnly, the child nodded. "I wish I was as old as you are. I wish my hair was like yours instead of—"

Reaching up, she grabbed a handful of the unruly red curls and yanked hard.

Mariah winced for her. "Yours is a lovely color. And it curls all by itself. Goodness, you can't imagine how much time I wasted tying rags in my hair, trying to make it curl." She laughed. "My mother used to despair of even keeping it neatly braided."

"Dorien calls me Fuzzball. Sometimes he calls me Rusty."

"My mother used to call me Stargazer. Whenever she tried to get my attention, I was always daydreaming, only she called it stargazing. Nicknames are often signs of affection."

"Is your ma dead, too?"

Plain speaking with a vengeance. "Both she and my father were drowned last winter," Mariah said quietly.

"I knew a boy that got drownded once. He went wading in his boots and a big wave caught him and drug him out to sea. He was real nice. One time he gave me a pencil."

At a loss as to how to respond to such a statement, Mariah resorted once more to gentle teasing. "Do you know, I find it hard to believe that someone who's only twelve and a half years old can produce such a splendid meal all by herself. Surely you had someone to help you? A fairy godmother? A team of talented elves? Confess now, you waved a magic wand over that chicken and it jumped into the pan and fried itself."

Evie giggled and quickly slapped a hand over her lips just as Mariah pulled up before the neat yellow house. Gathering the reins in one hand, she glanced across at her passenger and was saddened to see that the giggling little girl had already disappeared, leaving in her place a small, badly dressed child with a twisted foot and a gown so old that even the patches had patches.

She was about to suggest that Evie go find one of her brothers to carry in the basket when one of them stepped out onto the front porch.

"Morning, Miz Deekins."

Nodding, Mariah mentally raced through the alphabet, trying to come up with the right name. She was fairly sure he wasn't A or B, but she couldn't recall if this one was C or D.

"I'm Dorien. I come between Caleb and Evie.

Hi, Rustmop, where you been? I need a shirt ironed."

"They're still on the line," his sister said.

"Tell you what, you fetch in the clothes and iron me a shirt and I'll take in that mess of potatoes for you."

Fetch in the clothes? Iron him a shirt? Mariah fairly sizzled with indignation.

"Papa'll be home to dinner—I've got to get it on cooking."

"I already put the iron on to heat. It won't take you but a minute to do me up a shirt. Nick's waiting. Him and me are fixing to ride up to Kinnakeet."

"He's here?" Evie's eyes widened. Her face turned fiery red.

Mariah, not knowing what else to say—knowing only that someone should say something on behalf of the poor, beleaguered child—said, "I beg your pardon."

"Yes'm?" With a wickedly flirtatious look, Dorien sauntered out to the cart and swung the big basket of potatoes up onto his shoulder just as another young man stepped out of the house, a half-eaten wedge of cake in the palm of his hand.

"Real good cake, Evie."

Beside her, Evie let out a small whimper and ducked behind Mariah as if she were trying to hide. "Evie? What's wrong, dear?"

Mariah looked from the girl to her brother to the other young man, who was definitely not one of Maxwell's brood. Not with that hair. Not with that narrow, clever face and those wicked black eyes.

"Miz Deekins, this here's Nicholas Devereaux . . ." Dorien strung out the name, dancing out of the way when Nicholas Devereaux leaped down off the porch and pretended to swing at him. "McKenna," he finished. "We call him Old Nick."

Turning, Nicholas Devereaux McKenna swept her a bow worthy of a French courtier except for the smear of chocolate on his beardless chin.

Mariah was half tempted to curtsey. Fortunately, common sense intervened. These boys-on-the-edge-of-becoming-men would be gracing her classroom in a few days. Heaven help her, she was just now coming to realize what the women had been talking about at the pounding the other day.

Trouble. Sheer disaster. What this pair couldn't come up with between them wouldn't be worth doing. If she hoped to retain the upper hand, she'd better tread carefully.

"What about my shirt, Evie? We gotta get going."

Head down, Evie tried to slink past her, but Mariah reached out and caught her around the shoulders, drawing her against her side. "Surely you don't expect this child to drop everything just to wait on you, young man. Don't you have someone to do your laundry?"

"Surely do, ma'am. She does a right fine job of it, too, don't you, Rustyfuzz?" Dorien gave his sister a swat on the backside, still favoring Mariah with a smile that was just a little too pert for a boy his age.

She wanted to tell him he was too young to look at any woman that way, and besides, he didn't know her well enough. Instead, she heard herself saying, "I'd like for Evie to visit me some afternoon at the teacherage. Do you suppose tomorrow would be possible? Could you give her a lift, or should I call for her?"

"Rusty don't visit much, ma'am, but thanks for inviting her. Better hurry on that shirt, gal. Pa'll be home pretty soon, and you know how he gets if his dinner's not on the table on time."

Mariah closed her eyes and counted to ten. When she opened them, Evie was nowhere in sight. Dorien was just disappearing inside the house, the basket of potatoes balanced on his shoulder, and Waite McKenna's handsome son was leaning against a porch support, licking crumbs from the palm of his hand, his expression too innocent by half.

"I don't suppose a fancy lady like you would know how things is around here, ma'am. Women are supposed to work, not go lallygagging around all day making mischief."

Hanging on to her temper by a thread, Mariah spoke in measured tones, reminding herself that Nick McKenna was only a boy. His father's son, at that. "Nevertheless, you may tell Mr. Newbolt that I'll drive by tomorrow afternoon to collect his daughter. I'll bring her home in plenty of time to fix his evening meal, but I'm sure he'll be happy to spare her for a few hours."

Her back was still stiff as a poker a few minutes later as she cracked the buggy whip harmlessly in the air. She didn't believe in physical cruelty, but at this moment she would dearly love to—to kick something!

It didn't help to know that she might have opened the door to more trouble than she was prepared to handle. What if Maxwell took offense? What if he took out his displeasure by canceling her teaching contract?

He would hardly do that, she assured herself. He might be a petty tyrant, but he was, after all, a reasonable adult. Besides, it was too late to get another teacher out here . . . wasn't it?

But what if he took his displeasure with her out on Evie?

If ever a child needed a friend, she told herself, it was little Evie Newbolt. Mariah was determined the girl would have at least one.

Instead of driving directly to the teacherage, she turned toward the principal keeper's house, climbed out of the wagon, and wrapped the reins around the porch rail. She was on the verge of knocking on the door when she happened to glance over toward the double house.

There was a stack of baggage outside. Trunks stacked three high, topped with carpetbags and hatboxes. She was still staring a moment later when a tall young woman dressed in a fashionable purple silk gown and a feather-plumed bonnet stepped outside, pointed to a valise buried in the middle of the stack, and said sharply, "That one. Handle it carefully, now—watch out, you dolt! You nearly tripped over Precious!"

Precious?

A dog yapped. And yapped, and yapped, and yapped. Sarvice A. Jones bobbed up from behind the stack of luggage, loaded with parcels, and tried to dislodge the indicated valise without toppling the rest.

He didn't succeed. Mariah winced as the beautiful woman with the razor-edged tongue described the poor man's antecedents, prospects, and general lack of abilities. The dog continued to bark. Recalling her mission, Mariah knocked sharply on the door and waited.

Chapter Six

Mariah, her hand lifted to knock a second time, stared at the man in the open doorway.

"What is it now, Miz Deekins?"

Waite looked positively harried. His collar was loosened, his brows knotted as if he were hurting. Mariah murmured, "Perhaps I should come back at a better time."

"There won't be a better time." Things would only get worse, his tone implied.

"I see our new neighbors have arrived."

"Yes, they have, so if that's all, madam, I'll bid you good morning."

"No! I mean, yes—oh, for heaven's sake, may I come in?" He looked so harassed Mariah could almost find it in her heart to pity him, which was certainly a switch.

"Why not?" he said with a shrug.

It was hardly a gracious invitation, but she wasn't about to stand on ceremony. Once inside, she glanced around curiously. It was strictly a masculine room. There was an oak desk, three straight-backed chairs, a bookcase, and a small fireplace, but nothing at all of a personal nature except for the black uniform hat hanging on a set of antlers mounted on the far wall. Centered on the desk were two ledgers, three letters, three pencils, and a pen, all lined up with mathematical precision. Off to one side was a square glass ink bottle, filled and capped.

The room was obviously an office, yet Mariah had a feeling that the rest of the house would be just as barren, just as neat.

"Madam, I assume you had a purpose for this visit, so if you'll kindly state it and let me get on with—"

"Are you related to the Newbolts?"

"Am I *what*?"

"Related. Kin. To Maxwell Newbolt and his family."

Once again his thick brows came together in a ferocious scowl, and Mariah hurried to explain. "I need some answers, but I don't want to start off on the wrong foot."

Crossing his arms over his chest—he did that rather a lot, Mariah had noticed—he waited. Now that she'd had time to cool off a bit, she wished she'd taken the time to organize her thoughts before barging in and demanding answers to questions that were really rather awkward. "Yes, well," she murmured aloud, "I'm here now, so I might as well explain."

Not a word of encouragement. It was like trying to hold a conversation with a tree stump. Through the open window came the sounds of the yapping dog and the fussing woman, which didn't help at all.

"*Watch that corner! Don't drop that hatbox, you clumsy oaf! Hush, Precious, Mama's going to feed you in a minute.*"

Yap, yap, yap—yelp!

"*Well, I told you to hush!*"

Waite strode across to the window and slammed it shut. Despite the resulting stuffiness, it was a blessed relief. "You're wanting to know if I'm kin to Newbolt, is that the gist of it?"

"Yes, well . . . not entirely. The thing is, I've been told that nearly everyone on the island is related in some way or another to everyone else."

"Newbolt's from up north."

"But his wife was a native. I need to know if she was related to you, or any of her children." She dug a handkerchief from her reticule and delicately mopped her forehead.

"She was their mother."

Nonplussed, Mariah stared at him. "Well, of course she was their mother. You know what I mean. . . ."

"I might eventually figure it out if you were to get on with it."

Without waiting for an invitation, she plopped down in one of the spindle-backed chairs. "I've just come from there. From Maxwell's house. I met your son there, by the way."

"At Newbolt's? I sent him to collect the mail."

"Yes, well, I believe he and Maxwell's middle child are off to someplace with an unpronounceable name that sounds like Connecticut, but probably isn't."

"Kinnakeet. Post office just renamed it Avon. It's up the Banks a ways."

He looked mildly irritated, which prompted Mariah to get her questions asked before he threw her out. He looked perfectly capable of doing just that.

Yap, yap, yap!

"Hush up, Precious, it's only a nasty old cow. Watch that trunk, boy, you nearly scraped the leather on the doorframe!"

Three strides carried Waite to the door. He slammed it shut and then leaned his forehead against the cool surface, his inbred arrogance for once not in evidence. Seeing the defeated slump of his shoulders, Mariah didn't envy him for having to live right next door to such a noisily demanding woman.

Although, to give the woman her due, she was certainly beautiful. Black hair, not a strand out of place, skin the color of magnolia petals—Mariah hadn't been close enough to determine the color of her eyes, but they were probably every bit as lovely as the rest of her features.

Feeling hot and damp and rumpled by contrast, she steered her thoughts back to the subject that had brought her there. "What I want to know—and I assure you, Mr. McKenna, it's not mere idle curiosity—is why that child is dressed in rags, and why she's treated so shamefully by her own family. I was afraid to ask anyone else for fear they might be related and take offense."

"Dressed in rags?" He raked his fingers through his hair, as if to clear his mind.

"I'm speaking of Evie Newbolt, not your new neighbor," Mariah said dryly.

"Newbolt's girl is being mistreated?"

"I wouldn't treat Sally the way those boys treat their sister, and Maxwell's no better. They evidently expect her to do all their cooking and serving, and to wash and iron and carry heavy market baskets all the way from Mr. Cyrus's store. They leave her there and then ride off, letting her get home the best way she can with that foot of hers. What happened to it, anyway, if I might ask?"

"Who's Sally?"

Mariah blinked several times. "Sally? She's my maid. Was my maid, I should say. Not that she was a very good one. She was even more hopeless in the kitchen than I am, but then, neither of us ever had to cook before. We had Bathsheba."

Waite nodded gravely. "You had Bathsheba. Uh-huh."

Not being slow-headed, she picked up on his attitude right away. "You're thinking I'm spoiled, that I'm used to being waited on hand and foot, aren't you?"

"Is that what I'm thinking?"

"Well, of course it is, but what purpose, may I ask, would it serve for those of us who can afford to hire help to insist on doing for ourselves? How would poor Sally and Elmo and Bathsheba—and Pearl, who does the wash—how would they manage if the more fortunate among us refused to hire them?"

He leaned against a corner of the desk and crossed his legs at the ankle. His black uniform pants fit like a glove. Mariah plucked at the high collar of her shirtwaist as a fresh film of perspiration broke out on her overheated body.

"I see," he said in that slow, rolling brogue of his. "It's your civic duty to be waited on hand and foot."

"You're deliberately being obtuse, Mr. McKenna."

"Obtuse?"

"Muleheaded. Uncooperative."

"Don't expect company manners, madam, and

you'll not be disappointed. I've never been a sociable man." As if he'd needed to tell her that, Mariah thought, amused. "As to the Newbolt girl, if I had to venture a guess, it would be that she's still wearing her mama's frocks. After seven or eight years, things tend to wear out."

"I do wish you'd answer my questions in proper order. Still, that could explain it. Evie's clothes, I mean. But the boys are certainly well dressed. The eldest pair looked spiffy enough."

"Even out here on the Banks we have the mail-order catalogs." With a wintry smile, he lowered himself onto the desk chair. Mariah thought he looked as if he hadn't been sleeping well. "When things have to last through five owners," he continued, "it makes good sense to buy quality. But then, I don't reckon you know much about hand-me-downs, Miz Deekins."

Mariah wanted to scream at him that it was *Miss* Sawyer, not *Miz* Deekins. Not Miz anybody. Instead, she said firmly, "I might not know anything about hand-me-downs, sir, but that doesn't make me any less sensitive to the plight of those less fortunate than I."

Dear Lord, that sounded insufferably priggish. And at the moment she'd be hard-pressed to name anyone less fortunate than she. If she didn't actually die of starvation, she'd probably poison herself before she mastered the art of cooking even the simplest dish.

"It's hot as blazes in here," she grumbled, plucking at her collar again. Aside from a collection of insect bites, a few in embarrassing places, she had a heat rash. She itched.

Rising, her host crossed to the door and

propped it open with a polished brass doorstop. "Now, what else were you wanting to know besides why Maxwell dresses his brood the way he does?"

"You make it sound as though this were nothing more than idle curiosity. I assure you, it's not. That child has a problem, and if I'm going to help her, then I need to know more about her. Was she born like that? Her foot, I mean?"

"As to that, I couldn't say."

Mariah waited. The man was truly exasperating. Or maybe it was the weather. Or maybe it was both. "Couldn't, or wouldn't?"

"I don't know the answer to your question, madam. Is that plain enough for you?"

It was more than plain enough. If there was one thing she should be accustomed to by now, it was unpleasant interviews and uncooperative men. Ignoring her various discomforts, not the least of which was sheer, weary discouragement, she tried again. "Do you know how it happened?"

"How what happened?"

"Evie's foot."

"Madam, I told you, I don't gossip."

"Well, neither do I, but this isn't gossip! I want to know if something can be done about it."

"If it could, why, then, I reckon Newbolt would've seen to it."

Then again, Waite thought, *he might not.* The man saw to his own comfort, and that was about as far as he extended himself. Come to think of it, the meddlesome woman had a point—he had noticed a time or two that the Newbolt girl looked a mess. Nick had said something just the other day about the way she always ducked like a gun-

shy dog whenever she saw him. She and that lit-
tlest one—the one who had so much trouble spitting out his words—they weren't much like the
rest of the litter.

A light breeze drifted in through the back door,
carrying with it the sound of a rising surf, the
scent of coming rain. The schoolteacher rose up
tall and proud, just as if her frock weren't sopping
wet wherever it touched her body. For once, she
even had a speck of color in her face under all
those freckles. The first time he'd seen her she'd
struck him as too pale and cold-natured to be interesting, but that was before he'd seen her all hot
and bothered.

"Then, if that's all you can tell me, I thank you
kindly for your time. Good day, sir."

"Good day, Miz Deekins," Waite returned,
amused at her starchiness. It might be worth the
trouble to rile her up now and again, just to watch
the color come and go in her face. Before he could
catch himself he smiled at the thought.

She looked startled.

Don't be a fool, McKenna! Scowling again, he
said, "Rain's on the way. You might want to go
home and shut a few windows."

"I certainly hope you're right. About the rain, I
mean. A nice cool rain would be a real blessing,"
she said as she moved past him, her subtle, womanly scent tickling his nostrils.

He nodded. She might not think it was such a
blessing before it was over, but he didn't figure
she'd rest any easier for knowing they were in for
a real lambaster of a squall.

Before Mariah even reached the edge of the
porch, from an upstairs window next door came

the sound of a shrill, demanding voice punctuated now and then by a masculine rumble.

"I wonder if anyone ever told her she'll catch more flies with honey than she ever will with vinegar. Not that I think the advice would be appreciated."

Waite heard and shared her amusement, somewhat to his surprise. That and the warm scent of her skin triggered notions that had no place in his life. Just as she stepped down off the porch a gust of hot wind struck her, swirling her skirt up around her knees.

"Mercy," she exclaimed, swatting it down again. Laughing, she glanced at him over her shoulder and then looked up at the sky. The sun that had been shining so brightly only a little while ago was now hidden behind a roiling mass of black clouds. "Oh, my mercy," she gasped. Snatching the reins off the railing, she set out across the grounds at a run, tugging the reluctant mare behind her. Her skirt blew up over her knees. Sand peppered her limbs. She clapped one hand to her straw bonnet as the wind threatened to send it sailing out over the nearby marsh.

Waite stood in the open doorway and watched, wondering why he hadn't offered to go with her to unhitch the cart and see to the mare.

No, not wondering. Knowing damned well.

The woman was beginning to knock him off course. While he might not care all that much for women in general, he could still appreciate a nice ankle as much as the next man. Hers were small and neatly turned, from what he could tell in those fancy two-toned high-tops. He had a feeling the striped stockings he'd caught a glimpse of were silk, not cotton, and wondered how they'd feel to his hands if he were to . . .

With a soft oath, he turned toward the double house, where his new second assistant and his sister—not his wife, but his damned *sister*—were moving in.

Hardraker might be all right. The man had the sad eyes of a basset hound, but then, from what he'd seen of the woman, Caroline Hardraker, she was enough to wear any man down to the bone.

Catching sight of his first assistant scurrying around toward the back of the house, Waite called him over. "Have you sorted things out over there?" He jerked his head in the direction of the house his two assistants would be sharing.

"I'll be bunking in with Hardraker for the time being, so Miss Caroline can have my quarters," said Sarvice.

"Will someone kindly tell me what the bloody hell that female is doing here? The man's supposed to be married. One dependent, his papers said, with another one on the way."

"Yessir, only his wife's folks didn't want her coming to no place that don't have a real doctor, so they're keeping her home until the baby comes, then they'll send her on down."

"And that woman? The sister?"

"Seems she was wanting to get away. Mr. Hardraker offered to bring her down here with him for a spell."

"What the bloody hell does she think this is, some fancy resort? Tell her to try Cape May. Send her up to Virginia Beach if she wants to get away. She's got no call to come barging into my territory and setting everything onto its aft end."

"Yessir—that is, no sir. What I mean is—"

"And tie up that damned mutt before he spooks the horses. Oh, and Sarvice—you're first assistant keeper, not some snot-nosed lackey. The Lighthouse Service doesn't pay you four hundred dollars a year to fetch and tote for any spoiled city woman."

"Yessir! I mean, no sir!" Sarvice A. Jones's earnest face was red with a combination of embarrassment and exertion. Waite wondered, not for the first time, when the government had run flat out of common sense. The Lighthouse Service had always been a family affair, the duties usually passed on from father to son. His own father had been first assistant at Bodie Island before he'd moved down here as principal keeper.

Now they were bringing in men from farms and God knows where else. Hardraker had come all the way down from Maryland.

With a softly muttered oath, Waite dismissed the younger man after reminding him that he was on duty from midnight to dawn. And then he went inside to put yesterday's stewed turtle on to heat before heading out to light the lantern.

McKenna had been right, Mariah decided. They were definitely in for some rain. The surf was pounding hard enough to shake the house on its foundation, while thunder rattled every pane of glass in the windows.

She rocked, thinking of what a panic she would have been in only a short while ago, living here on the edge of the ocean, with a storm sweeping in from across the sound.

Instead of cowering in her bed with the covers

over her head, she had calmly unhitched the mare,
rolled the cart under the shed roof and given Merrily a rub and a handful of oats, then set about
shutting windows. She'd even remembered to see
to her chickens, wishing their new quarters were
finished.

It seemed that at the belated age of twenty-two
she was finally growing up. Which probably
meant that until now she'd been every bit as
spoiled and sheltered as Waite McKenna had ac-
cused her of being.

Well, of course she had. Still, better late than
never, she thought, pride and amusement mingling with only a tiny bit of uneasiness.

Or perhaps more than a tiny bit, she acknowledged as another blast of thunder caused her to
wince and grip the chair arms until her fingertips
turned white. Rocking faster, as if to outpace the
storm, she forced herself to take up the same
wretched bit of embroidery she'd been working
on for the past two years. The holly and pheasant
design was supposed to match the dining room
chair covers, only the chairs were long gone by
now, gracing someone else's dining room.

Probably with new covers. She didn't know
why she even bothered except that she needed
something to do with her hands, and sewing, at
least, wouldn't burn down the house as her attempt at making pancakes this morning had very
nearly done.

Start with a hot griddle, the recipe had said, so
she'd shoved several rich-looking sticks of split
pine into the rusty stove, and the next thing she
knew, there'd been sparks drifting out into the
room where the stovepipe joined the chimney.

To her list of things to bring up the next time she had occasion to speak to Maxwell she added a new range. And perhaps a bathroom. It wasn't that she was too proud to use a privy, but being eaten alive by mosquitoes the moment she stepped outside the door was rather discouraging, to say the least.

She made a mental note to see if Mr. Cyrus had any citronella candles. She could light one in each window, and a few in the privy . . .

And likely burn down the whole place, outbuildings and all.

Lightning flickered constantly, the cold white glare more than a match for the feeble yellow glow of her lamp. She bent over her square of linen and concentrated on finishing a lumpy, uneven satin-stitched holly berry in red silk thread. She should have thought to purchase more before she left home. Mr. Cyrus carried only black and white, in the coarsest cotton, saying that was all any decent woman needed. Poor man, she thought, amused. He'd probably be shocked to the core of his worthy soul if she should go in and ask for red silk thread.

Something—a branch or possibly a pine cone—struck the side of the house. She stuck her needle into the rumpled square of linen, laid it aside, and stared at the rain-spattered window.

It can't last much longer, she told herself. *Nothing lasts forever.* Reason told her that the storm would soon be over, the stars would come out again, and that despite the way it sounded now, the ocean wasn't actually sloshing up onto her doorstep.

She put away her sewing and took out her journal. "I'm not at all frightened," she wrote. "But I can't deny being lonely. A woman alone has a right to be lonely, as long as she isn't maudlin about it. Even little Evie has a house full of family. Carrie and Henry Lee have each other now. Ada and Lottie are probably together this very minute, planning what they'll wear to the wedding. Ada will probably wear her violet. It makes her look sallow. I never told her so, but perhaps someone should. Is spitefulness better than maudlinness? Is there such a word as maudlinness? Probably not. Perhaps I'll invent one."

She nibbled the cap of her pen, wanting to write something about Waite McKenna. Not knowing what to write. Not even to her own journal was she about to confide that she'd been dying to touch his naked skin ever since she'd seen him with his sleeves folded back over his forearms. He'd looked so warm, so hard, so golden, so . . . inviting.

"Waite McKenna continues to be a problem. I have a feeling, however, that his mind will soon be taken up by a more worrisome problem than the schoolteacher's alleged helplessness. Happy day!"

Capping her pen, she laid that and the leather-covered journal on her trunk-cum-table, lingering to stare across the grounds to the principal keeper's quarters. That was what it was called, she had learned the other day when she had gone to the post office on the off chance she might have received another letter. That was what *he* was called. The principal keeper. It had a solid sound. A permanent sound. Like a guardian. One who guards . . . one who keeps?

Lifting her gaze, she watched for the light to

cycle around. Six seconds. She had timed it. A brief flash, a longer wait, and then the whole cycle repeated itself. She was coming to think of the light itself as a sort of guardian. Even while she slept, it watched over her, bathing her in its light.

Maudlin. That was precisely what she was becoming. The thing was a simple lighthouse, that was all. Every coast had one, or so she supposed. Although to a ship at sea on a night like this, it might appear to be a guardian angel.

And then she got to thinking about the responsibility of keeping the lantern lit, rain or shine, year in, year out, in sickness and in health.

No, that was the marriage ceremony, wasn't it? For better or worse, in sickness and in health, till death do us part. . . .

"All I can say is that the sun had blessed well better be shining tomorrow," she muttered, idly scratching the rash that had shown up on her arm just a little while ago. If it didn't end soon she'd be reciting the multiplication tables to stay sane.

Marching into the bedroom, she drew the curtains, which were only plain white muslin but served the purpose, and proceeded to bathe by the light of a single candle. For a few minutes she allowed the cool night air to flow over her damp body while her mind strayed along pathways she had never quite dared to explore.

"Oh, for heaven's sake," she muttered. Tugging her nightgown on, she blew out the candle and crawled into bed. Tomorrow night she would make up her lapse by saying two prayers. Tonight, she was simply too exhausted.

It seemed she had barely fallen asleep when something brought her instantly awake again. The storm? The ocean? Naturally her first thoughts were of her worse fears.

And then it came again—the ungodly noise that had merged with a dream to become a nightmare. The whole house seemed to throb. It sounded almost as if someone were laughing, which made her wonder if she could still be dreaming. Cold sweat beaded her skin.

With no one but herself to depend on, Mariah eased her legs over the side of the bed, grimaced at the feel of sand underfoot, and tiptoed into the next room. The noise seemed to be coming from somewhere near the front door.

Whispers. A thump. And *laughter*?

It *was* laughter she heard. Snickering laughter!

Without bothering to light a lamp, she gripped the cool china doorknob, ready to fling open the door and confront whatever demons were waiting on the other side, when the knob itself began to vibrate against the palm of her hand.

She screamed. And screamed, and screamed.

And then the door was flung open, and just before she was swallowed up in a pair of iron-hard arms, she caught a glimpse of two shadowy figures streaking off in the direction of lighthouse.

He smelled like laundry soap, lamp oil, and clean male sweat. She had never felt so safe in her life, even though he was swearing up a storm.

"Waite?" Her voice was muffled against his chest. She wouldn't have moved away if her life depended on it. For all she knew, it did.

"It's all right," he said.

"Is it over?"

"Not yet," he said grimly, which wasn't particularly reassuring.

And then, to her distinct dismay, considering that she had so recently declared herself a competent, fully mature woman, Mariah burst into tears.

Chapter Seven

As if a dam had burst, Mariah wailed on and on. Noisily, messily, totally without dignity. Somewhere in the recesses of her mind lurked the knowledge that she should probably pull away, dry her eyes, and try to salvage something—any possible shred—of her self-respect.

"There, now, it's all over," Waite said, his voice a comforting rumble under the cheek that was pressed against his chest. Now that the first wild coming together was over, he held her stiffly, as if unused to physical contact, which made it all the more remarkable that nothing had ever felt quite so safe and wonderful as the hard body against which she was pressed and the large hand that was stroking her back, with awkward little pats between the strokes.

"I thought the house was f-falling in," she said, sniffling, wishing she had a handkerchief.

"Rosum."

"I beg your p-pardon?" She sniffed again and found a handkerchief being crammed into her hand. Dutifully, she blew, wiped, handed it back—and then thought better of it and reached for it again.

"I'll wash that. I do know how to wash a hand-kerchief. What is a rosum?"

"I reckon you'd call it resin. Pine juice that leaked out once upon a time and hardened. Same thing you use on fiddle strings. Around here, we call it rosum."

"I see," she said, not seeing at all. It seemed a good idea to remove herself from his arms, and so she did, and then wished she hadn't been in such a hurry. It had felt so good to be held.

"Boys have been known—meaning no harm, you understand—but now and again they might take a notion to tie a length of string onto a door-knob, haul it up real taut, and then rub it with a chunk of rosum. There's a trick to it, but done right, it can set up a vibration inside a house that sounds kind of like a bull's roar."

He obviously knew the trick. She didn't remark on that, but asked instead, "Is that what someone did to me? To my door?"

"It appears so."

"But why?"

Waite looked for a moment as if he weren't going to answer, but then he shrugged and said, "Sometimes when a boy's trying hard to grow into a man, he has trouble keeping his notions straight. He might do something real dumb, think-ing he's being smart. I guess testing the new schoolmarm seemed like a smart thing to do."

Mariah took a deep, steadying breath and tried not to think about the fact that she was standing here in nothing but her nightgown, in the middle of the night, with a gentleman she hardly knew. Back home, that alone would have been enough to wreck what little was left of her reputation.

"Well." She tried to sound composed. "I guess there was no real harm done, but shouldn't I report it to the authorities?"

"Consider it reported."

They stood a good six feet apart now. Except for the intermittent sweep of the light, it was pitch-dark, but she could tell even so that Waite's arms were crossed over his chest again. He reminded her of a fence with no gate.

"Do we have a sheriff?"

"We make do with Newbolt. Wreck commissioner comes down when he's needed. Otherwise, we more or less take care of our own affairs."

"In other words, whoever frightened me out of a year's growth won't even be reprimanded."

"I didn't say that." There was a wealth of meaning underlying the softly spoken words, with which Mariah had to be satisfied. She wasn't about to go chasing off after those two shadowy figures she'd seen running in the direction of the lighthouse.

"They'd just better not try it again," she said, trying to sound fierce. It would have helped if her voice hadn't trembled.

"They won't. I can promise you that."

From somewhere nearby, a night bird called softly, accentuating the darkness, the solitude. Mariah shivered, feeling the thin lawn of her gown brush against her body as a warm, wet wind began to stir. "I won't keep you any longer, then," she said, not even wondering how he had come to be there. "Thank you for stopping by."

Waite nodded solemnly, just as if there were nothing out of the ordinary with a man standing outside a woman's house, and her standing with him in hardly anything at all, in the middle of the night. Turning away, he strode silently through the sand toward the tower.

The rain had freshened the air some, but it hadn't soaked into the ground. Sand was like that. It could look wet on top and be dry as a bone a few grains under the surface. He thought about that, and then he thought about how different things sometimes were from the way they appeared, as he climbed the spiraling steps.

He seldom stopped on the landings, not even when he was carrying a five-gallon can of coal oil in each hand. Footsteps echoing hollowly on the gritty metal stairs, he reached the last stretch, from the watch room to the lantern room, and closed the door behind him. Drafts were funny things in a tower. They could funnel up and blow out a lamp, or they could make it flame higher until the glass was so sooted up it blocked the light.

Less than two hours to go before full daylight. After adjusting the wick, he stepped out onto the narrow balcony surrounding the lantern gallery. The first thing he saw there was the gander, lying dead outside the plate-glass enclosure. Neck broke. They did that sometimes, flew head-on into the glass. This time of year it was rare, though. He figured it for a pound-raised Canada that had gotten loose and become lost.

Fortunately, the glass was heavy enough to withstand a blow unless it was struck hard at just the right angle. Stewed goose for supper, he thought, and laid the carcass inside the door so he wouldn't forget to take it down with him. No point in wasting good meat, even out of season.

Some two hundred feet above sea level, the

wind was blowing a good fifteen knots. Rain had washed most of the salt haze off the glass. The light shone clear and clean behind the Fresnel lenses as they revolved, powered by the weighted chain that fed down to the base of the tower.

It was a solitary kind of life, for the most part, living out here away from the village, able to mount the tower whenever he wanted to get away. At least, it had been solitary, which he preferred, until they'd built that damned teacherage in between the marsh and the lighthouse grounds.

And now, in addition to that—in addition to a son who was determined to get into trouble at every turn—he had the Hardraker woman to deal with.

Leaning on the cold, damp iron rail, Waite stared down at the surf. It was churned up some, but not enough to stir up much sand off the bottom. By morning it would be clear as glass again, with the shoals visible all the way out to the Inner Diamonds.

It was a source of constant amazement to him how quickly the bottom could change. Let a hard nor'easter hang off the Banks for a few days and it would look like a different set of shoals by the time the water cleared up again.

The Outer Diamonds didn't change as fast, at least not to his knowledge. They lay offshore right there where they'd always been, for as long as anyone could remember. Waiting to trap any unwary ship riding southward on the Virginia Drift—the Labrador Current, some called it—or northward on the steady, four-knot flow called the Gulf Stream, which had once been known as the

Spanish Main for all the Spaniards that took advantage of it.

If a man ever stopped to think about how many lives depended on the light, the responsibility could wear him right down to the nub. So mostly Waite didn't think about it, he simply did it. Day in, day out. Year in, year out. It was a big enough responsibility to make a man both proud and humble.

He thought about it now, and then he thought about the woman who was also, through no fault of his own, a part of his responsibility.

The women. Two of them now, Lord help him.

Hardraker would have to keep his sister in line for as long as she was here. And that damned dog of hers. He was spooking the horses. Sarvice said the cow had nearly stopped giving milk. They'd be lucky if the hens didn't clench up and quit laying.

As for the schoolteacher . . .

He let himself think about her now that he was safely out of her range. He thought about the way she had felt in his arms. About the way she smelled, all warm and sweet and salty at the same time. About the way his body had reacted.

That had taken him by surprise. He was too old, long past that sort of thing. Unscheduled longings, hungerings. How the devil was a man supposed to keep a hell-bent, half-grown kid in line when he couldn't even manage to control his own urges?

He dwelled on that depressing thought for a while, until the sky to the east began to brighten. Then, reluctantly, because problems never seemed quite so immediate when he was looking down on them from some two hundred feet in the air, he scooped up the dead gander, closed and latched the door, and descended slowly to the cold, dank lobby that always seemed to smell of kerosene and wet masonry.

Nick was defiant. Waite knew the boy hated being taken to task, even when his conscience was eating holes in him. At least he had a conscience. Now and again, Waite had run across a man who didn't. In a case like that, there wasn't much hope of salvation.

"Did it make you feel more of a man, scaring a lone woman?"

"Ah, shootfire, Pa, we didn't mean no harm. Cyrus said you and him had done the same thing to Pearl Fletcher once, got her so riled up she come running out with her hair all rigged up in rags."

"That doesn't make it right. My Pa took a razor strop to my backside."

Nick's eyes took on a glassy look the way they always did when he knew he was in for a rough ride and deserved it. Against all reason, Waite wanted to haul the boy into his arms and hug him, something he hadn't done in many a year.

"So go ahead, beat me if it'll make you feel better," Nick said defiantly, and Waite sighed. He had no intention of beating him, but neither could he afford to slack off. Raising the boy alone, he had done the best he could, but for the first time he wondered if he'd been wise to pass on his own feelings toward women.

On the other hand, with the boy so close to the age Waite had been when, as a willing and eager participant, he had let himself be seduced by a woman who'd been visiting for the summer, a certain amount of wariness was in order.

Lord knows, Waite could have done with a warning all those years ago. Not that he would have heeded it. Once he'd gotten the bit in his teeth, nothing could have slowed him down. They had lain together, he and Miss Constance Devereaux of New Orleans, on the beach that first time, and then in the woods in a sheltered place where deer had flattened out the sedge grass, and in Cyrus Stone's storage shed, and on a pile of nets down at the landing one hot August night. He wasn't sure which time it was that he'd planted the seed that had produced the boy standing now before him, but he couldn't find it in his heart to regret a single one of them. Constance had been the highlight of his young life for a few summer months, before she'd turned into an anchor around his neck.

But Waite had never been one to complain. He'd charted his own course. And while he might have wished a time or two that things could have been different, he had never once regretted bringing a son into the world. Come close a time or two, but he'd soon gotten over it.

"You'll be fifteen in a few months," he said, sounding stern. Sounding as if he himself had never been fifteen and bursting with the lusty juices of youth. "Time you started acting your age."

Nick shifted his weight and sighed impatiently. Waite knew he had heard it all before, and that was a damned shame, but what was a father to do? He couldn't just let the boy run wild.

"Was Dorien with you?"

"I don't snitch, Pa."

"I appreciate that. All the same, when you finish picking and cleaning that goose, I want you to split a load of kindling and stack it out behind Miz Deekins's cottage. Hiram supplied her with enough oak to last her a while, but this time of year, she needs a quick fire for cooking."

"Way I heard it, she can't cook worth shucks. Dore said she near about ate everything on the table that night she took supper at their house."

"That brings to mind another thing," Waite said, and his son groaned. "What about that girl of Newbolt's? Miz Deekins says she works too hard."

Nick shrugged. "She's a girl, ain't she? You always said all a woman's good for is cooking and—"

"Dammit, boy!"

"Shootfire, Pa, I didn't mean nothing. Evie's just a little girl. She cooks real good, though. I wish we ate like Dore does, like every day was Sunday, with cake and gravy and all."

"I never saw you leave the table hungry. You want cake and gravy, go right ahead and make 'em. You know the way to the kitchen."

Nick scowled down at his big bare feet. Waite started to swear and thought better of it. He had taken great pains to set a good example for his son, and to let him know they didn't need any aggravating woman making their lives a misery, but maybe he'd overdone it.

Oh, hell, he didn't know. He was beginning to think he didn't know much about anything anymore. Keeping a lighthouse was a damned sight simpler than rearing a son. At least there were rules a man could follow. "Go clean the gander and hang it on the line. I'll set it on to cook directly I finish drawing oil."

"Evie's frying bluefish. I sort of promised Dore I'd eat supper with him tonight."

Waite didn't have the heart to object. The gander would be tough and stringy this time of year, and even if he thickened the stew with cornmeal, it never tasted right. Compared to fried bluefish it was damned poor fare. "Go along, then, but not until you've split Miz Deekins's firewood and scrubbed out the chicken troughs."

Mariah was hitching up her cart to ride into the village when her new neighbor came mincing across the grounds, picking her way past wiry patches of grass, sandspurs, and worse.

"You there," she called out when she was halfway across the clearing.

You there?

Mariah was out behind her cottage, but as the shed was set off to one side, she could see clear across the grounds. She waited until the woman was close enough so that she could see the color of her eyes—they were the palest shade of blue, like a midsummer sky—and then she said, "Good morning. I'm Mariah Saw—Deekins. Did you get all settled in?"

"Caroline Hardraker. Oh, for heaven's sake!" Caroline slapped at a mosquito, and then wrinkled her nose at the smudge on her white gloves.

Mariah had left off her gloves her second day in residence. After that, she'd started leaving off a petticoat and even her stays. Once she'd even left off her stockings, but the sand that had quickly collected in her shoes had been miserable. "They're not always this bad," she heard herself saying. Little more than a week on the island, and here she was defending it. It was a mark, she thought ruefully, of how very much she wanted to fit in, to belong.

Caroline managed to look both skeptical and disgusted without diminishing her flawless beauty. "Are you getting ready to go into town?"

"I'm not really sure you could call it a town, but I'm on my way to Mr. Cyrus's store. Would you care to go with me?" Of all things, she found herself feeling sorry for the woman, who was obviously not at all happy to be here.

Miss Hardraker took a wisp of handkerchief from her pocket and dusted off the seat, climbed in, and arranged her skirts around her. "I might as well. There's nobody interesting around here. Is there any decent place to shop?"

"I suppose that depends on what you need. There's Mr. Cyrus's store." If there were other shops, Mariah had yet to discover them.

"Is this all you have to drive? Father gave me a brand-new gig for my birthday, but of course I had to leave it home. Lord have mercy, but it's hot here!"

As much as she'd looked forward to the company of another young woman, by the time they reached the village Mariah's enthusiasm had begun to fade. Miss Hardraker had criticized everything from the light that kept her awake at night, to the messy animals that ranged freely on the grounds, to the smell of paint and varnish, to the slow-witted creature who didn't know the difference between a hatbox and a valise.

"That would probably be Mr. Jones," Mariah said, wondering if she'd been that bad when she'd first arrived. "I've found him most helpful, even if he's not much of a conversationalist."

"Conversationalist! Heavens, the man can't say a word without his tongue getting tangled, which is better, I suppose, than the rest of the people I've met. I can't understand a word they say, can you?"

Having been there over a week now—it seemed more like a month—Mariah no longer found the accent strange. And while she wasn't on visiting terms with any of the women yet, she was making progress. They seemed to be thawing toward her. She had high hopes of becoming a part of the community before very much longer.

"I'm expecting a guest for lunch today," she confided, turning off the lighthouse road toward the village. Merrily seemed reluctant to move above a walk. In this heat, Mariah couldn't much blame her. "I thought I'd see what I can find at the store—it's remarkable what you can find in cans these days."

Caroline looked at her oddly. She was holding a parasol over her left shoulder, and it reminded Mariah of a pink one her mother had set such store by, all those years ago. Sadness fell over her for a moment, dimming the sun, dulling the noise of all the birds feeding on berries and wild grapes in the edge of the woods.

"You do your own cooking?"

Well, thought Mariah, amused—that had certainly cost her the respect of her new neighbor. Would it help to admit that she wasn't very good at it?

"How long have you lived here? It's obvious from the way you dress and speak that you don't belong here any more than I do."

Glancing down at the skirt of her lavender dimity, Mariah had to smile. It was quite plain, for she was still in half-mourning, but even so, the quality would be evident to anyone who knew anything at all about fashions.

"Oh, I haven't been here very long. I came to teach school."

Oops. Another mark against her. Evidently Miss Hardraker didn't approve of women who were forced to earn their own living. Still, she felt obliged to issue an invitation. "You're welcome to come to lunch. My other guest is only twelve, but she's an interesting child. The only girl among five brothers—"

"Brothers? How old?"

"Well, let's see, I believe Able must be in his early twenties, and Baxter's not far behind. Then there's Caleb and Dorien, and I know Dorien's fourteen or fifteen—he's just before Evie. And then there's Franklin. He's seven. They're alphabetical, but not at all alike."

They passed two women walking, both dressed in plain print dresses, both with scarfs knotted at the back of their heads. Each carried a fish by the tail. Both women smiled shyly, and Mariah smiled right back, thrilled at the small sign of acknowledgment, if not actual acceptance. As she pulled up before Cyrus's store, an old man in bib overalls took the reins, howdied her, and slipped the reins over the hitching post.

Mariah was touched all out of proportion to the small courtesy. She wasn't sure if it was because of her new position or because the island men, with a few notable exceptions, were naturally courteous, but it felt good. After her treatment back home in Murfreesboro these past few months, it felt more than good.

She smiled her thanks and then said to her passenger, "Here we are. Mr. Cyrus's store."

Caroline Hardraker looked so horrified that Mariah turned and considered the store again. What she saw was . . . well, it was hardly up to city standards, but for a small country store, it was perfectly all right. Forgetting that she'd been almost as dismayed the first time she had seen it, much less seen the meager display of goods inside, she felt herself getting defensive. "They have wonderful onions, grown right here on the island. And soap and cheese and tinned goods and kerosene—even a few bolts of dress material."

Three little girls darted around the corner, skidded to a halt, and piled into one another, staring up at the two women. Mariah smiled, suspecting she would know them all by this time next week.

And then Mr. Cyrus asked from the door if he could help her. Climbing down, she left Caroline Hardraker twirling her parasol under an increasingly hot sun and entered the dim recesses of the store.

"Evie Newbolt's taking lunch with me today," she confided. "I was wondering what you might have that would be easy to prepare. I'm not very good at cooking yet."

"Taking lunch, huh?" The wiry man's eyes twinkled in a face weathered to the texture of tree bark. "That anything like eatin' dinner?"

"Not in my house, I'm afraid. Is the canned hash any good? I've never tried it."

By the time she left the store, Mariah was burdened with a variety of cans, a box of soda crackers, a wedge of cheese, a bottle of Hire's root beer, and a bunch of locally grown grapes. They wouldn't starve. Lunch would hardly be up to Evie's standards, but then, that was all to the good. Mariah had every intention of doing a bit of bartering. Her helplessness in the kitchen would serve to strengthen her position.

"God, how can you stand it here?" Caroline exclaimed as soon as Mariah was seated beside her.

"It's not so bad . . . only different. I've hardly been here a full week yet, but I think I'm going to like it just fine."

"You obviously don't belong in a place like this. What are you really doing here? Oh, I know—you said you were going to teach school—but tell me the truth, is it a man?"

"Is what a man?"

"It has to be a man. You're not actually bad-looking, even with your complexion and that odd-looking hair. Tell me the truth, did your family send you down here to keep you out of trouble?"

Amused, Mariah said, "No, did yours?"

Caroline looked away. As they turned off down the winding, tree-shaded drive path, she lowered her parasol, twirling it in her white-gloved hands. "I was fast. At least that's what everybody said. I wasn't, not really, but a woman can't sit home forever hoping some good-looking, eligible man will ride up and make her an offer. Do you have any beaux? God, have you seen that wonderfully wicked-looking creature next door? He's terrifying, isn't he? I wonder if he's married. Claude didn't mention a wife, but there's a half-grown boy around the place. Probably a chore boy. He was out back plucking a goose when I left."

In the rush of trying to keep up with the conversation, Mariah felt as if she'd tangled with a dust devil. Catching a glimpse of Maxwell's yellow house through the pines, she breathed a sigh of relief.

What, she wondered, would Maxwell make of Caroline Hardraker?

What would Miss Hardraker make of the magistrate?

Before she could come to any conclusions, the curly-haired brother came out to greet them. He was gnawing on a drumstick and Mariah remembered guiltily that she had eaten somewhat more than her share of Evie's chicken.

"Miss Hardraker, this is . . ."

"I'm Caleb, ma'am." Blue eyes taking on a definite gleam of interest, Caleb wiped his hand on the seat of his pants and extended it to the stunning brunette in the cart, only to be ignored for his troubles. Shrugging, he said, "Evie's setting dinner on the table. She's been chafing at the bit all morning. Pa told her you likely wouldn't come, but she said you would."

"You've already had dinner? But I was going to make lunch."

"We've not eat yet, but Evie don't go nowhere without seeing to our dinner first." He grinned, and Mariah thought what a wicked piece of work he was, just like the other Newbolt boys. Lazy— the women had called them trifling—and a great deal too charming for his own good.

Caleb turned and yelled for his sister. "Evie—comp'ny's come for you!"

Caroline rolled her eyes and pursed her lips.

Suddenly Mariah felt a sense of belonging that was all out of proportion to the length of time she had been there. Mr. Cyrus had actually teased her this morning. Two local women had nodded and smiled at her, and three little girls had looked at her as if she were a fairy princess. In spite of her complexion and her unfortunate hair.

And now Caleb Newbolt was yelling for his sister to come go home with her. That was acceptance . . . wasn't it?

Chapter Eight

Evie Newbolt sat swaying and bouncing in the back of the cart. Now and again she turned to steal a glance at the back of Miss Hardraker's head. Never had she seen lips so red, nor hair so black and shiny. She wondered if the woman polished it with a rag to bring out all those sparkly colors.

Miss Hardraker did most of the talking. Her voice wasn't nearly as pretty as her hair, but Evie strained to catch every word. She could scarcely believe she was actually riding in the same cart with two women from away, with their pale skin and their pretty clothes and their smooth, shiny hair. Strangers almost never came to the Cape, and two at one time—it was just about the most exciting thing that had ever happened!

She hoped everybody saw her. Just in case Velma Jean happened to be looking out her window when they rode past her house, she twisted around to face the front of the wagon and tried to look as if she were joining in the conversation instead of just being toted down the road like a sack of chicken feed.

Miz Deekins had pretty hair, too, but it was red. Not sweet-potato-pun'kin red like her own, but red all the same. Evie was partial to black hair. Her mama had had black hair. Indian black, some said. There was a lot of that along the Banks.

I'm fixin' to put my own hair up most any day now, Lawsy, I reck'n I'll have to order me some hairpins from the Montgomery and Ward. Evie imagined herself taking part in the conversation.

"How can you stand it here? I hardly slept a wink last night, it was so hot!"

Evie couldn't quite make out Miz Deekins's answer. The schoolteacher's voice wasn't nearly so carrying.

I'm fixin' to order me a new frock just like that one you're a-wearin', too. Red silk with little black pokey dots. I'm real partial to red.

Once they turned off on the lighthouse road, where no one was apt to see her, Evie turned back around and stared disconsolately at the lap of her best muslin. There was still a hint of blue under the arms and inside the pockets, but the rest had faded until it looked gray. A drab, dirty gray. She had asked for a new frock to wear to school, but her pa had pretended not to hear her. Truth was, she wasn't even sure he was going to let her go back to school this year. She'd gone two months last year, and five the year before. She could already read real good, but Pa said there was no use for a girl to get too much schooling cause it might give her notions above her raising.

". . . open windows . . . mosquitoes . . ." Bits and pieces of conversation drifted back to her, and Evie strained to hear.

Miss Hardraker talked an awful lot. Miz Deekins didn't talk as much, and when she did, it had a sort of soft sound to it.

They were talking about hair, and self-consciously, Evie touched her own wild crop. She had brushed and brushed, and then tried to tie it back with a bit of string, but the string kept getting tangled up in her hair, and then Pa had heard her swearing and taken a swat at her, so she'd let it go.

"You're welcome to have lunch with us, Miss Hardraker," Miz Deekins was saying, and Evie nearly fell off the wagon, thinking about eating dinner with two beautiful ladies and talking about clothes and hats and gentlemen callers, like in that novel Velma Jean had gotten from her cousin in Elizabeth City.

"I'm sure Claude will have arranged for a cook by now. I told him to find a cook and a house-keeper and someone to do the laundry, but you know men. If you want anything done right you have to do it yourself."

"Another time, then," Miz Deekins said, and seated in the back of the cart with her limbs dangling over the stern, Evie silently mimicked the refined tones. She tried to speak more like her father, but mostly she forgot, and the words came out sounding like her brothers, her cousins, her friends and neighbors.

Anuther toime, then.

"Ah-nothah tiime, they-an." She whispered it under her breath as Miss Hardraker got out and picked her way past sandspurs, cow flops, and horse muffins toward the second keeper's house.

Mariah patted the seat beside her. "Come sit beside me, dear. I'm sorry you had to sit back there, but—"

"I don't mind ridin' in the back," Evie said

shyly. Nevertheless, she slid down, moved quickly around to the front of the wagon, and swung up onto the seat for the last few yards of the ride. "I'm used to sitting back there. When Baxter drives me to the store, he don't like for girls to see him toting me around. He says it cramps his style."

The schoolteacher said something under her breath. She sounded angry, and Evie's guard came up. She hadn't grown up among five brothers without learning to be wary. When they reached the teacherage and drove around to the back, they both climbed down, and without waiting to be asked, Evie helped her unhitch.

"Thank you, Evie. Now . . . I've a confession to make, my dear."

Evie grew still and waited. She might have known it was too good to be true. Why would a woman like Miz Deekins be nice to someone like Evie Newbolt unless she wanted something? "You want me to put in a good word for you with Able?"

"A good word with . . . Well, no . . . you see, the thing is, I'm not very good at preparing meals yet. I was hoping you might offer to show me what I'm doing wrong."

For a moment, Evie wondered whether or not she could believe her. All the girls wanted to get in good with her brothers—at least, with all of them but poor Frankie. "Yes'm, I reck'n I could do that."

"And in exchange, perhaps I could help you find a better style for your hair—not that it isn't lovely, but I'm sure it must be trying, with the weather as hot as it is." Mariah tilted her head and studied the small freckled face before her. "You have such lovely eyes, it's a shame to hide them. Perhaps if we were to . . ."

And then, one thing led to another and the ice was broken. After all, they were both redheads. They both had freckles. More cropped out on Mariah's face every day. And they were both female.

Laughing at her own ineptitude, Mariah struggled to open the tins without mangling either the lids or her hands, while Evie looked over Bathsheba's handwritten recipes, explaining the various terms.

"A pinch is just what it says." She demonstrated with a finger and thumb. "This is how much cornmeal she means." She cupped one small hand. "And a glug—you know how it sounds when you pour buttermilk from a jar? That's a glug."

The meal was simple in the extreme, but at least it was edible. They talked about heat rashes and how to tell when an oven was hot enough to bake bread, and whether or not cucumbers and buttermilk could actually fade freckles.

After setting the kettle to heat, they went out into the backyard with a towel, a comb, and a pair of shears, and Mariah proceeded to trim "just a tiny bit" off Evie's bushy hair.

Unfortunately, the tiny bit kept growing as first one side and then the other had to be evened up. Before Mariah realized what was happening, the child was shorn like a sheep. Mariah felt like a criminal. When Evie shyly asked for a looking glass, she was tempted to say she didn't own one, but honesty won out.

"All right, but before you look, remember this— it will grow out almost before you know it."

Staring at her reflection in the oval, silver-backed looking glass, Evie's eyes grew round as marbles. Tentatively, she touched her head, and then tugged at one of the pointy little wisps that stood up all over her scalp. "Lordamercy, ma'am, you done cut it all off," she whispered.

"Oh, no, it's just that—well, I'll admit, it might take a bit of getting used to, but really, it looks—"

"Like a skinned polecat," chimed in another voice as Nick McKenna sauntered around the corner. Shirtless, shoeless, he was grinning from ear to ear.

Evie wailed and flung the towel over her head, and Mariah stepped in front of her, as if to defend her from bodily harm. What on earth had she been thinking of? She had never cut hair in her life. It had seemed like such a simple thing—trim a bit off here and a bit off there—the hard part came in making the two sides even.

"Come on, now—let me see what you've gone and done to yourself, Evaloonie."

"It's Eva*leena*," the child hissed, clamping the towel over her face.

"Sure it is, Evaloonie. Quit acting bashful, now, and let's see your scalp. Did you know you can get freckles on the top of your head? You ever see old Horace with his hat off? He's got freckles bigger'n a possum egg."

"Just go away and leave me be!"

"Nicholas, don't tease her." Mariah felt obligated to step in. "Evie, truly, your scalp won't freckle. You've got lots more hair than you think. It only feels sparse because . . . because . . ."

"Because you've flat out skinned her bald, Miz D."

Nick was still grinning, looking more like his father than ever, his lanky, broad-shouldered frame hinting at the man he would soon become.

Under the towel, Evie was sniffling and hiccuping. Mariah would have chopped off her own hand if it would have helped, but a bleeding stump wouldn't make the poor child's hair grow back one whit faster.

"Come inside, darling." Slipping an arm around the frail, shaking shoulders, she led the girl inside. Nick lingered just outside the door, and Mariah glared at him. "Haven't you done enough damage?" she hissed.

To give him credit, he did look somewhat contrite. "I split you some firewood. It's stacked right beside the oak."

"Thank you, but that doesn't make up for hurting Evie's feelings."

"I didn't mean to make her cry, and anyway, the wood's supposed to be for what me and Dore did last night."

"Last night?"

"Rosum-stringin' your house."

Before Mariah could respond, Evie flung off the towel, scattering red corkscrew curls in all directions. She glared at Nick and said, "Dore did that? Just wait'll I tell Pa!"

"Aw, Evie, you wouldn't tattle, would you?"

Crossing her skinny little arms over her flat chest, Evie said, "I don't know. It all depends."

Nick, his dark eyes beseeching in his thin, handsome face, said, "It don't look all that funny, honest. And anyhow, it'll be cooler. Your head won't sweat near as much, just wait and see."

Mariah, watching the byplay between the lighthouse keeper's son and the magistrate's daughter, reached three conclusions, the first being that Evie was infatuated with the youth. The second, that Nick didn't even see her as a girl, much less an interesting girl.

And the third was that Evie, now that her heart-shaped face could be seen more clearly, was on the verge of becoming a lovely young woman.

"I want to go home," Evie wailed softly as Nick loped across the grounds to his own house. She stared after him, her red-rimmed eyes anguished, and Mariah, watching her, wondered if she had ever been so heartbreakingly young.

The truth was, a few months ago she'd been even younger at nearly twenty-two than Evie was at twelve and a half. In many ways. Only she'd been too sheltered to realize it.

Before she drove her guest back home, Mariah insisted on washing what was left of her hair, confident that it could only help matters. Nothing short of shaving what was left of the prickly red stuff could make matters worse.

And so they went outside again, hidden between the shed and the cottage, and Mariah lathered Evie's head with scented soap and then rinsed it with rainwater. Three times, the way her mother had taught her. After toweling it dry, she went inside to fetch the mirror again.

"Oh, my . . ." Evie whispered, gingerly touching the short ringlets that framed her small face. "It don't look real awful, does it?"

"My dear, it looks lovely!" So relieved she was close to tears, Mariah dashed inside and came out with a Nile-green silk scarf and draped it around

Evie's shoulders. "You should wear green more often."

"Mama didn't like green. Mostly she wore blue. I think. It's been so long, I've near 'bout forgot."

Impulsively, Mariah hugged her. "Oh, and blue always seems to fade quicker than all the other colors, doesn't it? I know—it just so happens that somewhere in one of my trunks there are several dresses I never wear because . . ." She bit her lip, trying to come up with a convincing excuse. "Because I've been in mourning."

Evie lifted a pair of large brown eyes. "I know. On account of your husband. I'm real sorry, Miz Deekins."

"Yes, well . . . at any rate, they don't fit me any longer, and I'd be glad if someone could find a use for them. I do hate to see waste, don't you?"

And so it was decided. Evie would come to visit another day, and the two of them would go through Mariah's trunks and see what could be done with the things she could no longer use.

She could only hope the child sewed as well as she cooked.

That evening, after driving Evie home and waiting to see that Maxwell didn't blame the child for what had happened to her hair, Mariah's spirits began to rise. The haircut had turned out unexpectedly well, after all, but men could be so peculiar. Her own father had been shocked the first time she had worn a grown-up dress instead of her usual girlish gingham. When he'd noticed her newly developed bosom, as small as it was, he'd turned into an ogre overnight and began treating boys they'd known all their lives as potential enemies.

Poor Maxwell. It was a wonder he'd found time to write at all, much less such long, detailed letters. Dealing with that pack of rascals, Evie not included, must be quite a challenge.

Caroline Hardraker was waiting for her when she returned after driving Evie home. "Do you know what that brother of mine said to me?" she demanded. Still in the red silk, she looked hot and wilted. Thinking of the rashes she herself still suffered, Mariah was tempted to advise her that soda-water baths would help and that cotton was considerably more comfortable for summer, but she wasn't sure her advice would be appreciated.

"What did he say?"

"He actually expects me to cook for him!"

Slapping Merrily on the rump to send her scampering toward the cedar grove, Mariah had to laugh. "Then I hope for your sake you're better at it than I am."

"It's not funny! He really means it."

"So do I," Mariah told her, sobering. "Believe me, if I'm ever fortunate enough to have someone to cook for me again, I'll not take her for granted. Imagine, having to build a fire and stand over a range all day when the temperature outside is hot enough to poach an egg."

"Claude said he won't get paid for another month, and on four hundred dollars a year, he can't afford to hire a cook."

Compared to a teacher's salary, that sounded quite generous to Mariah, but she didn't voice an opinion. The man was expecting a child any day now, according to his sister. If he was the sole support of a wife, a sister, and a child, he would be wise to save where he could. She could personally vouch for the fact that living on a budget was more than a mere challenge—it was a near impossibility.

"Then what will you do?"

"What would you do in my place?" Caroline countered. In the late afternoon light, her pale eyes looked almost colorless, making her somewhat less beautiful, but far more exotic.

"Learn to cook. Given a choice between going hungry or doing for myself, I chose the latter. Already I know how to burn biscuits, cornbread, and potatoes. Once I've mastered the incineration of meats, I'll invite you over again."

Caroline looked shocked. Mariah was hardpressed not to laugh. To tell the truth, she felt a smidgen of sympathy for any creature accustomed to a nest of privilege who suddenly found herself cast out on her own. "Believe me, Miss Hardraker, you'll find that you can learn rather quickly when it becomes a matter of survival."

"Claude said more or less the same thing. He said I'd either have to sink or swim, but until Father gives his permission, I can't go home again. I ask you—is that fair?"

Fair or not, Mariah thought as she opened her journal that night, at least Caroline had a home to return to. Whatever she had done—and it must have been dreadful to set her own parents against her—she at least still had parents.

Sink or swim. Taking advantage of the slight breeze off the ocean, Mariah sat in the rocker, the unopened journal on her lap, and considered the unfortunate turn of phrase.

And then she considered her own situation. Terrified of water, she had chosen to come to an island because it was the only place that had offered her employment. Once here, she had done her best to fit in and make a place for herself.

At least once each day she forced herself to walk on the beach. She was even coming to enjoy feeding scraps to the gulls and picking up pretty shells. She had yet to find the courage to wet her feet in the shallows, but at least she could walk beside them without panic setting in.

She, who had never even boiled water for tea in her life, was learning to cook. She, who had always taken friendships for granted, was learning to reach out and make friends of strangers.

Tomorrow she would drive herself to church and the day after tomorrow she would drive herself to school and begin a career that, if she was lucky, would be her life until she was an old, old woman.

She didn't know whether to weep or rejoice. Uncapping her fountain pen, she wrote:

Caroline Hardraker. She's beautiful and terribly worldly, I suspect. Her gowns are expensive, yet not quite the thing. Do I like her? I'm not sure. I don't know what to make of her, so I'll not make anything of her yet. Does that mean I'm learning to be charitable? Not really. It only means I can't seem to concentrate on my new neighbor when there's so much else to think about.

Evie believes she's in love with Nick. Per-

haps she is. I hope not. Waite has dimples. I
wonder if he even knows it. When he smiles,
or almost smiles, which is as close as he ever
comes, there are two little creases in his
cheeks.

Be still, my foolish heart!

Closing the journal, she leaned back, closed her
eyes, and pondered the possibility of some great,
ambiguous force called Fate. Could it be Fate that
had sent her out here to this isolated place to save
Waite McKenna before he grew any more embittered?

Across the way in the principal keeper's quarters, Waite sat at his desk and carefully logged the
last entry of the day. Then he leaned back, waiting
for the ink to dry before closing his ledger.

The twenty-first day of August, the sun
rose at 5:07 and set at 6:23. It squalled some
last night. Less than a tenth of an inch of rain
in the gauge. Wind SSE, light. Picked up some
late in the evening, still out of the southeast.
There were seventeen sets of sails off the
Outer Diamonds, same as yesterday, most
headed south and waiting for the wind to
change. Two steamers passed bound to the
north. One schooner turned north again, will
likely come in through the inlet and try to
make it down the sound.

Hardraker's sister . . .

Here he had paused. It didn't seem right to set
out on paper that the woman had a voice like an

ungreased winch. She was Hardraker's problem, not his own. Still, if she didn't behave herself, he might have to have a word with her. She'd come prissing around him this morning, tossing her skirts and batting her eyelashes, like he was a prize and she'd just won the toss.

He'd set her straight quick enough. There'd been a time, back when he was young and full of juice, he might have been tempted.

No more. Once bitten, twice shy.

It occurred to him that the schoolteacher might set her on the right track. Closing his eyes momentarily, Waite allowed himself a brief smile. A mule was stubborn until you set him against a billy goat. Then you found out the mule wasn't so stubborn after all. He wrote:

> Hardraker's sister talks right much. Hardraker don't. Schoolteacher seems to be settling in. Sarvice set out another bottle, I reckon hoping to catch the interest of a woman somewhere. Poor fool. Signed, Waitefield A. McKenna, Principal Keeper, Cape Hatteras Light.

Chapter Nine

Waite stood on the tower and watched her set out on the first day of school. He was somewhat surprised she'd lasted as long as she had, but school would be the real test. Some of those boys, his own included, were too old to be going to school on the island. Newbolt had taken his eldest boy up north to a boarding school a few years back. The boy had beat him home on the mailboat. He'd sent Baxter off a time or two, but he hadn't stuck, either. After a few more tries, he'd given up and let them stay home. Hadn't even tried with Caleb.

Waite could almost sympathize with the fellow. It was past time he sent Nick off to the mainland, but the boy always kicked up a fuss whenever the subject of boarding school was broached. He plain didn't want to go. And so far, Waite had let him get away with it, telling himself the boy had missed so much schooling these past few years, what with first one teacher and then another one quitting before they'd even gotten started, that another few months here at home wouldn't hurt.

Maybe after Christmas, he thought. He'd miss him worse than he'd have missed his right thumb, but the boy needed proper schooling if he was going to make something of his life.

After Christmas, then, Waite promised himself. Even before that if Mariah Deekins didn't stick around.

Like a compass needle homing in on magnetic north, his thoughts veered off along a familiar course. Mariah.

He'd figured her for the type of woman who'd throw up her hands in surrender at the first little setback. He'd expected her to come running to him to complain about the mice, the bugs, the snakes, the weather—or those two young hellions scaring her half out of her wits in the middle of the night.

So far, she hadn't run. Either away or to him. He had to admit she hadn't even complained all that much. Compared to the Hardraker woman, she was tough as old boot soles.

Leaning on the cool, damp iron rail, Waite gazed down on the tiny cart moving off at a rackety pace along the lighthouse road. She was in a hurry today. Be interesting to see how fast she came back. He should have thought to tell her to unhitch and turn the mare loose in the woods during the heat of the day.

One of the boys would do it. They might not look after a teacher, but not a one of them would ever mistreat a horse.

Just as she turned off onto the main road, he saw her clap a hand on top of her bonnet when a gust of wind threatened to blow it off. He chuckled, picturing her jumping off the cart and chasing the damn fool thing into Jenette's Sedge.

He did like her dress, though. It reminded him

of an early morning fog, sort of gray with darker
trim. Same color as her eyes, only her eyes were
clear, like looking down through five fathoms of
rainwater.

She. Her. Funny thing . . . he seldom thought of
her by name. Tried not to think about her at all,
come to that, but she was damned hard to ignore.

Her name was Mariah, he did know that. He'd
seen it on a piece of mail, only the letter had been
addressed to Mariah Sawyer, not Mariah Deekins.
He'd heard talk down at the landing that according to Newbolt, she'd been married and widowed, all within a matter of months. There was
even speculation on whether it had been the chol-
era, the influenza, or a lingering sickness that had
killed the poor man.

Not that he'd lingered long, if Newbolt had the
story right. Some even said the man had died
under suspicious circumstances, but Waite didn't
put much stock in loose talk, knowing how folks
could take a few random threads and weave them
into five miles of gill net. They'd talked up a storm
when he'd married Constance, and then talked
some more when Nick had been born. Come early
he'd put it about, not that anyone had believed
him.

Still, something must have happened to cause
those shadows in the widow Deekins's eyes. He'd
seen her laugh, seen her smile—seen her scared
out of her wits—but he'd never seen her without
that small, lingering shadow of sadness.

Not that sadness changed anything. She was
still just another dislocated city woman. Good to
look at, but too frail to last.

High up on the tower, he gazed down on the

lighthouse grounds, on the neatly fenced gardens, the scattering of livestock, the two residences, the outbuildings. And in the distance, the small, red, boxlike auxiliary lighthouse.

His domain. His responsibility.

And then he looked over toward the tiny teacherage that was *not* a part of his domàin. Which brought his thoughts directly back to that woman again.

Dammit, this used to be the one place where he could come to rise above his worries! Now she'd even robbed him of his privacy.

He wondered what kind of a man her husband had been. Successful. He'd lay odds on that. But had he loved her? Looked after her properly? Spoiled her the way a woman likes to be spoiled? Had he pleased her in bed?

Had she pleased him? Was there fire enough under all those prim riggings to pleasure a man until he hollered out with it?

Waite shifted uncomfortably and switched his thoughts into safer channels. Such as why a young widow who wore well-cut gowns and had fancy dishes and big, gold-framed portraits of her folks had to earn her keep as a schoolteacher in a one-room school on the Banks.

Waite had known widows aplenty. Rhoda Quigley and Maggie Stone came to mind right away. They'd both lost their husbands in the same storm when their fishing boat had capsized trying to make it through Hatteras Inlet before dark.

Whatever tears the two women had shed had been shed in private. Once the bodies had been recovered they had buried their dead and got on with life, making do with what was left. Maggie had turned her home into a boardinghouse and set table for those who had need of her cooking.

Rhoda had her children. She fished her husband's nets, tended garden, and took in sewing. A fine-looking woman, she could have remarried. Instead, she made do with brothers, cousins, and neighbors whenever a man's help was needed.

The island bred strong women. Waite had spent more than a little while regretting that none of the McKenna men had had the good sense to marry one.

Forcing his mind away from idle thought, he examined the small crack he'd discovered earlier in the corner of one section of glass. He wasn't sure how it had happened. Cold rain on hot glass. That gander striking at just the right angle. Things happened, though. Sometimes a man never did figure out how, much less the why of it.

Collecting his polishing rags and the two empty five-gallon cans, he headed down the steps, nodding to Hardraker, who was cranking up the weights—panting and sweating and making heavy weather of the job.

Claude Eustace Hardraker, newly transferred down from the Rock Point Light in Maryland, was a tall man, over six feet, but he wasn't much bigger around than a flagpole. He had the saddest pair of eyes Waite had ever seen. Dark, sagging at the outer corners, like it wouldn't take more than a harsh word to make him weep.

The man was something of a puzzle. He was educated. Came from quality, that much was clear from the way he spoke, the way he carried himself. His sister acted like she was second cousin to the queen of England. Waite would very much like to know what they were doing down here, but all he said was "Mr. Jones has the duty from sunset to midnight. I'll take midnight till daybreak. Get a good night's sleep while you can." A suggestion of a smile lit his eyes. "Damned shame nobody ever figgered out a good way to stockpile sleep for when a man needs it."

Before her first day on the job was half over, Mariah wondered why she'd ever thought she could teach. She couldn't even command the respect of a handful of children, much less teach them anything.

First there was the muskrat someone had crammed into her desk drawer. She'd discovered it when she'd opened the drawer to put away her reticule. All that had saved her from a full-blown case of hysterics was the fact that the poor creature was even more terrified than she was.

Obviously, the whole class had been in on it. At least she hadn't disgraced herself by screaming. She'd been too shocked. It was little Franklin Newbolt who had come to her rescue while the three older boys on the back row were snickering behind their hands.

"He's real skeert, Miz Deekins," the child said diffidently, peering around her shoulder at the bristle of reddish brown fur showing through the crack. "You want me to take him down to the ditch and let him go?"

"If you can get him out without being bitten, I'd appreciate it." She'd been proud of her composure. Her voice had hardly even quavered.

"He won't bite me, ma'am. I'll hold him by the back of the neck like a cat and be real careful."

One of the other children raised her hand and said, "Frankie's real good with animals, Miz Deekins. He's got a pet crow that can almost talk."

Blushing, Frankie had inched his fingers into the partially open drawer. Skillfully avoiding a pair of big orange incisors, he had lifted the frightened rodent out. The little girls gasped in unison. The older boys called out advice, not all of it helpful. Four small paws scrabbled wildly, scattering pens, chalk, and a tablet. A scaly tail twirled frantically. Franklin, holding the frightened animal at arm's length, hurried outside, his shoes, a good two sizes too large, clattering on the bare wood floor.

"Well, now, shall we get on with our lessons?"

Evie wasn't there. She wasn't coming, or she would have come with Frankie. Taking a deep breath, Mariah pushed aside her disappointment. She would deal with the matter later. Ignoring the stifled giggles from the front row and the whispered remarks from the back, she nodded to the pretty child who had spoken up on Franklin's behalf. "We'll start with you—it's Alice, isn't it?"

"Yes'm. Alice May Scarbrey, ma'am. I can read and do my times tables all the way to the six-timeses."

"That's wonderful, Alice May. Now, suppose you all tell me your names, so I'll be sure I have them written down properly. Shall we start at the end?" She nodded to a girl in blue calico, with an enormous bow holding her two skinny braids together.

By the time she had heard from the children in the first two rows she was ready to tackle the back row, where three young gentlemen in various stages of adolescence lolled back on their bench and tried to look bored.

Two of them were already known to her. Maxwell's Dorien and Waite McKenna's son, Nick. The third, a plump young man named Oliver in a necktie that looked more like a hangman's noose, turned fiery red and tried to dig a hole in the floor with the toe of his boot.

It was Dorien who acted as spokesman. "We don't really b'long here, Miz D. Nick and me only come along to help out in case you had trouble with some o' the babies." He looked at Nick and grinned, and Nick grinned right back, pure mischief in their good-looking faces.

Mariah strived for an expression of tolerant dignity. Not that she felt dignified—nor tolerant, either, at the moment. She knew very well who she had to thank for that muskrat.

"Thank you, Dorien. Now, how many of you have finished the first three readers? How many the fourth?" She counted the raised hands and went on to try to discover who had studied what, to what effect, and where she had best begin.

Franklin came back and slipped into his seat. His high-tops were wet and muddy, his shirttail was out, and there was a pine straw stuck in his hair.

Mariah smiled, murmured her thanks, and continued to try to sort out her students according to grade level. Not until much later, when she was gathering her books to go home, did it occur to her that Frankie had not stumbled over a single word in dealing with the muskrat. Nor even when called upon to read the first page of *The Wolf and the Seven Goslins*, a clear indication that he stuttered only when he found himself in a stressful situation.

Muskrats didn't bother him. Neither did reading.

Which made her wonder about his life at home.

When the cart drove back to the lighthouse grounds late that afternoon, Waite was once more up on the tower balcony. He'd been measuring the glass so he could send off for a replacement, which would take forever, as it was a special kind of glass. Pausing, he gazed over the side, his shirttail fluttering in the brisk westerly wind, and admired the way she—Mrs. Deekins—Mariah—handled the frisky little mare.

Quickly he finished taking measurements and headed down. Come winter, he thought, she would need something better to drive. Most of the women walked wherever they needed to go. Some few drove. The men, for the most part, rode horseback. There were a few covered carriages on the island, but they were used mostly for solemn occasions like weddings or funerals.

Emerging from the door in the octagonal base a few minutes later, he raked back his hair and retrieved his uniform cap. He knew better than to wear it topside. He'd lost too many caps that way. Tucking his shirttail back inside his trousers, he told himself it was only polite to go over and inquire as to how her first day on the job had gone.

Mariah slung her chip-straw bonnet in one direction and her reticule in another, unbuttoned her shoes and kicked them off, then collapsed in the rocking chair. If she'd been put through one of

Mr. Goodrich's rubber clothes mangles, she couldn't have felt any more wrung out.

She wriggled her toes in her white silk stockings. After a moment, she reached up and pulled the pins from her hair, letting it tumble in damp clumps onto her shoulders.

Day one. Her contract called for a maximum of eight months, not including holidays and tide days, as long as she had a minimum of five students. It took the fees of at least five to pay her salary.

Heavenly days, she just couldn't do it. No one had told her when she'd first mentioned becoming a schoolteacher that the job would require the strength of a blacksmith, the wisdom of Solomon, and the patience of a saint.

By the time someone rapped on her door, she was almost asleep where she sat. It was still light outside, but the room was full of deep shadows.

"Mariah? Miz Deekins, are you all right?"

Oh, bother. The man had come to gloat. "Yes, of course, I'm perfectly fine," she called back. Sighing, she felt about with her toes for her discarded shoes.

Waite didn't stand on ceremony. He let himself in and stopped just inside the door. "Damn, what happened to you?"

Mariah gave up looking for her shoes and rose, forgetting she had let down her hair and unbuttoned the top four buttons of her high-collared gray twill.

Even in the shadowy room, she could feel his eyes moving over her hair, her throat—down over the gored skirt past the chalk smears and the wrinkles, lingering on her silk-clad toes.

"Yes, well . . . it's, um . . . warm, isn't it?"

"Hot as pickled peppers in here. Nice breeze up on top of the tower, though, if you'd like to go up."

His gaze caught on her face and stayed there. Mariah stared right back. She had the strangest feeling that something was happening, yet for the life of her, she couldn't put a name to it. Nothing she had ever experienced before had left her feeling this way—as if the air had been sucked right out of her lungs.

"Warm, you say?" she murmured. "No, I said that, didn't I? Is there truly a breeze?"

"Come see for yourself. That is, if you're not too tired."

They both recognized the challenge in the simple invitation. If she said she was too tired, he would look at her with that pitying expression he seemed to reserve for women of her stamp.

Whatever her stamp was.

If she said she wasn't, she'd be forced to drag herself all the way to the top of that monstrous tower. Why couldn't he simply let her swelter in peace?

If she'd had the slightest tendency toward claustrophobia, Mariah told herself a few minutes later, she would have run screaming right back outside again. The room at the bottom of the tower was round and damp, like a dungeon, though it was well above ground.

Still, it was cool. Wonderfully, chillingly cool! If only it weren't so musty, she could have stayed there for hours.

She gazed up toward the shadowy summit, and Waite touched her lightly on the shoulder.

"Don't look up," he said. "Just start climbing. There's landings to rest on if you need to stop. If you can't go all the way, I'll bring you back down."

In a pig's eye. If she had learned one thing in her first day of teaching—and actually, she'd learned several things—it was never to give the enemy a clear shot. Keep them off balance. Just when they expected you to veer right, veer left instead.

"After being cooped up all day, I'm looking forward to it. Shall I lead the way?"

He let her lead. Before she'd climbed the first few dozen narrow steps, she was regretting her bravado. The muscles in her lower limbs were quivering, threatening to knot up on her. She was sorely winded, and worst of all, she could practically feel his gaze on her backside. It made her self-conscious.

Which made her concentrate on not swaying her hips.

Which in turn made her move like one of those hinged wooden dolls on a paddle. "Oh, for heaven's sake!" she muttered.

"Stop here on the landing. We'll take a breather."

Without slowing her climb, Mariah said airily, "Feel free to stop if you need a breather, Mr. McKenna. You don't mind if I go on ahead, do you?"

Evidently, too much chalk dust clogged the brain.

"Suit yourself."

She suspected from the sound of his voice that he was grinning. It would almost be worth turning around to see, but if she hesitated for a single second—if she looked either up or down, or anywhere at all but straight ahead, she would surely perish. *Concentrate on breathing, Mariah. In, out, pause—in, out, pause.*

She was gasping like a beached whale. Or did whales gasp? They were mammals, weren't they?

Oh, drat, she was hallucinating.

"Slow down, Mariah. It's too much. You're not fit to—"

"I'm fit, dammit," she gasped. It was a sign of just how very *un*fit she was that she'd cursed out loud for the first time in her entire life. Or perhaps the second. Well . . . possibly the third.

Stiffly, she dragged her left foot up beside her right one. Daring a look upward at the rapidly narrowing tunnel, she saw that they'd come barely a third of the way, spiraling around and around . . . and around, and around. . . .

She gave up trying not to gasp, not to pant, and stood where she was, like a sodden lump of blancmange. If she'd deliberately set out to prove to Waite McKenna that she was every bit as frail and useless as he'd expected her to be, she couldn't have done a better job of it.

"You . . . win," she whispered.

"Beg pardon?"

Furious with the man for showing up her weakness, she whirled to face him and would have fallen if he hadn't caught her around the waist. As he was standing on the step below, his face was on a level with hers.

Mariah closed her eyes. Her face was red as fire. She could feel it burning. Her hair was sticking to her damp face, and there wasn't a breath of air to fill her tortured lungs. "I said," she gritted through clenched teeth, "if it's all the same to you, I believe

I'll wait a day or so before going all the way up to the top. I—my—that is, it's getting so dark, I couldn't really see anything, anyway."

She barely got the last word out before a spasm of pain grabbed the muscles of one of her legs. There was no way on heaven or earth she could keep from gasping aloud.

"What? What is it?"

"Nothing!" She bent over and grabbed her leg through layers of skirt, petticoat, and drawers, kneading with her fingers, biting her lower lip against the pain.

"Let me," Waite said, and before she could summon the strength to resist, he took over.

Chapter Ten

Waite brushed away her hands and said, "We'd better sit down. I should've known better than to—"

"It's only a cramp, for goodness' sake! I'm not dying!" It only felt like it. Nevertheless, she sat, and Waite took a seat on the step below. Almost as bad as the dreadful cramp was the way he was watching her in the dim light that fell from the nearby window, as if he expected her to faint. "I'll be all right . . . once I've . . . caught my breath."

Her lungs were bursting, her limbs were on fire—and all from climbing a few little bitty steps. Flopping over from the waist, she grabbed her leg and tried to press out the hurt.

Waite brushed her fingers aside. "Here, let me see."

She slapped his hands from her skirttail. "Stop that!"

"You want to hurt, or do you want help?"

"I can do it myself." Leaning against the curving masonry wall, he continued to regard her with maddening unconcern. Mariah thought, *I'm dying in agony and all he can do is gloat!*

"Leg cramps can hurt like the very devil," he observed.

Ignoring him, she battled her way through layers of skirt and underskirt, trying to get at the source of the pain. She squeezed, but it didn't help. "Oh, it . . . *hurts*," she muttered.

With a sigh of saintly patience, he reached out and lifted both her feet by the heels. Propping them on his knee, he folded back her skirttail, closed his hands around her calves, and then his fingers bit into the knotted muscle. "Where? Here?"

"Yesss! Make it stop," she begged. "Please."

His hands were magic. Hard, capable, warm, they manipulated the spasming muscles, smoothing out the knots, calming the stress, until within minutes all that was left was a residual soreness. "Oh, that's wonderful," she whispered.

"Woman in the village makes up a fine liniment. Mustard, onion, and turpentine, from the smell of it. I keep some on hand."

Mariah rolled her eyes. Waite chuckled. He continued to work on her, his hands gentler now, his strokes longer. It might have occurred to her if she'd been conscious of anything other than sheer relief that his strokes extended from her shoe tops all the way to her knees. She could only lie back, her elbows propped on the cool metal surface, oblivious to all but the exquisite absence of pain.

"Heavenly," she murmured.

Long moments passed before something in the quality of the silence made her open her eyes. He wasn't looking at her. He wasn't even looking at the silk-clad limb stretched out across his lap. Instead, his eyes were closed, his face flushed in the most extraordinary way under his mahogany tan, as if he, and not she, were the one in pain.

Abruptly, she jerked both feet off his lap, smoothed down her skirt, and sat up straight. "That's much better. If it's all the same to you, Mr. McKenna, I believe I'll go back downstairs now. There's really no need to go all the way to the top. I'm feeling much cooler now."

They both stood at the same time. He was so close they were almost touching. To regain her composure, she turned and stared out the narrow window at the lavender, gold-streaked sky. "However, I do thank you. For your consideration, I mean . . ."

She tried to sidle past him, but there was no room. In the small space, his body seemed to radiate heat, strength, and a raw sort of masculinity that bore no resemblance to the well-dressed, cologne-scented variety she was accustomed to dealing with. Her father. Henry Lee. Maxwell.

Impossible to imagine either Henry Lee or her father living in a place like this. Even Maxwell didn't really belong here. Remembering the impression she'd formed through his letters, and how far off target it had proved, she smiled.

"Something tickle you?" he asked.

"No. Well . . . perhaps my own thoughts. This does seem to be my day for learning things."

He preceded her down the stairs, telling her to grab his shoulders if she felt faint. She could have told him that the very thought of grabbing his shoulders made her feel even fainter, but she didn't. Instead, she slid her hand down the painted iron rail, placing her feet carefully on the small metal steps that spiraled downward, and kept her gaze focused on the top of his head.

He'd left his hat in the anteroom below. His

hair was thick, a bit too shaggy, as if he cut it himself when he happened to think about it. She'd never seen hair like that before. Dark around the edges, a sort of sooty brown, the top layers bleached bright gold by the sun. Nick's was like that, only the gold was even paler. With those dark eyes, both McKenna men were striking.

"Doing all right?" he asked when they were halfway down, stopping and turning toward her. She nodded, picturing Waite as a child. His hair would have been bleached pale even then, his skin burned brown from racing along the shore skipping shells, diving through waves, riding others ashore, the way boys still did. Without adult supervision, totally without fear, shrieking for the sheer joy of living.

What if something happened to one of them? Lord, it didn't bear thinking about.

"Mariah?"

"What? Oh. Yes, I'm fine, thank you," she said breathlessly as they reached the gritty floor.

"You never got to feel the breeze."

"No, I—but it's much cooler, even here, than it is outside."

"Yes, it is," he said quietly. She smiled up at him and discovered that he was smiling, too, and her last rational thought melted like river mist under a hot summer sun. He was staring at her mouth, which made her gaze drop to his mouth. He had a beautiful mouth, his lower lip full and firm, his upper lip narrow, the bow sharply chiseled.

"Is what?" she murmured. "Oh. You mean cooler."

It occurred to her that she'd seldom met a man

so comfortable with silence. Was he even capable of carrying on an extended conversation? And if so, what would he have to say for himself? Instinct told her there was more to the man than met the eye.

Not that what met the eye wasn't enough to engage any woman's interest.

Mercy, she was getting all hot and bothered again! Amused at the notion, she brushed past him and stepped out onto the granite steps and into the steamy heat. "There might be a breeze at the top," she said, "but there's certainly none down here."

He merely nodded. Evidently the heat didn't bother him. Did anything bother him? she wondered. Anything besides schoolteachers who had the misfortune of not being island-born?

The air smelled of salt marsh and some powdery sweet fragrance. Boneset, perhaps. It grew freely along the road. Long lavender shadows reached out across the grounds, leaving patches of peach-colored sand in between. A golden haze had settled over the wall of low forest that separated the lighthouse community from the village. Seagulls, their white wings gilded by the setting sun, drifted lazily overhead, silent for the moment, while, a few hundred yards away, the ocean whispered quietly to the shore.

Not long ago, Mariah mused, she would have felt threatened by the nearness of so much open water. Now she could sit quite comfortably on the shore, enjoying the sights and sounds and scents. She was even making friends with one particularly cantankerous seagull, who wasn't above begging for a crust.

I'm making remarkable progress, if I do say so my-self, she thought, and, bracing her shoulders, she lifted her skirt, descended the granite steps, and struck out across the sand, wary of sandspurs and horse manure.

Without a word, Waite matched his long stride to her shorter one. She racked her brain for something intelligent to say to him, but nothing came to mind. He seemed perfectly comfortable with the silence; but then, lighthouse keeping, she suspected, was a rather solitary occupation.

"Well," she said brightly as they approached the teacherage. "Thank you again for . . ." For what? Testing her once more and finding her wanting? She shrugged. "For thinking of me. About the heat, that is."

"You said you'd learned things at school today. I thought teachers were supposed to know all there was to know."

Mercy! Was the man actually instigating a conversation? Unwilling to waste the opening, she said, "A good teacher never ceases to learn. Only today I learned the difference between a grass whistle and a finger whistle. One will summon a horse, the other won't."

"Depends on your whistling style and the horse's training."

Her style, when it came to whistling across a blade of grass, sounded more like a sheep breaking wind than anything else she could imagine.

"Yes, well . . . fortunately, I'm not required to whistle very often. I've been told that my pucker is all wrong." He grinned broadly at that, and she marveled at the improvement.

"How do you call Conk?"

"Merrily"—she stressed the name, her eyes glinting with good humor—"comes running as soon as she sees me step out the door."

"You've been bribing her." His eyes were sparkling, too. He hardly looked like the same bird of prey who had landed on the deck of the mailboat not too long ago, ready to send her back to where she had come from.

"Turnips. I'll have to try something else when this year's crop runs out. Mr. Cyrus suggested dried apples."

They were standing on her doorstep, both flushed and damp with the unrelenting humid heat. "And?" he prompted.

"And?" She studied his brows, which, like his thick eyelashes, exactly matched the underlayer of his hair. Dark, sooty brown without a smidgen of red.

"And what else did you learn today?"

"What else? Oh, yes. I learned that a desk drawer is not the favored habitat of the muskrat." He nodded solemnly at that, which made her wonder if he'd played the same prank as a boy. What a rogue he must have been. What had happened to change him? "And I learned that Maxwell has no intention of wasting a good education on a mere daughter."

Waite locked hands behind his back and stared off at the cedar grove, where half a dozen ponies grazed on the wild grass that grew there. He could have told her that. He was only sorry she'd expected otherwise. Nick had told him what she'd done for the girl—tried to do, at any rate. From the sound of it, she'd damn near scalped the child, but he knew her well enough by now to know her efforts had been well meant. "Do you want me to talk to him?"

"About Evie?"

He could tell she was surprised by the offer. Hell, so was he. "I could remind him that the village looks to him for guidance. They don't, but he thinks they do. He'll believe me. I might tell him that if he won't send his own daughter to school, others might follow his example, and there aren't enough boys to make up the difference. We'd have to close down again."

Waite would prefer not to get involved. It wasn't his battle. But the way she was looking at him, you'd have thought he'd never done a decent, unselfish thing before in his life, and that stung his pride. "I'll have a word with him," he said, stepping back, deliberately widening the space between them. "But don't go expecting any miracles."

"No, I won't. And thank you. For that, I mean, and—and everything else."

He left her then, striding across the grounds toward the tower, telling himself it wasn't weakness he was showing. The woman was still here on sufferance as far as he was concerned. It wouldn't be fair to her or to anyone else to let her think otherwise.

He was halfway home when the Hardraker woman came out onto the porch and waved at him. "You, there! Mr. McKenna! Come here, please!"

Swearing under his breath, Waite was tempted to ignore her, but she'd only screech at him. If there was one thing that riled a woman, it was being ignored. Constance had been the same way.

When whining didn't work, she'd set in to cry, and when that didn't do it, she'd screech at him, which drove him to escape her ranting, either by climbing the tower and locking the watchroom door or racing his horse along the shore, as if he could outrun his troubles.

"Yes, ma'am." He reached for his hat, then decided to leave it on. He was in uniform. A man in uniform wasn't obliged to kowtow to every blessed female on the island. It only seemed that way.

"You have to do something about my windows. There's a tear in my window netting, and the Jones boy won't repair it. I've told him and told him, and now I can't even find him!"

"Did you ask your brother?"

She tossed her head, and he had to admit, it was a fetching gesture. Like a filly flirting with a young stallion. "Oh, him. He's not speaking to me. Besides, he likes seeing me miserable."

"Keeper Jones"—Waite stressed the title—"is on duty. His duties don't include doing odd jobs for visiting females. The netting was inspected the day before you came. It passed."

"Precious doesn't like being confined in my bedroom, and I must say, I think it's unreasonable to expect—"

"Madam, if your blasted dog tore your mosquito net, then I suggest you either pin it together and make do or burn citronella candles in your bedroom."

They both issued a few more statements, none of them particularly helpful. Waite noticed her dress, that it was silk, bright red, and tightly fitted to her voluptuous body. And that it had the smell of material that hadn't been aired often enough.

He bade her good day, cutting her off mid-whine. Wives and children were one thing, he fumed. Sisters were against the law. He was pretty sure there must be something in the regulations forbidding a man from housing a sister in the double keepers' quarters.

Sarvice A. Jones siphoned oil into the storage tanks, put away the gear, noted the gallonage, and then collected basin, soap, and towel and headed for the back stoop. He dipped a bucket of water from the cistern, removed his shirt, and began lathering the smell of kerosene off his skin. He reeked of the stuff. He'd almost as soon burn lard. It stunk, but at least the stink didn't linger.

Seeing him there, Waite crossed the space between the two houses and joined him. He thumbed toward the second floor. "The lady's been complaining again."

Sarvice shot him a resentful look. "Don't do nothing but."

"This time it's about her window screen. Dog tore a hole in it."

"Reckon if I was to tear it bigger, a fish hawk might fly down and carry the little bastard off?"

"Who, the dog or Miss Hardraker?" Waite took out the cigar he allowed himself after supper each evening. Tonight he just might have two. This time of evening, the mosquitoes were bad. Smoke helped.

"It just don't seem right for a woman that looks like a blessed angel to carp all the time. Reckon what turned her so sour?"

Waite shrugged, already tired of the subject. He'd informed both his assistants of just how far their duties extended. What they chose to do in their free time was their own business. "Have you seen Nick around lately?"

"Saw his horse out by the cedars. I think he's gone down to ride a few before it gets too dark."

Waite knew he meant waves, not horses. Horses were transportation. For racing along the beach, too, but mostly for transportation. When the seas were right, rolling in all the way from the second bar, riding the surf was a temptation that was hard to resist.

It had been years since Waite had taken the time, but it wasn't something a man forgot. It might help flush out his brain to swim out, mount a few big combers, and ride them all the way to the shore. Feeling the surge of power might help him forget the powerlessness of being at the beck and call of two women, neither of them welcome.

The two men began a discussion of the work being done to rebuild a beacon south of the lighthouse. They were still talking, Sarvice drying his arms, Waite enjoying the last of his cigar, when a cart came racketing up the path.

"Newbolt," Waite said. "What the hell's he got stuck in his craw now? I'd better go see."

"What do you want me to do about the Hardraker woman's window net?"

"No point in making her too comfortable, is there?"

"McKenna." Maxwell Newbolt greeted the man coming around the corner with a barely perceptible nod. "I've come calling on your guest."

"My guest?"

"Miss Hardraker. Would you care to let her know I'm here?"

"Tell me something, Maxwell. How's your window netting?"

"My—my what?"

"Oh, nothing. Just a notion I had." Grinning broadly, Waite stepped inside the double quarters and yelled up the stairs. "Miss Hardraker, you have a caller."

He could have taken the opportunity to mention the Newbolt girl's schooling, but it had been a long day. He didn't feel much like getting in the middle of another set-to. Brushing past the magistrate, Waite headed for the tower, reasonably certain that none of his problems would follow him there.

Mariah watched Maxwell's cart drive onto the grounds, saw him pass by her own door and stop at the house where Caroline Hardraker was staying. She felt an overwhelming sense of relief.

Maxwell and Miss Hardraker? What an intriguing combination. She wasn't even aware they'd met, but then, she'd been in school all day. Caroline Hardraker didn't strike her as a woman to idle away her time with a book or a set of watercolors.

After a supper of boiled potatoes and fried egg—the potato was perfectly done, but the egg was more scrambled than fried—Mariah settled in the rocker with her journal on her lap.

Today was the first day of school. I taught very little, but learned more than I can digest. Children are fascinating creatures with a wealth of imagination, but no real meanness that I can detect. I can tolerate pranks—at least, I believe I can learn to tolerate most pranks. What I cannot abide is meanness. It strikes me that it's extremely mean-spirited for Maxwell to keep that child home for his own selfish reasons.

She chewed on the cap of her pen. Maxwell and Caroline? She knew what he saw in her. Caroline Hardraker was a beautiful, well-dressed, if rather petulant woman who came from "away." Which seemed to be the criteria Maxwell used to judge the worth of any individual, because if it was only beauty he was looking for, there were enough pretty girls in the village to please the most discriminating man.

As for what Caroline Hardraker saw in Maxwell Newbolt, that was another matter. He was twice her age. A fussy, prosy, pompous little man who was tolerated by the natives of his chosen land only because they were too well bred to be openly rude.

Well . . . perhaps not all of them. She knew of one native, at least, who didn't mind at all being rude. The trouble was, he could be equally kind. It was almost as if he'd deliberately erected a protective wall around his gentler feelings.

Or perhaps he had no gentler feelings.

And perhaps you're imagining things, she told herself. *You hardly even know the man.*

But she wanted to. There. She'd admitted it. She might have become an accomplished liar with others, but she refused to lie to herself.

Touching the nib of her pen to her tongue, she wrote:

Stopped by the store on my way home. Everyone calls it that. The Store. As if there were only one. For all I know, that may be so, but I suspect there are others.

I do like Mr. Cyrus. One can look into his eyes and tell that he knows far more of the world's foibles than he'll ever admit to, and views them with tolerance. He adds extra candies for the children's pennies, and counts out eggs by the baker's dozen.

Rhoda Quigley came in while I was there. What a lovely woman. It has nothing to do with her features, or her style of dressing, which is rather plain, but more appealing, I must say, than red and black polka-dotted silk for a hot August day.

The people I've met, for the most part, have a natural sort of dignity which is rather wonderful. I believe they're beginning to accept me. Perhaps it would help if I spread the word that I managed to bake a panful of almost acceptable biscuits this morning for breakfast. Once I scraped off the bottoms, they weren't at all bad. Thank goodness for Rhoda's fig preserves.

By the end of her first full week of teaching, Mariah was somewhat more confident of her abilities. Her two oldest boys had become so engrossed in the War of 1812 they'd forgotten they were sophisticated men-about-town long enough to ask a few intelligent questions.

She made a mental note to dig out her own copy of Moore's *History of North Carolina*. There were great gaping holes in their knowledge of what a large part their own little island had played in the formation of the nation.

Frankie Newbolt read an entire chapter of the third reader without missing a single word. His grasp of numbers, too, was truly remarkable. And Maxwell had said he was *slow*?

Mercy, the man must be blind. She was considering trying the boy on *Sanford's Intermediate*. It was rather advanced, but then, so was Frankie in some respects.

Evie had started attending class halfway through the the week. There was something so endearing about the child, Mariah couldn't help but be drawn to her. She was not a brilliant student; barely adequate, in fact, but there was a sweetness about her that was irresistible.

The poor child had been stricken with a paralyzing self-consciousness when Nick McKenna had teased her about her hair, which, Mariah was proud to note, was truly flattering once one got over the initial shock. It would grow out again, she'd assured her, and frequent trimming would keep it from becoming unmanageable.

All in all, Mariah decided as she removed her bonnet, her shoes, and her stockings, she'd had a successful week. Now, if only she could manage to bake a batch of biscuits that didn't look, feel, and taste like plaster, she would be happy.

Or if not happy, she thought, lingering by the window to gaze out at the man striding toward the tower, at least reasonably content.

A gust of wind blew a bucket off the fence post.

One of the chickens set up a fuss. Sarvice A. Jones, as good as his word, had built her a tidy hen house, the yard wired over so that hawks and raccoons couldn't get at her small flock.

From the looks of the sky they were in for a blow. Perhaps another dry shift. After a mere two weeks on the island, she was coming to be almost as weatherwise as a native. But then, the weather was so much a part of everything here, far more so than back home in Murfreesboro.

Gathering the towels and undergarments she had washed out earlier from the line, she thought how strange it was: The house she had grown up in—the people, the shops, the church, the college—it all seemed so far away now. As if nothing existed but this small elbow of land jutting far out into the Atlantic, exposed to the whims of nature.

And I'm a part of it all, she marveled. Once I've weathered one of the winters I keep hearing so much about, I'll consider myself, if not a native, at least the next best thing.

It stormed the very next evening. There was no lightning, no thunder, only wind and a strange, impending feeling as she tooled her cart into the shed and unfastened the traces. She dumped oats into Merrily's feed box, but the little mare only snorted and took off toward the cedars the moment she was free. The frogs in the marsh out behind the house and those in the nearby ponds all fell silent in one stroke, as if directed by an unseen conductor. No chuck-will's-widow to be heard. She'd grown used to the nightly chorus now and missed it. There wasn't even a gull to be seen, but then, they had to be *somewhere*. The world hadn't simply ceased functioning.

Mariah made her supper early. Bacon, eggs, cold biscuits, and coffee. Her best effort yet. She pulled her rocker to where she could see the tower. The intermittent sweep of the light was oddly comforting, and she thought about how unreasonable that was, for what on earth could a lighthouse do if she needed help?

It was the man, of course. Waite McKenna. The light was a constant reminder that he was nearby, even if he had avoided her for days.

Or perhaps she'd only fancied that. She'd seen him at a distance, once riding through the village on that great ugly gelding of his when she was on her lunch break, taking her cheese sandwich and apple out on the schoolhouse steps. Twice she'd caught sight of him going about his duties here on the grounds.

She would have thought he'd come by to see how she was faring, in view of the storm. But he hadn't. Not that he was under any obligation, regardless of what he'd told Maxwell. Still, one would have thought common decency would have prompted him to look in on a neighbor, knowing she was all alone.

She watched the light fade completely from the sky, going from a sulfury yellowish gray to black with a sliver of cold light on the horizon. There'd be no evening star tonight. No moon, either. The wind blew sand in horizontal clouds across the clearing, and then the rain set in.

Waite battled his conscience while he went about securing the lighthouse property against the coming blow. With the wind out of the northwest blowing a steady thirty knots, a full moon on the horizon, even though it couldn't be seen, and flood tide rolling in, they'd be in for some wash-over before the night was done. Sound water had already beaten all the way up in the creeks. The marsh was full.

He refrained from glancing over at the teacher-age and wished he could direct his thoughts as easily as he could his gaze. What was there about the woman? She wasn't nearly as pretty as Constance had been. There were prettier women in every village on the island, and not a one of them set his teeth on edge the way she did.

He didn't know what it was about her that got under his skin. The way she talked or the way she walked—the way she dressed, all buttoned up to her chin and down to her wrists. The way she smelled, like soap and wildflowers and a woman's special scent.

He'd seen her laughing with some of the children outside the schoolhouse the other day when he'd passed by there. They liked her.

Hell, he liked her himself.

The Hardraker woman had ridden out with Newbolt again just before dark. He wondered if she knew she might not be able to make it back before morning if the road flooded.

At that, he had to smile. The magistrate's reputation meant almost as much to him as his dignity. What would folks think if he were to entertain a lady overnight?

Or maybe the woman was trying to compromise him. Waite still couldn't figure out what she was doing down here. She sure as hell didn't like it here. From one or two things her brother let drop, he thought she'd been sent down here to keep her away from an unsavory connection.

Waite emptied the chicken troughs and set them up inside the henhouse so they wouldn't wash away. He saw to the rest of the animals and collected whatever might blow or wash away, then went on back inside.

He should have gone over to the teacherage. It wouldn't hurt to ask if she needed anything. That was only being neighborly.

The trouble was, it might not stop there. All week he'd stayed away, but he couldn't help but see her coming and going about her business. Every morning she marched down to the shore with a teacup to collect gravel for her chickens. Sarvice had told her the layers needed shell in their mash.

From the tower he'd seen her lingering on the beach, staring out over the water with her clothes blowing against her body like one of those fancy figurehead carvings. When her hair blew across her face and she reached up to brush it away, he could almost feel it tickling his own skin.

Cut it out, McKenna. You've traveled down that road before. It's a dead end.

Constance had been a beautiful woman. Dark hair, dark eyes, full red mouth, and a body made for a man's pleasure. The Hardraker woman was cut from the same bolt of cloth, only she was somewhat bigger all around. Her hair was more of a blue-black, but she had that same look about her, as if she knew exactly what was on a man's mind and took pleasure from the knowing.

Mariah was as different from those two as a bog

lily was from one of those hothouse orchids he'd seen once in Norfolk. Every bit as delicate, too. He'd known the first time he'd ever laid eyes on her that she wouldn't last out the fall, much less the winter.

Which made it all the more exasperating that he couldn't seem to get her off his mind. Couldn't climb the tower without remembering the feel of her leg in his hands, without smelling that certain scent she wore. A scent that, mingled with the heat of her body, could churn him up inside until he could scarcely stand up without embarrassing himself.

He'd even started dreaming about her. At least, dreaming about a woman and waking up hard. Randy as a goat.

Damnation. In a man his age, it was downright disgraceful. He'd thought that by staying away, by not getting close enough to touch her, to smell her, to see the way her eyes went dark when she was angry and sparkled like rain when she was tickled over something—he'd thought that would be enough to put her in her place.

It hadn't.

A gust of wind struck the side of the house, causing the shutters to rattle. Swearing, Waite sat down and shucked off his boots, rolled up his pants legs against the rising tide, and a moment later he lit a lantern and set out across the grounds to the teacherage.

Chapter Eleven

Mariah was terrified. Rigid with fear. She had long held a dread of storms. Not the actual storm itself so much as the noise. Lightning would be all very well without the thunder.

Which only went to show what an irrational creature she was.

Something struck the side of the house just then and she flinched, visualizing a torrential river sweeping toward her, uprooting trees, toppling houses, sweeping helpless creatures to destruction. She stared blindly at the yellow glare of lamplight, thinking, *It's only the wind. It won't last much longer. The water won't come into the house, else it never would've been built here.*

Oh, what a fool she'd been to think for one moment she could spend the rest of her life on an island. How could she, when water—any body of water bigger than a goldfish bowl—had figured in so many of her nightmares, ever since she'd been pulled out of the Meherrin by her heels, more dead than alive?

And then to have her parents drown in that same river . . .

Wind shrieked. Mariah shivered. There was no thunder, thank the Lord for small blessings. She was ready—or as ready as she'd ever be—to meet her fate. Fully dressed, right down to her best gray kid shoes and her hat with the rose and plume, she sat rigidly in her bed, clutching her reticule, which had been crammed with everything that wouldn't fit in her valise, which she'd also packed and placed on the bed beside her.

Let the storm rage. Let the tides come. Thank God her bed was made of wood and not iron. Wood floated. If worse came to worst, she would simply paddle her bed to high ground.

Between concocting wildly improbably plans, she sought comfort in the fact that at least the grounds would be swept clean. No more dodging cow patties, horse muffins, and chicken splotches—not to mention the misdemeanors committed by that yapping little dog.

She had almost managed to muster up a shaky smile when the window blew out. Glass shattered. Curtains whipped in the wind like a pair of maniacal ghosts. Lamps flared and then flickered out, and Mariah screamed and jumped from bed. Oblivious to the glass crunching underfoot and the rain that peppered her face, she snatched up her valise and reticule and was out the door without a single thought as to where she was going.

As if there could be any question.

Head down, she leaned against the powerful wind and set out. She'd gone only a few steps when cold water began to seep into her shoes. "Oh, God," she whispered prayerfully. "Don't let me drown, please don't!"

When a beam of light swept across the grounds, she froze, staring at the sea of dark, restless water where no water should be. Knowing it was there was one thing. Seeing it was altogether different. *Oh, my heavenly days, a body could get lost and walk right out to sea!*

Stop it, Mariah! It's only the ocean running over.

Suddenly the sky split open. The blinding flash was followed almost immediately by an earth-shattering boom. She waited, her heart lodged somewhere in the region of her gullet, until she could see the faint yellow light from a window again, and doggedly slogged her way through the shin-deep tide toward the sanctuary of the principal keeper's quarters.

Toward Waite McKenna.

In between sweeps of light from the tower and blinding flashes of lightning, it was dark as pitch. She couldn't see an inch in front of her face. Which was probably just as well, she thought with a little yelp as something brushed past her ankle.

Fighting wind, blinded by rain, she waded toward the light, her sodden skirts swept sideways by the rushing tied. There was more than one swampy pond nearby, but none between her and her goal.

"Don't you dare blow out your lamp, Waite McKenna," she whispered fiercely. What if she wandered off course and stumbled into one of those half-hidden, backwater ponds, never to be heard from again? What if she stumbled and was swept away?

Whatever happened to the new schoolteacher?

Gone, just like all the rest.

"Stop it! It's only water, for heaven's sake!"

Her hat blew off and she grabbed at it, missed, and nearly lost her valise in the process. Muttering a litany of prayers and desperate promises, she

leaned into the howling wind and tried not to
think of all that was hidden under the rising water
as she made her way, step by tentative step. She
had barely covered a third of the distance when
she slammed head-on into a solid wall of flesh.

"Whoa, steady on, there."

The deep voice came out of the darkness, and
weeping, laughing with relief, she flung her arms
around her savior. "Waite! Oh, thank you, Lord,
thank you!"

Waite felt something firm and heavy strike his
backside. A pair of slender arms managed to get
a stranglehold around his neck. It was raining fit
to sink the ark. He was already soaked clean
through, and so, he suspected, was Mariah. As
her place was closer than his, he scooped her up,
baggage and all, and waded the few yards toward
her front door.

She didn't utter a single protest. Once inside, he
set her down, shut the bedroom door to cut off
the draft, and lit a lamp.

Squinting against the sudden glare, he turned
to where she stood, rooted to the spot where he'd
left her. Hadn't moved a muscle, as far as he could
see. "Mariah?"

Nothing. Not so much as the blink of an eye.
Her face couldn't have been any paler if it had
been whitewashed. As for the rest of her . . .

Judas Priest. She might as well not have a stitch
of clothes on, for all the good they did her. He
could see the layers as plain as day. The ridge of
her whatchamacallit, with the rows of whalebone
around her middle. The lump of a tie at her
waist . . .

And her bosom, what there was of it.

Calling himself a miserable lowlife didn't help. There was no way he could tear his gaze away from her chest. She was small all over. Skinny as a fence post, in fact. He could have covered her bosoms with his palms and had room to spare, but with those hard little nubbins standing out against the thin wet cloth of her gown, he couldn't seem to stop the pictures from forming in his mind. All he could think of was bedding her, which was the last thing he would ever do, even had she been willing.

Which she wasn't. Never would be. He'd never deluded himself that he was the answer to any woman's prayer.

"I thought I'd better come see how you were faring," he said, his voice gruff with swallowed emotion.

"I—I—" She gave it up after the third *I*. She was shaking so hard it was no wonder she couldn't get her words out, but at least she was reacting.

"Sit down while I find a blanket or something. I'll get a fire going and make some coffee." he dragged the rocker over beside her and gently shoved her down onto the seat when she didn't seem inclined to move.

Quickly he set about reviving the coals. He added several splits of pine, a chunk of oak, and a stick of lightwood to get it going. He located the coffeepot, found her coffee grinder, checked the drawer, which was half full, dumped it into the basket and filled the pot half full of water.

Then he headed for the bedroom to see where the draft was coming from, returning a few moments later to drape a quilt around her shoulders. His hands lingered there, as if to lend her the heat of his own vital body, but then, with a quiet oath, he turned and left.

Mariah sat and shivered. Couldn't have moved if her life depended on it. Somewhere in the back of her mind drifted the thought that she was in good hands. She was freezing, but safe enough as long as she stayed where she was. Waite had put her there. If he came and moved her, then she'd move. Not before.

You're acting like a doll, you stupid ninny. Like an empty-headed china doll!

She felt the heat begin to seep into her bones. Heard movement from the next room. Heard the coffeepot begin to simmer, and then the noisy *blurp-blurp* when it began to percolate. Waite came back just as the rich scent of freshly made coffee began to fill the room.

"All secure," he said. "Wind's dropped off some, swung around to the nor'east. She'll likely blow for a day or so, but the tide'll be falling off before daylight. Moon's already halfway up."

Unable to move a muscle, Mariah stared at him helplessly. She was covered with goose bumps from head to toe. Her shoes were ruined. Her clothes felt all clammy against her body, and she was about as embarrassed as she'd ever been in her entire life.

"M-m-moon?"

"Directs the tide. It's already commencing to ebb, but with the wind the way it is, it'll be a while yet."

Mariah stared at him unblinkingly, as if every word he spoke made perfect sense. "D-did you fix m-my window?"

"Covered it with a blanket. I'll get Sarvice over

first thing. He's handy with tools. I've got spare panes on hand. Don't reckon it'll bend regulations out of shape to give you a couple."

"I'll p-p-pay," she said, and then, "Oh, d-d-drat! I'm just so cold!"

Solemnly, he poured her a cup of coffee. The coffee was black, bitter, and thick as tar. She shuddered.

"It might be a tad strong."

"There's sugar in the bowl." She nodded to the sterling-topped cranberry-glass sugar bowl gracing the hideous varnished table.

"Full of ants. They give it a sour taste when you bite into one, thinking it's coffee grounds."

"Oh." It was a mark of her distraction that she never even questioned him. She sipped, shuddered, and grimaced. Waite leaned his backside against her table, studied the portraits of her parents, and sipped his own coffee. She told herself that her mama's best Wedgwood cup looked ludicrous in his big, work-hardened hands, but it wasn't true. For all his toughness, his rudeness, his utter lack of polish, there was a natural dignity about the man. She'd seen it in more than one of the native Bankers. As if they knew precisely who they were and weren't at all concerned with what the rest of the world thought of them.

She envied them their confidence.

Waite turned her mattress for her. With the rain coming from another direction now, he told her that fresh bedding and the blanket over the window would suffice to keep her dry the rest of the night. He swept up the broken glass and lit her lamp, and then regarded her critically, as if she were a horse he was considering putting down.

"Don't look at me, I'm freezing," she muttered. Which made about as much sense as anything else she'd said or done all night.

Slowly, he shook his head. Standing not two feet away, he opened his arms, and like a bird homing in on its nest, she leaned into them, tucked her head in the crook of his shoulder, and closed her eyes.

"I can't be cold, it's only August," she murmured.

"You're wet," he said, and they stood there like that, wrapped in each other's arms, for minutes or hours or possibly days. Time lost all meaning as warmth began to creep into her bones. She was aware of cold feet inside squishy shoes. Of hard, warm hands stroking her back, cupping her bottom, moving up her sides and around to her chest and . . .

Warmth splintered through her body. She uttered a knotty little gasp, and his hand grew still, all except for his thumb, which stroked across her bosom once . . . twice . . .

Oh, my mercy!

And then he released her and stepped back, just as if he hadn't laid a hand on her in a place where no hand had ever been laid before. "Take off those wet clothes, mind you," he said. "Else you'll take a chill. I'll bank up the fire to take the edge off the air. Come morning, go stand beside it to get dressed."

Mariah wondered if he was going to hear her prayers and tuck her in. She could picture him doing those things for a small motherless boy, and that surprised her. That she could visualize a younger Waite and his infant son. Somewhere along the way, her opinion of the man had undergone a rather thorough metamorphosis.

Not to mention her opinion of herself.

Her rooster had a faulty crow. She'd hardly slept a wink, or so she told herself, when the wretched thing commenced squawking the next morning, sounding as if he'd strangled on his breakfast.

At last the weather had improved. The air was balmy, although the sky was still gray. Just as Waite had predicted, the tide had gone down, leaving only random puddles and swollen marshes. Mariah took down the blanket Waite had nailed over her window, her mind going over all that had happened. The way he'd held her and touched her. The way she had looked up at him, startled, to find him gazing at her mouth. She'd thought for a moment he was going to kiss her, but he hadn't.

Clutching the wet blanket against her cheek, she leaned against the wall and sighed. Through her uncovered window there drifted a complex scent that was salty, muddy, and spicy, and not entirely unpleasant.

Like the man himself, she mused. Salty, earthy, and spicy.

She'd barely had time to brush out her braid and put her hair up before Maxwell Newbolt came rapping on her front door. Giving an impatient twist to the last of her hairpins, she hurried to let him in. "You've caught me at an awkward time. The house is in a mess after last night's storm. I assure you, I'm not always this untidy, sir."

"Never mind, my dear. I'll send Evie to help

you clean up after she's done with the wash."
And without waiting for her protest, he set to pacing and complaining. "Impossible weather, simply impossible! I'll never get used to it, if I live here a hundred years. In Philadelphia, where I come from, the weather's more civilized. At least a body knows what to expect."

"Snow and ice, you mean. I read about last winter's blizzard."

He made a noise with his teeth and tongue that she'd always found rather disgusting. That thought made her feel churlish because, after all, he had come all this way, and so early, too, just to be sure she'd survived the storm.

So she offered him coffee. "Waite made it last night. I'd better warn you, it's strong."

"McKenna? What the deuce was he doing here last night?"

"Seeing about my broken window."

"A window broke? Where?" He looked around. "Glass is dear as hen's teeth. Like everything else, it has to be shipped in, and then cut to size."

"Not in here, in my bedroom, and you needn't worry, Mr. McKenna said he'd take care of it. Mr. Newbolt, while I really do appreciate—"

"Call me Maxwell, my dear. We've gone far beyond the formalities, after all."

"Maxwell," she said reluctantly. "I really do appreciate your stopping by to look in, but I'm sure your time is far too valuable to waste where it's not needed."

Her mother would have been horrified at her lack of manners, but then, her mother had never met Maxwell Newbolt.

"You don't have to thank me, my dear. I had to

drive Miss Caroline home, anyway, and thought I
might as well stop by while I was in the neighborhood."

"Caroline Hardraker?" The Maryland beauty
and the Philadelphia dandy? Well, why not? Both
were as out of place here on the Banks as a pig
at a tea party.

"Miss Caroline was, um . . . stranded, you
might say. I—that is, my daughter kindly offered
to share her room."

In spite of feeling dull from a largely sleepless
night, Mariah could barely restrain her amusement. Poor Evie. Poor Caroline! Mariah hadn't
seen the child's bedroom, but judging from all she
knew of the Newbolts, it was probably a pallet in
a pantry.

A shaft of sunlight broke through the clouds,
glinting on a patch of water in the middle of the
sodden grounds. And there, leaping off his front
porch and striding across the wet sand, was the
man she'd lain awake thinking about until all
hours.

"Oh, here comes Mr. McKenna now," she said.

Maxwell twisted around, endangering the
seams of his snug-fitting coat. "What's he doing
coming over here so early? You'd think he'd have
enough to do seeing to his own affairs." He posi-
tioned himself in the doorway, as if to bar the
way.

Mariah stood silently by, hands clasped at her
waist, and watched the confrontation unfold.

"Newbolt," Waite said politely and, with the
sheer force of his presence, forced the other man
to step back. "Mrs. Deekins, glad to see you looking hale and hearty this morning."

Was that a compliment? The last thing she felt was hale and hearty, but it was probably better than being told she looked limp and languishing.

Waite had left off his coat and wore only his black uniform trousers and a white shirt, the collar open, the sleeves turned back, a faint scorch mark on the yoke. Mariah thought he looked perfectly magnificent, but then, as she'd already demonstrated, her judgment was open to question.

"I've come to see to Mrs. Deekins's welfare, McKenna, you needn't bother. I'm sure you have plenty to keep you busy."

"Inspections done, wicks trimmed, tanks refilled," Waite replied pleasantly. "I left Mr. Jones cranking up the gears and Mr. Hardraker seeing to the dog's business. Everything's in hand."

"Yes, well—I was just about to take Mariah home with me while I send someone to mop up her bedroom floor. I'm sure it's a mess."

He was?

"What, you haven't seen her bedroom yet? Oh, it's a right fair mess, all right. I swept up most of the glass, but the floor boards're already buckled. Comes from building the place right on the edge of a swamp. Bad location. Too damp."

Maxwell grew red in the face, which didn't help his looks at all. "I didn't ask for your opinion, sir."

"Might be better if you had."

"There's nothing wrong with the location. In a place like this one must make do with what's available, unlike my home in Philadelphia, where we have the best of—"

"The best of everything. Yeah, I know. I've heard how the streets are paved with gold so that your poor don't even have to beg, they just bend over and claw off a chunk of sidewalk."

"Don't be facetious, McKenna!"

"Facetious? How do you spell it? I'll have to look that one up."

He was a truly wicked man, Mariah thought, amused, irritated, and, yes—hungry as a bear. Poor Maxwell, he didn't even know when his limb was being pulled.

Maxwell sputtered for a moment, and Waite said gravely, "I reckon our poor'll have to go on living on collards and croakers and walking on sand until you can figure out a way to put us on a par with Philadelphia." He turned to Mariah, who didn't miss the twitch at the corners of his mouth. "Madam, if you'll step into the bedroom with me, I'd like to take a few measurements."

"McKenna! Have you no shame?"

"Yep. Shame, a measuring tape, and a good supply of window glass." He led the way to the bedroom, a matter of five steps, with Mariah right on his heels. "Oh, by the way," he called over his shoulder, "Miss Hardraker says to tell you she'll be delighted to take supper with you again tonight, and this time she'll bring her dog. The damned—begging your pardon, Mariah—but the thing yapped all night long. I think he sleeps with her. Reckon he missed her last night. You like dogs, Newbolt?"

Considering its inauspicious beginning, the rest of the day turned out surprisingly well. Mariah, having had enough of the bickering between two men who were old enough to know better, shooed them both out the door. Neatly dressed for school, she set about cleaning up as much of the mess as she could before it was time to leave. When Waite and Sarvice came back carrying two panes of window glass and a variety of tools, the sun had cleared away the last of the clouds and Mariah had swept up the last few splinters of the broken glass. The rest of the cleaning would have to wait until after school.

In the process, her hands had suffered a few mishaps. Two cuts, a broken fingernail, and a set of blisters that had broken and burned like the very devil, the latter of which came from wielding the heavy broom.

It was Waite who discovered her injuries and jogged across the clearing, to return moments later with a jar of some foul-smelling ointment. "Miss Agnes makes it up. Won't tell what she puts in the stuff, but it seems to work. Why the devil didn't you say something?" he demanded.

"Would that have cured anything? For heaven's sake, Mr. McKenna, I'm not a child. I do know a blister, and a few small cuts aren't likely to prove fatal."

"They can be. Why do you think Hardraker's here?"

"To take the place of your previous second assistant, who hurt his foot and had to leave. Why didn't he use Miss Agnes's miracle cure?"

Waite, holding her small hand in his much larger one, scowled as he stroked a greasy forefinger across her wounds and then across her palm, where one of the cuts was located.

Mariah caught her breath, remembering the way she'd felt last night when his thumb had strayed across her breast. This was only her hand, for heaven's sake! She told herself it had to be the salve. It certainly couldn't be the man himself. All the same, what had stung so badly only moments before now tickled in a way that affected parts of her body that had never even come close to a broom handle or a shard of glass.

"Stuff didn't smell to suit him."

"What?" she murmured breathlessly.

"Miss Agnes's ointment. Some say it's made from mice dung, butter, and turpentine—" She snatched her hand from his, curling her fingers into her palms, and stared up at him in horrified wonder. "But I doubt it. Not many cows on the island give milk rich enough to make butter. Most likely it's just herbs and tallow."

Wretched man. He had to know what effect those eyes of his had on a woman. Dark as sin and twice as tempting. "I've got to . . . If you're sure you don't need me here, I'd best be on my way. My classes . . ."

The schoolhouse, as it turned out, had suffered little more than a few leaks from what Mariah referred to as the storm until some of the older boys started laughing and swapping tales about what they called *real* storms.

Mariah could only hope they were exaggerating. Fully a third of her students were missing, but she called those present to order and set each group to its assigned task. While they worked, she compiled a list of books she intended to ask Maxwell to order for her, including a few select novels. It was never too soon for children to learn that reading could be enormous fun.

Evie was, as she had earlier discovered, no great

scholar, but she was such a delight. Seeing the way she'd made use of the green scarf Mariah had given her to enhance a faded and much-mended calico, Mariah was reminded again of her vow to do something about the way the child dressed. Now that her great mop of unruly hair was gone, she was really rather pretty. Or if not actually pretty, at least far more attractive, with a promise of growing into a piquant style of beauty that was, to Mariah's way of thinking, far more attractive than mere prettiness.

As neither Nick nor Dorien had returned after the noon break, Mariah drove Evie and Franklin home, using as an excuse the book list she had compiled. "You'll enjoy reading about Jack London, Franklin; and Evie, I'll lend you my own copy of—" She broke off as Maxwell, looking particularly magisterial, strode out to the cart. "Good afternoon, Maxwell. As you can see, I've brought your children home. If you've a moment, I'd like you to look over this list of books I'll be needing."

"Evie, there're chickens to pluck and dress. Franklin, fill the wood basket. Scat!" He clapped his hands together and both children slid down off the cart and hurried into the house.

"Now, madam, if you don't mind, I'll ask you to stop filling my daughter's head with all your foolish notions. I've agreed to let her attend classes because . . . well, because she's my daughter, after all, and it's only right to set a good example."

Why, you pompous, prating, posturing, pious . . . prig!

"However, if you, madam, continue to lead her astray, then I'll be forced to keep her home."

Mariah was speechless, but only for a moment. Regaining her wits, she stated in firm tones, "I've never led anyone astray in all my life, sir. If you mean my encouraging her to make the most of herself, why then—"

"Evie's a cripple! That's all she ever will be. She's a good child, and useful, but if she gets her head stuffed full of all sorts of nonsense, why, then, she won't even be of any help at all!"

Mariah didn't have a whip. Had seldom used one, in fact, considering a slap of the reins sufficient to impart her wishes. If she'd had one in her hand right now, however, she'd have been tempted to use it on the sorry specimen of manhood standing beside her cart.

Looking down on him, she said repressively, "You, sir, are the most miserable excuse for a father any child ever had the misfortune to possess. As for your eldest boys, I couldn't say, but you don't deserve two such wonderful children as Evie and Frankie. And now, if you'll excuse me, I'll be on my way."

She whapped the reins lightly across the little mare's croup, and Merrily leaped and then settled into her usual leisurely pace. That was about all the sandy ruts would accommodate anyway, which was perhaps just as well. The way she felt right now, Mariah could have won a steeplechase, cart and all.

Halfway home, she met her two truants. Judging by appearances, they'd been racing along the shore. Flushed, windblown, and wet to the knees, they pulled aside to allow her to pass, both grinning and bowing as low as they could without tumbling off their horses' backs.

In a better frame of mind, Mariah might have taken their tomfoolery, and even their truancy, in stride, but after her sleepless night and on top of that her interview with Maxwell, she was in no mood to beat around the bush. "I have a few words to say to you two young men, and you'd do well to hear me out."

"Now, ma'am, it wasn't our fault—" Nick began, when Dorien broke in.

"No, ma'am, it surely wasn't. See, we heard there was this whale out on the beach, and I said to Nick, I bet that'd make a dandy exhibit for Miz Deekins's biology class, and him and me, we decided to check on it to see if it was dead and all. Mostly when they wash on up shore that way, they're goners."

"All washed up, you might say," put in Nick, with the same dancing light she'd noted more than once in his father's eyes.

"Trouble is, there weren't no whale. What it was, was a bundle of net washed up that—"

"Boys! Forget about the whale. I'm sure your reason for not being in class this afternoon is perfectly sound." She was sure of no such thing, but she fully intended to use their guilt for her own ends. "It's about Evie and Frankie. I've noticed you both tease them incessantly, and I want it to stop. They're sensitive children, and you're both old enough to know better. You, Dorien, you're their brother, for heaven's sake! You should be looking out for them, not making things more difficult."

"Ma'am, I'm not their brother," said Nick, and Mariah waved an impatient hand.

"I'm speaking of basic decency. Not only are

you demanding, and not the least bit helpful so far as I can see, you both tease Evie until the poor child is on the verge of tears. Don't you even realize how cruel that is? Don't you know how much it hurts to be taunted by someone you love, when you're twelve and a half years old and need so badly to be accepted?"

There was a mumble of response that could have been most anything. Mariah chose to take it as acquiescence.

"Now, I want you both to promise me you'll be kinder. All you have to do is treat others as you yourself would like to be treated. That shouldn't be so difficult, should it?" Mariah had been drilled on the Golden Rule before she could even understand what it meant.

Nick looked at Dorien.

Dorien looked at Nick.

"I reckon I'd better go fish that dead eel out of her bed before she climbs in," Dorien said.

"And me, I reckon I could tell her she don't really look like a boiled onion. Come to think of it, she looks more like a boiled rutabaga. Same color, don't you think so, Dore?"

Mariah's eyes flashed fire; her lips thinned. Before she could say something unbecoming to her position, she snapped the reins and drove off.

Perhaps she wasn't meant to be a schoolteacher, after all. Surely a good teacher wouldn't be tempted to scalp a pair of her own students.

Chapter Twelve

That night she settled into bed with her journal. Wearing white gloves, her hands liberally smeared with Miss Agnes's evil-smelling miracle cure, she wrote, "I'm changing. Too much salt air? Possibly. I'm beginning to feel things I've never felt before, to think things I've never thought before. Sad to say, I'm also beginning to want things I can never have."

Lulled by the now familiar chorus of frogs, chuck-will's-widows, and the ever-constant sound of the surf, Mariah left her worries behind. She tried and failed to recall where she'd been a year ago on this particular day, but memories of the past seemed to have merged into a dreamy collage. More laughter now than tears, thank heavens. Which must mean she was nearing the end of her time of mourning. Earlier today when she'd seen a pretty young woman with a child hanging on to her skirttails and another one in her arms, she'd even found herself growing angry at her parents for robbing her of a chance of ever having babies of her own.

An image of a small, towheaded boy with devilish dark eyes appeared in her mind just before she drifted off to sleep. A full moon shone through her neatly repaired bedroom window, opened to let in the light breeze. But she never heard the whispered voices outside, never even heard the muffled curses when one of the stealthy intruders ran into her clothesline.

"Swear to God, Dore, she's tryin' to hang me!"

"Shhh, if she wakes up and starts screamin' and your pa catches us, he'll do worse'n that."

"You take the other end o' the house, I'll take this here window. We'll count to twenty, startin' now."

It came out of a dream like the roar of a thousand lions. Mariah, her heart pounding, sat up in bed, wondering what had awakened her.

And then she heard it again.

She opened her mouth to scream, but no sound emerged. Even had she screamed loud enough to shatter glass a mile away, no one could have heard her above the most hideous noise in the world. Blasting from right behind her head, it echoed back and forth through the house. *Whooo-ooo-woo . . . whooo-ooo-ooo.* Like a train whistle, only there wasn't a train within a full day's journey. *Whooo,* and then a little bleat and it started up all over again.

Drenched with perspiration, she felt deathly cold. Her pulse was racing like a runaway horse, her heart pounding in her chest. "H-help," she whispered.

Dear God, what was it? Was the world coming to an end? She didn't want to die all alone!

Suddenly her limbs came alive and she leaped out of bed and snatched up the basque top to her gray twill, which she'd left out to air. Hastily pull-

ing it on over her nightgown, she rushed outside
barefooted, her braid flopping against her back,
conscious of only one goal: reaching Waite Mc-
Kenna before she died.

She was halfway across the ground when it occurred to her that the hideous roaring had ceased.
Slowing her footsteps, she listened intently, every
sense alive to the terrifying possibilities. Which
was no doubt why she happened to hear the muffled snickers coming from behind her house. And
the sound of a familiar voice saying something
about her mare.

About Merrily?

Oh, for heaven's sake, they'd done it to her
again!

Whirling in her tracks, Mariah marched back to
her house, arms pumping, a militant gleam in her
eyes. "When I lay hands on you two," she
shouted, "you'll not be able to sit a horse for the
next six weeks!"

She was angry enough to do it, too—whale the
living daylights out of them—despite the fact that
she didn't believe in corporal punishment. Despite
the fact that either boy could have stopped her
with one hand tied behind him. One way or another, she was going to tame the pair if it took
her until the day after forever!

Before she even reached the door, she heard the
sound of horses racing off down the lighthouse
road. Horns, she thought. They'd tooted horns
through her window, or else come up with some
other brand of devilment, like that resin string
thing.

Giving them the benefit of the doubt, she told

herself they had only meant to startle her. They couldn't have realized how the sound could become a part of a terrifying nightmare, coming as it did when she was sound asleep.

All right, so perhaps she wouldn't beat them. Nor would she tell on them, because they would never respect her for that. Tossing her jacket aside, she slammed shut the five small windows in the house, hooked the door on the inside, and crawled back into bed. Not until she had pulled the spread up over her did she feel the sand.

"Oh, botheration!" She'd forgotten to dust off her feet. But if she did that, she would have to change her linens, and by then she'd be even wider awake than she was now.

So she slept, sand and all, until her rooster greeted the morning with his horrid attempt at crowing. She knew now why the widow Wallis had been so generous in sharing her chickens. The wretched thing started squawking before the sky even began to pale.

The dwindling days of August were swelteringly hot, but remarkably pleasant nonetheless. Mariah went about her duties cheerfully, trying to pretend she wasn't hoping to catch a glimpse of Waite McKenna. For a next-door neighbor, he certainly made himself scarce.

She finally met Miss Agnes, maker of potions, tonics, and poultices, deliverer of babies and layer-out of the dead.

"New schoolmarm. Got the itch, ain'chee?" the tall, dark-skinned woman said by way of greeting one morning in the post office.

"Who, me? Oh, my neck, you mean. And, well . . . this is poison ivy, I believe, on my hand." By now, Mariah had become accustomed to the island way of plain speaking.

"Stump water'll cure them blisters. Sody powders'll do your neck a mought o' good. Come by on yer way home."

Mariah stared at the old woman's narrow back as she set off down the road on foot. *Stump water? Sody powders?*

Within three days, her various itches were gone. Not only that, she had three bars of homemade bayberry soap and a cream to lighten freckles, of which she now had a plenteous supply.

In exchange, Mariah had given the healer access to her personal library, comprised of textbooks from two years of preparatory school and four years of college, her mother's gardening books, and her collection of favorite novels.

She'd been rather amused when the woman, who looked to be half Indian and a hundred years old, had selected *Jane Eyre* and *The Tenant of Wildfell Hall,* by two of the Brontë sisters.

Caroline Hardraker was a frequent visitor after school hours. Not a particularly welcome one, for by that time of day Mariah was usually exhausted. Teaching, while it had its rewards, was not quite the sinecure she had envisioned.

On the days when Caroline rode out with Maxwell in his cart, often tossing a triumphant glance over her shoulder if Mariah happened to be outside, Mariah took advantage of the opportunity to remove her stays, put on her oldest pair of shoes, and walk over to the beach. She was cultivating a relationship with a certain seagull, who was cocky as could be, considering he had only one leg. She took him slivers of bacon, and in return he declined to rend the flesh from her fingers with his sharp, hook-tipped bill.

She saw Waite only in passing. Invariably, he tipped his hat if he happened to be wearing one and nodded if he didn't. She got a warm feeling all over whenever she happened to see him and told herself it was only this oppressive, relentless heat.

And knew herself for the accomplished liar she had become.

Sarvice A. Jones joined her one afternoon. He had evidently been examining the temperature of the water, for he'd been kneeling at the very edge when she'd walked down to the shore with her teacup.

The man had turned out to be surprisingly good company. He was fairly well read and even possessed of a sense of humor, but he was so terribly shy she had to work hard to draw him out.

Which she did, if only because she had come to enjoy meeting challenges.

"My folks had seven sons," he confided after several minutes of probing on her part. "All took to farming 'ceptin' me. My ma wanted me to take up preachin', but I never felt the call. I could've read medicine or law—my uncles would've 'prenticed me—but I wanted to go to sea. Only trouble is, I get seasick somethin' awful. Cousin with the Lighthouse Board, he got me this job, an' it suits me right well. Some says the jobs are handed down from father to son, but all my pa has to hand down is a seventh of a hog farm over near Ahoskie. Mr. McKenna says he'll recommend me whenever I want to move up. He's a fair man, he is."

After he left, Mariah lay on her back on the shawl she'd brought for just that purpose and stared up at the tall, spiral-striped tower. She thought about Sarvice A. Jones and the mysterious force that could lift a man out of one life and plop him smack-dab in the middle of another for no discernible reason.

Perhaps the seemingly random patterns of life weren't so random, after all. Mr. Jones was happy here. And so, for that matter, was she, she reflected with some degree of surprise.

She thought about her first contact with a native Banker and how he'd tried to frighten her into turning back. Fortunately, she'd been too stubborn to run and too proud to go crying to him with the least little problem, as he'd fully expected her to do. The one time she'd asked for his help was on behalf of someone else, which wasn't the same thing at all.

"Weak city woman, my foot," she murmured, smiling, her eyes closed against the glare reflected off the water.

The late afternoon sun beat down unrelentingly. At this rate she'd be one big freckle before the summer was done, but it did feel good to lie here, baking her bones. Healing aches of the spirit as well as aches of the body. There was something soothing about hearing the sound of the surf, feeling its power.

Which meant that either she'd lost her wits or she'd found them. Either way, it felt good.

Eyes still closed, she smiled. A moment later, a shadow fell over her face. She opened her eyes, blinked away the spots, and stared up at the for-shortened figure towering over her.

"Don't tell me I fell asleep." Struggling to sit up, she expected the offer of a helping hand, but instead of offering, Waite stepped back, his hands clasped behind him.

Lord, he was an impressive man! A different species entirely from the timid creatures she'd known back home. Henry Lee Ball was a regular spindle-shanks compared to . . .

Her gaze drifted down the lean, muscular form, and she felt a film of moisture collect and trickle down between her breasts.

"Tide's coming in," he observed.

"No! Is that a fact? I thought surely after coming up so high last week it would stay out for the rest of the summer." Was all this silliness coming from her mouth? She'd been warned to wear a bonnet. Now she'd gone and baked her brain.

"Know what a tide line looks like?"

"Isn't that some sort of fancy seaman's knot?" From silliness to facetiousness. *Not at all becoming, Mariah.*

Waite pointed to an irregular line of seaweed, shells, and broken grasses some dozen or so feet behind her. "High-water mark," he said. His expression hadn't changed at all since he'd arrived. She wondered if he could close the door on his thoughts at will, and decided it would be a handy talent to acquire.

"I'm impressed," she said quietly.

"You'd soon have been submerged."

"But surely—"

"Only a fool sleeps below the high-water mark on a rising tide."

"I wasn't asleep," she lied.

"You snore when you're awake?"

"I wasn't . . . was I?"

He grinned then, and it was as if the sun had come out from behind a dark cloud. "Buzzed, more like. The way a bee does when he's hunting nectar."

She was flustered. And embarrassed. And sandy, and hot, and frazzled. "Oh, for heaven's sake, you always seem to catch me at a disadvantage. Honestly, I'm usually not this inept."

Without an invitation, Waite hiked up his trousers and sat beside her, leaning back on one muscular arm. An errant breeze tossed his bleached thatch of hair, and Mariah watched, entranced, as he brushed it back with his other hand. He had beautiful hands. She had never before realized how very sculpted a man's various parts could be. His forearms. His thighs. His features . . .

"Sarvice said your nose was getting red again."

Before she quite realized what she was doing, Mariah had crossed her eyes in an attempt to see for herself. Waite laughed aloud. She joined in, because it sounded so good, and discovered that it felt even better. Laughing with someone else.

Besides, Mr. Jones was right—her nose was red again. Which wasn't particularly funny, but she felt like laughing, so she did.

Felt like taking off her shoes and digging her feet into the warm sand, and then wading in the clear turquoise water to cool them again.

Of course, she didn't do any of those things. All the same, gazing into Waite's eyes as their laughter trailed off, she felt a sharp-edged awareness that was becoming a bit too familiar. As if all the colors in the world were suddenly brighter, the scents sweeter, the sounds more musical.

"I heard the boys were out blowing conchs last night. I hope it didn't wake you up."

"Blowing conchs? You mean . . . shells?"

"Knock off the nipple, blow through the channels, it makes a dandy horn if you've got the wind for it. Takes a right powerful set of bellows. You didn't hear anything?"

Rather than lie outright, Mariah asked him to draw her a picture. Waite smoothed out an area of sand and with a forefinger, drew a lopsided form she identified as a whelk. "You cut right here and blow from here," he said, and sand blew from his hand onto her skirt when he shifted his weight. "Sorry," he said, and brushed at it.

The feel of his hand through two layers of skirt made her catch her breath, and seeing her reaction, Waite flushed and apologized again. For a man who wore arrogance like a second skin, he looked awkward and embarrassed. Endearingly so, she thought, even as she watched the familiar walls come up again.

He rose and, moving carefully downwind, brushed the sand off his hands and seat. "Well. Just thought I'd better warn you, ma'am."

Ma'am? You laugh with me, gaze into my eyes as if you'd never seen a pair of gray ones before? You touch my breast and kiss me with your eyes, avoid me for days, and then you call me ma'am?

Waite touched his brow as if to tip his hat, then turned and walked away. Mariah watched him, wondering what made seeing a man walk, his various body parts working in smooth harmony, so very fascinating.

Maxwell strutted like a rooster. Henry Lee had walked as if afraid of wrinkling his clothing. He'd always been something of a dandy.

Waite strode across the earth as if he owned it.

Forcing herself to turn away, she stared at the surf and realized that he'd been right. The tide really was coming in. There was a certain impatience to the wave patterns that hadn't been there when she'd first arrived. Each wave came higher up onto the shore before it receded, and before it had washed completely out again, a few more piled in on top.

Some days she felt like that. As if before she could settle one thing, six more took its place, piling one on top of another until she simply gave up trying to deal with it all and walked out here to the shore.

"I've made a place for myself here," she wrote that night.

In a small way, I'm beginning to feel at home. Miss Rhoda asked me just yesterday if I used something special on my hair to make it shine the way it does. I told her chamomile and a boar-bristle brush covered with a square of silk. Mother taught me that. Papa always loved Mother's hair. He said it reminded him of clematis seeds, all silky and curly. I'm surprised he even knew what they looked like,

but I'm learning that people are full of surprises. They're not always what they appear
at first glance.

Caroline and Maxwell seem to be hitting it
off quite well. Caroline seems less tense, if no
less discontented. She's gaining weight, although I'm not sure she wants to. The seams
of several of her gowns are straining about
her waist. Perhaps it's true what they say
about sea air and appetites. My own is gar-
gantuan, but that might be because I manage
to cook an edible meal only about three days
out of a week. Though tonight's fish turned
out rather well, even though it was too salty.
Must remember to thank Mr. Stone.

*August 31, 1886. Wind brisk, SSW. Offshore
traffic light today. Three sharpies fishing in the
bight. Not much being caught lately. Rollerson
said porpoise factory probably won't clear $8,000
this year. Sun rose at 5:09, set at 6:19. Schoolteacher holding up better than expected.*

Waite thought about saying more, then decided
against it. An official log was no place for personal
observations, even though chances were no one
would ever read it unless there was a disaster and
it was called into evidence.

He wrote because there were limits to a man's
capacity for self-containment. He'd never been
given much to talking, nor had his father before
him. Conversation was a habit. Nick seemed to
have developed it from somewhere, the Newbolt
boy most likely. But one day soon Nick would

leave home, first to go off to school and then to make his own place in the world. Waite wouldn't insist he take up lighthouse keeping if he'd a mind to try his hand at something else. Either way, though, he would marry. Nick liked women too much, even at his young age, to remain single and stay out of trouble.

Waite knew all too well that his son was his biggest weakness. He'd had the complete raising of the boy. Living out here away from the village, there'd been no kindly woman next door to take a hand.

God, he loved him, though. Nick was bright and good, for all his mischief, but Waite knew he would have loved him just as well if he'd been slow and homely and needy.

If he'd been slow and needy, Waite might have stood a better chance of keeping the boy around longer. As it was, he'd do well to prepare himself to be alone. Get ready once more to face all the hollow places inside him that had yet to see the light of day. Over the years, having Nick around, having the responsibility of his work, he'd been able to plaster them over until they hardly showed to the outside world. Once he was alone again, and older, too, the plaster might not hold so well.

Loneliness. All his life he had practiced being alone. You'd think by now he'd do a better job of it.

The earthquake struck just before ten o'clock that night. Waite was up in the tower, or else he might not have been quite so aware of what was happening. An oil can he'd left beside the stairway to take down toppled over and rolled noisily down the steps. Masonry creaked, but held solid except for the dust that fell from the cracks. And the noise! The noise was almost worse than the drunken swaying. All the creaking and groaning, as if the whole structure were about to collapse.

Waite hung on, held his breath throughout the ten or fifteen seconds until the world grew still again. There wasn't a doubt in his mind what was happening, which surprised him, for he'd never before experienced an earthquake.

Once he was fairly certain things had settled down, he examined the lens as well as he could by lanternlight. As far as he could tell there was no damage, but come tomorrow he'd have to give it a thorough inspection from top to bottom. He hadn't forgotten what lightning had done a few years back.

Mariah. God, she'd be terrified! All alone there. Asleep, more than likely. Her lamp had gone off some twenty minutes ago.

Pulling the watchroom door to behind him, Waite practically ran down the stairs. Another tremor, a minor one, struck when he was halfway down. He hung on to the railing and waited, listening, his heart still, his breath held painfully in his lungs.

Dust fell. Nothing more. Breathing again, he raced down the remaining steps. There were two more episodes before he reached the teacherage. Both were minor. All he felt was a momentary sense of dislocation, but he could picture Mariah, paralyzed with fear, afraid to light a lamp for fear of fire.

His heart all but stopped beating again. If anything happened to Mariah—!

Chapter Thirteen

~~~

There was a lamp lit in the bedroom, but no light showing from the rest of the house. Waite called out softly, afraid of startling her, half expecting her to come hurtling out to meet him. The house itself, being small and of solid frame construction, should be safe enough, unless . . .

"Mariah? It's all right now, it's over."

Waite prayed to God it was over. He wasn't sure what to expect. He had read about an earthquake in Venezuela ten years ago that had killed sixteen thousand people. One in China back in the 1500s had killed nearly a million. He'd heard there were places on the West Coast that shook several times a year.

"Mariah, can you hear me? I'm coming in."

Her door was hooked. He rattled it, willing to break the flimsy wire latch if he had to, but it wasn't necessary.

"What on earth are you yelling about? Shouldn't you be trimming wicks or performing some other keeperly task?" Holding the lamp in one hand, she opened the bedroom door.

If she'd stood on her head and started reciting multiplication tables, he couldn't have been more stunned. Hadn't she even felt it? Was he the only one who realized they'd just experienced a bleeding *earthquake*?

Mariah wasn't quite as composed as she appeared. Underneath her yellow silk wrapper, her heart was thumping noisily in her chest. This time, however, she was determined not to allow those wicked young hellions to ruffle her. They'd tried turning her house into a bass fiddle with a string and a bit of resin. They'd blasted conch shells through her windows in the dead of night. Heaven only knew what they'd done this time, but whatever it was, she was not about to let on she'd been frightened, only to realize it was Nick and Dorien at it again.

"Mariah, unlatch your door and let me in."

"At this time of night? Whatever for?"

"We've met far later than this," he reminded her, sounding slightly less grim.

"I was on my way to bed."

"I won't keep you. I just need to look around to make sure your chimney's not about to fall down. I understand masonry can be a problem."

"My chimney? What on earth did they do this time, hitch a mule up to my house and try to pull it off the foundation?"

"What? Who?"

As if he didn't know. "You know who, and I didn't say a word. I'm not complaining, Waite, honestly I'm not. In fact, I'm pretty sure I'm making progress. Just this morning, Nick helped the young O'Neill boy with his arithmetic, and Dorien brought me a lovely bouquet of lilies and cattails from the edge of the freshwater pond. It wasn't his fault that cattails always make me sneeze."

"That damned . . . Unhook the door, Mariah.

With or without your permission, I'm coming in. Consider it a part of my duty."

"I am not one of your blessed duties," she practically shouted, but all the same, setting the lamp on a table, she unhooked her door to keep him from tearing it off the hinges.

Impatiently, Waite stepped inside, brushing against her in the process. Sparks flew. Mariah caught her breath as another cage full of wild birds began to flutter inside her breast.

The first thing he did was light another lamp. It was then she noticed that both the portraits Sarvice A. Jones had put up for her were now hanging crookedly on the wall. And that the Wedgwood vase of wildflowers on the trunk by the window had toppled over and was probably leaking water on her winter woolens.

She gathered up the wilted blooms and found a towel to blot up the water while Waite straightened the heavy gilt-framed portraits. The cup she'd used for cocoa earlier had toppled off the table and was lying in several shards on the floor.

"Oh, no," she whispered, and knelt to pick up the broken remains. "This was my mother's wedding china."

Waite glanced at her curiously, then went on examining the place where the stovepipe joined the brick chimney. "Leastwise, it wasn't your own."

"Well, of course it was mine." She stroked the delicate handle of the broken pearlware cup. "I don't suppose they meant any real harm," she said, but she was beginning to believe they did indeed wish her harm. Three times in less than a month they had come in the dead of night to torment her. To frighten her into leaving.

Suddenly the spirits she'd fought so hard to keep up began to sink. Still on her knees, she struggled unsuccessfully to hold back the tears. She'd sworn off crying more times than she could remember, because in the end tears didn't change a blessed thing, but now and then, usually when she was tired and discouraged, doubts crept in.

What in the world was she doing way out here on this forsaken little island? *He* didn't want her here. He'd made that plain enough right from the first.

As if sensing her distress, Waite took her by the arms and lifted her to her feet. "There, now, you're all unsettled. You're not even making sense, but that's all right. The main thing is, it's all over now. There were a couple of small quakes after the main one. You might not even've noticed them down here. I was up on the tower when the first one struck. I thought she was about to come crashing down, the way she was swaying."

He was still holding her, and while she had no idea what he was talking about, she wasn't about to make an issue of it. He smelled of coffee, lamp oil, and something else, something that struck her as being essentially masculine. She savored it, along with his warmth and strength, but then his words sunk in and she leaned away and stared up at him. He thought *she* wasn't making sense? "You say the lighthouse was swaying? But . . . why?"

It was Waite's turn to look puzzled. "Why? The earthquake, that's why. What the devil did you think it was?"

"It wasn't Nick and Dorien?" she whispered.

His eyes widened, then narrowed. His jaw took on that carved granite look that had grown all too familiar, from the time he had landed on the deck of the mailboat and invited her to leave. "I don't believe so, not this time. Not that they wouldn't have given it a shot if they'd thought about it, but an earthquake—that's a stretch beyond what even that pair can manage."

An earthquake, she mouthed silently. "Oh, my mercy . . ."

His arms eased, and he held her away from him, searching her face, which suddenly felt stiff and cold instead of warm and wet. "Mariah, for what it's worth, I'm sorry."

When she could gather enough breath to speak, she said, "For what? Waite, I seriously doubt if even you have the power to make the earth tremble."

Which was not precisely true. At this moment, she had every reason to believe he could do just that. If he held her much longer . . . looked at her the way he was looking at her now . . . she might very well take off and fly a few circles around the moon.

"I meant for the boys. I reckon I've not set the best example, but I truly never meant—"

She laid a finger over his lips. "Shhh. You don't have to apologize for Nick and Dorien. They're old enough to take responsibility for their own acts. I assure you, I'm tough enough to take anything they can dish out."

"Oh, aye, that you are. Tough as mullet gizzards," he mocked softly. "A body can see that right off." His eyes moved over her face, dwelling on the smattering of freckles on her short, straight nose, moving on to her lips. Even there he noticed a single freckle. As if drawn by some mysterious magnetic force, he lowered his face to hers. Just before his mouth touched her own, Mariah could have sworn the earth trembled once again. Overwhelmed by sensations she had never before experienced, never even imagined, she simply shut her eyes tightly and let it happen. She could actually feel the shape of his lips on hers. Seeing them and feeling them were worlds apart, she thought wonderingly with her last glimmer of reason.

Breath mingling, flesh against flesh, he kissed her thoroughly. If Mariah had thought she'd been kissed before, she'd been sadly mistaken. His hands were on her back, one high, one low, but it was as if he were touching her everywhere. One by one, and then all at once, pulses began hammering in her body. Flesh swelled and urged and throbbed. Like a ripe peach bursting at the first penetration of a knife blade, she felt her juices begin to flow, sweet and heady and intoxicating.

Something stirred against her belly, and she reached down to brush it away and then froze.

Oh. Oh, my!

"Sorry," he whispered hoarsely. "I never meant to—that is, I only came to see if you were—"

"I am," she assured him in a thready little voice. Disengaging herself from his arms, she stepped back, relieved to discover that she could stand unaided. "Safe, that is. And thank you. For offering to comfort me."

This was *comfort*? She felt a slightly hysterical urge to laugh. If what he'd offered was comfort, then heaven help her if she ever got any more comfortable.

Face flushed, Waite left, after assuring her that he'd send Sarvice over to check out her foundation the next morning, to be sure her house hadn't slipped from its moorings. Mariah watched from the door as he strode across the clearing. In the moonlight his white shirt seemed to float above the earth, and she stared after him till the last glimmer disappeared.

Waite McKenna. A cold, stiff, humorless lighthouse keeper, of all things!

Knowing sleep would be long in coming, she took out her journal, uncapped her fountain pen, and held it poised for several minutes, her head tilted thoughtfully at an angle.

And then she set both pen and journal aside. What could she write, after all? That after all these years she had finally experienced lust?

Because that was what it was. She'd heard it whispered about, read oblique references to such things in the racier novels she had shared with her three best friends, but the written word bore scant relation to the real thing.

So. Tonight she'd undergone two new experiences. Lust and earthquakes. Of the two, lust made a far more profound impression.

Sarvice A. Jones was on his hands and knees examining the underpinnings of her house the next morning when Maxwell drove past with Caroline Hardraker. She called out a cheery greeting, and Mariah, her arms full of damp woolens to hang on the line, waved back. Sarvice bumped his

head trying to scramble to his feet, then blushed
to the tips of his generously proportioned ears.

"I do believe there's a match in the making,"
Mariah observed. She had awoken feeling, of all
things, cheerful and optimistic. And not entirely
because it was Saturday and there was no school
today, either.

"He just wants a housekeeper. He won't treat
her right, Miz Deekins, but she'd never believe me
if I was to tell her that."

Sarvice looked so doleful, Mariah paused at the
corner of the house, a basket of clothes pegs on
one arm, several of her best woolens on the other.
"Do you think so?" was all she could think of
to offer.

Sarvice stared after the disappearing cart for a
few more moments and then knelt and crawled
back under the house. Thoughtfully, Mariah
pegged her slate blue with the military braid and
the dark green suit to the line. They'd been on top
of the rest of the garments in her trunk and had
collected most of the water that had dripped
through when the vase had overturned.

Maxwell and Caroline Hardraker?

Sarvice and Caroline?

Oh, poor Sarvice.

Mariah had just finished feeding her chickens
the remains of a luncheon of cold hard biscuits
and scorched bacon when Nick and Dorien raced
past her on their way to the beach. She'd noticed
before that the older children, and some of the
younger ones, too, rode along the shore, evidently
using the lighthouse as some sort of a marker for
their informal horse races.

With nothing better to do for the rest of the afternoon but grade a stack of papers, scrape the burned crust from the bottom of her best skillet, and try her hand at making an omelet for supper, she strolled after them.

They were long gone by the time she came in sight of the water. The tide was out. Somewhat to her amusement she was becoming adept at keeping up with such things. There was a wide expanse of hard pink sand, now marred with the tracks of several sets of hooves. In the distance she could see two horses, their riders bent low, flying through the edge of the surf, and suddenly it struck her as the most glorious pastime imaginable. Racing along the beach. Actually daring to ride a horse through all that frothy, turquoise water.

"Miss Sawyer, I hardly know you," she murmured, shading her eyes against the glare.

"Who's Miss Sawyer?"

Startled, Mariah spun around and nearly tripped over the man standing just behind her. "You will creep up on a person!"

"Ever try stomping in soft sand?"

"You could have spoken."

"I just did."

"Oh—you know what I mean!"

Waite was at his most informal, his white shirt open at the throat, the cuffs folded back to reveal those powerful bronze forearms—plain black trousers hugging his lean, muscular flanks. He was barefoot, and he was grinning. A barefoot and grinning Waite McKenna was a sight to behold.

"Shouldn't you be doing something more

important, or is a lighthouse keeper's life all play and no work?"

"Just come from fishing over in the freshwater ponds."

"What, with a sea full of fish right at your front door? Maxwell says the fish in those mudholes aren't even fit to eat."

"They're all right if you skin 'em. Sarvice comes from farm country. He's right partial to freshwater bass. Lately, he's been moping around, and I figured maybe he was homesick."

Mariah had a good idea why the first assistant was feeling depressed, and it wasn't from homesickness. But that was his secret and not hers to reveal. All the same, she was somewhat surprised that Waite would set aside his precious dignity long enough to fish in what was essentially a puddle in the midst of a swamp.

She said as much.

"Oh, I still enjoy watching a cork bob on the end of a cane pole. Haven't done a whole heap of it since I grew up. Nick keeps us pretty well supplied with table fish, but with a third man to share the duty I can afford to take a few hours off now and again."

It occurred to Mariah that she'd seldom seen him in quite this mood before. Chatty, relaxed, not so stiff and standoffish.

Not that he'd been all that standoffish the night of the tide, or last night, either, but that was different. Late at night, the drama—the stress of the moment . . .

"Well. It seems Miss Hardraker is settling in nicely. It wouldn't surprise me if she became a permanent resident."

As quickly as that, Waite's good humor was gone. "I wouldn't count on it. Even Newbolt's got better sense than that."

"To marry her, you mean? Sarvice—by the way, what does the A. stand for?"

"Ask him if you want to know."

"I'll do that. Anyway, he said Maxwell wasn't good enough for her. Why do you suppose he said that?"

Waite cut her a sardonic look. "You're supposed to be a smart woman. Figure it out for yourself."

Just then the two boys, mounted on a pair of smallish, shaggy Banker ponies no different from the ones that ranged free on the island, came loping up, winded, laughing, looking so wonderfully carefree that Mariah found herself wishing she could have grown up as a boy in this wild, Swiss Family Robinson–style paradise.

A gust of wind blew her skirt across Waite's legs, blew her hair, which was forever escaping its pins, across her face. Raking it back, she laughed and squinted up at her two students. They were handsome lads, hovering on the brink of manhood. Both would be sent off to school on the mainland this year or the next. There was much to be gained by the venture, but something to be lost as well, she thought a little sadly.

"There's stovewood to split. I've hauled the big dory. Her bottom's fouled bad. She'll need scraping down," Waite said to his son.

"Yessir, and then can I ride up to Kinnakeet with Dore? We've been invited to take supper with Cap'n Hooper."

"Cap'n Hooper's daughters, more likely," Waite said. "Get on with your chores, then."

The two raced off, shouting in an excess of high spirits. Mariah said wistfully, "I wonder where they get the energy. August has to be the most debilitating month of all."

"September now. Bad month for storms."

She glanced at him and discovered that he had resumed that closed-in look, which was a shame. She'd come to look forward to the rare occasions when he let go enough to actually carry on a conversation. As a rule he was as stingy with words as a miser.

"Spoilsport," she said, hoping to tease his good nature back again, but he'd already turned away and was striding back toward the lighthouse as if he'd wasted all the time he could spare.

Drat the man! A week ago—perhaps two—she would have simply considered the source and discounted his grouchiness, but now she knew better. She'd seen the softer side of Waite McKenna and she wanted it back.

It was nearly ten that night when Sarvice A. Jones rapped on the door and then let himself inside the principal keeper's office. Waite had been trying to finish up the paperwork required by the Lighthouse Board, a task he usually put off as long as possible.

"Miss Caroline's ailing," the young first assistant blurted out. Hat in hand, he stood just inside the door, his earnest face screwed into a mask of concern. "This morning I heard her in there a-groaning and carrying on, and I called out to see if she needed anything, but she just said a bad word and cut loose in the chamber pot."

"Cut loose? Hell, man—"

"Vomited, I mean, not the other. She was real sick, I could tell. I went down and dipped her up a jug of fresh water and took it back upstairs, but she wouldn't let me in. You reckon it was that corned beef we had last night? I scraped the mold off, but you never can tell. City women has delicate constitutions, you said so yourself."

Waite swore. This was all he needed. A sickly woman on his hands. "Did you speak to her brother?"

Sarvice nodded vigorously. "Yessir, but he just said it weren't none of my business and I was to let her be."

"Then my advice is, let her be."

"You don't think I ought to send for Miss Agnes? She could come like she was just paying a call. Maybe if she saw some spots or something she could offer her a potion. I heard tell the measles takes some folks like that. Hot fever, sick to the stomach, red spots and all."

"She looked fine to me when she went riding out with Newbolt."

"What if she spreads it around?"

Impatiently, Waite shut his ledger and capped his inkstand. "In the first place, we don't know if it's catching. In the second place, if it is, she's already spread it. In the third place, I've had the measles and so have you, and it's flat out none of our business. The sooner she goes back to where she came from, the smoother things will run around here. If that damned dog of hers keeps me awake one more night, I'm going to parboil the little bastard and eat him!"

"Yessir." Sarvice looked almost as miserable as if he were coming down with something himself.

"The cistern weren't damaged none last night, but the dipping vat's got a crack in it. You reckon we're going to get any more of them earthquakes? They're sayin' it near about ruint Charleston, down in South Carolina."

"I heard. First thing in the morning, see what we've got in the paint locker. The boat'll need a fresh coat once Nick gets her scraped, and then we'll have a go at patching the dipping vat."

Sarvice let himself out, and Waite stared down at the logbook. Last night he'd written only that what appeared to be an earthquake had struck at 9:50 P.M., and was followed by a number of smaller tremors, and that there'd been no damage as far as he'd been able to determine without closer inspection.

Some of the internal fractures that had occurred back in '79 when lightning struck her might have opened up some. He hadn't seen any sign of it this morning when he'd gone over the entire structure, but there was no way of knowing. The wall was three layers thick.

As for what else had happened last night, he'd thought long and hard. And then he'd dismissed it as unimportant. It wouldn't happen again. He couldn't afford to let down his guard, not when he had a job to do and a son to raise.

Every man, Waite figured, should undergo marriage once, or else the world would soon run out of people. But he'd done his share. He'd as soon leave the marrying and breeding to other men, from here on out.

As for Mrs. Deekins, she might or might not be inclined to have another go at it. Either way, it was no skin off his nose. When and if he ever got to the point where he was tired of living alone—which might conceivably happen once Nick moved away and set out on his own path—why, then, he would find himself a decent island woman, one who didn't expect more than he had in him to give her.

Hell, he'd almost forgotten how to kiss, it had been so long. Not that there hadn't been women since Constance, because there had. A man had to have release, after all, but that seldom involved any kissing, much less making promises that couldn't be kept. Or speaking a lot of pretty words that were forgotten come morning.

Leaning back in his chair, Waite idly rolled the steel-tipped pen between thumb and forefinger, thinking about last night. About what had happened when he'd raced down from the tower and gone tearing off across the clearing in the aftermath of the quake.

She'd looked so damned beautiful in that yellow thingamabob she'd been wearing, with her hair hanging down her back like a garnet waterfall.

A garnet waterfall?

Flinging down the pen, he swore, raked back his chair, and stood. Hardraker had the first shift tonight, but Waite suddenly felt a powerful need to feel the wind in his face, to gaze down on a world that was both familiar and safely removed.

Chapter Fourteen

The church was small, crowded, and unbearably hot. Caroline Hardraker, looking pale but determined, had been collected by Maxwell and sat on the bench alongside the entire Newbolt family, which, according to Mariah's way of thinking, was tantamount to a declaration. In purple silk with matching plumes on her hat, she looked hot and uncomfortable, if far more elegant than any other woman in the congregation.

Mariah had driven to church by herself. The moment she took her seat on one of the back benches, Evie slipped off the end of her father's pew and joined her there. Maxwell turned and glared, but short of creating a disturbance there was nothing he could do about it.

And while Mariah admired the girl's newfound courage, she only hoped it didn't get her into trouble. Perhaps Caroline would act as a buffer.

Evie scooted onto the bench and looked up with a grin. She was wearing the dress they had refashioned together, with the help of one of the local women. "Don't it look fine? Papa was real mad, but I think he was ashamed to say much on account of Miss Hardraker was there," she whispered. "She's there a whole lot. I don't like her much." And then the girl slapped a hand over her mouth.

Remonstrating her with no more than a gentle frown, Mariah sat back to enjoy the sermon. Eventually, she told herself, things would have to sort themselves out. Evie and her family. Maxwell and Caroline. And poor Sarvice A. Jones.

The service was endless and boring, the preacher having chosen to belabor an obscure point concerning the deceits of the world, the flesh, and the devil.

Mariah was still trying to come to terms with her own deceits. Passing herself off as a widow was no small crime, even though she honestly hadn't intended to deceive anyone. Besides, according to the mores of society, she wasn't entitled to her father's name. She had impulsively adopted her mother's family name with no thought of any possible consequences. What had followed was no fault of her own, she rationalized

Oh, no? You could have set the record straight.

What, and lose my position?

All the same, you're living another lie.

Then I'll just have to live it, won't I? It's either that or starve.

Uncomfortable under her burden of guilt, she allowed her mind to be lulled by the drone of the preacher's voice. After a while she stifled a yawn. The sweet chatter of songbirds drifted in through the open window, pierced now and then by the distant sound of gulls and the raucous cawing of a crow.

"That's Indigo," Evie whispered. "He follered Frankie, begging for a goober. He can almost talk."

Mariah smiled. The smell of salt air, warm pines, and some subtle flower fragrance mingled with the scent of lye soap, varnish, and warm humanity was not at all unpleasant. Life, on the whole, she decided, was good.

Seated several rows ahead of her was Waite McKenna, easily recognizable by the width of his black-clad shoulders, the dark-edged gold of his hair, and the fact that he was the tallest man on the bench. Nick sat stiffly beside him, his paler hair wet and slicked back, looking surprisingly mature in a white shirt with a wrinkled collar and a black necktie.

Beside her, Evie sighed. The poor child was staring, her feelings plain as day to anyone who cared to look. Mariah tried to recall who had said "It is impossible to love and be wise." It could have been one of the Brontë sisters, but she rather thought it was Sir Francis Bacon.

Come to that, wasn't she herself proof of love's folly?

The sermon eventually meandered to an anticlimactic finish. The congregation waited until first the preacher and then Maxwell and his family filed out. Both men took up positions just outside the door, where they proceeded to greet the emerging congregation.

Mariah was amused. Gracious, did Maxwell oversee the church as well as everything else in the community?

Not particularly eager to face her father's censure, Evie hung back. Out of sympathy, Mariah stayed with her. "Oh, these are pretty," she murmured. Someone had brought a jug filled with

wild bracken and pink flowers and set it on a
table in the rear of the church.

"Swamp mallers. Some calls 'em marsh mallers."

Mariah, who had breezed through a single se-
mester of botany, said, "I believe they're related
to Mother's Rose of Sharon."

And then it was time to go. The congregation
had scattered, some riding, most walking. While
his sons collected the family's transportation,
Maxwell delivered himself of the opinion that
there was entirely too much wriggling and
scraping of feet and that, ragwort or no ragwort,
sneezing shouldn't be tolerated during the reading
of the Lord's word, and that he would post a notice to that effect.

*How could I have ever fancied the man, if only
through his correspondence?* Mariah marveled. She
smiled and offered him a greeting. Solemnly, he
tipped his hat, a fine brown beaver, then glared
at Evie and jutted his elbow for Caroline, who
was evidently invited to take Sunday dinner. Little
Frankie, with a strained grin at Mariah, trotted
along behind and barely managed to scramble up
onto the wagon bed before his father slapped up
his mare.

Not until days later would it occur to Mariah
that it was her careless remark about the pretty
flowers in the church that prompted Evie to beg
her brother to take her to the freshwater pond so
she could collect a bouquet for Miss Mariah that
Sunday afternoon.

And Dorien, mischief no doubt already sim-
mering inside his handsome head, quickly lured
Nick into joining them on the expedition. And because Nick had a battered old skiff in the pond

nearest the lighthouse, they chose that particular
pond to visit.

The lighthouse pond, while it was home to a
variety of flowering vegetation, also contained
hoards of turtles, a few of them snappers, but the
rest mostly mud sliders. It was the turtles that
brought about the catastrophe.

Not unexpectedly, the most desirable blossoms
were on the far side of the pond, or else Evie
could have picked to her heart's content without
ever leaving the bank. Once she'd discovered that
Nick was to be a part of the outing, she had kept
on her church finery despite her brother's teasing.
It was enough that he had agreed to humor her.
If she smudged her gown with mud and never
got to wear it again, it would still be worth it.
Neither one of them had even called her Rustmop
or Evaloony.

They set out across the still, dark water, Dorien
in the bow, Nick paddling from the stern, with
Evie seated in the middle. The skiff was barely six
feet long. Evie forced herself to stare at the patches
of pink among the cattails and rushes, and not at
the handsome young man paddling them across
the pond without so much as a splash. It was her
solemn belief that Nick could have walked across
the water and gathered the flowers for her had he
so desired.

"Man, look at that big 'un!" Dorien called their
attention to the granddaddy of all mud sliders.

Nick flashed a broad white grin. "Lookee yonder at the one that just popped his head up. He's
a snapper, wouldn't you say, Dore?"

"Shootfire, he's got to be three foot across if he's

an inch! Better not let him grab hold of the paddle
or he'll pull you over."

"Get your fingers out of the water, Evie,"
warned Nick.

"Uh-oh, he's comin' after us!" cried Dorien.

As both boys had been feeding table scraps to
the pond's residents for years, they were perfectly
familiar with the turtles' habit of approaching and
begging for food.

Not so Evie. She seldom ventured this far from
home. Clasping her hands in her lap, she drew
herself up into as small a package as possible and
stared wide-eyed as dozens of snakelike heads
converged on the small skiff. When Dorien suddenly scooped up one of the creatures and flung
it onto her lap, she screamed and jumped up. The
boat lurched, and before either boy could grab
her, she toppled over the side.

Mariah saw it all. She'd just come out the door,
headed to the beach to collect gravel for her chickens, when she'd noticed Maxwell's cart with Evie
and her brother. Expecting Dorien to deliver the
child for a visit, she had lingered outside the
house, then wandered down the road toward the
pond when they stopped there instead.

She'd seen Nick jog down to join them, watched
the three of them shove off from the shore in a
skiff not much bigger than a copper hip bath, and
wondered if they were intending to go fishing on
the Sabbath. She wouldn't put it past either boy,
but she was rather surprised that Evie would take
part in any such secular activity.

She had just reached the edge of the pond when
Evie flew over the side. Both boys were reared

back, howling with laughter, slapping their thighs and whooping great gales.

Horrified, Mariah shouted a warning. They didn't hear her. Skirt about her knees, she raced to the edge of the pond and, without giving a single thought to the depth of the water or the fact that she couldn't swim a stroke, plunged in— boots, bonnet, and all. "I'm coming, Evie, I'm coming!" she gasped, flailing like a sternwheeler headed down a waterfall.

Waite had been up on the tower balcony. He'd seen Nick emerge from the house and head down toward the pond, and wondered if the boy had finished washing the dishes before he'd set out. They had rules concerning chores. Nick didn't always abide by them.

Next he'd caught sight of the Newbolt boy and his sister wheeling down the road, and when they'd stopped at the pond instead of riding on to the teacherage, he'd muttered, "Oh-oh. Something's up."

Waite had eaten more than a few snappers out of that pond. Put in a barrel and fed on cornmeal and greens to clean them out, they were about the sweetest meat a man could want. But that pair wouldn't be going after snappers with a girl along. No, sir! Something didn't square up.

He was down the stairs and out the door in record time. Whistling up one of the horses grazing on wild clover, he swung aboard and took off at a gallop, just in time to see the schoolmarm hurl herself into the pond.

"Judas priest," he muttered. "What in bloody hell is going on here?"

It was Waite who waded out and dragged both

females up by their skirttails. A stricken Dorien hauled his sister back aboard the skiff, and Nick, his face pasty white, began racing for shore. Waite waded ashore carrying Mariah. Her eyes were closed, but she was breathing. Gasping, spitting up water, in fact. He'd have done better to throw her over his shoulder, head down, and bring up any water she'd swallowed that way, but his arms refused to give her up. He cradled her, carrying her along the road toward his own house. They both stunk. His clothes were plastered to his body with mud, as were hers. There was a strand of duckweed across her bosom, which called attention to the two small nubbins pressed against her bodice.

Hastily, he averted his eyes. "Easy, easy," was all he could think of to say. She was starting to shiver. The temperature was somewhere in the high eighties. When she opened her eyes, she stared up at him as if she didn't recognize him.

"Mariah? It's all right, I've got you now."

"Evie?" she rasped. Her eyes were as wide as if she'd just seen the gates of hell.

"She'll do just fine. The boys have got her ashore already. They're loading her onto the cart to take her home. Nick covered her with his shirt. He's holding her—she'll not likely take a chill before they get her home."

And then she started crying. No ladylike sniffles, not even the self-pitying sobs his wife used to employ to help her get her own way. Mariah flat out howled. She wept like a child, noisy, openly, as if she were hurting. Waite told her again that she was all right, that Evie was all right, and that those two limbs of Satan would regret

the day they'd ever taken the girl out in that
damned leaky cockleshell of Nick's.

She looked awful. Her face was so pale her
freckles stood out like nutmeg on a bowl of clab-
ber. He carried her directly to his place. It never
even occurred to him to take her to the teacherage.
The Hardraker woman could look after her while
he rode after Miss Agnes.

And then he remembered that Caroline Hardraker was still at Maxwell's place.

"Sarvice," he shouted s soon as he got within
shouting distance. "Ride down the ridge and fetch
Miss Agnes, and then send word to Newbolt's for
Miss Hardraker to get on back home. Tell Hardraker he's got the duty until you get back!"

The first assistant goggled at the wet and
muddy pair dripping all over the freshly scrubbed
floor, then took off at a run, mounted a pony with
surprising agility, and galloped off down the road.

Waite carried Mariah through to the kitchen.
She needed warming first of all, then he would
see to cleaning her up some. If Miss Agnes or the
Hardraker woman wasn't here in time to take
over, so be it. It wouldn't be the first time he'd
had to do for a woman. He'd all but delivered
Nick himself, the midwife being out on another
delivery. Ever since that time he had borne the
burden of guilt for his wife's death, although the
midwife had later assured him that no one could
have saved her. She'd started bleeding inside, and
before anyone realized it, she was gone.

And now he had another needy woman on his
hands. "Mariah? Stop crying. It's all over and
you're no worse for the wear. Didn't do your frock
much good, but I reckon you've got others."

He tried for a lighter note, but it didn't seem to help. She was still crying, not so noisily now, but softly, hopelessly, as if she'd lost everything in the world instead of just one pretty gray dress. And a bonnet. Her shoes would never be the same, either. There was mud etched in every seam of the fine gray kidskin.

Draping a towel around her shoulders, he knelt and unfastened her high-tops, shucked them off, and then stared in consternation at the filthy silk stockings.

I shouldn't be doing this, he thought. *I don't need this.*

But *she* needed it. Needed to feel clean and dry and warm again. Needed to feel safe.

"You can't even swim, can you?"

She sniffed and shook her head. It was the first real reaction he'd gotten out of her. He was encouraged. "So you jumped in the pond after the Newbolt girl without knowing the depth of the water—without even being able to swim. Is that right?"

She nodded and sniffed again, and he pulled out his handkerchief, forgetting that it was every bit as wet as she was.

Lord help him, and he'd thought her weak? Frail? A city woman who couldn't survive in a place like this? At the rate she was going, that might be true, but it wouldn't be for lack of courage.

Much later that evening, after Waite had finished describing every aspect of their character, or lack thereof, as well as their ultimate destination, he listened while Nick and Dorien explained that all they'd been trying to do was take Evie to where she could fetch a bunch of flowers for the teacher. The thing with the turtle hadn't been planned—it had just sort of happened. It had never occurred to them that Evie couldn't swim, even though, self-conscious about her affliction, she'd never gone to the beach with the other children.

And besides, as Nick said ingeniously, the pond was no more than five feet deep at the deepest part. Everybody said so. Nobody actually knew, but everybody said so.

"Five foot of water over ten foot of mud. And Miss Evie's about . . . what? Four-foot-three?"

"We didn't think. Honest, Pa, we didn't mean no harm."

Waite had more to say on the subject, finishing up with the fact that Nick would be going off to boarding school as soon as he could make arrangements.

A sorrowful Nick was dismissed, shoulders drooping, head hanging. Waite wondered how he was going to be able to let the boy go. Unlike the Newbolt boys, Nick wouldn't be coming back again on the next boat. He did know that about his son—that while he might get up to any amount of foolishness, he would never disobey a direct order from his father. He was solid as ironwood at the core.

Miss Agnes had arrived and assured him that Mariah would come to no harm. Caroline Hardraker had come, reluctantly, and lent a hand. "Good Lord, I don't see what all the fuss is about. So she fell into the water. She's not going to melt, is she?"

Waite, unable to hide his disgust, left the three women alone in the kitchen. Caroline Hardraker . . . now, there was living proof of his theory about women. If she and Newbolt made a match of it, he could almost find it in his heart to feel sorry for the pompous little prig. She'd make his life miserable. And while those two younger children needed a mother, he had a feeling she'd be worse than no mother at all.

He was still standing on the back stoop, wondering how he could muzzle that damned dog next door, when first Caroline and then Miss Agnes emerged from the kitchen. "I told her she could go home," said Caroline. "There's nothing wrong with her that a good bath won't cure. Whew, her clothes stink! It's enough to make a body sick to her stomach!"

The wrinkled old midwife, who had delivered generations of island babies, lingered at the edge of the porch, gazing after the proud woman still dressed in her purple churchgoing finery. "Been sick to her stomach a lot, ain't she? Takes some women thataway, mostly of a morning. Your woman was the same way." She shook her head, refusing the money Waite offered her, refusing a ride back home.

"The Lord, He give me a good pair of feet. If I don't use 'em, He might take 'em back." She cackled, shook her iron-gray head when the Hardrakers' dog started up again, and strode off toward the road, as sprightly as a woman half her age.

Mariah, feeling drained by her ordeal yet oddly relieved, as if a weight had been lifted from her shoulders, stepped out onto the stoop several minutes later, carrying her wet things as if they were contaminated. Caroline had gone across to the teacherage and returned with a change of clothes. She'd chosen the oldest, most unbecoming gown Mariah possessed, one she usually wore only for housework, but at least it was warm and dry. After the clammy feel of what she'd been wearing, she was glad of anything that wasn't wet and reeking of mud.

Her hair was still damp. She could hardly wait to wash it and rinse it until the odor was gone. "I haven't thanked you for pulling me out. Thank you, Waite."

He grunted in response. She was still pale. She should be put to bed, no matter what those two women said, but it wasn't his place to order her there.

"I did try, you know . . . not to be a burden, I mean. I know Maxwell said that I was to go to you with any problems—" He dismissed that with an impatient gesture. "But I also know how much you resent having to look after whoever happens to be living in the teacherage."

"You need to be in bed."

"I will be, just as soon as I bathe, wash my hair, get myself a bite to eat and ride over to see that Evie's truly all right. The poor child could've drowned."

"Dammit, woman, you could have drowned! Didn't you stop to think of that before you went sailing off into the water like a damned fool?"

"Are you calling me a fool?" Her feelings still abraded, Mariah snapped, "Nobody asked you to pull me out! I would have come through just fine! The water wasn't even over my head, and be-sides—"

"How would you know that? You couldn't even manage to stay upright."

"Could I help it if my skirts billowed out and I lost my balance?"

"The boys were already reaching for Evie to haul her back into the skiff when you grabbed at her and nearly knocked her under again."

She looked so stricken, Waite could have bit off his tongue. He tried to make up for it, but it was too late. She had already mounted her high horse. Head up, eyes red-rimmed from crying and from pond water, she said, "I'm sorry I dripped all over your kitchen. If you'll leave it until later, I'll mop the floor for you, but right now I—" Her voice began to wobble, and she teared up again, and Waite swore.

"Go home, Mariah. Go to bed."

He watched her make her way, stiff as a bowsprit, holding the basket away from her so it wouldn't drip on her skirt. What a woman, he thought. And what the devil was he going to do with her?

Chapter Fifteen

The first week of September, traditionally a time of bad storms, drifted by without incident. Mariah's days settled into a routine that was both satisfying and encouraging. She enjoyed teaching, she truly did. What's more, she'd discovered that she was good at it. Murfreesboro's loss was Buxton's gain, she thought smugly.

Evie seldom missed a day of classes. And while she read well ahead of her age, the poor child couldn't subtract six from a dozen. She placed Turkey in the middle of France and, when Mariah gently corrected her, shrugged her bony shoulders as if to say, *What difference does it make? I'll never go there.*

Which was probably true. Sad, but true.

Franklin read every book on the advanced shelf and borrowed her personal copy of *Modern Science of the Nineteenth Century*. Maxwell scolded her severely for encouraging his daughter in her foolish waywardness, but he'd ordered the books she'd requested, all the same.

Caroline Hardraker continued to take supper with the Newbolts on Wednesday and Friday evenings and dinner after church on Sundays. She continued to ridicule the magistrate behind his back until Mariah lost patience and suggested that if she disliked the man so much, one would think she'd avoid his company.

Caroline had burst into tears, blurted something about Mariah's not understanding, and rushed off. Mariah, staring after her from her own doorway, told herself she really ought to go after the woman and draw her out. Sometimes talking about one's troubles helped lighten the load. She had a few troubles of her own she wouldn't mind sharing, but she didn't dare. She could imagine the response if she announced that not only was she not a widow, she'd never even been married.

That not only was she illegitimate, she was a liar as well.

That not only was she all of the above, she was the world's greatest fool, for hadn't she gone and fallen in love with a man who gave her no encouragement whatsoever—a man who ran hot and then cold, who was reputed to despise all women, city women most of all?

Of course, she could have explained that Murfreesboro wasn't all that big a city. Hardly more than a country village, in fact, although it did have a number of lovely homes, several fine businesses, and a highly respected college.

But what was the use? For the sake of any future children if for no other reason, no decent man would marry a woman in her situation. And whatever else he might be, Waite was a decent man.

Standing at the corner of the teacherage that evening, a basin of chicken scraps in her hand, she sighed and watched as Sarvice trudged across to the tower to light the lantern, with Caroline's little dog following in his footsteps.

It was that time of day. Lamplighting time. Her chickens were ready to go to roost, and here she was, withholding their supper while she indulged in another daydream. She'd never been particularly prone to daydreams before. But then, she'd never met a man like Waite McKenna.

Sarvice had told her that chickens didn't need to be fed three times a day, that once was sufficient. Earlier, he had brought her a plate of freshwater bass, skinned and baked with potatoes, onions, and bacon, which she'd had for her supper.

He'd offered to bring her a turtle and even to clean it out for her first. Heaven only knew what that involved. She had declined his offer. Having only just managed to master the art of frying fish and chicken, she wasn't about to tackle cooking turtles. However, she'd allowed him to linger and talk about Miss Caroline, which he seemed to enjoy. About how beautiful she looked in all her silk finery. And how, though she was getting noticeably stouter, he worried about her. About how he was afraid she might marry Mr. Newbolt and live to regret it, because nobody truly like the man, they only tolerated him out of the kindness of their hearts.

Which was more or less what Mariah herself had concluded. Sarvice was right. Maxwell was a prig. He had no more sensitivity than a lump of clay. He was proud of his two eldest boys because they were big and handsome and popular with all the girls. He treated his daughter like a servant and was embarrassed by his youngest son. As for

Caleb and Dorien, she hadn't quite made up her mind. She rather suspected that pair was more than a match for him. But it was anyone's guess how he would treat a wife, should he ever choose to remarry.

On the ninth day of September, which happened to be her twenty-third birthday, not that anyone knew or cared, Mariah celebrated by asking Sarvice his middle name. "I'll tell you mine if you'll tell me yours," she teased.

He blushed, which didn't make a whole lot of difference, as he was red-faced, anyway. Tan of hair, large of ear, red of face, he was not an unhandsome man when one took the trouble to study his features.

"It's America," he said. He'd come by to bring last week's *Herald and Examiner.* "I was borned on the fourth of July."

Mariah swallowed a hoot of laughter. "I think that's—well, I think it's wonderful!"

"What's yours?"

"What's my—oh, you mean my name. Nothing quite so grand, I'm afraid. I was named after an elderly friend of my father's who was rich as Guernsey cream. The old man didn't have any family, and Papa hoped he might remember me in his will, but he didn't."

"What was his name?"

"You'll not laugh?"

"No, ma'am, I'd never do that," the first assistant keeper said solemnly.

"It's George."

His lips twitched. There was a gleam in his tan eyes, but he nodded soberly. "Miss Caroline's middle name is Alice. She's not married, but she's going to have a baby, and her folks sent her down here on account o' they didn't know what else to do with her."

Mariah's jaw dropped. She sat down suddenly on the chopping block without regard for any splinters she might collect. "Sarvice, you can't know that."

"Yes'm, her brother told me so. He offered me fifty dollars if I'd marry her, and if I didn't want to keep the baby, he said he'd take it up to Virginia and find it a home."

"Oh, dear, no wonder the poor man looks so sad all the time."

"Him and his wife is expecting their first any day now. He don't know what to do, and Miss Caroline, she's not making it no easier, making up to Mr. Newbolt like she does."

"Does Maxwell know? About the baby, I mean?"

"As to that, I couldn't say. Seems like if he was wanting to marry her, though, he wouldn't wait around much longer. She'll be coming out of the sickness 'fore long, but then she'll start poking out in front so everybody'll know."

"How do you know so much about it, if I might ask?"

"Like I told you, my ma had seven of us. Half my brothers is married with young'uns of their own, all living right there on the farm. A man notices things like that."

One would think a woman would notice, as well; but then, Mariah had been an only child. She hadn't been on intimate terms with her friends' families. "What about Waite? Does he know?"

"Yes'm, he put it together from her bein' sick every morning and from something Miss Agnes said. He said it weren't none of our business and that if I was smart, I'd keep away from her. Him and her, they never hit it off real well."

No, Mariah mused, they certainly hadn't. She'd wondered about that, because men liked pretty women, and Caroline was certainly that. As for Caroline, one would have thought that of all the men available, Waite would have been her choice; but then, perhaps she preferred a man she could control. That would certainly leave Waite out of the running.

Sarvice left her to go begin cranking up the weights, and Mariah lingered, reluctant to go back inside her sweltering cottage. She felt as if she ought to do something for the poor woman, only she didn't know what. She did know, however, what it felt like to be desperate and alone.

But before she could make up her mind whether or not to interfere, Waite joined her, looking handsome, hard, and not entirely aloof. At least she'd made some progress there. Perhaps in a few years she might even tease him into admitting that he liked her just a tiny bit.

Having decided against hurling herself into his arms, Mariah finished feeding Merrily her daily treat of dried apples, pretending a nonchalance she was far from feeling. "My, a little rain would certainly feel good, wouldn't it? I've been considering sending off for one of those new electric fans I've been reading about."

It would have to be one that ran on kerosene. There was no power on the island.

"Might get more than rain by the end of the week."

"Men and their empty promises," she teased. He didn't respond. He might pretend he was made of iron, but she happened to know better.

Perched on the tail of the cart, she brushed a few seeds from her skirt, wishing she were wearing something more becoming than her old yellow dimity, but at least she'd put away her drab grays, lavenders, and blacks. "You might be interested to learn that I no longer scream and hide my head under a pillow at the first crack of thunder." Determined to tease him out of his sober mood, she grinned up at him. In a weak moment, she'd told him about shutting herself in a trunk in the attic when she was a child.

"That's progress. Any more fears to conquer? Mice? Snakes? Water?"

She shrugged, her smile fading. "I nearly drowned when I was six. My parents did drown. Together. Just last February. So my fear of water might take a while longer, but yes, I'm making progress."

"I'm sorry, Mariah. I didn't know."

She shrugged. "How could you? Everybody back home knew, of course. Most of them were there when it happened. The river froze over. It hardly ever does, at least not hard enough to skate on, but that didn't stop my mother."

He looked as if he didn't want to hear it, but now that she'd started the telling, she needed to say it. She'd never talked about it.

And so she told him how Lydia Sawyer—Lydia Deekins—had gone sliding out onto the ice that sunny winter afternoon in her red velvet cloak and her new galoshes—laughing, some said. And how George, who everybody knew still doted on her, had yelled and told her to behave herself and come on back. And how Lydia had called him an old sobersides just before she'd flung up her hands and disappeared.

"Papa went after her, running right out onto the ice, even though it was cracked all around, and everybody was yelling at him to wait and get a plank or a rope, but he didn't. So he fell through, too. They went out in boats and broke the ice with poles and oars, but it wasn't until nearly a week later that . . ."

Her voice shook. She smiled, but her eyes were wet and her chin was wobbling. "Sorry. I thought I could get it all out, but I guess it's still too soon."

Waite's expression had shifted into something akin to awe. He swore softly under his breath. "You dived headfirst into the pond, with a history like *that*?" He'd suspected she might be afraid of water. Hell, anybody who'd seen the way she stood back from the surf, the way she drove on the other side of the road whenever she passed the pond, would know something was out of kilter.

He was tempted to wrap her in his arms and cry with her, but if he did he might never let her go, and that wouldn't do. It would never do. So he mumbled some excuse and left her there, because staring down at the sun glinting off her garnet-red hair, shining clean through those wet, rain-colored eyes of hers, he wanted so much to take her in his arms and hold on to her until all the hollow places inside him and all the hurt inside her went away. Wanted it more than he'd wanted

anything in a long time—so he walked off and
left her there.

The weather, though summer was coming to a
close, remained miserably hot. Mariah was wringing wet before she could even finish getting
dressed each morning. The men grumbled because
fishing was slow. The women fretted because the
men were worried. Even the children seemed
more restless than usual.

However, Nick and Dorien, to her surprise,
showed some slight improvement in their behavior. Mariah suspected it had to do with a combination of things—guilt over the incident at the pond
and the threat of being sent off to school.

On a day when heat waves were dancing off
the sand by eight o'clock in the morning, when
three people came down with what Miss Agnes
called heat fever, and when Mariah ate cold soup
from a tin for breakfast because she couldn't bring
herself to build a fire in the range, something happened that took her mind completely off the
dreadful weather.

Evie missed school. When Mariah drove by her
house that afternoon to see why, she found the
child in the backyard taking in clothes. She called
out a greeting and Evie spun around. Before she
could hide her face or roll down her sleeves, Mariah saw the bruises on her arms and the red mark
on one cheek.

"Oh, my dear, what happened?"

Evie turned away, mumbling something about
tripping and falling down the back steps, only Mariah didn't believe it for one minute. That mark on
her cheek could only have been made by a hand.

"Ma'am, my papa don't like for me to have company."

"Bosh! I've visited here before. You've come to see me at my house. We've cooked together and sewed together—I thought we were friends."

Evie went on unpinning and folding shirts, her face averted. It was all Mariah could do not to throw her arms around the child, who was trying too hard to act as if nothing were amiss.

"Evie, if there's something you want to tell me, you know I'll do my best to advise you. And I never tell tales out of school. Nor in school, either."

Her little joke fell flat. Evie picked up her clothes basket and turned toward the back door without speaking, her limp more pronounced than ever.

Feeling helpless, Mariah watched her go inside. She didn't follow, but she couldn't help but wonder about all those stalwart male Newbolts. Not Frankie, of course. And not Dorien, either, because she was pretty sure that, while the lad might be thoughtless and full of mischief, there was no real meanness in him.

As for the other three, she simply didn't know. Caleb, from all reports, was fishing with one of the local men and saving up for a boat of his own. The eldest two, as far as she could tell, did nothing at all. Evidently, they considered being handsome and charming enough to justify their existence.

But what if a streak of meanness lurked under all that good-looking, easygoing charm? What then?

Mariah knew she had to do something, but

what? She could hardly report her suspicions to the local law. Maxwell *was* the local law. He wasn't the type to believe ill of his own sons.

Could Evie really have tripped and fallen?

No. Not when the marks of four fingers and a palm were right there for all to see.

She drove home slowly, lost in her own thoughts. The swamps were silent, as if all the frogs had left. The birds, too, were quieter than usual. On the way she passed several children out calling "Precious! Here, Precious!" and she roused from her thoughts long enough to wonder why.

The why, she soon learned, was that Caroline's dog had been missing since early morning. Evidently he'd been let out to do his business and then wandered away while Caroline was suffering her morning wretchedness.

Mariah felt as if she should join in the search, but all she could think of was Evie. So she told herself that the poor little dog had probably crawled up under one of the houses to escape the heat. Sooner or later it would turn up safe and sound. Tomorrow, if he still hadn't come home, she would join in the search, but for now every child in the village was out looking. They knew the woods far better than she did.

That night she blew out the lamp, undressed, and bathed in cool water. She was tempted to pour the basinful over her head, but she'd been warned all her life that going to bed with a wet head brought on lung fever, stiff joints, and possibly even madness.

Madness, at least in its milder forms, was an ever-increasing possibility.

"I'm worried about Evie," she wrote in her journal. She'd changed into her nightgown and moved the rocker away from the living room lamp to escape its heat, which meant she could barely see to write. "Someone has hurt the child, and she won't say who. Why won't she tell? Is she afraid? Embarrassed? So many questions arise, most I've never even had cause to consider. I need to talk to someone, but who?"

Distracted, she closed her eyes and listened to the soothing sound of the surf. It occurred to her that she could have written something about poor Caroline's plight, but even being pregnant and unwed paled in comparison to cruelty to a child.

With a sigh, she opened her eyes again and wrote, "Caroline's dog is missing. Could have wandered off into the marsh. Sarvice says there are wild boars in the woods that will eat anything. Does that include dogs? Poor noisy little wretch, I hope he's found quickly.

"It's too hot to breathe tonight, and I'm far too perturbed to sleep. Perhaps a walk on the shore will have a calming influence."

Waite dropped his clothes on the sand and stood there for several minutes, letting the soft night air caress his nakedness. The sea was calm, the tide dead low. There was a storm in the offing, according to the latest word from the weather station at Hatteras. He'd suspected it even before the news had come in. Felt it in his bones. On his skin. In the very air he breathed.

There were fewer birds in the air today. Some went deep into the woods, some headed across the sound. So far there wasn't a cloud in the sky.

A half moon and roughly a billion stars shone down, reflecting off the water, making the night almost as bright as day. But the storm was coming, all the same.

Flexing his shoulders, he strode down to the water's edge, waded out hip deep, then dived into an incoming wave.

For perhaps a quarter of an hour he swam, using a powerful overarm stroke learned before he'd reached the age of five. He followed the shoreline, first north and then south, reveling in the tug of hidden currents. When he felt himself beginning to tire he waited for a wave and rode it more than halfway in before it disintegrated. Then he stood and made his way ashore.

She was just coming over a low rise when he saw her. Another man might have taken her for a ghost dressed in flowing white, but not Waite. He'd have known her anywhere, even without all that long, glossy dark hair.

For a minute he considered going back out to sea, waiting for her to get tired of standing there and go back, but there was a strange devil riding him tonight. The same devil that had driven him to swim alone at night, something he'd forbidden Nick to do. The same devil that had kept him awake more than a few nights these past few weeks, wondering about her husband. About their life together. About whether or not she'd been one of those women who enjoyed the marriage act, or if she'd only tolerated it.

Redheads, some men said, were supposed to be passionate. Waite wouldn't know. He'd never had one. If he'd had to venture a guess, he'd say this one was cooler than any Nordic blonde. Constance, with her Creole coloring and hew New Orleans roots, had surely been passionate until pregnancy and disappointment had wrung all the passion out of her.

The tide surged around his hips, undermining his footing. "Oh, the hell with it," he said, and, never taking his gaze from the woman, he strode ashore.

Chapter Sixteen

Mariah stood transfixed by the figure that rose from the sea. She was dreaming, of course. Or the heat had affected her mind. She'd resisted pouring the basin of cool water over her body, head and all, yet she must be suffering a moon spell—a sea-spell—*some* kind of spell. Because that was surely a Viking king walking up from the sea, moonlight glittering on the crown of his pale hair, on every polished facet of his magnificent muscular body.

He hesitated. She hesitated. and then they both began walking again, he up from the shore, she down to the shore, until they met where the sand was hard and damp, their footsteps glittering with a strange greenish glow. He was her lighthouse keeper, of course. A part of her had realized that from the first, but as long as they were both in thrall to the same dream, Mariah didn't even try to resist him.

He was beautifully formed. Strange and shad-owy in places, but completely beautiful. They halted, not touching. As the night breeze tossed her flimsy gown against her heat-damp body, she allowed her gaze to flow over him until she had looked her fill. Her eyes traced the line of his pow-erful limbs up from his high-arched feet, past

something dark and mysterious, over the ridged
flatness of his belly, lingering on his golden-haired
chest. His shoulders were far wider than any part
of her own body—she'd known that all along.
And enormously strong. His arms hung at his
sides, utterly still. Boldly, she lifted her gaze to
his fathomless eyes. He made no move to touch
her. And then she reached up a tentative hand
and touched the hollow of his cheek.

Somewhere it must have been carved in the pil-
lars of time that he would hold her in an embrace
here on the shore under a half moon, his heart
thundering against hers like a thousand racing
stallions. That he would sweep her up into his
arms and carry her higher onto the broad, flat
beach, into the very shadow of the tower, and lay
her on a bed of sand that still held the heat of the
day's sun.

The scent of the sea and of warm flesh and laundry soap drifted up around her. She became dimly
aware that he'd laid her on his shirt.

Did Viking kings wear starched white shirts?

Did it really matter?

Neither of them spoke. Lying on his side next to
her, he traced the line of her jaw with one finger,
followed the throbbing pulse down her throat,
and then he was cradling her breast in the palm
of his hand.

Mariah breathed out a sigh and forgot to
breathe in again.

Her eyelids drifted shut, yet she could still see
him as clearly as if they were open wide, as if it
were broad daylight. When his hand moved below
her waist to caress her belly, his fingers brushing
the floss of her private place, she caught her

breath in a shuddering gasp. For one endless moment, neither of them moved. Was it her own heart she heard pounding in her breast, or was it his?

Or was it the sea?

She felt his heated touch on the cool flesh of her thigh, yet both his hands were on her breasts. Felt it surge against her once more, hot and hard and satiny smooth. He shifted slightly. She opened her eyes to gaze up at him just as he reached down and parted her thighs.

Her gown was twisted up around her waist—she was dimly aware of that, but far more aware of the raw, heedless compulsion that drove her to touch, to feel, to lift her hips off the hard, warm sand and seek her fate.

Strange . . . so strange . . . I knew it would be like this—this wild, sweet achy feeling—oh! Yes—yes—touch me there!

She shifted again, rose up to meet his exploring hand, conscious of heat and moisture and hardness. Pleasure swarmed around her, so near—never quite touching—and then came the pressure. It stung a little, but she wanted more of it, only . . .

Warnings whispered in her mind. She ignored them. This was right! She loved him, and surely he cared for her, too. How could he do these things if he didn't love her?

Restlessly, she moved against him and heard the quick, hoarse sound of his indrawn breath. What she felt now was more pressure than pleasure, yet she would die if he stopped.

He won't marry you. No decent man will ever marry you. What if he gets you with child? What then?

Hush! Take what he offers. It's all you'll ever have, but at least you'll have had this much.

"Stop—I can't—something's not right," she panted, and just like that, the spell was broken. The world stopped spinning and she was back on earth, lying in her nightgown on a bed of sand and a rumpled shirt. She was sticky, scratchy, aching, and mortally embarrassed.

Waite rolled off her immediately. He groaned. Sitting beside her, he drew up his knees and stared out to sea. She could hear the harsh sound of his breathing even above the noise of the surf.

Cool air settled on her bare limbs, chilling her in spite of the heat of the night. Reaching down, she tugged her nightgown over her as best she could, but it wasn't enough. She still felt . . . naked.

She wanted to die. To evaporate like a wisp of fog under a blazing sun. Knowing that was hardly likely, she forced herself to sit up and brush the sand from her hands, her face, her . . . everywhere.

How could you do such a thing, Mariah Sawyer?

But how could I not?

You know very well where lustful behavior leads! You, of all people, know the tragedy that can result from such selfishness!

For the first time she could almost understand what her parents had done. They had to have felt this same compelling magic.

But they'd both been fully aware of the risks they were taking, and had chosen to take them anyway. Waite didn't know about her past. Once she told him, he wouldn't want her anymore.

For the sake of her heart, Mariah told herself

that what she'd mistaken for love was only lust. A pure and simple case of physical infatuation.

Not that there'd been anything either pure or simple about it. The first time she'd felt it, when Waite had kissed her and touched her breast, she'd told herself it was love, but Mariah knew her biology. She'd read the book. And nothing she'd ever read could have prepared her for this wild, heedless fever that had struck without warning.

Lust, she thought miserably, was what often resulted in a child being born. A child who could have no real place in society. A child who would be called illegitimate without ever having transgressed the law.

"I'll have to leave," she said quietly.

"I'll see you home."

"No, I mean—here. The island. My position."

"Why?"

"Well . . . because."

She stood and then Waite did, too, and retrieved his clothes from where he'd flung them earlier. They were damp and sandy, and so was he. And so was she, and it was all his fault!

No, it wasn't. They were equally to blame. They and the moon and the sea. And this strain of wildness she'd inherited from her parents, just as she had inherited her mother's features and her father's coloring.

Waite struggled into his trousers, tossed his shirt over one shoulder, and followed her when she headed over the dunes. "Why did you lie?" he asked her.

At first he thought she hadn't heard him. With

the tide turning, the surf was beginning to pick up. "Why, Mariah?"

Refusing to look at him, she kept on walking. He didn't dare touch her, not when he was still hard and needy, and mad as hell about it all. "You've never been married. You're not a widow."

"You know nothing at all about me."

"I know damned well you've never lain with a man before. I know you're as much a maiden as the day you were born. I know no man could have been married to you and kept his hands off you— I know that much," he said bitterly.

She stopped then. They were halfway between the tower and the teacherage, alone except for the pony that whickered softly in the darkness. Every few seconds, the beam of light swept overhead, not touching them, making the night still darker by contrast.

"Then you might as well know the rest, hadn't you? And then you can go to Maxwell and he'll send me packing, and everyone will be happy. Is that what you want?" Her voice sounded raw, as if it hurt to speak. In the faint moonglow he could see the crooked trail of tears on her face.

"What happened tonight doesn't concern anyone but you and me. I want—no, I need to know the truth, Mariah."

Halting, Mariah lifted her face to the sky, closed her eyes, and drew in a deep, shuddering breath. Head held high, she said, "My parents were never married. That is, my father was, only not to my mother. They moved to Murfreesboro the year before I was born, and everyone took us for a decent, respectable family. Papa was president of the bank. Mama organized the Orphans' Benevolent Society. She gave wonderful parties, mostly for charity, and everyone loved her because she was so pretty and full of fun. Some people said they spoiled me because I was their only child. I never thought so, but Papa did allow me to go to college even though Mama thought it was silly because I'd never need to make my own way in the world."

She laughed, the sound hardly recognizable even to her own ears. Waite remained silent, waiting for her to continue. He didn't touch her. She would have shattered if he'd done that, and he probably knew it. "Well. I think I told you they drowned. Papa died trying to save Mama. He really did love her, even if he had no right—even if they shouldn't have . . ."

Her voice broke and then faded. She took another deep breath and said all in a rush: "It was Papa's lawyer who discovered the truth when he was trying to sort out his estate. He hadn't left a will, and you know—you know . . ." Desperately trying to maintain a fragment of dignity, she managed to get through the rest of the shoddy little melodrama.

About how she'd had a home, but no money. How she'd been hired to teach school before the truth came out, and then lost both her home and her position when it did. How she'd answered the advertisement from Maxwell and, in a moment of rebellion, used her mother's name, which was the only name that was legally hers to use, according to her father's lawyer.

"I never actually lied about being a widow. Maxwell discovered the discrepancy in names and drew his own conclusions. And I let him believe it, which is as good as lying. Or as bad."

Through it all, Waite remained silent. She couldn't look at him, and so she didn't know what he was thinking. Wouldn't have known even if she'd been staring him in the face in broad daylight.

Which was probably for the best.

"So there you have it. The sad little saga of a shameless spinster schoolmarm. If you don't want me to teach Nick, you have only to say so. I'll speak to Maxwell tomorrow. I should have done it a long time ago."

"Mariah, listen to me—"

She flung her hair over her shoulder, and in the momentary swash of light he caught a glimpse of her brittle smile. "I do despise self-pity, don't you? But I want you to know, I'm working on it. It's next on my list after thunder and water, and now that those are taken care of, I'm ready to—"

He caught her by the shoulders and shook her hard. She was almost glad he did, because she *hated* herself in this frame of mind! Mostly, she avoided it—self-pity—because really, she'd been most fortunate. What if she hadn't gotten a degree? She could have been doing other people's laundry, which would have been disastrous— she'd wash whites with colors and scorch everything she tried to iron, and—

When she started to laugh this time, Waite drew her into his arms and held her, rocking her gently until she broke off with a single sob. Neither of them felt like talking any longer. Waite felt his sexual nature begin to stir again, so he released her and began guiding her toward the teacherage.

"Wash the sand off and change your nightshift, but leave your door unlatched. I'll be back."

She looked at him, against all reason daring to hope, but he shook his head. "No, not that. You need something to help you sleep tonight. I keep some brandy on hand for emergencies."

When she started to protest, he said, "I want you to sleep late tomorrow. I'll send Nick out to pass the word that the teacher's ailing, so the children will know to stay home."

"Oh, but I'm not—"

"You'll need to rest up. There's a storm coming up the coast, the kind that takes some getting ready for. Now go wash the sand off, and we'll take things one at a time."

Back in the stuffy confines of her small blue room, Mariah bathed, changed into a clean dry gown, and brushed the sand from her hair. She dabbed cologne on her wrists and throat, and then washed it off again in case he thought . . .

But he didn't come, and he didn't come, and after a while she went to bed, too discouraged to hope any longer.

He'd changed his mind about her. Well, what else had she expected?

Mariah slept until the sweltering heat woke her up the next morning. The rooster had done his truncated best, her laying hen had announced her daily achievement, and she dimly remembered hearing a dog bark and thinking that either Precious had been found or another dog had taken up residence in the neighborhood.

With a groan, she covered her eyes and dozed for another few minutes before finally dragging herself from bed. At first she thought it was Sunday, but there was her best bonnet, right where she'd left it after church yesterday.

Which meant it must be Monday. Which meant she was late for school!

And then she remembered it all. Everything. Every mortifying word and deed.

If she'd thought it was even faintly possible, she'd have wished herself back to the beginning so that she could start all over again. To the day she'd arrived on the island. Or perhaps the day she was born?

Listlessly, she wandered into the other room, and there on the trunk by the window was a bottle with several ounces of spirits. Beside it was a note that said simply, "Sorry. You were asleep. W."

Well, drat! If she'd had the energy she would have wept. Or cursed. Or at the very least kicked something and probably broken a toe.

There wasn't a cloud in the sky. So much for the promised storm. She was actually disappointed. A storm, at least, would have taken her mind off her problems, which seemed to have multiplied overnight.

She was still feeling listless, headachy, and undecided as to her course of action when Evie arrived later that day with a basket of food and another of socks to darn. "Miss Caroline's gone to visit Pa again, and it's only Monday," she announced dolefully, "so I made Dore take me with him when he rode out after dinner. He don't much like Miss Caroline. Baxter and Able, they like her just fine, but I don't and Dore don't and Frankie don't. Caleb, he don't say much. Mostly he's worried about when the fishin'll pick up again.

Frankie said once the wind shifts, he'll have more spot 'n' sea mullet 'n' speckled trout than he can haul in, but don't nobody pay much attention to Frankie."

She paused for breath, and then she said, "Miz M'riah, you don't look too good."

"Fortunately, I don't feel nearly as awful as I look," Mariah assured her, smiling in spite of her throbbing head and scratchy eyes. Disappointment and hot, restless nights weren't known for their beautifying effects. "What have we here?" She lifted the napkin covering the larger basket and expressed her delight over the sweet potato biscuits, watermelon rind preserves, and cold ham.

"We heard school was out today on account of you were ailin'."

"I do believe I'm already feeling better," Mariah declared. "Why don't I make us a pot of tea and we'll share an early supper."

As the afternoon passed, the sky clouded over and the wind and water both began to rise. Evie and Mariah, intent on far more important matters, hardly even noticed. They spoke woman to woman of things every girl should know, such as how to deal with spots and the monthly stomach cramps that Evie had heard whispered about but had not yet experienced.

They talked about men—boys, in Evie's case—and how underneath all the braggadocio, most of them were as insecure as anyone else, and must be tolerated until they grew up and became civilized. They talked about pianos and parlor organs.

And finally they talked about the advances in medical technology that made it possible for someone with Evie's affliction to be fitted with a special cork-soled shoe that would even the length of her limbs, and of possible exercises that could help. "Caleb asked Pa about sending off for one of them special shoes once, but Pa said it weren't no use puttin' money in nothing like that when my feet's still changin' size. He says to remind him and he'll think about it once I stop growin'."

Mariah swallowed her immediate reaction. Neither of them had mentioned the bruises still visible, and she reminded herself that trust had to be built slowly, one brick at a time.

Evie pulled another of her brothers' socks from the basket, poked the darning gourd into the toe, and set to reweaving the hole. The wind had been whining and whistling for some time. Mariah first noticed it when a bucket that had been turned down over a post near the shed blew off with a clatter. Both young women glanced up, startled, Evie with a sock in one hand, a needle and thread in the other; Mariah with a lap full of the beans she'd been shelling.

Just then the rain began, not with a sprinkle but with a solid sheet of water. The sky was a dark greenish gray, and Mariah glanced at her watch. It was only a few minutes past four. She'd lit a lamp earlier when she'd noticed Evie squinting over her task.

"When was Dorien coming for you?" Mariah asked. "When it slacks off, perhaps I'd better hitch up and drive you home. Imagine—the sky was perfectly clear when I stepped outside to feed the chickens just before you arrived."

Evie limped over to the window. Her eyes grew round as marbles. "Miz M'riah, come look."

And Mariah did. "Merciful saints in heaven, what's happening?"

"Sea tide's running over again. Able said there was a storm on the way, only he said it likely wouldn't get here before tomorrow. I better get on home. Pa'll skin me."

"You can't go out in this. What on earth was your brother thinking of? Surely he'll come for you before long."

"Dore, he said he was headed up the beach. He'll likely not remember."

"But your father—"

"Oh, Pa won't be thinkin' of nobody but Miss Caroline. She's tryin' to make him marry her. Leastwise, she hasn't said so right out, but a woman can tell. When he's around, she fusses over me and carries on about how a little girl needs a mother, but once he leaves the room, she don't even like me very much. And I don't like her, either. She don't even treat her dog nice."

"Oh, Lord, poor little Precious. He disappeared yesterday, and I forgot all about him, and now, with water everywhere—"

"Mr. Jones found him. He said he was muddy an' all full of briars and ticks, so he gave him a bath and a bowl of cow's milk, but Miss Caroline whupped him all the same. If he was my puppy, I wouldn't ever whup him. I don't like whuppings, do you?"

At the moment, what Mariah would have liked most of all was a dose of Waite's medicinal brandy, never mind the headache that would result from it. It would have to wait, though. "No, I don't, dear. As for the tide, I'm beginning to get used to it by now. The other night when we had all that awful lightning and thunder, the water came almost up to my doorsill."

The truth was, she would never get used to it. At the moment, her inclination was to stand up on a chair and scream for help, but that probably wouldn't set a particularly heroic example.

"We don't never have to worry about tide. Pa's house is built on a real high ridge."

"Yes, well . . . my house is built on the edge of a swamp."

"I reckon we better lay your dresses up on your bed to keep the bottoms from gettin' wet if it comes inside. We can set ever'thing else up on chairs and dressers."

Mariah got the idea, but surely it wouldn't come to that. Any moment now the rain would stop and the wind would die down, and then the water would go back where it belonged.

However, she calmly set about doing what Evie suggested because she was an adult and there was a child here who looked to her for guidance.

They worked together as darkness fell. The rain continued to beat deafeningly against the house. From time to time Mariah thought she heard horses racing past, and once she glanced out and saw lanterns bobbing over on the shore, but by then she had more than enough worries of her own. The tide was still rising and the rain was still falling. Evie was calm as could be, which made Mariah ashamed of herself, because as busy as she was, she'd managed to chew her fingernails to the quick. They'd just grown back after the journey out on the mailboat.

By the time Waite came for her, she had emptied her trunk, piling the contents on her bed along with the gowns that had been hanging in a corner of her room. She'd removed the bottom drawer and set it on top of her dresser, following Evie's instructions. Rain was beating in around the windows. Evie found towels, twisted them into ropes, and spread them along the sills. There were two leaks in the roof, but Evie said if the tide was coming in anyway, there was no point in setting out pots to catch the drip, which Mariah thought was eminently sensible. And said so, with scarcely even a tremor in her voice.

Neither of them heard the pounding on the door. Suddenly it was flung open, and Waite, accompanied by a gust of wet, howling wind, burst inside.

"Are you all right?"

"I—I think so," Mariah said breathlessly. Lord, the man was magnificent, even soaked to the skin with his hair dripping over his face.

"Then come along. We'd best get the two of you out of here. My place is bursting at the seams, but it's on higher ground, and it's as sound a place as any you'll find on the island."

Mariah's eyes rounded. Evie, standing in the bedroom door, nodded mutely. Waite looked from one to the other and said, "Miss Evie, I'll carry you, since you're the shortest. Tide's cut some sand out, and I wouldn't want you to disappear. Mrs. Deekins can hang on to my shirttail and you watch to see she follows along behind us."

"Bursting at the seams?" Mariah repeated.

"I'll watch her real good," the child said earnestly.

"Survivors. Ship foundered in the bight. Might be another one out there. Durants and Big Kinnekeet stations have called in all men, but they've both got their hands full. We're handling those close by.''

With a sweeping glance around the two rooms, he nodded, then swept Evie up in his arms. ''Follow me, Mariah,'' he said, and she knew she would have followed him to the ends of the earth, more's the pity.

Chapter Seventeen

Not until they reached the keeper's quarters, where several lamps were lit, did Mariah realize that Waite had been injured. There was a strip of white sheeting wrapped across his chest, clearly visible under his shirt. But before she could inquire about that, she was distracted by the babble of voices coming from the back of the house.

Sarvice America Jones poked his head through the doorway and said, "Nick says he needs you to set a feller's collarbone."

Without a word, Waite left the two women standing there, cold and wet and frightened. "It's all right, Evie," Mariah tried to sound reassuring, but she was sorely in need of reassurance herself.

"I hope nobody drownded. Last winter they say Mr. McKenna had to go out in his boat and pick the crew of the *Rebecca Mary* right off'n the rigging when she broke up off the point."

There was a fire burning brightly in the grate, despite the hissing of raindrops from the chimney. Evie led Mariah over to stand in front of the small brick opening. They were both soaked to the skin from the short journey across the grounds.

"What about the Lifesaving Service? Aren't they supposed to do that sort of thing?"

"Mostly they work through the winter months. Other times, they live at home. They'll go out—times like this, ever' able-bodied man that's got his own folks took care of pitches in—but it takes longer when they're not living at the station."

Mariah warmed her front, then turned and warmed her backside, lifting her bedraggled skirt to allow the heat to get through to her limbs. Steam arose, and she stepped away from the hearth. "Surely there's something I can do to help."

"They'll be hungry. Could be some that needs doctorin'. I'll help."

"My dear, it might be better if you were to stay here." She looked around, finding nothing more comfortable than a straight-backed chair.

From the kitchen at the back of the house came the sound of a groan and then a masculine yelp. Evie gave a satisfied nod. "Popped it right back in place," she said. "I seen it happen before. Miz M'riah, I growed up in a house full o' menfolk. There's not much I've not seen nor done when one o' my brothers is ailin'."

"Which is more than I can say, I suppose." Mariah surrendered gracefully. "Come along, then, we'll see if we can help out."

A few feet away from the orderly front room, chaos reigned. The small, overheated kitchen was crowded with strangers, some talking a mile minute, some staring numbly at the wall—one clutching his hand and swearing softly under his breath. The same words, over and over.

"Ma'am, you ortened to be here," Sarvice said.

"I need whuskey! My shoulder's busted wide open!" one of the rescued seamen called out.

"Long as you're here, ma'am, hold this for me, will you?" Sarvice, finished with sewing up a long gash in a seaman's upper arm, held out a roll of bandage while he dusted powder along the jagged wound. Her stomach threatening rebellion, Mariah took the roll and stood by for further instructions.

Over the next few hours she bandaged, helped splint, consoled, and helped feed the five lucky seamen who had made it to shore from the wrecked coaster. Three others had perished. When she agreed to write a letter for one of the victims, others quickly chimed in, wanting letters written, telegraphs sent, and she promised that as soon as everyone was taken care of properly she would find paper and pen and take down their messages.

Evie was kept busy boiling coffee and baking and splitting biscuits, filling them with cold meat, mustard, and cheese. Her clumsy gait didn't seem to hamper her in the least.

Nick was invaluable, bringing in pails of water from the cistern, gathering stacks of bedding from upstairs to make pallets near the fires, finding a supply of dry clothing, and then helping the men change behind a hastily erected screen. When a shingle blew off the roof of the house next door and struck a window, breaking the glass and allowing rain to blow into the room, it was Nick who made temporary repairs. Mariah was beginning to see why the lighthouse crew kept a supply of glass on hand.

A groan from close by alerted her and she grabbed a basin and held it for the poor devil who'd gulped down too much raw whiskey on top of a bellyful of salt water, then tenderly wiped his face with a wet cloth sweetened with peppermint oil, as her mother had done for her more than once when she'd been sick with a stomach ailment.

She hardly had time to glance up when Waite left the house. When she found a moment to ask after him, Sarvice told her he'd gone down to the shore to see if he could spot any more survivors.

"In this storm? Isn't that dangerous?"

"If it weren't stormin', there wouldn't be no reason to search. Can't launch a boat till morning—maybe not even then, less'n things calm down some. Wouldn't even get out past the breakers in these seas."

Mariah could hardly believe anyone in his right mind would be out there in all this wildness, much less consider launching a boat. "But the beach—everything's flooded," she protested.

"There's high places. He'll wave a lantern and wait for a break in the wind to see if he hears a shout. He's carryin' a line and a life ring." And without skipping a beat, he added, "I don't reckon Evie said nothing about Miss Caroline. She'd not come home last time I checked."

"She was visiting Maxwell. Evie left after she'd cooked dinner. She said they were looking through the catalog, pricing pianos and parlor organs."

They spoke softly, but with all the noise both outside and inside the room, there was little chance of being overheard. "Then I reckon he'll be obliged to marry her," the farmer-turned-lighthouse-keeper said dolefully. "It's done gone past midnight already."

"You mean her brother will insist? Where is he, by the way? Out helping with the rescue?"

"Standing watch in the tower. Times like these, with the wind and all, one of us always rides out the storm up there in case the lamp goes out."

"But surely Mr. Hardraker doesn't think Caroline's been compromised just because she spent a night away from home."' Could a pregnant single woman be compromised all over again? Did it really matter? "In this storm, with the roads flooded, he couldn't possibly expect her to risk drowning when she's safe on high ground."

"There was time enough before things got too bad if she'd wanted to come home. The tide come up fast, but ever'body knew it was coming. Even when a storm don't strike head-on, there's usually some tide."

"Yes, but Caroline might not have realized—"

"Newbolt did. She knew what she was doing, all right. If you ask me, she done it a-purpose."

There was nothing Mariah could say to that. She suspected Sarvice had it right. If what he'd told her was true, the woman desperately needed a husband, and this was as good a way as any to trap one. The irony was that Maxwell, from talk she'd heard in the village, was every bit as anxious to find a wife, which should have worked out to both their advantages, only Mariah had a feeling the two of them would make a terrible match.

"Poor Evie," she murmured, and went to rinse out the basin. Pausing beside Nick, who was tapping the barometer and frowning, she said quietly, "I don't think we need to be quite so generous with the whiskey, do you? Everyone seems to be recovering. A few of them are beginning to show signs of overindulgence."

He flashed her a grin that was surprisingly adult, and it occurred to her that overnight he had turned from a prank-playing youth into a mature young man. "They'll call for it. I'll water it down some, or add it to coffee. Weather's not all that cold, but when a man's been through something like this, he needs a jolt of liquid heat to set him on his feet again."

"I'd say it's more apt to set him on his back." She nodded to indicate a burly seaman who had toppled over where he sat against the far wall and was snoring loudly.

"That'n had more than most. Pa had to cauterize a place that got tore up real bad when a barrel o' salt meat come down on his shoulder and busted it wide open. Not enough whiskey in the world to take the sting out of carbolic acid on a raw wound." He flexed his own bony shoulders, glanced past her, and said, "Pressure's startin' to rise. Reckon the worst is over."

"I hope you're right. It's still dark as pitch outside, and the wind sounds as if it's going to come right through the door."

"Almost as scary as a rosum string or a pair o' conchs, huh?"

As tired as she was, Mariah had to laugh at that. "Even scarier than an earthquake." There was a silent understanding between them that Mariah found profoundly affecting.

Evie hobbled past, holding the big gray enameled coffeepot with both hands wrapped in a towel. Her face was paler than usual, and it occurred to Mariah that the child should have been in bed hours before now.

Evidently, Nick thought so, too. "Evie, you better set a spell now, else you won't be fit to cook breakfast," he said quietly, removing the heavy pot from her hands.

For one stark moment, the young girl looked up at the handsome youth, her heart in her eyes. Mariah ached for her. There were some problems that no amount of womanly advice could solve.

And then, in a gust of warm, wet air, Waite came in through the back door, his shirt plastered to his body, the bandage she'd noticed earlier stained with blood. "Wind's shifted," he said tiredly. "Tide's startin' to back down. Nick, pour me a jar of coffee and throw a few biscuits in a poke, and I'll take 'em up to the tower. I doubt if Hardraker thought to take anything up with him."

Mariah's concerned gaze followed him as he crossed to the stove, lifted a lid on the enormous soup pot, and set adrift in the room the heavenly aroma of ham and tomatoes.

One of the men called out, "I'll take a bowl o' that there soup if you're offerin'."

"Me, too," chimed another.

"Yeah, me, too."

Nick said, "Sounds like they like your cookin', Rustmop."

Evie blushed and ducked her head. "It's only just a ol' hambone I found in the cool house, with 'maters and onions and beans." The enticing smell of food seemed to underline the feeling of camaraderie in the cluttered room. At least it helped overcome the smell of the wet clothing that hung from makeshift drying lines, from the backs of chairs, and from nails all around the walls.

Mariah had no notion of how much time had passed. Minutes turned to hours, which, for all she knew, could have turned to days. The wind had subsided to a low, nerve-wracking whine, which nevertheless was an improvement. The last time she'd noticed, it had been howling like a thousand banshees. Rain still beat against the windows in bursts, but it, too, had lost some of its driving force.

Busy tending the superficial cuts on the hand of a wiry little man who looked too old to be earning his living as a seaman, Mariah allowed her tired mind to touch briefly on Caroline and Maxwell, wondering if there would be an interesting announcement once the emergency was past.

She wondered if Caroline had told Maxwell about her condition. Her desperate need of a husband was understandable, but Mariah knew better than most how miserable it was to live a lie, even knowing that the truth would mean an end to her dreams.

Oh, the webs we weave, she mused tiredly. Her thoughts turned to Nick and the side of him she'd seen tonight. Even as a newcomer, one heard things and saw things and formed certain opinions. There were fewer than a thousand people on the entire island, scattered among several villages—only a few hundred in Buxton—but it hadn't taken her long to discover that Waite McKenna had scant respect for outsiders and none at all for what he termed city women. And that his son took after him in that respect.

Perhaps it was endemic on the island. Maxwell's sons—the eldest two, at least—seemed to think that women were put on earth to serve men's needs. She rather thought Caroline Hardraker might change a few opinions in that particular household. Time would tell.

Meanwhile, she was beginning to believe she might have been mistaken about the McKennas. But there again, time would tell.

The scent of coffee, whiskey, wet garments, and carbolic acid blended with the aroma of hambone soup as Evie, ignoring Nick's advice, began ladling out steaming bowls.

"O'er here, gimpy. An' bring me some whiskey while ye're at it."

The words fell into a sudden pool of silence. Nick's head came up. Slowly, he turned and speared the survivor with eyes that were as cold and hard as any Arctic ice. "I hope I misheard what you just said, mister." His voice was quiet. Too quiet.

"Soup. All I wants is some o' that there soup and some whiskey," the man whined.

Mariah held her breath. It seemed as if everyone in the room was doing the same. Evie, her face pale with exhaustion, looked both embarrassed and resigned. She began to dip another bowl of soup. "I don't know what went with the whiskey bottle," she murmured.

"No," said Nick.

"Son," Waite said, his voice a quiet warning.

Mariah stepped between them and took the bowl from Evie's small hands. Turning to the seaman, she said, "Here you are, sir. If I were you, I'd mind my manners. Tempers are inclined to be short under the circumstances."

The man took the bowl, not meeting her eyes. "Sorry, boy," he muttered. "Didn't mean no harm. Reckon I've had me enough whiskey after all."

"It's not about the whiskey."

"I said I wuz sorry, didn't I?"

"I don't need your apologies. Miss Newbolt does."

"Nick, don't," Evie wailed softly. Mariah thought the whole matter would be best dropped, but this didn't concern her, it was between Nick and the rescued seaman. Or the seaman and Evie.

Or Evie and Nick . . .

"Sorry, ma'am—uh, Miss," the man finally grumbled.

The night ended, as nights inevitably did. Mariah sat up in the bed she'd shared with Evie, feeling stiff and rumpled, and, after sorting through the events of the evening, rose and hobbled stiffly across to a window. From the floor below she could hear the sounds of snoring, sleepy muttering, and the occasional thump as the household came awake.

Outside, the sky was an incredibly lovely shade of pale turquoise, touched here and there with small pink clouds. Impossible, she thought. The world couldn't change so swiftly.

Yet she, of all people, should know that it could indeed, and sometimes did. She looked around at Waite's bedroom. She'd slept in his bed. Those were his books on the shelves—more of them than even she possessed. There was a locker at the foot of the bed, but nothing of a more personal nature. What a very private man he was.

She sighed.

"Pa's gonna kill me," Evie said tearfully behind her.

That was the sound that had woken her, Mariah realized. The child had been sobbing quietly. She hurried across the room and knelt to take the frail young girl in her arms. "Darling, he won't! He'll be so glad you're safe and sound, he'll—"

"Kill me. I'm ruint. I weren't there to cook his supper and I weren't there to make his breakfast, and he'll know I been out all night, and—"

"Evie, listen to me. There was no way you could possibly have gone home. Even before the rain started, the tide was up over the road. By the time we thought to look out, the storm was already upon us, don't you remember? Besides, Miss Hardraker probably cooked supper." Evie just looked at her. "Well . . . perhaps not."

"Tide always comes up fast. Ever'body knows when one o' these storms comes up from the Caribbean"—she pronounced it *Carry Bean*—"we're in for a mommickin' even if it don't hit square on. If it passes offshore, we get sea tide. If it comes up over by the mainland, we get sound tide. There's just too much water and not enough land."

"All the same—" Mariah began, but the child refused to be consoled.

"I knew it was coming. I shouldn't never have left home, but Dore said he was fixin' to ride out and look at the surf, and I asked him to take me and drop me off at your place, and we got to talkin', and Dore, he forgot to come back, and now Pa'll be mad at him, too."

There was no reassuring the child. To Mariah's way of thinking, there'd been no wrongdoing at

all, under the circumstances, but Maxwell was a
stickler for propriety. "I'll simply tell your father
that you spent the night with me. There's certainly
nothing out of the way about that."

"He'll know we didn't stay over there."

"How could he know that?"

" 'Cause ever'body knows whenever the tide
comes up, the teacher's house is like to be floated
off the pilings. There was talk about building it
too close to the marsh. Some said it weren't set
up high enough off the ground, but Pa said it
settled lower on account of the ground's soggy
there."

Mariah didn't know whether to be angry or
amused. That would explain why her floor always
felt as if it sloped to the back. It probably did. The
blooming place was sinking in the muck!

"Shall we see if there's water in the pitcher? My
face feels as if it'd been slept in."

Evie managed a tearful chuckle at her feeble
joke. They washed and brushed as best they could
with the meager provisions. Mariah didn't have
a single hairpin left. Goodness knows what had
become of them. She braided her long, poker-
straight hair, straightened her shirtwaist, and
shook out the worst of the wrinkles from her
stained skirt. Her shoes, of course, were ruined
and still wet, but she wore them anyway.

By the time they arrived downstairs, Nick was
waiting.

"G'morning, ma'am—Evie. If you're ready,
Rusty, I'll ride you home. Ginger don't mind
wading."

Ginger was his pony, Mariah did know that.
She also knew he rode like the wind, usually

whooping and hollering like someone from a Wild West show. But it was a sober Nicholas who stood before them this morning. "Nick, is everyone all right? Did anything else happen after we went up to bed?"

Is your father all right? she wanted to ask, because if he wasn't, then nothing was right with the world.

"Sherman—he's the one with the busted-open shoulder—he's come down with a fever. I thought I'd ride Evie home and then see if Miss Agnes would come look at him. The others, far as I can tell, are no worse off than they were last night, 'ceptin' maybe for a few swollen heads from too much drinkin'."

"Where's your father?"

"He's gone up with Sarvice to check over the tower. We had a piece of glass that was already cracked. It's real special; takes a while to get a replacement ordered and sent out. Claude come down about five and turned in, he's plumb wore out. Didn't even think to ask where Miss Caroline was."

Nick shot a quick look at Evie, who was fingering a neatly darned place on her skirt, but he addressed his words to Mariah. "Ma'am, it's a right rough bunch in there. Coal haulers from up north. I can see you home if you're ready, else you can stay here in the office until Pa gets back."

Such chivalry from a lad who had done his best to drive her away? Mariah, marveling at the change brought on by the emergency, declined his offer. "I'll stay until either your father or Sarvice comes back in case one of the men needs something. You go ahead—I know Evie will feel better once she's explained to her father why she wasn't able to get home last night."

Nick looked skeptical. Evie looked miserable. Mariah could only take one thing at a time and hope for the best. If she had to deal with Maxwell, then deal she would. No father would want his daughter to risk drowning just to get home in time to cook his supper. And after all, hadn't Caroline been stranded there, as well?

Stepping outside, Nick whistled. A moment later a shaggy sorrel came trotting across the sodden grounds from the nearby woods. Apologizing for not having a saddle, he lifted Evie onto the horse's back and then swung up behind her. It occurred to Mariah as she watched the pair ride off that the poor child wouldn't be doing too much worrying about her father, not with Nick's arm around her waist.

The yard was filled with puddles, the road, as far as she could see, still submerged. The shrubs, mostly yaupon and wax myrtle, looked as if they were cowering amid the sparse patches of wild grass that had been flattened by wind, rain, and tide. Everywhere she looked there was debris, mostly broken branches. A few bits of lumber had washed up and lodged against the garden fence. Halfway between the keeper's houses and the teacherage she saw something that looked almost like a nest box.

"Oh, my mercy, my poor chickens!" She'd forgotten all about them. Bending over to untie her shoes to wade across and see if they'd been blown away, she heard one of the men call out from the kitchen. "Ma'am, if you're not busy, could you come look at my foot? I think it's festerin'. It feels hot and throbs something fierce."

Her chickens, it seemed, would have to wait their turn. She was still at it—changing bandages, handing around cold biscuits and hot coffee, and offering to get word to families, when one of the men—the same one who had called Evie gimpy—summoned her to examine the place on his hand where he'd torn it on a bit of stranded cable.

Arming herself with a roll of bandage and a jar of carbolated ointment, she went to examine his injury, telling herself the man couldn't help being a stupid fool. Some people were insensitive. It didn't mean they were intentionally cruel.

She leaned over to take a closer look and felt something brush against her hip. The room was crowded, and some of the men were beginning to move around, to see to their own needs. "It's badly bruised," she murmured. "Let me wash the dried blood away and we'll see what it . . ."

Feeling something touch the small of her back, she reached back to swat it away. Someone behind her laughed. Feeling a hand close over her buttock, she gasped and stood up, wondering if she could have imagined it. But then she felt her skirt and petticoat fall back into place and realized that someone—she didn't know which one—had carefully lifted them while her attention was engaged, folding them up over her back when she'd bent over.

She jumped back, spinning around to glare at the culprit. Every man in the room was watching her. "You wicked, ungrateful wretches!"

One of the younger seamen began to laugh. Reaching out, he caught her around the waist.

"Them's about the purtiest drawers I seen in many a day, ain't that right, Cornie?"

And then everything seemed to happen at once. Waite appeared in the doorway, looking like nothing so much as an avenging angel. "Get your goddamned hand away from her!" With one blow, he knocked the man cold. Then, turning his attention to the man with the injured hand—the one called Cornie—he lifted him by the shirtfront and said in a voice that was too soft, too calm, "As soon as the road's clear, you're moving out, the lot of you. I don't give a damn in hell where you go. You're not staying here."

"Hey, we didn't mean no harm, mister. It ain't like she's your wife or nothin'. We wouldn't disrespect no married lady, but the other feller said she's a widder woman."

"Shut your filthy mouth," Waite said with the same quiet intensity, while Mariah stood, aghast, beside the door. "The liquor's where you won't find it. There's food on the stove and coffee in the pot. If you want anything you'll have to get it yourself, because from now on, you're on your own. Be ready to move out as soon as the roads are clear."

Then, his dark eyes blazing in a face that could have been carved from stone, he extended his arm to Mariah and escorted her from the room.

Chapter Eighteen

She could have wept. When Waite opened her door and Mariah saw her slimy floors and the muddy watermark on her bright blue walls, she could have sat right down and cried her eyes out.

But of course, she didn't.

"I'm sorry, Mariah. It'll scrub off."

"I suppose the house could've washed away. Or perhaps that would've been an improvement." A gulp of laughter that was half sob escaped her. "I'll help clean up."

"You'll do no such thing. You're injured, you haven't slept—you haven't even taken time to change your dressing, have you? What happened, anyway?"

"It's nothing. Just a scratch."

She had a feeling he would have said as much if his chest had been split wide open and his heart removed, like one of those awful sacrificial rituals she'd read about in a recent archaeological report.

They stood there in the wet, musty room, brown eyes searching clear gray ones, each yearning for something for which neither of them dared reach out. Mariah said, "Well, then . . . I'm sure you have dozens of things that need doing right now."

"Nothing that can't wait."

"Waite, there's no need, honestly. I might be only a helpless female, but I do know how to mop a floor." She managed a rueful smile. "In another few years, I might even get good at it."

"About that lowlife, what he did—what he said—"

She reached up and placed a finger over his lips. "Don't. It was embarrassing, but I'm not so fragile I can't survive a bit of embarrassment. We both have better things to do than worry over trivial matters." She wanted to erase the dark scowl from his face.

"Yes, but—"

"Hush, now. The first thing you have to do," she went on without pausing, "is change that bandage. Have Sarvice help you. He's surprisingly good at it."

"Yes, ma'am." The scowl faded some, but didn't quite disappear. "I'll get back over here directly. And Mariah—in case I forgot to thank you—"

She interrupted him. "For allowing you to rescue me from the storm? If you want to show your appreciation, then go home and go to bed. And don't set the alarm for half an hour! Look at you, you're worn to a frazzle!"

Mariah heard with a sense of wonder the voices of her mother, her teachers—Bathsheba and even old Elmo. All those who had looked after her and admonished her while she was growing up. And now, without knowing quite when it had happened, she'd become a full-fledged adult, entitled to scold others for their own good.

After waving Waite off, she lingered in the doorway, gazing out over the changed landscape.

The tower still stood, like a tall, stark guardian angel, but most of the low dunes were gone, washed clean away. There were small channels cut through the sand. The marshes were beaten down, and a scrubby cedar that only yesterday had stood on the edge of the marsh was uprooted. Several pines were broken off. The pungent smell of crushed foliage and drowned earth reminded her of the flowers near the pond, and she wondered if any of them had survived.

Probably not, but they'd come back. The wonder was that she herself had survived. Not only survived her first tropical storm on this fragile barrier island, but made herself useful.

Waite was halfway across the clearing when he suddenly turned back. Lord, he was beautiful, she marveled, waiting until he came closer to ask if he'd forgotten something. Sunlight glinted off his thick, golden hair. Barefoot, exhausted, his clothes little more than filthy, sodden rags, he was still the most magnificent man she'd ever known. If another storm had come roaring up from the Caribbean that very moment, she was quite certain she couldn't have moved to save her soul.

But the storm that struck was of another kind, far more devastating than mere wind, tide, and rain. Without saying a word, he reached out and pulled her against his body, crushing her against his wet shirt, his bloodstained bandage. She thought she heard him groan, but then he was kissing her and nothing else registered, neither sight nor sound nor scent. With a rough magic that swept her under its spell, he claimed her, body and soul, using weapons against which she had no defense. While his hands moved restlessly over her back, cupping her nape, pressing her soft belly against his hardening loins, his tongue broke the seal of her lips and began to explore, gently at first, then forcefully. Not until she was clinging to reason by a fast-unraveling thread did he lift his mouth from hers.

He looked stunned, but no more than she did.

As if helpless to resist, he lowered his head again and began brushing his lips back and forth over hers, soft, moist flesh dragging over soft, moist flesh. Helplessly, she strained against him, standing on tiptoe. Wrapping her arms tightly around his neck, she pressed closer, wanting more. Wanting all of him. Wanting things she only dimly understood, and wanting them *now*.

Several moments passed before she realized that he was carefully lifting her arms from around his neck. Wilting in shame, she let him set her away.

"Mariah, I'm sorry—I didn't mean—"

"Don't say it. Just don't you dare say anything! It's—it's the storm, is all. Heightened emotions—it always happens."

It had never happened to her before. She might hide her head under a pillow and wait it out, or play her mother's piano, crashing chords loud enough to drown out the thunder, but she had never forgotten herself so far as to want a man's hands on her breasts, on her most private parts.

And she'd wanted it, oh, yes, she had. Wanted him to do those things to her that he'd done that night on the beach, things that had made her feel as if rainbows were blooming inside her body.

"I have work to do," she said sternly, "and so do you." Stepping back, she brushed a hand down her skirt, as if smoothing the wrinkles there would somehow make all the untidy wrinkles in her life disappear.

The look he gave her could have burned through stone. It certainly did little to restore her poise. Good heavens, she thought, contemplating the rigid set of his shoulders as he strode away, splashing through puddles, kicking aside storm debris—as if she hadn't managed to muddle up her life quite enough without committing this ultimate folly.

While Mariah looped her skirts up, knotted them about her knees, and set to cleaning up the sodden, smelly mess left behind by the receding tide, Waite made arrangements to remove the contingent of survivors to the village. Rhoda Quigley had room enough to house the lot until a boat could come for them. He would warn her to set a few rules. Seamen who'd been shipwrecked, injured, and under the influence of too much medicinal spirits could be tough customers.

He paid the bill in advance from his own pocket, knowing the men had nothing but the rags on their backs. Eventually there might be insurance money, but it would go to the shipowner, not the crew. Little, if any, would find its way to the Outer Banks. Not that anyone expected to be rewarded for hauling survivors ashore. Still, Rhoda lived close to the bone. There weren't many boarders at the best of times, and this crew, once they got over their initial shock, would eat her out of house and home before she could get shed of them. They'd damn near emptied his own larder in the few hours they'd been under his roof.

Waite followed a routine he'd maintained for as

long as he'd been in charge of Cape Hatteras light. After any storm, there was always enough to do to keep all hands busy.

Enough so that he didn't have time to waste dwelling on what was happening—or rather, on what he was afraid had already happened to him. Methodically, he inspected and made notes on the damage. There were shingles missing from both roofs and one bent lightning rod. Sarvice located two sections of garden fence nearly a quarter of a mile away. The lifeboat he'd hauled up for caulking and repainting had been stove in by a tide-driven set-net stake. More work to do.

The tower, thank God, was still sound as far as Waite could tell, but the rain had beaten in through the damaged section of glass. There was seaweed draped over the balcony rail—it had been one hell of a blow—but she'd managed to survive the lightning strike a few years back except for a few internal cracks, and the earthquake last month that had done little damage. She was a tough old lady. If anything ever brought her down, it would be the sea.

Only after he'd made the rounds and written his meticulous reports did Waite allow himself to consider the problem of Mariah.

And problem she was. God help him, he was falling in love with the woman. It was happening to him all over again. He could have sworn he'd outgrown such foolishness before he'd ever reached his majority. Evidently he hadn't learned a damned thing. At the age of thirty-three, he had no more sense than a baby loggerhead fresh out of the egg.

Not even as much. At least a baby turtle had

sense enough to make for the safety of the sea the minute it hatched and crawled up out of its sandy nest. Didn't matter where on the shore the nest was located, the little blighters always headed instinctively for the open sea, scrambling to escape flying predators.

Evidently, Waite thought with bleak amusement, his own survival instincts, if he'd ever had any, had shut down. Not even the example set by his own mother had been enough to keep him from making the same mistake his father had made. She'd lit out for the mainland before Waite had even turned six and had never been heard of again as far as he knew.

There was just something about Mariah he found impossible to resist. Part of it was the way she looked—the way she dressed, all buttoned up prim and proper. She even smelled different from most of the women he knew, not like plain lye soap and honest cotton, but like silk and sachets and soft, sexy nights.

Constance had liked a heavy perfume. Mariah's was more subtle. He didn't know about his mother. It had been so long ago. . . .

She'd been from somewhere up north. He could no longer remember her face, much less the sound of her voice, but he did know she'd had a different way of speaking. Constance had grown up in New Orleans. She'd had an accent all her own, and it was different, too. Like sorghum pouring slow from a pitcher. Like melted butter.

That is, until after they were married. After that it hadn't sounded quite so fine.

Waite would be the first to admit that he still found something foreign and exotic about the few city women he'd met since his wife had died. They came down to the Banks now and then. Every few years one or two would show up, and rumors would fly, mostly among the younger men who hadn't seen much of the outside world.

After the war, a number of Yankees who'd been billeted on Hatteras Island with the Union troops had come back, looking for easy pickings. Found some, too. Bought up acres of land for little or nothing. Occasionally they'd brought their women with them. It was always good for speculation and conversation. Growing up in a place where everyone knew everyone else, and most of the folks were kin, novelty had its appeal.

Waite had done his share of looking and speculating over the years. As a single man, he liked looking at pretty women as much as the next man. Until recently, he'd been content to look without touching.

The trouble was, Mariah looked like a city woman and smelled like one and sounded like one. What she didn't do was act like one. And that was damned disobliging of her. He'd been wary right off, but then, what with one thing and another, he'd let her slip in under his guard, and now he was caught. Trapped like loon in a gill net. He wanted her worse than he wanted his own freedom, but having her and then losing her would be worse than not having her at all.

And lose her he would, in the end. It was his worst fear. Because he was finally coming to understand that the weakness was not in the woman—she was a lot stronger than she looked. The weakness was in himself. Evidently the McKenna men lacked whatever it took to hold on to their women. God knows what it was he was lacking. He had honestly done his best with Constance, but in the end he'd lost her. Lost her even before Nick was born. She'd told him more times than he could count how much she hated him for trapping her in this hellhole, and that as soon as the baby was born she was leaving, going back to New Orleans where there was music and restaurants and carriages, where folks knew how to treat a lady.

In the next room, the brass Seth Thomas ship's clock struck seven bells. There was still a broad streak of light in the western sky. Waite heard the dog next door tune up and figured Sarvice must be around somewhere. He heard Nick let himself in the back way and lift the lid on the pot on the stove.

"Pa? You in there?"

"Here, son. Finishing up the day's report. You've been gone a long time. Any trouble with Newbolt?"

Nick wandered in with a cold biscuit dripping fig preserves. "Boy, things is sure a mess over on the sound side. I been helping Maggie Wedbee round up her pigs. Never did find the old sow. One o' the winders blew out of Miss Agnes's back room and wet a whole mess of stuff she had strung up to the rafters. I nailed a tarp over it and told her I'd come back tomorrow and put her a new glass in. We still got some, don't we, Pa?" He bit off two-thirds of his biscuit and wiped a dribble of syrup from his chin. "Bunch of privies washed over on the back road. Me'n some of the boys been hoistin' 'em up. Boy, the place is gonna stink to high heaven in a few days."

"What about Evie? Did she get home all right?"

Nick frowned. "I run into Maxwell and Miss Caroline headed in. He was bogged up to his axle and swearing up a storm. The roads is still a mess. Don't know why he even tried to get out. Miss Caroline looked like she was fit to spit, and Evie . . ."

"What about her? Was there any trouble?" Waite didn't give much of a damn if Maxwell's cart sunk all the way to China, but he was concerned for the girl. Mostly because Mariah was concerned, and without knowing why he should, he trusted her instincts.

"I don't know, Pa. Lately, I've had me this feeling—I almost asked Dore about it, but then we got off on something else. Mr. Ebbie's sharpie come ashore and we had to roll her a ways on logs—it took seven men and one ox, but we got her overboard again. Caleb, he'll be fishing shares on her come fall. Pa, if I could find somebody to take me on, you reckon I could fish instead of going off to school?"

"You were going to tell me about Evie."

The boy scratched his armpit. He crossed and then recrossed his legs, slinging one big bare foot across his knee. "Y'know, Pa, she acts like she's scared of him, but he's her pa, so that don't make sense. But I'll tell you what I did see. I saw him kick that little dog of Miss Caroline's the other day when she weren't looking. Kicked 'im right off the porch for peein' on a ol' rag rug. Did I tell you Abel and Bax have signed up for the Lifesaving Service? I think it's on account o' they don't much like the notion of Miss Caroline movin' in."

Waite shook his head. "Hell of a reason," he

offered, thinking it was about time those two lay-
abouts did something worthwhile. "Keep an eye
on the girl, will you? Mrs. Deekins is worried
about her."

The sun was barely up the next morning when
Waite came back from turning off the lamp and
saw the trunk on the porch of the double keeper's
house. From an upstairs window he heard the familiar sound of a dog yapping and a woman
screeching.

He groaned. Damned if he hadn't had about all
he could take of that female. If Newbolt wanted
her, he'd better fetch her quickly, because if he
didn't, Waite was going to crate her up and ship
her back where she came from. He had a hunch
her brother wouldn't put up too much of a fuss.

Before Waite could disappear inside the house,
Caroline Hardraker came outside, still wearing a
wrapper with her hair in a braid down her back.
She plopped a bulging valise on top of the trunk
and turned to go back inside when Sarvice A.
Jones emerged from the other door. Spotting him,
she cried, "Hitch up the cart! I'm leaving here just
as soon as I finish packing!"

"Ma'am?"

"Well, don't just stand there gawking! I told
you what to do, now see to it!"

"Ma'am, the mailboat won't be running today.
You don't want to get all packed up and then
have to—"

"Yes, I do! I'm going all the way to California,
where nobody knows me and I don't know a living soul, and if I never see my family again, that's
just too bad! They all hate me, anyway. Everybody

hates me! Just because—just b-because—" She
burst into tears. Waite watched, amazed, as his
first assistant quietly took charge and led the hysterical woman inside. Just before the door closed
behind them, she turned and began wailing all
over the poor man's clean white shirt.

Judas priest, what next? Waite wondered.

He sat at his desk a long time before he uncapped his inkwell and commenced to write in his
journal. "September 15, 1886. Sun rose 5:24. Haze
to the SW, wind calm, sea still churned up from
storm. South Beacon down again. Will send Hardraker to make repairs."

The poor fellow would likely welcome a chance
to get away. Waite wondered if he'd slept through
his sister's tirade. Probably so used to hearing it,
it didn't even register.

There was a clicking sound, and Caroline's dog
came into the room. Nick must have left the door
open. Absently, Waite reached down and
scratched the small fellow's ears, and then
scooped him up and went on contemplating his
logbook.

Sarvice was a surprising man. There was more
to him than met the eye. Considering the length
of time he'd been here, Waite was beginning to
believe he'd never even known the man. He
thought about the three people living next door
for a spell longer, then he gave the pup's ears a
final scratch, set him down, and finished his log,
reporting a steamer and two schooners headed
south, none headed north. "Some trouble with the
survivors taken in the night of the storm. I blame
the whiskey, not the women."

*   *   *

A short while later, Mariah dragged her rocking chair to where she had a clear view of the keeper's quarters while she ate her breakfast. Not that she was hoping to see anyone in particular; it was just that whatever current of air there was came though the open door, and it was already breathlessly hot.

She had worked herself to a frazzle the day before and was far from finished. She still had a clothesline to put up and damp things to hang out before they mildewed. Once the roads had time to dry out, she would ride into the village to see about Evie. She couldn't forget the sight of that poor little waif, perched up on top of Nick's Ginger, the mare wading hock deep in tide. The child had looked so worried.

A squabbling from out back reminded Mariah that she'd lost her rooster. Something had washed up against the coop and torn a hole in the wire, allowing him to escape. Or allowing something to crawl through the hole and get to him, but she didn't want to think about that, she really didn't. Still, she'd miss that strangulated croak.

She'd found a small snake in her bedroom, too, and while she wasn't exactly terrified of the things, she didn't want to think about that, either. Or about the fact that the door was gone from her privy and she'd forgotten to retrieve her slippers from under the bed and now they were ruined.

The truth was, there was so much she didn't want to think about, she had trouble finding somewhere to focus her mind. Nick had told her the night of the storm that school wouldn't be kept for the next few days because all hands would be needed to help clean up after the storm, and besides, fishing was generally good after a hard blow. She had already learned that fishing took precedence over schooling.

She was wondering how the schoolhouse had fared when Waite came out on the porch across the way. Clutching her coffee cup to her breast, she gazed to her heart's content, wondering why she had told him not to come back. Told him she didn't need his help.

She'd been disappointed when he'd taken her at her word. Perhaps she should walk over and see if he needed help with his houseguests. Or his bandages . . .

And perhaps not.

While she indulged her fanciful imagination, she saw Sarvice come out on the porch of the double keeper's quarters and strain to lift a small trunk. One of Caroline's trunks, if she wasn't mistaken. Precious raced back and forth between the two houses, yapping his silly little head off. Mariah wondered briefly what the trunk was doing outside in the first place and why Sarvice was dragging it back in.

And then she began wondering if Caroline was actually going to marry Maxwell, and why she hadn't set her cap for Waite instead, who was all any woman could want and more.

But then, Sarvice was a nice man, too, Mariah mused. If a woman was going to do something so foolish as to fall in love, she could do a lot worse than to lose her heart to a kind man like Sarvice America Jones.

Personally, she wouldn't have had Maxwell on a bet. As for Waite, he wouldn't have her. Of course, Sarvice A. might not have had her, either, once he learned of her irregular situation.

Mariah had taken to thinking of her situation as irregular rather than illegitimate. After all, she'd done nothing illegal. To be sure, she'd lied, but it was more by omission than by commission. Perhaps . . .

"Perhaps nothing!" Rising so fast she almost overset the rocking chair, she turned away. She had far more to do than mope.

Across the way, Waite stepped off his front porch and headed toward the teacherage, his shoulders braced as if for a battle. He'd scarcely reached the low place where water still stood when Sarvice emerged from the double house, waved him over, and then set out to meet him.

Almost relieved by the intervention, Waite turned and waited for the other man to join him. "Trouble?" he asked, seeing his first assistant's expression.

"Thought I'd better tell you I'll be getting married as soon as I can get the paperwork done. I'd be obliged if you'd help me with it, seein' how I've never done it before."

Chapter Nineteen

Determined to be at least half as self-sufficient as the native Banker women, Mariah sweetened her mare with a handful of dried apples the next afternoon, and, deeming the roads sufficiently safe, hitched her to the cart and set out for the village. She had several errands in mind. First a visit to the post office, not because she expected a letter but because the local women tended to linger there, making it a good place to hear the latest news. After that, she would go by Mr. Cyrus's store and purchase the few items on her list.

Then, if Caroline still wasn't home, she would take herself to Maxwell's house. There was no point in beating around the bush. If Maxwell intended to marry Caroline, someone was going to have to talk to her about Evie. As far as Mariah could determine, the woman had shown no interest in anyone but herself, but at least she might stand as a buffer between Maxwell and his daughter. It was obvious no one else was going to intervene.

Mariah made up her mind that if Caroline couldn't be drafted to the cause, she would simply have to turn to the authorities. Just which authorities, she couldn't have said. The governor, perhaps. She'd met him once when he'd come through Murfreesboro on a campaign junket. In this particular case, she could hardly turn to the magistrate.

It was all of forty-five minutes later when she turned off onto the road that led to Maxwell's house, carrying with her a faint sense of puzzlement. She'd thought they were coming to accept her, these islanders with their somewhat aloof sense of dignity. But the women at the post office had been rather standoffish today. Finally, after her first few pleasantries had been ignored, she had asked point-blank about storm damage in the village.

"No more'n usual," one woman had said after making busywork of retying her apron. "Roofs been patched before, floors've been scrubbed before." Then, to her friend—or perhaps her sister, they looked enough alike—she added, "I had me a good crop of collard greens, though, 'fore the tide come up over 'em."

They'd all laughed at that. Mariah had never grown a collard in her life, nor even cooked one, but she'd laughed, too. She wanted so desperately to be friends with these women she'd first met at her pounding and was slowly coming to know through church and their school-aged children. She missed having close friends.

"Well . . . I suppose I'd best be getting on," she'd said, hoping they'd ask her to stay, to visit with them awhile longer.

They didn't, but one old woman, her twinkling blue eyes nearly lost in a net of wrinkles, murmured, "Don't pay no mind to what's being said, child."

Somewhat confused, Mariah smiled her thanks and left.

Mr. Cyrus, when she stopped in at his store, drew on his pipe for several long moments before he greeted her. As if he weren't quite sure he knew her. He didn't have this, and he didn't have that, and he was fresh out of the other. "Folks stocks up before a storm," he explained. And then, almost reluctantly, he admitted to having a few Irish potatoes in the back room, and said he was out of salt pork, but he'd send over a side of fish in the morning after his eldest had fished their nets.

Urging Merrily to a trot a few minutes later, Mariah told herself that she was probably imagining things. After all, she had a roof over her head. She had food. She had a respected position in the community—for the moment, at least. What more could a body want?

Don't ask. You're not to even think about that man until you can do it without getting all achy-chested and watery-eyed!

There was a woman sweeping Maxwell's front porch. It wasn't Evie, and it certainly wasn't Caroline, who wouldn't know a broom from a button hook unless each was labeled.

"Good afternoon. I'm Mariah Deekins," she said cheerfully, climbing down from the cart and looping the reins around the gatepost. The woman regarded her steadily. "The schoolteacher," she added helpfully. Still no sign of acknowledgment. "I have the three youngest Newbolts in my classes?" This was getting to be ridiculous!

Finally the woman tipped her head in a regal nod. Mariah wondered if she was expected to curtsy. Who *was* this creature? She wore her steel-gray hair braided across the top of her head like a coronet. Plainly dressed, she was extremely tall and as suntanned as any fisherman. Her piercing black eyes and square jaw were rather formidable, but she bore herself with the dignity of a bishop in full regalia.

"I've . . . um, come to see Evie. Is she at home?"

"Kitchen. I'll fetch her out to you."

"Don't bother. I know the way. I'll just go in and surprise her." Still wondering who on earth the woman was and why she didn't introduce herself, Mariah frisked on up the steps and walked briskly into the house. It was neat as a pin. She might have known a small thing like a hurricane wouldn't dare disrupt the orderly Newbolt household. Even the yard had been freshly swept.

Perhaps the gray-haired woman was the new housekeeper. If so, it was an encouraging sign for the future. Maxwell must finally have seen the light. Caroline's doing, no doubt. Miss Hardraker wasn't about to ruin her pretty hands for any man.

"Evie? It's me—Mariah. I've come to see . . ." *Dear God.* "Oh, Evie, darling, what happened?" But Mariah knew immediately what had happened. Dropping to her knees, she gathered the child into her arms.

Evie didn't say a word, nor did she yield herself to sympathy. There was a stoicism about her that was more touching than any amount of tears would have been.

I'll kill him, Mariah vowed silently. *If it's the last thing I ever do, I'll make that man rue the day he ever laid a hand on this child.*

There wasn't a speck of doubt in her mind that

Maxwell was responsible for the black eye, the
swollen lip, and the bruises on both those poor,
skinny little arms. "Where's your father, Evie?"

"Gone to meet the wreck commissioner," came
the lifeless reply.

"I want you to pack your things right now,
dear. You're going home with me. If your father
objects, I'll deal with him. I'm sure I can make
him understand."

She was sure of no such thing, but she'd vowed
to protect this child, and protect her she would.

"Aunt Fee's come to look after us," Evie said
dully. "Frankie fetched her."

"Is Aunt Fee the woman sweeping the front
porch?"

Evie nodded. "It don't really need sweeping. I
already swept it this morning. She's only looking
out to see when Pa comes home so I can go hide
in the toilet. He won't foller me there."

"This Mrs. . . . Fee?"

"Her whole name's Ophelia. She's not my real
aunt, but we always called her that. She and my
ma was cousins. Frankie snuck out to her house
last night when Pa took one of his spells."

"Let me speak to Mrs. Ophelia, then, dear. And
I really would like for you to go home with me."

"I reckon I'll stay. Pa won't bother me none as
long as Aunt Fee's here, and she won't leave until
Dore gets home."

Mariah didn't know what the woman expected
Dorien to do about the situation. Evidently it had
been going on for some time, with no one making
the least effort to stop it.

Ophelia Bennette met her in the front hall, arms
crossed over her flat bosom. Her bearing indicated

that she'd made up her mind about something. "I'm a plainspoken woman, madam. I don't listen to gossip and I don't spread it, but I've given that man his last chance. Now I'll be taking those two least ones home to stay with me. My cousin was a weak woman—some said she was a fool, and I'll not argue with that, but what she done is done, and there's no undoing it. Them two young'uns is nothing to do with Maxwell. I can't say about Dorien. He's not got the look of a Newbolt, but then, he's not got the look of his ma's folks, neither."

Mariah opened her mouth to speak and then closed it as the meaning of her words sunk in. She couldn't think of a single thing to say in the face of such a revelation, but she must have murmured some sort of a response, however inarticulate.

Ignoring her, the woman said, "Maxwell, he knows Evie and Frankie ain't his, and it burries into him like a grub-worm into a punkwood log. That Hardraker woman got him riled up the night of the storm, and then left him to simmer till he'd worked up a good head o' steam. He took it out on Evie, her bein' the weakest. Franklin, he come a-running for me."

"Where is Frankie? Is he all right?"

"He'll do. I left him there at my place with the dogs. He's a good boy. Smartest one o' the lot. That don't set well with Maxwell, neither, 'cause for the most part, his own blood kin's not got the brains of a dippin' gourd."

"Oh, those poor babies," Mariah whispered. "Do you know if Maxwell's going to marry Miss Hardraker?"

"What, and her with a bun already in the oven?

Even Maxwell knows better than to poke his fist into a hornet's nest twice. He was fixin' to, all right. She spent the night of the storm here. Can't say which bed she slept in. Don't matter none now. Evie didn't come home at all that night, and Maxwell, he was ireful over that, and when that woman went and told him about the fix she was in, Frankie says he took her home—rode out before the roads was even clear—and then he come back home and went to brooding. Frankie, he stayed out of the way. Evie, she couldn't."

Mariah was sick at heart, thinking it was her fault, that she should have kept the child with her until she could bring her home and explain, only then he might have taken out his spite on poor little Frankie.

No wonder the child stuttered. It was a wonder he spoke at all. "I can take one or both of the children. I don't have a whole lot of room to spare, but we'll work out something."

"No need. I got me this big old empty house. My man died seventeen year ago next month. Lifesaving Service. Drownded tryin' to rescue the crew off'n the *Liberty Rose.*" She spoke calmly, but Mariah could sense a wealth of hidden pain behind those few words. "If you want to come visit with the young'uns, Dore'll bring you. He's the trustiest one o' the lot."

After telling Evie she'd come to see her in a day or so, Mariah drove off, pondering over the many ways in which the lives of the innocent could be blighted. She'd been half tempted to tell Ophelia Bennette the truth of her circumstances, and then to seek out Maxwell, tell him her story, and let

the chips fall where they would. Waite knew. The
rest of the world didn't matter.

Before she put her teaching career at risk, however, the matter of those two children must be
settled. Maxwell was a monster hiding behind a
cloak of respectability. Didn't anyone else know?
Had he managed to fool an entire community all
these years? Was everyone in the whole wide
world living a lie?

That night she wrote in her journal:

I can't believe how very mistaken I was in my
earlier opinion of Maxwell Newbolt, formed
solely on the basis of a few letters. The wretch
deserves to be pilloried before the whole village, but of course, that will never happen.
I'm almost glad Evie and Frankie are not his.
Or could I have mistaken Mrs. Bennette's
meaning?

No, I'm sure I didn't. Perhaps their true
father was a noble gentleman who was lost
at sea before he could make an honest woman
of Mrs. Newbolt.

And then she muttered, "That doesn't even
make sense! The woman was already married."

Mercy, life was such a messy business.

"I'm glad they can turn to their Aunt Fee," she
wrote finally. "What a remarkable woman! I think
I like her."

Then, putting pen and journal aside, she fell to
thinking about the man she'd vowed not to think
about any more than absolutely necessary. The
trouble was, he was impossible not to think about.
He knew the worst of her situation and yet he

hadn't condemned her, unlike certain others who had quickly revoked lifelong friendships once her irregular situation had come to light.

Or perhaps he had. He hadn't been to see her in almost twenty-four hours.

Too tired to do any more cleaning and too restless to think of sleeping, Mariah went over in her mind everything that had occurred to her since the night she had unburdened herself to Waite.

Had he treated her any differently after that? She didn't think so. Of course, hours and whole days went by without her seeing him, but he was busy. He had his work. And, too—he had kissed her.

Could he have kissed her because he thought she was easy? Knowing no decent man would ever marry her, could he be thinking of making her his mistress? Men did that sort of thing. Women, too. Sometimes they even went so far as to pretend they were married . . . .

Stop trying to analyze the world and everyone in it, Mariah George Sawyer! Your mother warned you that too much education addled a woman's brain.

But then, what would be so wrong with reaching out for whatever happiness she could capture, considering everything she would be denied?

Mariah spent the following day airing out the schoolhouse, which had suffered only minor damage, mostly rain beating through the windows and down around the stovepipe. Just as she was finishing the cold luncheon she'd brought with her, Nick and Dorien rode up. Seated on the front steps, she'd been enjoying the last of the cold tea she'd brought to wash down her bread and cheese.

"Oh, good, you're just in time to help unstick a stubborn window." She wanted to know about Evie and Frankie, but thought it best to work up to the matter diplomatically.

Nick slid off his pony, not bothering to hitch it to the flagpole, and went inside to deal with the window. Dorien dropped down onto the step beside her. "Ma'am, I want you to know I don't blame you none for what happened to Evie the other day."

"Blame *me*?"

"No, ma'am, I don't. Even without you keeping her out all night, Pa would've found some excuse to take out his meanness on her. I used to think it was on account of her being—you know—crippled, but it ain't that."

"Merciful saints—"

"I think he could've got her leg fixed up when she was a baby, but he let it stay, just to spite Ma. When I asked him once if he couldn't do something, he said there weren't no point in buyin' her a special shoe when her feet's still growin'. But I'm gonna get her fixed up, once I save up enough money. Miss Agnes says there's a doctor there in Norfolk that works on folks with Evie's trouble, but I'll have to take her to him, and it'll cost right much."

"I'll help. Oh, please let me help!" She had yet to be paid her salary, but that wasn't important. If she had to sell everything she owned, which wasn't all that much, she would gladly do it to see that child made whole and happy.

It was a measure of Dorien's concern that he

didn't refuse her offer. "Bax and Able'll put in once they start drawing pay, but Cale's got him this girl he's all the time moonin' over, and a boat he's aimin' to buy shares in, so me'n Nick, we planned it all out. We'll both save up ever' penny we can, and between us, we'll keep watch over Ev and Frankie. Pa, he takes these spells . . ."

Mariah nodded, indicating that she knew about Maxwell's "spells."

"If Pa makes me go off to school, Cale said he'll hold off on putting fishing money into the boat and put in what he can, and with Aunt Fee looking after 'em till I can get Evie fixed and make a place for 'em on my own, it's gonna be all right."

Mariah was flabbergasted. This boy, not yet fifteen years old, had taken charge and settled the matter all by himself. Or at least with Nick's help, which was even more amazing. Yesterday they'd been playing pranks on the new teacher, stuffing muskrats into desk drawers, tossing turtles on laps, and blowing conchs in the middle of the night.

Today they were shouldering more responsibility than many adults ever had to bear.

Nick came outside and reported the window unstuck. Mariah looked at him with new respect. He promised to mix up a batch of salt and wood ash and mend the cracks in the stovepipe where rain had beaten in, and as there was no more room on the front step, he leaned against a live oak and propped one bare foot against the trunk. "You tell her yet, Dore?"

Both Dorian and Mariah spoke at once. She said yes, and he said no. And then she said, "Tell me what?" Mercy sakes, what else was there to tell?

Surely Waite hadn't told anyone about her irregular situation.

Nick shrugged. He seemed to be having trouble meeting her eyes. "Nothin' much. Just some talk that's going around. I told ever'body it ain't true, 'cause I was there and I ought to know, but them men—the ones Pa pulled out of the surf, that was there in the kitchen that night? One of 'em's saying some stuff about how you was sashaying around, showing off your garters, and how he got his hand up your skirt and how you—"

Mariah gasped. The color drained right out of her face, making the freckles she'd tried so hard to bleach with buttermilk and cucumbers more visible than ever. "He said *what*?"

"Ma'am, he'd been drinking. Him and the others, they got 'em a gallon o' white likker from somewheres. Nobody believes a word of it, but I thought you ought to know what's going around."

"Good Lord in heaven," Mariah sputtered. She tugged at her high dimity collar, which had suddenly grown too tight. Bright circles of color blossomed on her cheeks.

"Ma'am, don't pay it no mind. It's not—"

"Miz Deekins, it's not that bad. Folks talks, is all."

"But everybody's been so friendly," she wailed. "I thought—I thought they *liked* me!"

"Shootfire, ma'am," said Nick, digging his bare toes into the soft sand. "Don't nobody put no stock in talk like that, leastwise not for long. We all like you just fine. Pa says, for a city woman, you're about as stout and hearty as they come, and Pa ain't much for sweet talk."

Outrage veering dangerously close to hysteria, she swallowed the urge to laugh. Stout and hearty? That was Nick's notion of sweet talk? That boy had been under his father's influence far too long. It was time the McKennas had a few lessons in the proper way to treat a lady.

"Don't worry none, Miz Deekins. Just leave ever'thing to us," Nick said, and what else, she wondered, could she do?

They rode off then, with Dorien sitting sideways on his barebacked pony and Nick poking at him with a fist. Showing off. Children again. Yet, amazingly enough, Mariah really did feel better. She felt fairly certain Evie's and Frankie's well-being was in good hands.

As for her own reputation, well . . . time would tell.

Waite, his patience badly frayed, was mending the wire on Mariah's chicken coop when she tooled her cart around the corner. He'd had to undo the mess she'd made of it with shoestrings and what looked like a scrap of veil off a hat, and start all over again.

Why was he even bothering? he asked himself. He hadn't signed up to mend any chicken coops. Dammit, when had his calm, peaceful life begun to come unraveled? The day he'd gotten his first look at the woman when she'd come in on the mailboat?

He'd been so sure she wouldn't last out the week, but she had. Which meant he'd had time enough to take a second look, and when he had, he'd liked what he'd seen—liked it a little too much. First thing he knew, what with one thing and another, she'd managed to work her way under his skin until now he couldn't go an hour without wanting to see her.

Which was the reason he'd tried so hard to avoid her. Because he couldn't look at her without wanting her, wanting her the way a man wanted a woman, naked and in his bed. He spent more time than he could afford thinking of all the things he wanted to do to her. With her.

Hell, he couldn't even get a decent night's sleep anymore without waking up damp and sweating, his heart thundering in his chest and his rod standing up stiff as a flagpole. Knowing what he knew about her didn't make a particle of difference. She was a good woman, an honest woman— too fine to tangle up with a McKenna man.

He watched her drive up, her hair, shiny as polished bronze, slipping out from under her bonnet. She tried so hard to look neat and prim, but it never lasted long. Right now she had a streak of soot on her face, and he'd bet she didn't even know about it.

Without a word, he reached for her hand, helped her down, then unhitched the cart and gave the mare a handful of oats. There was talk in the village. Evidently, the boy who'd brought the wreck commissioner to interview the crew the other day while Waite had been up in the tower had a loose jaw. They'd stayed in his kitchen all morning, and because Waite didn't much like his house full of strangers, he'd stayed away.

Now he wished he hadn't. He didn't know all that was being said in the village, but he had a pretty good idea. They were a rough crew, so rough he'd changed his mind about sending them over to Rhoda's boardinghouse. When he'd told her he'd keep them until the boat came in, she'd tried to give him back his money, so he'd commissioned her to cook up a bait of dinner and he'd sent Nick over every day to collect it. At least they'd eaten well.

But he was sorry about the talk.

He cleared his throat, wondering if he should even bring it up. Maybe he should spare her that. It would die down in a few days, anyway. "Mariah, I came to tell you—"

"I saw Nick and Dorien today."

"You did? Did Nick say anything about—"

"The children? Yes, he did, and I met Aunt Fee, too. My, what a—a staunch woman! Anyway," she hurried on, smiling brightly—a little too brightly, come to think of it—"I'm pretty sure that among the four of us, we have everything under control. The boys were wonderful. You should be proud of your son."

"I am proud, but it's not that—I mean, I'm glad everything's under control, but . . ." What was under control? He sure as hell wasn't.

"But what? I'm sorry—what were you going to say?"

What was he going to say? Damned if he could even remember, with her standing so close he could smell her skin, see the tortoiseshell hairpins sliding out from under her bonnet, touch the tiny freckle on her lower lip.

"Waite?" She touched his arm and his skin came alive. It was the damndest thing he'd ever experienced.

"Yeah. Well, what I was fixing to say is that Sarvice and Miss Hardraker are wanting to get

married, and I'd like you to—that is, Sarvice asked
me to ask you if—"

"Sarvice and Caroline? Merciful heavens, the
mind boggles." She smiled. And then she began
to laugh.

"I don't see what's so blamed funny."

"Neither do I," she gasped, and laughed all
the harder.

"Mariah! Dammit, stop that!" He took her by
the shoulders, scowling down at her damp, freckled, heat-flushed, soot-smeared face, and then
every shred of common sense he possessed sunk
without a trace. "God help us all," he groaned,
just before he covered her mouth with his.

Chapter Twenty

The sun settled slowly behind the woods to the west, trailing a wake of purple shadows. Neither Waite nor Mariah saw. Swarms of mosquitoes emerged from the nearby marsh, bent on attack, and were ignored for their efforts. She was like a magnet to him—like magnetic north to the needle of his compass. All he could think of was Mariah. The way she tasted. The way she felt in his arms. The things she did to him without even trying.

Using his thumb and forefinger, he pressed her jaws apart, the better to tap her sweetness. He began to kiss her as he had kissed no other woman, not even his wife, because he hadn't known how to kiss a woman so thoroughly when he was a callow youth, and had never cared enough since to learn.

With Mariah, it was instinctive. Kissing her was compulsive, an act both of frustration and desperation. And because he wanted her more than he had ever wanted any woman—wanted her with the single-mindedness of a man obsessed, a man too long denied—he went on kissing her that way, the thrust of his tongue a surrogate for the thrust of his loins.

And just in kissing her he came closer to losing

control than he had since the summer when, as an eager, inexperienced lad he had been introduced to his own sexuality by a beautiful, experienced young woman from New Orleans.

This time, he told himself, *I'll have her. This time there's no turning back.*

Spreading his legs, he cupped her hips and pressed her against his swelling groin, a deep-throated groan escaping him as she began to twist against the hard ridge trapped between them. Driven by the sweet intoxication of desire, he found her breast and worked it until he could feel her peak and harden.

Take her, the lust in him whispered. *It's what you both want, so why not let it happen?*

Because she was defenseless, reason argued. An innocent caught up in something beyond her experience. One of them had to remain sane, and he was the one with experience in matters of the flesh. If he took her now, he would never be able to let her go. And if he tried to hold her against her will, she would soon come to hate him, just as Constance had grown to hate him, and he couldn't go through that, not again. Not with Mariah.

Stealing himself, he dragged his mouth from hers, ignoring the demands of his own flesh. "This is not what I came for." *Liar, liar!* "Mariah, I never intended for this to happen."

Blinking as if she'd just awaken from a long, deep sleep, she whispered, "I know. I understand."

"I only came to tell you—"

"About Caroline and Sarvice." She sounded so calm. How the devil could she sound so calm when he was still reeling? "Well," she said with a sigh, "you told me."

"I did?" Dammit, she didn't have to recover all that quickly!

Schooling himself to some semblance of composure, he said, "Yes, well . . . like I said, I thought you might be interested."

With the delicate wave of a hand, Mariah dispersed the swarm of whining insects drawn by the scent of heated flesh and attar of roses. "I suppose it's for the best. He cares for her, and she truly needs a husband. Still, one can't help but be sorry for the both of them. Where will they go? How will they live?"

Waite moved to stand behind the cart, embarrassed by his body's unflagging enthusiasm. "The, um . . . I believe the plan is to leave on the next boat out and go to Maryland to be married." He studied her face, noticing that the wild-rose flush that had bloomed so briefly in her cheeks had faded. Still, he suspected he'd been the one to put it there and was proud of such power.

And was sorely ashamed of his pride.

Mariah opened a lard stand and scooped up a handful of oats, but the mare had already gone, so she fed it to the chickens. "I suppose they'll come back here."

"For a year or so, at least."

"Somehow, I can't see Caroline being happy here." They might have been discussing the weather, but Waite wasn't fooled. She was as rattled as he was, but women were better at managing awkward social situations.

"As a keeper's wife, you mean." He sounded

defensive, but hadn't meant it that way. At least
he didn't think he had.

"That's not at all what I meant. She'll be better
off with Sarvice than she ever could with Maxwell, but I'm not sure she has it in her to be happy
anywhere. Some women don't, I believe."

Waite suspected she was talking about one
thing and thinking about something else, but hell,
so was he. "Do you have it in you to be happy,
Mariah?" He regarded her steadily, watching as
questions formed behind those clear gray eyes.

Questions to which he had no answers.

"I believe I do," she said thoughtfully. "Con-
tented, at least. Which reminds me, Waite—if I'm
going to go on living here after—I mean, with—
well, you know what I mean. If I'm allowed to
stay, we're going to have to come to an
understanding."

"You're staying. There's no question of that."
One way or another, she was staying, he'd see to
it. Still, he understood what she was getting at.
Understood more than she might think.

He understood that she was a decent woman
who'd had one bad break after another. That, having lost her home and all her friends, she was
lonely, and being lonely, she was vulnerable. He
understood that through no fault of her own, her
reputation, not to mention her livelihood, was at
stake, because, fair or not, once there was talk
about a woman, folks watched her like a hawk.
And because he'd taken her under his roof the
night of the storm, there'd already been talk.

So he would see that the record was set straight
about what had happened and what hadn't. If he
had to crack a few skulls in the process, he would

definitely do that. But if word ever got out about the other, it was going to take some doing. Folks might not hold a woman's illegitimacy against her—she'd had no say in the matter of her birth, after all. But lying to them was something else. Using a false name was like a ship sailing under false colors.

With any luck, she could keep her past where it belonged—in the past—but from here on out there couldn't be so much as a whisper of doubt about her character, because shifting a single grain of sand could bring down an entire mountain.

Which meant he'd have to stay away from her.

Which also meant he might never get a decent night's sleep again, but at least his conscience would be clear. "You said something about coming to an understanding. I expect you mean that as you're a single woman and I'm a single man living off apart from the village, folks might try to make something out of nothing."

"Oh, but that wasn't—I mean, we're not exactly—"

So what I was thinking is, it might be better from now on if I send Hardraker to see to your needs." He waited for a protest, but none was forthcoming. He could tell by the way she looked at him that it wasn't what she wanted to hear, but it was all he had to offer. All he could honorably offer any woman. "With Sarvice gone, we'll be working double shifts. If you need anything, send word by Nick. You'll see him every day in school." He attempted a smile, but it wasn't particularly successful. "Leastwise I hope you will. The boy's got a stubborn streak in him."

"Oh? I wonder where that came from," Mariah

said caustically, lifting her head in what her father used to call her Princess Prissy posture. And then he did smile, and it reached all the way to his eyes and broke her heart, because she knew what he was trying to tell her. He might as well have spoken aloud.

Don't count on me, Mariah. Men don't marry women in your situation.

Damn and blast her situation! To hide the tears that rose far too easily these days, she stared out at the ocean. With the beach washed flatter than ever, a wide band of it was visible, stained purple now by the setting sun.

He moved from behind the cart and turned to leave, and she said to herself, *Who needs him, anyway? Who wants him? Let him go!*

"Well," she said brightly. "So Caroline's going to be married. I thought surely she and Maxwell would make a match of it." So much for letting go.

He paused and turned around. She willed him to retrace his steps, but he didn't. Shrugging, he said, "Too much alike."

"Maxwell and Caroline?" She fanned her overheated face with a limp, lace-trimmed handkerchief and surreptitiously blotted her eyes. *Don't go. Please don't leave me like this!*

"Ship can't have but one captain."

"And you think they'd both insist on being in control?"

"Don't you?" Waite knew he ought to leave before he got in any deeper, but she was a hard woman to walk away from.

"I don't know about that, but I do know why Maxwell won't marry her."

"Because a smart man don't get bit by the same dog twice."

"I simply meant that Maxwell would expect her to earn her keep, and she'd expect to be waited on hand and foot."

"Like I said before, they're too much alike."

"Well, if that's the case, Caroline and poor Service should get along just fine, then, because they're nothing at all alike. She'll run him ragged, and he's far too nice a man for that."

"I wouldn't count on it," Waite said quietly, and nodded politely, just as if he hadn't kissed her senseless and broken her heart only moments before. "Well . . . I've got some repairs to see to," he said, and walked off, hands in his pockets, watching his feet carry him away from her.

As September merged with October, the weather remained all but perfect. A light breeze from the northwest brought relief from the relentless heat and humidity. With each passing day the sky became a clearer, deeper shade of blue. Before her the sea spread out like a rumpled blue counterpane, edged with white lace ruffles.

Mariah, refusing to mope over matters beyond her control, took to walking the shore again. She was determined to be happy if it killed her. In one of her mother's best pearlware cups she collected beach gravel each day for her laying hens. She practiced skipping clamshells on the surface of the water, to the great amusement of the younger children who played there. Five skips, the current record, was held by little Betsy Casey. Mariah's score was a big, fat goose egg, but that didn't keep her from trying. Or from laughing

along with her students when she failed again
and again.

She made a point of not glancing up at the
tower balcony, where as often as not a silent figure
stood gazing down. But she knew he was there.
She knew he watched her. Knew it and thought
angrily, *Stubborn, stubborn man!*

And sometimes she even thought, *Damn you,
Mama and Papa!*

On a sleepy afternoon when her class had been
cooped up in the stuffy schoolroom just a tad too
long, someone came by and yelled through the
door that the drum were in. The resulting exodus
left behind scattered books, slates, a hair ribbon,
and two pairs of shoes.

Knowing it was pointless to call them back, Mariah closed up and went home. On the way, she
passed several of her younger boys whipping
something in a creek. Drums?

"Elliot, what's going on?" she called out.

A skinny eleven-year-old lifted a long wire,
brought it down on the surface of the creek, then
stood back while several of the younger children
scooped something from the surface of the dark
water.

"We're just swarping minnow, Miz Deekins. For
the drum."

Swarping minnows. M-hmm. For the drum.

Intrigued beyond all reason, Mariah followed
the same group of children when they passed her
cottage some ten minutes later. Carrying a bucket
and several coils of line, they trotted out onto a
sandy point that jutted out into the sea just south
of the lighthouse, and Mariah, hurriedly anchor-

ing her bonnet with a hatpin, went after them.
Evidently, this was something important.

A drum, it seemed, was a fish. A channel bass,
to be more precise, and just now the sea was
stained wine red with a large school of the things.
She watched as the older boys lined up at the
edge of the water, each holding a heavy line coiled
in one hand, and hurled the baited end out well
beyond the breakers.

She saw half-grown boys haul in fish almost as
long as they were, and cheered along with the
others when little Frankie, fishing between Nick
and Dorien, managed to drag one of the pink and
silver drumfish into the wash. Throwing down his
line, he dashed out into an incoming surf and fell
belly down on the flapping fish, holding on to it
with both arms lest it wash back out to sea, and
everyone laughed.

Mariah cried. But that was nothing unusual. She
cried a lot these days. Over butterflies. Over her
crazy old one-legged seagull. Over Nick's lifting
Evie up on Ginger and leading her to her Aunt
Fee's house one day when it started raining just
as school let out.

She was in love with her children, in love with
the island, in love with the people, who seemed
to her to be far more real and honest than any she
had ever known before.

Two days after the first run of drumfish, Rhoda
Quigley invited her to join a quilting circle. Once
the weather cooled off, the widow said, the
women gathered to crochet, quilt, and drink yaupon tea, a local beverage for which she was rapidly acquiring a taste. She offered to bring cookies,
but Rhoda told her not to disfurnish herself, by

which she gathered that word of her cooking skills had spread.

Miss Agnes came often to trade her herbal wares for more of Mariah's books, which Mariah assured her she was welcome to borrow with no need to barter. But pride was strong in these self-sufficient people. So she gradually acquired a life-time supply of tonics, washes, unguents, and herbs good for everything from spots to sprains to windy bowels.

She had learned that many of the islanders were great readers. Once the day's work was done, as Miss Agnes said, there was little else to do but gossip or read, and reading wasn't as apt to get a body in trouble.

Mariah could certainly vouch for that fact, although whatever tales had been spread about her by those wretched sailors had long since died down.

The weather remained perfect, an invitation to being outdoors, and so she walked for miles along the beach after school, collecting shells and bits of driftwood, which she arranged in circles, thinking that when spring came, she might even plant a few flowers. She told herself she wasn't hoping to see Waite, but each day that passed without a glimpse of him made her ache all the more inside.

The days when she did see him were even worse. He would wave from his porch, or from the tower balcony, and she would wave back, wondering what he would do if she were to race up all five thousand of those wretched steps, tear off his clothes, and have her way with him.

She wasn't entirely sure what her way was, but she suspected that once she stripped him naked, the way he'd been on the beach that night, then things would evolve of their own momentum.

But she wasn't quite that desperate. Not yet.

Of Maxwell she saw nothing at all. He'd gone off on the boat that had carried the storm survivors and come back nearly three weeks later on the mailboat that had brought the newlyweds and Mr. Hardraker's family.

None of the Newbolt children ever mentioned their father, and Mariah thought it best not to ask. Best not to rake over those particular coals again.

She had welcomed the newcomers with a pie she had baked herself. Raisins in an egg custard that hadn't quite set, in a crust that was only slightly scorched, but tough as flannel. Sweet, shy Emily Hardraker had thanked her effusively and offered to let her hold the baby, a red, wrinkled, wigglesome little bundle that everyone, even Caroline's dog, Precious, seemed to dote on. Mr. Hardraker was still as silent as a sphinx, but he smiled a lot these days, mostly at his tiny son.

Sarvice smiled a lot, too. He appeared to be thriving in his role as husband, and Mariah could only hope his bubble didn't burst too quickly. Caroline was as haughty as ever. She had taken to bossing everyone in the double quarters except, oddly enough, for her husband. She referred to him now as Mr. Jones, which was a great improvement, Mariah considered, over "Boy" or "You there!"

Toward the end of October, just as the fishermen were beginning to complain that the fish weren't coming up into the sound at all this fall, the wind shifted, bringing about an end to the clear warm weather. After the third day of fierce northeast winds with a heavy overcast but little rain, Mariah was ready to return to Indian summer.

But instead of moderating, the wind blew even harder. Sand raced across the grounds, piling in little drifts against the smallest blade of grass. Wind whined around the corners of the house and down the chimney. The seagulls seemed to love it, lying on the air for long moments with only the occasional twitch of a feather.

The horses hated it. With their rumps to the wind, they stubbornly ignored calls and whistles, and even the promise of a treat. Mr. Cyrus told her she could always tell when a weather change was coming because of the way the cows were facing. East for good weather, west for bad. The only trouble was, she could never remember which direction was which.

The three lighthouse keepers were kept busy with their duties, which included shoring up the funny, boxlike red signal house some distance beyond the tower and replacing the hooks on all the shutters on both houses, as well as keeping the tower lamp burning. They were still at it that evening when the rain started coming down, solid sheets of it blowing horizontally, beating in around window frames.

Sea tide was running over again, which made matters worse. Increasingly restless, Mariah felt as if she were entombed in a cold gray cocoon, the only sound the constant drumming of rain and surf and wind, the only distraction her own imagination.

"I'm considering building an ark," she wrote in

her journal after an early supper of tinned soup, which she didn't even bother to heat.

It's only October, but I'm beginning to understand what Waite meant when he said few city-bred women could stand the winters here. It's not the weather I mind, it's the isolation.

But it's not that, either. It's more the wanting and not being able to have. My, doesn't that sound petulant? One would think that after being told in so many words that our friendship was ended, I'd have accepted it, and that would have been that. Instead, I waste time daydreaming, a singularly unrewarding pastime. I'm quite ashamed of myself. I'm sure I never spent nearly as many hours dwelling on the way Henry Lee's hair curled around his ears, or the way his eyes crinkled at the corners when he smiled.

I've forgotten if they did or not, or even if he ever smiled, although I'm sure he must have. Smiled, that is—not crinkled. There've been so many changes lately. When I first moved into the teacherage, I was a woman alone in a man's world, a risky proposition at best, especially for one in my *irregular situation*. Now we number three men, three women, a boy, and a baby (and soon to be one more).

S. and C. remain a mystery. I wonder what really goes on between those two. I've come to believe S. is both a realist and a romantic. He's not a handsome man, but he's not unhandsome, either. I only hope C. appreciates him, for I suspect he's far better than she deserves. At least I've discovered who wears the pants in that family. When C. whines, S. has only to lift an eyebrow and she sweetens immediately.

As for the two male residents of the principal keeper's quarters, one is resigned to being sent away to school after Christmas, the other seems to have no problem ignoring whatever it was that once existed between us. And something surely did. I can't have imagined it all.

W. has a scar on his chest where he was injured the night of the hurricane. I saw him without his shirt last week—I'd been visiting Emily and the baby and he'd been baling out his cistern, shirtless, shoeless, hatless, and perfectly magnificent. I believe he actually blushed when he saw me. I was tempted to flirt—would have if I thought it would thaw out this awful glacier that's grown up between us. I want the man. I lust for him. I ache and long and lie awake in a swelter, thinking of all sorts of wicked acts I'd like to commit on his body. Believe I must be depraved, if not actually demented.

As the remaining daylight began to fade, Mariah set aside her pen and journal. The rain had finally slacked off, but not enough for a walk on the beach. Besides, with the mixture of tide and rain covering the ground, she'd probably sink to her knees in quicksand and ruin yet another pair of shoes.

Which was an indication of just how far she'd

come in a few short months—that she would think of plunging into all that water without a qualm other than ruining her shoes.

Restlessly, she sorted through the winter gowns she had packed away last February. Slate blue. Dark green. Brown. Every one of them was so wretchedly drab.

Suddenly she felt like wearing red! Red would look ghastly with her hair, but she wanted it anyway. The brightest red imaginable. And maybe even a red hat. That would show him.

"Widgeon," she whispered. "You silly, pathetic widgeon."

Standing by the window, she stared out at the gathering darkness, allowing the sweep of light from the tower to settle her thoughts. Counting always helped. Counting the seconds between sweeps of light.

Counting the times he had kissed her, the times she had kissed him back . . .

She was still watching when she heard a faint shout and saw what appeared to be a piece of tarpaulin come sailing down from the top. Light flared and fluttered. A head and shoulders appeared briefly on the balcony, barely visible through the gloom.

Without a second thought, Mariah snatched up her skirts and set out at a run, not even aware of the quickening sand underfoot.

Chapter Twenty-one

Winded before she was even halfway up the stairs, Mariah paused and leaned against the wall, one hand over her pounding heart, her gaze focused on the metal door near the top. If she could have caught her breath, she would have called out.

Waite was up there alone. She knew because she'd seen Sarvice set out on his horse less than an hour ago, bound on an errand, no doubt, for his wife. And Mr. Hardraker was at home. She'd seen his lanky silhouette pass by a lit bedroom window not half an hour ago.

Wind howled outside the tower. Inside, it sounded like a thousand caged lions. Catching her second breath, Mariah bounded up the remaining steps and struggled to open the heavy watchroom door. Pulling it shut behind her, she didn't even wait to hear it catch, but hurried up the last set of steps, ignoring the cramps in her legs and the stitch in her side. Bursting into the lamp room, she cried, "Waite, where are you? Are you all right?"

Wind screeched around her like a banshee, tuggin at her wet hair, her sodden skirts. Light danced in wild, eerie patterns as a lantern on the floor flared and sent up a stream of black smoke.

All around her, moving in slow, mesmerizing patterns behind a revolving set of lenses, hundreds of pinpoints of light held her momentarily spellbound.

And then someone swore and yelled over all the noise "Dammit, shut the door!" and the spell was broken.

Blinking, she peered around at the man struggling to hold a billowing sheet of canvas. One corner was flapping inward, making a noise like gunfire. Rain beat against the dark glass walls surrounding her. Throughout all the chaos, those magnificent crystal prisms continued to rotate in slow, orderly fashion around the flickering lamp at the center.

Suddenly everything went wild. A loosened corner of tarpaulin whipped free of Waite's grasp, sucked inward by the downdraft from the open doors below, and knocked over the lantern beside the doorway.

Oil spilled. Flames streaked across the floor. Frozen in horror, Mariah screamed, and then Waite shoved past her, jarring her from her momentary trance, and she began stamping them out. From somewhere below she heard the sound of pounding footsteps, then of metal grating against metal. There was a loud slam, and the wind died out almost immediately.

In the sudden stillness she became aware of the sound of rain beating against the small enclosure. The air reeked of smoke and oil and something that reminded her fleetingly of wash day back home—the scent of cloth scorched by an overheated flatiron.

And then Waite was kneeling beside her, beating at her legs, and she cried, "Stop that!"

"Your skirt—"

"I'm all right!" Between the rain and the tide, she'd been drenched on the way over, but evidently there remained one dry scrap of fabric somewhere on her person. In treading on the flames, she must have managed to singe something.

"Stand still," he barked, still on his knees. He looked like a wild man, with his hair plastered to his head and his hands black with soot. He was fumbling up underneath her skirts—she could feel his hands up there—and for the life of her, she couldn't think why he was doing it, much less why he shouldn't.

As countless pinpoints of light continued to perform a dizzying minuet all around them, she felt a surge of nausea and told herself it was shock. Or the altitude. Or the stench of oil and scorched cloth.

"It was the door, wasn't it? I didn't take time to close it properly, and I'm sorry, oh, I'm so sorry." She realized she was wringing her hands and made herself stop. And then she realized he was still on his knees, with his head up under her bedraggled skirts, and she slapped her skirts back in place and stepped back.

Slowly, Waite stood. He was winded. And filthy. In the dim, flickering light she could barely see his expression, but she didn't need to see it to know it would be relentless. Unforgiving. *I could have burned down the whole lighthouse. Ships could've been wrecked. Lives could've been lost . . .*

Never mind that the lighthouse was built of

brick, with little wood involved, or that the light was still burning brightly. She could have caused a serious accident. He could have been badly burned or fallen to his death. "I'm sorry. I'm so very sorry," she whispered, and then had to repeat it louder over the roar of wind and rain. "It was all my fault." Ashamed of the careless impetuousness that had nearly caused a disaster, she hung her head.

He said "Yes, it was," and her spirits, already sagging, slumped like lead in her breast. "But not entirely," he added.

She dared to look up at him then. Hoping. Needing his forgiveness; knowing she didn't deserve it. *Dear Lord, I've mucked up again, haven't I?*

With a gentleness she had no right to expect, he reached out and tucked a straggle of wet hair behind her ear. His fingers trailed down her cheek, and then he began to speak. Calmly, as if she were one of his shipwreck survivors and he was afraid she might suddenly collapse, he explained about the cracked glass that had yet to be replaced, which had shattered and fallen out when a sash had been caught by the wind and slammed back, and how he'd come up to make temporary repairs until the new section of glass could be installed.

"With the wind dying down, I thought a tarpaulin would serve until morning, when there's more light to work by."

"I thought I heard you cry out," she said, her eyes and her heart saying something altogether different. Something that begged to be put into words. Words he'd as good as said he didn't want to hear.

"Probably cursing. I reckon the wind carried the sound. The job needed two men, but Hardraker's standing midnight to dawn. I didn't want to keep him up here until all hours."

He looked exhausted. Wet and tired and sooty and beautiful, and she loved him more than she even knew how to love. No rhyme or reason to it, she simply loved him, that was all. But for her pride, she'd have told him so long before now.

Oh, yes, her bloody, miserable pride.

"Are you sure you're not in pain? The flames—"

"Waite, my clothes are soaking wet. Besides, I managed to stamp out the fire almost as soon as it flared up. I'm sure if I'd been burned, I'd be the first to know."

"Sometimes, what with shock and all, it takes a while for the pain to set in. Mariah, I think you'd better sit down and let me take a look."

"In the dark? I broke your lantern, remember?"

"The wind did that."

"But I let the wind in."

"That you did," he said, but he didn't sound angry, more as if he were teasing her. Some of the tension that had set her to trembling began to ease. Not that she had stopped trembling, but then, that might have something to do with the way her left leg was beginning to throb and sting. It was as if she could feel her own heartbeat there between her shoe top and the ruffle of her drawers.

"If you're worrying about your modesty, I can tell you it was too dark under your skirts to see much."

"I'm sure there was nothing to see." She closed her eyes and tried again. "No flames, I mean."

"Well, madam, something up under your petticoats was burning, because it sure as hell felt hot enough when I rubbed my hands down your legs."

He thought she'd been on fire and he'd tried to beat out the flames with his bare hands without even thinking of the danger. Her heart swelled painfully, beating in time with the increasingly painful sensation in her lower limb.

"Mariah—"

"If I was in danger, then so were you. Your hands would've been . . ." She reached for his hands to prove that neither of them had suffered any real harm. They were so filthy that at first, in the dim light, she didn't even see the redness on his palms.

And then she did. "Oh, God," she whispered, aghast that he'd been burned, and that it was all her fault. Not even thinking of her own rapidly growing discomfort.

He pulled his hands from her grip—she'd been holding him by the wrists—and said gruffly, "My turn. Lift your skirt."

She uttered a little gasping noise that was closer to tears than laughter. Or perhaps both. "I beg your pardon."

In the center of the lamp room, the lens continued to revolve. The myriad points of light continued to flare and fade, never quite leaving them in complete darkness. Waite knelt again and felt her skirt, and it was as sodden as she'd claimed, but all the same, he lifted it and her petticoat, too, and then he swore softly under his breath. "I knew it! Were these silk?"

"Were what silk?"

"Your stockings."

She leaned over, and it didn't even strike her as comical that he was on his knees, his face hidden under a canopy of bedraggled muslin and once-white ruffles, and she was bent, bottom up, staring at her own lower limbs. "They're ruined," she wailed softly. "My last pair of striped silks."

But by now the pain had increased until she was fairly certain the damage had not stopped there.

"Come on, then, I'd better carry you home. Salt water burns like the very devil on raw flesh."

The thought of salt on her wounds brought a fresh surge of nausea washing over her, but she protested, "Not with those hands, you'll not carry me."

"Nothing wrong with my arms. Hold on a minute," he said. After doing something with the tarpaulin and ropes, he ushered her from the lamp room. He would have carried her down the stairs, all the way to the bottom, but she wouldn't allow it. She'd brought this on herself, and caused him injury in the process. So she went first, and he carefully shut the watchroom door behind him, making her feel guilty all over again.

At the rate they were piling up, she would need to make a list of all her reasons for feeling guilty, or else she might be tempted to forget a few.

The door at the base of the lighthouse stood ajar. She'd forgotten to close that, too. Stepping outside, she paused to gaze out over the expanse of black water.

Dark, treacherous water. . . .

She shuddered. It had still been light when she'd set out—just barely. Now, in the shadow of the tower, there was no light at all, only a fleeting reflected glow when the revolving beam swept through the rain. It wasn't terribly cold, but she was shivering hard.

He came up behind her, and she was aware of his body heat even with the increasing pain of her own burns. His hands must have been hurting him every bit as much, but she wasn't about to apologize again. It wouldn't assuage her guilt.

"Ready?" he asked.

"I still don't think you—"

"Mariah, stubborn woman, listen to me. You don't want to wade home."

"Maybe I need to. You're hurt and we've left a mess up there that will have to be cleaned up, and I feel so awful because it's all my fault for being careless." Her father had scolded her more than once as a child, warning her of the dire consequences that could follow a single reckless act.

The words couldn't have been more prophetic.

With a flash of whiteness that Mariah took to be a grin, Waite swept her up in his arms and headed down the last few granite steps. "Don't fret. You came rushing out in the rain and tide because you thought I needed a hand."

"All the same, I should have taken time to close the doors behind me."

"Next time you'll know."

"But Waite, I—"

"Hush. I can't tote and fight at the same time. If you're bound to fret, then do it quietly."

Sarvice rode onto the grounds and, seeing the

couple, came to meet them. "Trouble?" he asked, and briefly Waite explained.

"I'll take the rest of your watch. Caroline's got a headache. She's already gone to bed, so it's not like I've got anything better to do." With a tug of his cap, he turned and headed for the tower.

Mariah said, "Waite, this is embarrassing. I'm perfectly capable of walking. I walked down the stairs, didn't I? And that after running practically the whole way to the top."

"Wait'll your legs seize up on you. Even without the burns, you'll not have an easy night of it." She started to object, and he shushed her with a little squeeze. "Now quit trying to argue. You don't have your wind back yet." His voice came from deep in his chest. She could feel it, just as she could feel his heart pounding beneath her cheek. Drawing in a lungful of his distinctive scent, comprised just now of wet clothing, lye soap, lamp oil—and whatever it was about him that always made her pulse rate triple—she settled her head into the hollow of his shoulder and tried not to think of his raw hands.

It was simply heavenly to be in his arms again, whatever the reason.

"All the same, I'm too heavy for you to carry. You really should put me—"

"Put you down so you can deal with all the critters you're apt to meet on the way? Rats bigger than a full-grown cat, and snakes? Muskrats—snappers? All the things that live in the swamp until they're flooded out?"

"I'm sure they're more afraid of me than I am of them."

"Then how about the pit toilets and the animal

droppings the tide washes over? Think about all the animals that are around here, and the rest of it. Then think about if you want all that washing up against your raw flesh."

Her toes curled inside her ruined, pointy-toed shoes. Put that way, she wasn't quite so eager to be set down.

"Having a few second thoughts, hmmm?"

He was teasing her, and she was tempted to defy him and demand to be set down anyway, but there was enough truth to what he said to give her pause. Besides, by then they'd already arrived at her doorstep.

She reached out and opened the door to spare his hands, and when he shouldered his way inside and lowered her to the floor, he did it slowly, never once taking his eyes from hers. And she knew then, as surely as she knew her walls were blue, that his burned hands and her aching limbs weren't all he was thinking of.

"I have some—" she started to say.

"You'd better—" he said at the same time.

She tried again. "Miss Agnes—"

"I know. Sit down, I'll get it. Better yet, go lie down. I'll bring a lamp and see to the damage before I leave."

"Don't forget your hands," she called after him as she headed for her bed before she collapsed. She might look steady as a rock on the outside, but inside she was quivering like molded gelatin.

Waite lit the lamp on the trunk, tipped over one of the miniatures and righted it again, then turned toward the cabinet. Mariah thought he looked rather like a bull in a birdcage in her cramped, cluttered little cottage, and loved him all the more.

Modesty was the last thing on her mind by the
time he rolled her onto her stomach on the bed
and folded back all the layers of wet garments.
She protested that his hands needed tending first,
but he said they weren't all that bad, and proceeded to ease off her shoes—her last decent pair,
now ruined like all the rest. She peeled off her
melted silk stocking. Frowning over her shoulders,
Mariah watched in the yellow lamplight as he un-
tied the ribbons at her knees and shoved her ruffled drawers halfway up her thighs, the better to
see the extent of her injuries, or so he said.

He poured water from the pitcher into the
basin, washed his hands with her scented soap,
then emptied the water and poured fresh.

"I'm running out of shoes," she said, because
she was edgy and self-conscious and hurting, and
didn't want him to know any of it.

"Rinse 'em good, set 'em out to dry, but not by
the fire. They'll stiffen up some, but if they're
good leather, you can work 'em soft again."

They were certainly good leather, considering
what she'd paid for them. She didn't know why
she'd even brought it up, because shoes were the
last thing on her mind at the moment.

Nerves. The prickly, shivery feeling of having
him so close, his hands on her body again, his
breath warm on her skin.

He set the basin of water, warmed with water
from the kettle, on a chair beside the bed, and
then he proceeded to wash away the sooty shreds
of silk clinging to the bright pink skin of her calf.

She demanded to see his hands when she
caught him grimacing. The blisters were clearly
visible in the palm of his right hand, but his fin-

gertips seemed untouched, and when he began to smooth Miss Agnes's Miracle Heal-all on her limb, he told her he was treating his own injury in the process.

He stroked both limbs, claiming the stuff worked on cramps as well as burns, which she didn't believe for one minute, but it did feel good. It cooled the fire, if not the dull throbbing, and who was she to say it wouldn't prevent muscle cramps?

The intimacy of the scene was not lost on her, either. The man bending over her backside, his capable hands stroking and stroking her limbs, was breathing audibly. She didn't think it was from carrying her all the way from the lighthouse, either. He'd had time since then to collect his breath.

Feeling his touch linger on the dimple at the back of her knee, she gasped, "That tickles!"

"Good. Proves your senses are still in working order."

They were in working order, all right, and she thought he knew it. That was the trouble—they were working entirely too well. She was feeling things that had nothing at all to do with a patch of reddened flesh or a few cramped muscles—feeling things she had promised herself she would never again allow herself to feel, because for her they could lead nowhere.

"Mariah . . ." Waite's deep drawl was scarcely audible over the drumming of rain beating down on the roof.

"You should go home," she whispered. "I'll be just fine now."

"It's raining," he said, just as if he'd never been

wet before. As if they weren't both soaked to the skin and beginning to feel the chill.

"I have a raincoat," she offered. And then, picturing the impractical garment that was good in a light sprinkle, utterly useless in a real rain, she said, "But perhaps you'd better stay a little longer, just until it slacks off again."

It was the beginning of the end, and they both knew it. Or the end of the beginning. No more polite bantering. No more pretending that they were neighbors, nothing more. That they hadn't thought about what it would be like ever since that night on the beach—since long before that, if truth be told.

"You know what will happen if I stay?" he asked, his eyes shadowed, unreadable.

She nodded. Rolling onto her side, she made room on her narrow bed. "I want you to stay, Waite."

"I won't ask you to marry me."

"I wouldn't, even if you asked," she said quietly, knowing she was lying, feeling as if she were being cut up inside, as if her heart had turned to shards of broken glass. "I'll take whatever you offer and ask for nothing more, I promise."

It would be enough—it would have to.

"God, Mariah, if only—"

"Hush. Shhh, take off your wet clothes and get under the covers before you catch cold."

He laughed, but it was a ragged sound, as if he were hurting every bit as much as she was. "Fat lot of good that'll do me, with you wet as a mackerel."

So she started to undress. Neither of them pretended to be unaware of what was about to happen. Waite helped her with her buttons, and she kissed the knuckles of his poor injured hands. He smelled of Miss Agnes's salve, and so did she, but he told her her hair smelled like roses and rain, and she wanted to believe him, although she thought all traces of the attar of roses she sprinkled on her hairbrush must have long since washed off.

When he was undressed and standing before her naked as the day he was born, she thought about that night on the beach and told herself that this time he knew the truth about her. This time it would happen. There was no more reason to hold back.

Shivering, eager, apprehensive, she held out her arms and he came down beside her on the narrow bed. "Maybe we'd better put the mattress on the floor," he said, his voice husky with need. "Not so far to fall."

She had already fallen so far, a few more feet wouldn't matter, but she scrunched back some more and he worked himself closer, each trying to protect the other's wounds.

Waite wanted it to be sweet and gentle, for her sake. He was determined not to hurt her. He'd never taken a virgin before, but he knew—at least he'd heard—it could be painful for the woman.

He began to kiss her, and thought again how right it felt—how right it had felt the very first time he had touched her lips, knowing even then that it would never serve. He was no good for a woman, like his father before him.

But still, it did feel right.

He tasted her and parted her lips with his tongue, and she let him explore, and when he felt the tentative touch of her tongue inside his mouth, he nearly went over the edge.

He tore his lips away, swallowing hard, steeling himself not to rip into her body, spill his seed, and collapse like a rutting animal. The little whimpering sounds she was making deep in her throat made him want to pleasure her until neither of them could think about tomorrow.

"Easy, easy, love," he murmured when he felt her hands flutter down his back to grip his buttocks.

He moved until his face rested on her breasts and he took one small nipple in his mouth, tugging on the hardening nub, stroking it with his tongue.

She gasped and surged upward. "That feels—I never knew—never dreamed—ah, Waite . . ."

He reached down and found her with his fingers, and she was wet and hot and swollen for him, and he groaned, gently exploring her, caressing her. The spicy scent of desire filled his nostrils. The feel of her body, like satin—like velvet—like heaven—was nearly his undoing.

He would never let her go—ever! Somehow, he vowed, he would make her happy. Or die trying. One thing he would never do was let her go. . . .

"I wanted to take it slow," he whispered, his voice hardly recognizable even to his own ears.

"Oh, please," Mariah cried. "I want—I want—"

Mariah wasn't entirely certain what it was she wanted, but she didn't want it to be slow. She was awash with an urgency, a heedless need to *do something!*

Waite spread her thighs, cupping her womanhood with his palm, and she rose against his hand, straining eagerly for the completion she sensed was close—so close—it only needed . . .

"I'll try not to hurt you," he rasped, and she felt something blunt press against her most private part, and instinctively she lifted her hips.

He entered her slowly. He was trembling, as if under a tremendous strain. When he stopped, she almost wept, but he said, "No—wait a minute—sweetheart, this might hurt."

But waiting was not a possibility. Her body was in command now, and her body thrust upward and took him in, absorbed the stinging pain, the sensation of being filled too full, and then something began to happen that overshadowed all that.

He began to move inside her, slowly at first, and then rapidly, and she clenched muscles she never knew she had—to hold him in or keep him out, she never knew which—but her arms were holding him, too, and then he began to shudder and cried her name aloud, and she felt as if she'd almost touched the rainbow!

Almost . . .

But not quite.

"I hurt you," he whispered, and, lifting his weight, he rolled over onto his side, taking her with him. They were still joined in that most remarkable way, although it felt different now. Like music she could see but not hear. Like a parade she'd run after but never quite managed to catch.

Waite mumbled something about going home—about work to be done—and she started to protest, but before she could think of how to make him stay there, he was snoring.

"Well," she whispered. And with a deep, shuddering sigh, she closed her eyes and shifted closer. She felt wet, but still warm and . . . nice.

It wasn't quite the word she wanted, but it would do.

Nice . . .

Chapter Twenty-two

With the wind blowing fitful bursts of rain against her bedroom window, Mariah squinted one eye open and tried to judge the time. It was still gloomy outside. Far too gloomy to be up and about. What she needed was another few hours of sleep, but one of her legs was stinging like the very devil—and both were cramped. In fact, she felt as if she'd been riding horseback without a saddle. Not only that, she was pressed between two walls, and one of them was definitely not made of pine.

Waite. There'd been a fire in the tower, and Waite had brought her home, and . . .

For several moments she lay there, her nose pressed against a warm, living throat. With one arm curled between her own breast and a hard, masculine chest, the other one draped over a man's naked waist, she went over the past few hours in her mind.

And then, reluctantly, she opened her other eye. On the off chance she was dreaming, she really didn't want to wake up.

However . . . "Waite?" she whispered.

"Mmmm." He flopped over onto his back, eyes closed, and nearly tumbled off the edge of the bed. Mariah studied his features in the gray morning light, memorizing them for all the tomorrows when he wouldn't be waking up beside her. As if her heart hadn't memorized them long before now.

There came the intrusive *rap-tap-tap* of a woodpecker, and she stretched and yawned. She felt the call of nature. She was hungry, too—quite starved, in fact, for she'd skimped on supper, and here it was tomorrow already.

Moving carefully, she extricated herself from the embrace of the man sleeping beside her and crawled over the covers to the foot of the bed. She swung her leg over the rail and reached for her wrapper just as the woodpecker started up again.

Breakfast . . . she would make him breakfast. Biscuits and—

"Mariah, are you in there?"

Merciful saints in heaven, it was Maxwell!

Quickly knotting her sash, she smoothed her hair with her fingers and hurried to the door before he woke the entire neighborhood.

"What on earth—when did you get back? Is everything all right?" Her first thought was of Evie, but then, Evie was no longer living with her father.

"What, you're not up and dressed yet? You've less than an hour to get to class."

"Maxwell, what do you want? Has something happened?"

"You might say that. Open the door, *Miss Sawyer*, unless you want the whole world to hear about your sordid little deception."

"My sordid little . . . How did you know?" Casting a worried glance at the bedroom door, she was forced to step back when Maxwell brushed past her and came inside. From a remote corner of her jumbled mind came the thought that he was dressed in the exact same suit he'd worn when he'd met her at the mailboat that first day. Rusty brown, the pants too tight, and his cravat a good ten years behind the fashions.

She shook her head, wondering if she could possibly be lying in her Jenny Lind bed back in Murfreesboro, dreaming a whole new life for herself. If so, it cried out for a bit of editing.

"Well? What have you to say for yourself?" The magistrate flapped a handkerchief over the seat of her rocker, pinched the snug thighs of his trousers, and seated himself. The look on his face made her want to throw something. Preferably him, and preferably out.

"Maxwell, I haven't even had breakfast yet. Could this wait until later? If it's about Evie, then I think you have some explaining of your own to do."

He turned red and started to bluster, and she thought, *Ah-ha! That fixed your wagon fair and square, didn't it?*

But before she could move in for the coup de grace, the door opened behind her. Waite emerged from her bedroom, shirtless, shoeless, his trousers on, but just barely.

She rolled her eyes. "Oh, for heaven's sake," she muttered. "If this is a dream, I want you both to know I'm wide awake now, so go away! Don't either of you say another word. I want you both out of my house, and then I'm going to go back to bed and sleep until things begin to make sense again."

Maxwell's eyes bulged, making him look rather like a frog. He started to bluster. "Now, see here!"

"No, *you* see here."

"Mariah, sweetheart, I think we'd better tell him, don't you?"

"Tell him what? That you spent the night here? That we—"

"That we're going to be getting married just as soon as we can make the arrangements."

"But we're—"

"Hush, sweetheart. Don't be shy, now. He'll have to know sooner or later, so why not—"

"*Miss Sawyer!*" Maxwell roared.

Both sets of eyes swung his way. Mariah's legs suddenly began to throb painfully. "You know?" she whispered.

"I know everything," Maxwell said ominously. "In case you weren't aware of it, I traveled out on the same boat with the men who were staying in the keeper's quarters the night you and my daughter were there."

"But that—" Mariah began, when Waite quelled her with a single look.

"There was no impropriety there, Newbolt, and you damn well know it. You charged me with the welfare of your teachers. I did what any sensible man would've done under the circumstances."

Mariah tried again to butt in. "Yes, and—"

"Oh, and I suppose she's told you all about how she was run out of her own hometown in disgrace, and how she lied to get a teaching position, and how she's only a ba—"

"I think we'd better step outside, if Mariah will excuse us." Waite took the smaller man by the elbow, his fingernails white with the force of his grip, and steered him toward the open door. Maxwell had no choice but to go, for even shirtless, bootless, his eyes still heavy from sleep, the keeper radiated the kind of authority the magistrate would never possess.

Two strides, and they were at the door. Mariah hurried after them. "Yes, but I—"

Never actually lied, she was going to say when Waite politely closed the door on her statement. The last thing she heard was Maxwell blustering about giving her until the end of the week to be packed and gone. She waited and waited, but they didn't come back. When she looked outside, Maxwell's cart was gone and so was Waite's horse. His shirt and boots were still in her bedroom.

Well, she thought, angry, aching, wanting to cry but too stubborn to give in to weakness. *Well!*

She was going to be late for class. There was no time for breakfast, even if she could have choked down a bite. She was sore in places she wouldn't have thought possible, which made getting dressed a real chore, but what was even worse was trying to work up her courage to drive to the village. How many people had Maxwell told? Did everyone know? Were they all whispering about her?

Oh, Lord, not again.

With a film of Miss Agnes's Miracle Heal-all over her burn and a pair of cotton stockings to keep from smearing it onto her petticoat, she reached for her shoes. She didn't have a decent pair left, but perhaps if she could manage to pin a smile on her face and hold it there long enough, no one would look at her feet.

She did take extra pains with her hair, though, securing it in a prim knot above her nape. There was entirely too much of it, and it was straight and slick and heavy so that her knots always came down before the day was over. She really must consider having it cut.

A hundred questions skittered across her mind as she drove briskly through the village, for once oblivious to the sight of red-leafed creeper vines, starchy palmettos, and giant, sprawling live oaks festooned with beards of Spanish moss. *It's not the end of the world*, she told herself. *It only seems that way now, but you'll survive. You've been through difficult times before, remember?*

Taking comfort in the fact that most of her students had waited for her, Mariah led them inside, removed her shawl, and waited for the whispering and scrambling to cease before she rapped a ruler on her desk for attention.

"Now, back row, you were to be prepared for a quiz on mental arithmetic. We'll have that right away. Third row, you were to read the fourth chapter of *Swinton's General History*. We'll discuss it after the arithmetic quiz. The rest of you may place your papers on my desk, take a book from the shelf, and read quietly for the next half hour."

Evie's eyes were glowing. She did notice that. Frankie was fidgeting, and Alice Tolar was scratching several spots that looked suspiciously like . . .

Well. That will hardly be my concern, Mariah told herself.

Dear God, how could she leave these children? These babies and soon-to-be-adults and all the in-betweens, with their big, snaggly teeth and their scrapes and bruises and their bright, eager eyes.

And even worse than having to leave them, never knowing whether or not their young lives were fulfilled, was the pain of having them learn of her disgrace. A teacher should be above reproach, respected by all; otherwise how could she ever hope to inspire children to want to learn?

By tomorrow they'd all be whispering about her. Snickering. Saying she was no better than she should be. And what did that stupid phrase mean, anyway? She'd heard it all her life—probably said it a time or two herself. Just how good *should* one be?

To start with, one should try to avoid being a bastard, she thought bitterly. Or, if unable to manage that feat, one should at least have the decency to avoid contaminating decent people.

As for committing the sin of fornication . . .

She sighed, the arithmetic book open in her hand. It hadn't felt like sin at the time; it had felt like love. Still did, for all the difference that would make.

"Now, Dorien, suppose you tell me what percent of your weekly income you would have spent on apples if you earned seven dollars a week and you bought five apples a day at three cents each."

And while the boy screwed up his face and concentrated, Mariah gazed out the window at the dense, stunted forest that had looked so strange to her the first time she'd ever seen it, and thought, *I'll miss it all. The sights, the sounds, the scents. But most of all, the people.* She wasn't sure quite what it was that set them apart—maybe it came from being so vulnerable to the elements, so dependent on the sea for a living and on each other for all else—but she prayed a small portion of their sturdy independence had rubbed off on her in the brief time she had lived among them. She was going to need it.

When the bell rang, courtesy of Franklin, she saw her students out the door for what could very well be the last time. She said good-bye just as she always did, fighting back the temptation to hug each one and whisper to each some special word of encouragement. She could only hope that in time they would forget her disgrace and remember her with a modicum of kindness.

After packing her books and few personal belongings in the cartons she'd brought with her for that purpose, she drove herself home, praying she wouldn't meet anyone along the way. She couldn't have borne it if they turned away from her—her erstwhile friends. Her quilting group. Mr. Cyrus at the store.

I will not cry. This time I will not shed a single tear!

But by the time she finished unhitching her cart, went inside, and got a handful of dried apples for Merrily, who would now go back to being Conk, the tears could no longer be contained. She sniffled and sobbed, wiping her tears on her sleeve because her hands were sticky from the apples and dusty from throwing a handful of cracked corn to her chickens. She would give her laying hen to Caroline and Sarvice. She owed them a wedding gift.

Once back inside, she took a deep breath, washed her hands, and got on with her packing. Three hours later, she was still at it. The sky had darkened, unnoticed. Suppertime had come and gone. There might be a few tear trails on her cheeks, but she had finally done all the weeping she intended to do. When Waite arrived, she was standing over the crate she'd dragged in from the shed and padded with crumpled paper, a teacup in her hand, wondering who she could get to crate and ship the portraits to her once she found out where she was going. And how she could afford to ship anything anywhere, as she had yet to be paid for her first quarter's teaching.

"Oh—hell, damn, and blast," she muttered.

"Madam, I'll allow my wife to go on teaching if she's of a mind to—I'll allow her to burn my suppers—I'll even allow her to distract me when I should be working, but I'll not allow her to out-swear me."

She dropped the cup she was holding. It broke into three pieces. "At this rate, I'll not have a single teacup left," she said, forcing herself to turn and smile. "You startled me."

It was all Waite could do to keep his hands at his sides. She looked a mess. Her hair was a mess, her face was a mess, all tear-smudged and dusty—her hands were filthy and trembling, and the tip of her nose had turned red.

And God help him, he loved her so much it flat-out scared the wits out of him. "What are you doing? You don't need to crate things up just to move across the way."

"Waite, don't. I appreciate what you did this morning—telling Maxwell we were going to be married, I mean—but we both know you don't have to marry me. Just the thought that you'd offer means more than you'll ever know, but I can't allow you to ruin your own life."

He said something extremely rude, and she laughed, only it sounded more like a sob. "I'm almost done now. Do I need to make a reservation on the mailboat?"

"Just tell me why you want to go. If it's because you don't want to teach anymore, you don't have to. I make more than enough to keep a wife in comfortable style."

"Oh, but I—"

"If it's because you don't want to live here on the Banks, I reckon I can understand."

She flung out her hands, as if he'd exhausted her patience, and he thought, *Here it comes. I've heard it before, but this time I'm not sure I can bear it.*

"Waite, I adore teaching. I love it here on your island, you know I do! But how can I stay when— well, you know what I am. Not even you can change that."

She turned away. He saw her shoulders sag, then stiffen, and she said, as if it were the most ordinary thing in the world, "I'm a bastard, to start with, and a—a fornicator. If that doesn't disqualify me, I don't know what will. Grand theft? Murder?" She picked up another teacup and began wrapping it in newspaper.

"Who you are, madam, doesn't have one damned thing to do with what your parents did. Maybe they didn't go by the rules. I reckon you could say they lived a lie, but I'll lay you odds it never felt like a lie while they were living it. And if they hadn't done what they did, then you never would have been born, so don't blame your parents."

"They lived in sin! I was conceived in sin, don't you understand?" She slammed the teacup into the crate, and the sound of breaking china was loud in the sudden silence.

He reached out and took her in his arms then, her back rigid against·him. "Who made you judge and jury? Listen to me, Mariah, there's sin in all of us. We do the best we can, and we learn from our mistakes. And we help one another when help's needed." Some of the stiffness left her then, and he took hope.

"I hate to leave Evie—"

"Don't worry about Evie. She'll be just fine. If you want to worry, woman, worry about me. If you leave, I'll go back to being what I was before you came. You wouldn't want to wish that on the world, would you?" He leaned his head down beside hers. "What, was that laughter I heard?"

"No, you wretch, it was not!"

But it was. Tears and laughter and joy, and a budding radiance that felt like sunrise and moonrise and all the lighthouses in the world. "Waite, could we really—do you honestly think we could . . ."

"First answer me this. Do you think you could stand to spend the rest of your life in a place like this?"

"As long as you love me, I can live anywhere. An igloo—a tree house—a boat in the middle of the ocean. If you're there, then that's where I want to be."

"Then yes, ma'am, I do indeed. But if you still need some convincing, I've got plenty of time. Sarvice owes me two weeks."

She turned and buried her face in the front of his shirt. Her arms came around his waist and she was either laughing or crying again, he couldn't tell which. He found her chin and lifted her face, and he still couldn't tell which, but she was the most beautiful sight he'd ever laid eyes on, tears, dirt, freckles, and all. And he told her so.

"I really ought to leave. I've been fired, after all."

"And rehired. I had a talk with Newbolt, and we came to an agreement. You're going to go on teaching as long as you want to. His misdeeds'll not be reported. He's going to hire him a woman to look after his house, and Baxter and Fee are going to take Evie to Norfolk to see the doctor. To give him credit, the man's heartily ashamed of himself. I think. Leastwise, he made the arrangements while he was gone, before he went out to that college of yours. What's a golden report, by the way?"

Distracted by something in the way he was looking at her, she said, "Oh—nine-tenths average, no absents, perfect deportment."

At that he let out a bark of laughter. "You? Perfect deportment? How many of those things did you win?"

"Earn, not win, and I earned seven."

He laughed some more until she covered his mouth with her hand. "Waite, does Maxwell truly mean it? Will Evie have to go back and live there when she comes back from the doctor?"

"As to that, I can't say. Dore and Nick'll be going off to school after Christmas, so if Fee wants to move in and manage things, there'll be room. Now, no more talking, all right?"

"But what about—"

"Shhh. Any woman who wins seven golden reports for perfect deportment ought to know better than to argue with her intended."

"I haven't intended yet. I mean, I don't—that is, I haven't said—"

"But you will, won't you?"

She looked at him helplessly and hopefully, and there was nothing he could do except demonstrate a few of the reasons why she had to marry him. He could never in a million years explain it in words. He'd never been any good with words. So he kissed her, and then he kissed her again, and somehow they ended up standing beside her bed. As he unbuttoned her gown, he heard her stomach growl, and he laughed. "You want something to eat?"

"No—that is, maybe later. After . . ."

"After what?"

"*You* know!"

"After I lay you down and make love to every square inch of your body? After I make you scream with pleasure and yell my name loud enough to scare the crows right out of the trees?"

"Will I do all that?" she whispered, her eyes widening in anticipation.

"I'll see to it. If it takes all night. I'm nothing if not a patient man."

"Well . . . all right, but Waite—"

He kissed her slowly, lingeringly, as he slid her gown and chemise down her arms and cupped her small breasts in his hands. "What?" he said hoarsely.

"Hmmm? Oh—it's just that I don't think there are any square inches on my body."

With another shout of laughter, Waite McKenna swung his woman up into his arms and settled her in the middle of the narrow, sagging bed, where he loved her with great tenderness and passion while a beam from the nearby tower swept over them, silently blessing their union.

Epilogue

Mariah sprawled on top of her husband, staring at his shadowed jaw. Who would ever dream how exciting it could be to watch a man shave his beard? Or to watch him chop wood, his bronzed muscles glinting in the sun? Or merely to watch him sleep?

"Waite?"

"Mmm." He didn't wake up.

"You're awfully lumpy, did you know that?"

"Mmm?"

"Bumpy. Knobby. And getting knobbier by the moment."

He didn't make a sound, but she thought she saw the corners of his mouth move. "Waite?"

"Mmm."

"Why do you suppose it makes you so sleepy when it always makes me want to talk?"

"It?"

She squirmed a little on his knobby-and-getting-knobbier body. "You know . . . IT."

He shifted slightly so that she settled deeper into the space between his thighs. One of his hands just happened to fall onto her behind. "Want to talk, do you?" he murmured drowsily

"Well . . . I feel good. When I feel good, I want

to share it, and one of the ways to share good feelings is to talk about them."

"You're right."

"Then you're awake enough to talk to me?"

"Right about feeling good. You do." He didn't open his eyes, but his lashes twitched.

Oh, she loved it when he teased her this way, but right now, she truly did want to talk. She'd been leading up to it for days. "Nick's growing up. Did you know he and Evie are writing to each other?"

"No. She tell you that?"

"She has me check her spelling when she writes back. She misses him."

"Well, hell . . . so do I," Waite said plaintively, and Mariah knew he was feeling a bit put out because Nick very seldom wrote letters home. She thought it best to change the subject.

"Caroline said they're leaving in August."

"Mm hmm."

"I'll miss them, but at least we'll have the dog." That great, shaggy monstrosity that was half Precious and half heaven only knows what. "Waite! Wake up!" She knew very well he wasn't truly asleep. At least not altogether asleep. At least, not all parts of him. "Did you ever ask Sarvice what was in that bottle?"

"Bottle?"

"You know, the one she keeps on the mantel— the one with a piece of paper inside it?"

"*He* keeps."

"He keeps, she keeps—what's the difference?" And when he feigned sleep again, she tickled his chin and mused, "You know, it's strange, but I've noticed what whenever she gets that tone in her voice—you know the one I mean—Sarvice can glance over at the bottle and she sweetens right up again. It's the oddest thing . . ."

He smiled. If there was one thing about Waite that drove her wild—and actually, there were several—it was his way of smiling when he was pretending to be asleep.

"Well, anyway," she said, determined to get it said this time. She'd been trying for days to work up her courage. "I probably won't be teaching again next year."

"Hmm?"

She swatted him on the shoulder and he grabbed her wrist, carried it to his lips, and kissed the place where her pulse was fluttering. "Aren't you even going to ask me why?"

"Why?"

"Why what?"

"Why aren't you going to be teaching again, and why are you making such heavy weather of telling me? Love, it's your decision, you know that. If you want to teach, then do. If not, I don't mind having you underfoot all day. You're not particularly useful, but you're certainly decorative."

"Wretch!" Laughing, she moved to slide down off his powerful body, knowing even as she did that he wouldn't let her go. It was a game they'd played more than once. "If you must know, I won't even be decorative much longer. By September I'll be big as a house. I'll be waddling like a duck and—"

As quickly as that, the game was over. She was suddenly lying on her back staring up at Waite's grim face. She'd never seen him so pale, not even

standing in church at his own wedding, when his
hands had trembled so hard he'd dropped the
ring twice before he could slide it onto her finger.

"You're not . . ."

In that one moment, Mariah thought her heart
would break. Wordlessly, she nodded. "Don't ask
me to say I'm sorry. I can't."

Turning away, he sat on the edge of the bed,
his head in both hands, as if he were terribly tired.
Or discouraged. She ached to reach out to him,
but didn't dare. She had hoped . . .

But then, Waite already had a family. He had
Nick. And she did, too, in a way, only it wasn't
the same. Nick was nearly grown now. She hadn't
known him as a baby.

Besides, she already loved the tiny life growing
inside her. Waite's baby. A part of her, a part of
him, forever joined.

He turned to her then, and if she didn't know
better she would have thought he was terrified.
"Waite?" she whispered.

"If you die and leave me, how can I go on
living?"

And then she understood. Constance, his first
wife, had died after giving birth to Nick. And
Waite thought . . .

He was afraid. "Darling, listen to me. I'm not
going to die. I have no intention of dying for at
least fifty years. I'm strong, don't you know that?
I might not be island-bred, but that doesn't mean
I'm not tough as nails. Look at all the things
I've—"

With a groan dragged from the depths of his
soul, he gathered her into his arms. If she didn't
know better, she might have thought the wetness

on his cheeks was tears, but it was probably what he called "glow." The night was warm for May.

"I think you'd better lie down," Waite said, his voice rough with concern.

"I am lying down."

"First thing tomorrow I'll see about getting a woman in from the village to—"

"You dare get another woman and I'll—"

"No, you don't understand. I don't want you lifting a hand. I'm going to take such good care of you—"

"Waite."

"We can move to the mainland, closer to a physician so that—"

"Waite, hush. I'm not going anywhere. Miss Agnes will do just fine. Now, if you really, really want to make me feel better, you'll come back to bed and hold me until I fall asleep. I do get sleepy a lot. Miss Agnes says that's a sure sign."

They argued some more, and she could see that he was truly frightened for her. It took a while, but she finally managed to reassure him. One thing she had discovered once she'd broken through the hard shell that had grown around his heart—the man had the most remarkable capacity for loving.

So they held one another. Tenderly, at first, and then not quite so tenderly, not that either of them complained. A long time later, they both fell asleep. Outside, a chuck-will's-widow called for her mate. The surf rolled in as it always had and probably always would. And the lighthouse blessed them with its steady, reassuring beam.

Please turn the page

for an exciting sneak preview

of Bronwyn Williams'

next historical romance

ENTWINED

coming from Topaz

in 1998

December, 1887
Western Connecticut

It had been nearly two years since he'd last been home. The hedges had grown shaggy. Absently, Brand noted the fact, but his mind was on matters of far graver import. Not until he turned off the main road onto the long, hilly drive to the house did he take in the sad condition of the land. Lingering for a moment, the cold wet wind howling around him, he stared out across acres of rock-walled pasture toward the distant hedgerow.

A peppering of blackbirds, startled by his presence, scattered over the treetops. There'd been a time when the hills had rung with the sounds of three boys, the smallest scarcely big enough to hang onto his new pony, as they raced helter skelter across these same fields, calling challenges back and forth.

Poor Liam. The news was going to crush him. He'd always idolized Galen. The youngest by eleven years, Liam had been the tender-hearted one. Spoiled by their mother, his boyhood battles fought by his two elder brothers, he'd had an easy time of it growing up. Maybe too easy.

Shoulders sagging under a burden of grief and exhaustion, Brand continued on his way, searching his mind for a gentle way to break the news. But there was no gentle way to tell Liam that Galen was dead. Lost at sea. That the *Mystic Wings* had gone down with all hands somewhere in the North Atlantic.

Brand had sailed immediately after they'd received the news. He'd spent these past four months searching, hoping against hope to find some trace of survivors. Now, in spite of the shadow of doubt that against all reason still persisted, he could wait no longer to tell Liam.

They would hold a memorial service. Brandon, Liam and Liam's new wife, whom Brand had yet to meet, and perhaps their few close neighbors. Mr. Kondrake. The staff, of course. Old Everette, the farm manager, who'd taught all three brothers to ride.

God, he wished there was some way he could cushion the blow. Perhaps the woman, Fallon—the girl Liam had been so hellbent to marry he couldn't wait for his brother's approval—perhaps she could offer some comfort. According to Galen, who'd been in great demand by the ladies ever since he'd changed out of knee pants, a woman's touch was a purely magical thing.

Personally, Brand wouldn't know. Except for a few brief affairs that had involved comfort of an entirely different sort, he'd been far too busy building his own small empire to learn much about the species. He'd left that particular area of expertise to his two younger brothers.

Noticing a gate hanging by a single hinge, he frowned. Come to think of it, it wasn't the first sign of neglect he'd noticed since turning off the main road. Evidently, managing a large farm, even with a reliable staff, wasn't quite the sinecure Liam had imagined. He'd been eager enough to take over after their father's death. So eager, in fact, that both Galen and Brand had signed over their shares in the prosperous farm and gone to sea, instead. In truth, they'd both been drawn more to their mother's seagoing heritage than their father's legacy of horse breeding.

But marriage should have settled the boy. Brand had never met his new sister-in-law, but according to Liam's letters, her name was Fallon and she was beautiful and passionate beyond belief.

And expensive, opined Galen, who'd met her a few weeks before he'd headed east to join Brand in the seaport town of Mystic. They'd had a laugh over that, both finding it hard to imagine their baby brother wed and settled. He was only twenty-one. No, twenty-two now. Time had a way of slipping past when a man was busy building a shipping business.

Distracted, Brandon rode into the yard, dismounted and looked about for someone to see to his horse. He waited for a few minutes, then shrugged and walked the poor animal toward the large rock-walled barn.

The barn was deserted. Not a single creature, four-legged or two-legged, to be seen anywhere. The feeling that had been quietly growing in the back of his mind ever since he'd turned off the main road could no longer be ignored. Something was wrong.

Something was terribly wrong.

The coach car reeked of stale cigar smoke and unwashed bodies.

With sleet beating against the windows, fresh air was out of the question. The train began to move, and Ana braced herself, still half expecting to be dragged off onto the siding. The porter had pointed out an empty seat near the front, but then he'd been called away.

This was no Pullman car. It was only coach, but it would serve. It would have to serve, as it was all she could afford. Clutching her valise with one hand, she took a tentative step forward, steadying herself on the seatbacks as the train picked up speed. Careful not to hurry, not to do anything that would arouse suspicion, she swallowed her fear, only to have it stick like a dry biscuit in her throat.

Outside, the steam whistle broke into a scream, and she gave a startled yelp. Someone laughed. Someone else made a sly remark. Ignoring the clammy feel of wet petticoats slapping against her limbs, of wet shoes squelching with every step, she made her way down the aisle to the empty sea at the front of the car, imagining dozens of pairs of accusing eyes boring into her back.

But then, why should they accuse? How could they know?

Dear Lord, how could they *not* know? Surely something so horrendous couldn't be hidden so easily.

With cold, trembling knees, Ana Gilbretta—no, Ana Hebbel now—lowered herself onto one of the empty seats. The woman across the aisle turned away and looked pointedly out into the inky darkness speeding past the window.

Ironically, it was the same woman who had prompted her to buy a ticket to a place she'd never even heard of. Only moments before the train had pulled out, Ana had dashed into the station, breathless and terrified, to demand a ticket for the train that was just now ready to depart. She hadn't cared where it was bound as long as she was on it. Her only thought had been to get away.

"End of the line?"

"Yes, please," she'd gasped.

"That'll be twenty-nine dollars, then."

While she was digging in her reticule for the wad of money she'd brought with her, counting it for the first time, a slender, heavily veiled woman had pushed in front of her. "One way to Elizabeth City in North Carolina." The woman had sounded agitated. She'd glanced over her shoulder toward the door, ignoring Ana as if she weren't even there. "Did you hear me? Hurry, you dunce!"

Under any other circumstances, Ana might have been offended by such rudeness, but compared to what she had done, rudeness was a very small sin. Tallying up the amount of money she had with her, she'd stepped forward the moment the veiled woman had hurried away to board the departing train and said, "Elizabeth City, one way, please, and hurry."

The ticket agent had gawked at her. "Land's sakes, I never even sold a single ticket to that place before this. Now all of a sudden everybody wants to go there. They having a ladies convention down there?"

Ana had forced herself to smile and nod, but feared it was a ghastly effort. Still shaking his head, the agent had taken her money and handed over a strip of cardboard just as the train had let loose one short blast, signaling its imminent departure. Grabbing the ticket, she'd snatched up her valise and run.

Where on earth was she going? She'd never

even heard of Elizabeth City. What on earth would she do there?

Turning her head toward the window, she shut her eyes in an effort to shut off her thoughts. What was done, was done. The die was cast, as her husband would say.

Would've said.   Her late husband.

TOPAZ

SEARING ROMANCES

☐ **TEMPTING FATE by Jaclyn Reding.** Beautiful, flame-haired Mara Despenser hated the English under Oliver Cromwell, and she vowed to avenge Ireland and become mistress of Kulhaven Castle again. She would lure the castle's new master, the infamous Hadrian Ross, the bastard Earl of St. Aubyn, into marriage. But even with her lies and lust, Mara was not prepared to find herself wed to a man whose iron will was matched by his irresistible good looks.   (405587—$4.99)

☐ **SPRING'S FURY by Denise Domning.** Nicola of Ashby swore to kill Gilliam Fitz-Henry—murderer of her father, destroyer of her home—the man who would wed her in a forced match. Amid treachery and tragedy, rival knights and the pain of past wounds, Gilliam knew he must win Nicola's respect. Then, with kisses and hot caresses, he intended to win her heart.   (405218—$4.99)

☐ **PIRATE'S ROSE by Janet Lynnford.** The Rozalinde Cavendish, independent daughter of England's richest merchant, was taking an impetuous moonlit walk along the turbulent shore when she encountered Lord Christopher Howard, a legendary pirate. Carried aboard his ship, she entered his storm-tossed world and became intimate with his troubled soul. Could their passion burn away the veil shrouding Christopher's secret past and hidden agenda?   (405978—$4.99)

☐ **DIAMOND IN DISGUISE by Elizabeth Hewitt.** Isobel Leyland knew better than to fall in love with the handsome stranger from America, Adrian Renville. Despite his rugged good looks and his powerful animal magnetism, he was socially inept compared to the polished dandies of English aristocratic society—and a citizen of England's enemy in the War of 1812. How could she trust this man whom she suspected of playing the boor in a mocking masquerade?   (405641—$4.99)

*Prices slightly higher in Canada

Buy them at your local bookstore or use this convenient coupon for ordering.

PENGUIN USA
P.O. Box 999 — Dept. #17109
Bergenfield, New Jersey 07621

Please send me the books I have checked above.
I am enclosing $_____ (please add $2.00 to cover postage and handling). Send check or money order (no cash or C.O.D.'s) or charge by Mastercard or VISA (with a $15.00 minimum). Prices and numbers are subject to change without notice.

Card #_____ Exp. Date _____
Signature_____
Name_____
Address_____
City _____ State _____ Zip Code _____

For faster service when ordering by credit card call **1-800-253-6476**

Allow a minimum of 4-6 weeks for delivery. This offer is subject to change without notice.